*More . . .*

THIS IS A WORK OF FICTION. THE AUTHOR IS
AWARE OF THE ANACHRONISMS AND AMBIGUITIES
IN THE SOCIAL AND CULTURAL PUNCTUATION OF
THIS BOOK, AS HE IS AWARE OF DISTORTIONS
OF TIME AND GEOGRAPHY.

# TRUE CONFESSIONS

## JOHN GREGORY DUNNE

**P** A KANGAROO BOOK
PUBLISHED BY POCKET BOOKS NEW YORK

Distributed in Canada by PaperJacks Ltd., a Licensee
of the trademarks of Simon & Schuster, a division of
Gulf+Western Corporation.

POCKET BOOKS, a Simon & Schuster division of
GULF & WESTERN CORPORATION
1230 Avenue of the Americas, New York, N.Y. 10020
In Canada distributed by PaperJacks Ltd.,
330 Steelcase Road, Markham, Ontario.

Published by arrangement with E. P. Dutton
Library of Congress Catalog Card Number: 77-22126

ISBN: 0-671-81988-7

First Pocket Books printing October, 1978

Trademarks registered in the United States and other countries.

Printed in Canada.

# NOW

None of the merry-go-rounds seem to work anymore. There is a Holiday Inn across from the coroner's office. And Lorenzo Jones is our mayor.

"Imagine a pickaninny mayor," Frank Crotty said. "My son is very tight with him." He chased a digitalis tablet with a swallow of water. "And brags about it."

"I see your boy's picture in the paper," I said carefully.

"His Honor, the Judge," Crotty said. He didn't bother to disguise his disgust. "The champion of the poor."

"A good-looking lad," I said. It didn't seem quite enough for a member of the bench. I tried again. "Nice teeth."

Crotty digested that one for a moment.

"That's what I always wanted in a son," he said finally. "Good teeth. He has a lot of nice shoes, too. Forty-two pair, I think. So he can chew good and he can walk good. Never has to worry about wearing out the soles. Think of it, forty-two days and never the same pair of shoes. And the teeth all white and no holes in them either, that the food can hide in and cause the cavities. Yes, that's what I always wanted in a son. A good walker and a good chewer." He poured himself some coffee. "With a shine mayor as his best friend."

I made a pass at the check, but not serious enough to fool him: he was the visitor in from the desert, after all. I get along good—the pension from the department, the social security, some savings—and I could handle lunch in a Chinese restaurant, but Crotty, he looked like he could handle it better. He always liked Chinese restaurants, Frank. They were cheap, he always used to say. Which meant he ate on the cuff. A holdover from the days he used to work Vice in Chinatown. A meal on the cuff and a twenty in a fortune cookie and Frank would let the Mah-Jongg game in the back survive for another month. Live and let live. It was the same with Frank's suits. He knew the head of security out at Warner Brothers and Crotty would buy Sidney Greenstreet's old suits after every picture for a dollar each. Which was why he was usually dressed in white, Frank.

"Speaking of the mayor," Crotty said, "Bingo McInerney died."

Bingo McInerney. He was Lorenzo Jones's partner out of the Wilshire Division when they were both in the department. It was with Bingo and Lorenzo that it all started that day twenty-eight years ago. Bingo would be hard to forget. Bingo McInerney and Lorenzo Jones.

"Black and white in a black-and-white," I said.

"Oh, that's grand, Tom, that's grand," Crotty said. "Black and white in a black-and-white." He snapped his fingers for a check. "Bingo always knew how to drive that coon crazy. 'Knock, knock,' I heard him say to him one time. 'Who's there?' the pickaninny said. Smiling, you know, like him and Bingo was the best of friends, making with the knock-knock jokes all the time. 'Dee,' Bingo says. 'Dee who?' the coon says. And in the swellest dinge accent you ever heard, Bingo says, 'Dee po-lice.'" The laughter caught in Crotty's throat and he began to cough. "Oh, my," he said as

4

the choking subsided. "Oh, my. Like it was yesterday I remember it. And it still makes me roar."

"Poor Bingo," I said, not really meaning it. He was a knucklehead.

"It was the cancer that killed him," Crotty said. "A tumor the size of a football. They could have kicked a field goal with it, one of them little Greeks could, that kicks the field goals on Sundays."

Crotty rubbed at a spot of soy sauce on his suit. Still white, but a double knit now. And the hair blown like he was wearing a toupee, and the aviator glasses and the white shoes that had the shiny gold buckles that didn't buckle anything. And the manicure. He had more than the social security and the pension, Frank, and the Medicare that paid for the digitalis tablets. You treat people right and they treat you right and you can retire in very nice shape. The golden rule of the police department.

"He come to the funeral, the shine," Crotty said. "Hustling the votes. I thought Bingo's ma would start having her period when he kissed her. And eighty she is if she's a day. Telling her that him and Bingo was what America is all about."

"It's an election year, Frank."

Crotty was counting the tip, avoiding my eyes. I knew what he wanted to say. "If it hadn't been for him and Bingo, Tom . . ."

"If it hadn't been for a lot of things, Frank." Suddenly I was tired.

"You think about it then?"

"Occasionally."


## 2

Actually I think about it all the time. I even went down to 39th and Norton last week. Or maybe it was a couple of weeks ago. At my age you lose track. It was the first time in twenty-eight years. I remember the sign on that vacant lot. CRIME SCENE SEARCH AREA NO TRESPASSING. The photo car was there and the assistant coroner's car and the fingerprint car and Bingo McInerney and Lorenzo Jones in their black-and-white, they had answered the call. It was a funny neighborhood, 39th and Norton, twenty-eight years ago. You couldn't even call it a neighborhood, really. A couple of bungalows, the rest of it empty lots and a pile of weeds. There was a beat-up Hudson Terraplane with no axle sitting on one of the lots. No engine, either, and all the felt seat covers cut away. This woman who lived around there had been the first to see Lois Fazenda. She had gone out to buy a bottle of milk and when she turned up Norton, she saw this pair of legs sticking out from under a bush. That's all she saw, the legs. With all the toenails painted brown. Not that the lady going out for milk noticed that. It turned out later she was banging the guy in the grocery store, which was why she never had her milk delivered. Her husband got it in the basket during the war and the guy pushing milk down to the grocer's was only too willing to help her out. But that's another story.

Anyway, when I got there, Crotty was bending over the second half of Lois Fazenda. The top half. She was naked as a jaybird, both halves. There was no blood. Not a drop. Anywhere. Just this pale green body cut in two. It was too much for Bingo. He took one look at the top half and spilled his breakfast all over her titties, which is a good way to mess up a few clues. Not that it bothered Crotty. "You don't often see a pair of titties nice as that," was all he said. Respect for the dead, Crotty always used to say, was bullshit. Dead is dead.

One thing before I forget, the memory being what it is. That's Lois Fazenda's nickname. The Virgin

Tramp. Howard Terkel down at the *Herald Express* always claimed it was his scoop, that name. He picked it up from a bartender in Long Beach, Howard said. But the fact is, it was me that dreamed that one up, and there hasn't been a day the past twenty-eight years that I haven't regretted it. He was a funny little guy, Howard. He couldn't get with a case until he could pin a catchy nickname on it. The Lipstick Slaying was Howard's, and The Soda Pop Killer and The Hibiscus Murder. If you were a corpse and there was a palm tree in the neighborhood, then you were going to be The Coconut Caper to Howard. Vampires, he liked when there was a killing, and werewolves, too. The funny thing was, even with a girl cut in two and the top half having a great pair of boobs, Howard still couldn't find the hook. He tried the werewolf angle first, then the vampire, but they didn't catch on, and after Lois Fazenda was identified, calling her a "play-girl" somehow didn't seem enough. One thing Howard could be and that was a pest, and he nearly drove us nuts asking all sorts of questions about that Hudson Terraplane, as if all we had to look for was a werewolf carrying a spare axle. So Crotty says to me, "Think of a nickname and get him off our back."

"The Magic Pussy Murder," I said.

"Uh, uh," Crotty said. "Send him down to Long Beach. Nothing Howard likes better than prowling around Long Beach, interviewing soda jerks."

"The Sliced-Up Slit Case."

"Be serious."

"The Missing Clit Caper."

"Tom . . ."

"The Virgin Tramp . . ."

Tilt. "And don't forget to mention Long Beach," Crotty said. I didn't. The next day Howard's story began,

7

The *Herald Express* learned exclusively today that Lois Fazenda, playgirl victim of a vampire slaying in the shadow of the Los Angeles Coliseum, was known as "The Virgin Tramp" in the chic haunts she frequented in the Long Beach area. . . .

A chic haunt in Long Beach, Crotty said, was a place where the bartender didn't wear a tattoo.

But the joke was on us. Because the really funny thing was that if I hadn't come up with that name, we would have had a nice quiet little homicide that would have drifted off the front pages in a couple of days. But "The Virgin Tramp" brought us a lot of attention we didn't need, and with the attention came the heat, and then it got out of control and a lot of things happened that never should have.

Anyway. 39th and Norton two weeks ago. It's a Jap neighborhood now, Jap and middle-class colored. No empty lots, no bungalows, no Hudson Terraplane. The Neighborhood Association has put up streetlamps that look like gaslights and there are topiary trees and over on Crenshaw there's a Honda dealer and a Kawasaki dealer and Subaru and Datsun and Toyota dealers. The colored all have Jap gardeners and the Japs have colored cleaning ladies, and right where Frank Crotty said, "You don't often see a pair of titties as nice as that," there's this Jap-style house and just about on the spot where we found Lois Fazenda's bottom half, this Jap family has put up one of those little cast-iron nigger jockeys.

Son of a bitch if they haven't.

3

I knew I'd get to 39th and Norton eventually, because I drive a lot these days. Trying to put it all back together about me and Des. Over to Boyle Heights usually, where we grew up. The signs today are all different in Boyle Heights. It's one big body shop now. Acapulco Wrecking. Azteca Body Repair. Carro Latina. Not like when Des and me were kids. Boyle Heights was tough mick then, just like it's tough Mex now. Cops and priests, that's what the Heights was famous for. And drunks, hod carriers and bookies. A few stickup men, an occasional shooter. The priesthood, that was a way out. And the department. Boxing was the way I got out. I was the terror of the schoolyard at Saint Anatole's. The enforcer. The smart guys ran the pitch-penny games and put the market value on the bubble-gum baseball cards—three Ross Youngs for one Joe Dugan—and if any kid didn't like it, I put him on the grass. At home I used to lie in bed and try not to listen to the old man grinding away at the old lady in the next room, him drunk and her saying, Glory be to the Father and to the Son and to the Holy Ghost, as it was in the Beginning, is Now and Ever shall be, World Without End, Amen. It made you think a bit about how much fun it was to fuck, and so I used to lie in bed and imagine a bell ringing and the microphone coming down into the ring and some guy in a tuxedo pointing his finger at me and saying, ". . . the welterweight champion of the world." Anyway, I joined the navy when I was seventeen. Some old petty officer in the recruiting office said I could join the boxing team and avoid sea duty and fuck Chinese girls, which is pretty much what I did for six years. None of the Chinese girls ever said the Gloria. Four years straight I made the quarter finals in the China navy championships, but when the tough boys came in, I stuck and ran and made sure I didn't get knocked out and bet on the other guy. The funny thing was, I always knew I couldn't fight much. I had bad hands and no punch and I always had trouble making the weight.

The rap on me after I got out of the navy and turned professional was that I liked to hit all right, I just didn't like to get hit back.

You're just like your father, the old lady used to say to me. I guess she meant no good. She had other plans for Des. He couldn't have been more than three when she had him spelling all the Holy Days of Obligation. *A-s-c-e-n-s-i-o-n T-h-u-r-s-d-a-y. I-m-m-a-c-u-l-a-t-e C-o-n-c-e-p-t-i-o-n.* The priests loved it. I remember our pastor, Monsignor Shea. The monsignor was a man of a few firmly held opinions. Like the Jews killed Jesus and you named your first daughter Mary and your first son John. When my cousin Jerry got baptized, Monsignor Shea wouldn't pour the water on his head. "Jerry!" he said, that big harp voice booming through the sanctuary. "What kind of name is Jerry? You ever heard of a Saint Jerry? It's a name for a tap dancer."

And that was that. Except to the day he got killed breaking up a strike at the Ford plant in Pico Rivera in 1937, my cousin Jerry was always called Taps. There were a lot of guys like Taps Keogh in Boyle Heights, hard guys with not too many brains, good only for strike breaking or doing heavy work for Frankie Foley. Frankie was king of the Heights when me and Des were growing up, a real Public Enemy. Girls, protection, every now and then a hit. They made his life story into a Jimmy Cagney movie, although it was more Cagney than Frankie. I mean, I used to do errands for Frankie and he never wore a tuxedo and a wing collar and spats and a gray fedora like Cagney wore in the movie. And he was never good to his ma and the freckle-faced kid brother who wanted to be an altar boy. Then he got burned on a Murder One rap and he got life in San Quentin. I used to see Frank occasionally when I delivered bad guys to Q. He'd become the queen of the joint. The fag Cag, Des called him. The story made him laugh.

The house where Des and I grew up is still standing, which should tell you something about Boyle Heights. All I can really remember about the house is when the priest came to call. The priest would be there to take the parish census and he and my mother would sit there and drink tea and talk about living saints. She should have been a nun, my mother. She set great store by living saints.

"Tell me about Maureen Delaney, Father. Does she still come to the Sodality Meetings?"

"Never misses, Mrs. Spellacy."

"It's grand, as crippled as she is, with them wasted little limbs. Grand."

"You give her the Blessed Sacrament and you see her shining little face all scrubbed nice and clean to receive the sacred body and blood and she makes you feel you're doing her the grandest favor in the world."

"A living saint, Father," my mother said. I think now she was wondering if living with the old man qualified her for living sainthood.

"Not like some, Mrs. Spellacy." Then the knowing nod. "With the patent-leather shoes." Reflecting the underwear in the gleam is what he meant.

"Marie O'Connor," my mother said, with that special whisper she reserved for scarlet women.

"No names, Mrs. Spellacy." No slander from the lips of Father.

The subject was quickly changed. "Tell me, Father, Tommy's bowels are all plugged up. Would you recommend the castor oil or the milk of magnesia?"

Father folded his hands over his stomach. His advice was sought more often on matters of purgatives and politics than it was on questions of doctrine, and he gave as much thought about what laxative to take as he did about what Protestant or Jew politician to vote against. "The castor oil, Mrs. Spellacy. Oh, yes, a grand laxative, simply grand, like a physic. That's the ticket, no doubt about it at all."

"That's high praise for the castor oil, Father, coming from a man like yourself with such a fine intellect and such grand grammar." A little more tea in Father's cup. "And tell me about Tyrone O'Keefe."

"He's still all covered with the bug powder, Mrs. Spellacy."

Another living saint, Tyrone O'Keefe. Because of the tremendous growth of sanctifying grace in his soul.

My father wasn't a living saint. Nor was his grammar very grand. He used to take Des and me on the streetcar over to Lincoln Park to ride the merry-go-round. It was working then. He was a snappy dresser, the old man, poor as he was, always jingling the coins in his pocket and smiling a lot. He had that sweet harp smile when he was drunk, but then he was pissed so much, he never lost it, even when he was sober. Which was like every other Feast of the Assumption. He wasn't much with the words. I remember when Uncle Eddie Keogh died. Him and the old man did dig-and-toss work for the Southern Pacific, and the old man took me and Des to the wake over to Sonny McDonough's funeral parlor on Boyle Avenue. That was before Sonny merged with Shake Hands McCarthy and McDonough & McCarthy began to plant every stiff in the county, even branching into fox terriers. Uncle Eddie was stretched out in his fifty-dollar coffin, wearing the black suit that Sonny had sold Aunt Jenny as part of the package, although she didn't know the suit didn't have any back and that Uncle Eddie was naked from the waist down under the coffin top, Sonny McDonough even then being into low overhead. Aunt Jenny was crying and everyone was saying, "Didn't Sonny do a grand job, Eddie looks like he's just received Holy Communion," and Jenny throws herself on the old

12

man and says, "Tell me what kind of man he was, Phil, you knew him better than anyone," and the old man with that beautiful mick smile looked down at Uncle Eddie, lying there wearing Sonny's fifty-dollar special, and finally he just took Jenny's hand and he said, "He was a good shoveler, Jenny. Not a fancy shoveler, mind, but a good shoveler."

High praise from Phil Spellacy.

# 4

The first Tuesday of every month I go see Mary Margaret. Mary Margaret is my wife. She is in Camarillo. Not to put too fine a point on it, Camarillo is a state mental institution. There is nothing really that wrong with Mary Margaret. She talks to the saints, is all. Especially to Saint Barnabas of Luca. Now being an ex-cop and all, I've done a lot of legwork on this Saint Barnabas of Luca and to the best of my knowledge he doesn't appear on any saints' roster I've been able to dig up. I thought I had a lead when the Pope gave the chop to Saint Philomena a few years back, but Barnabas of Luca doesn't even appear on any morning report of former saints.

Barnabas first showed up after Moira was born. Moira is our daughter. Little Moira she was called. I suppose if a little elephant is little, then Moira was little. Poor Moira. When she was thirteen, she was 161 pounds in her stocking feet. A walking Hershey bar.

"What's that you got stuffed in your face, Moira?"

She never lied, even then. "Tootsie Roll, Dad."

"Jesus."

A tear rolled down Moira's face and some Tootsie Roll juice gathered at the corner of her mouth. I think she had a Mars Bar in there, too.

13

"You took the Lord's name in vain, Dad."

Moira is Sister Angelina now. A perfect name. Short for angelfood cake. She never misses a family funeral. Fourth cousin once removed and there's Moira, looking like a black battleship in her nun's habit, knocking out the rosary louder than anyone else.

"Hail Mary, full of grace,
The Lord is with thee.
Blessed art thou among women
And blessed is the fruit of thy womb. . . ."

(This is where Moira really belts it),

". . . JAY-SUS."

It takes a lot of effort, the rosary, so Moira is always first at the eats table afterward. A little shrimp, a little ham, easy on the potato salad, a dumpling or two. Chocolate eclair? Don't mind if I do. Twice. It's like they starve her at that convent between funerals.

"How's Mom, Dad?" says Moira, eyeing the platter of deviled eggs. "I sent her a spiritual bouquet for Christmas."

"She'll appreciate that, Moira."

"How's Kev?"

Kev is my son. I've lived with Kev and his wife Em since the last time Mary Margaret went to Camarillo. I make Kev nervous. He suspects I know all about his girl friend. I do. I was just keeping my hand in. To see if I had lost my touch. Kev is in the religious-supply game. That's what he calls it. The religious-supply game. Scapulars, mite boxes, statues. And those cheap gold-leaf chalices with the fake emeralds and rubies that he flogs to parents whose sons are getting ordained. There was an article about Kev once in *Church Supply Quarterly,* with a picture of him holding up a new

14

chasuble, and under the picture the line, "A Pioneer in the Design of Double-Knit Vestments." Anyway, the pioneer was always going off to religious-supply conventions in Las Vegas, not that I ever heard that Vegas was a gold mine for double-knit chasubles. Em thought it was grand, of course. Kev going to Vegas all the time, keeping on top of the latest developments in altar linen. But as I said, once a cop, always a cop. So one night there I decided to follow Kev when he told Em he had to go to an affair honoring Monsignor Barney Carey on the occasion of his twenty-fifth anniversary in the priesthood.

"I whipped up a new silver chalice for him," Kev said.

"Silver," Em said. "Because it's his twenty-fifth."

You couldn't say Em wasn't quick.

"And the monsignor doesn't know it yet, but they're giving him a new car. A Buick LeSabre. Red."

"What are they thinking of, Kev?" Em said. "Hungary and Albania and all those Polish countries going over to the Communists and they're giving him a red car. Black is what priests drive."

"They got a deal from Fuzzy Feeney over to Feeney's Buick," Kev said. "Red was all he had."

"It'll be a convertible next," Em said. "And the sunglasses."

I knew Barney Carey from the old days when he was a curate at Saint Vibiana's. He ate on the cuff more than Crotty. So I was surprised he only got the red LeSabre. I figured Barney Carey good for a whole Buick dealership, easy. Not that Kev hung around long at Barney's catered affair. He slipped out after the presentation of the silver chalice and headed over to the Valley. I kept a block behind. As I said, just keeping my hand in. He turned south on Winnetka and into the lot of a building called the Ramada Arms. In the space for apartment 6C. The rest was easy. The occu-

15

pant of 6C was one Charlene Royko and she was a computer programmer for National Cash. Twice married and also banging a utility infielder for the Angels. Which was why she only played ball with Kev when the Angels were on the road.

I hadn't lost my touch. Not that I told any of this to Mary Margaret when I went to Camarillo the first Tuesday of every month.

"How's Kev?" Mary Margaret said.

"Getting his innings in."

"And their boy?" Mary Margaret said. "Has he made his First Holy Communion yet?"

"Fourteen years ago."

"That's grand, Tom," Mary Margaret said. "Napoleon always said that the day of his First Holy Communion was the grandest day of his whole life. With all his honors. Did you know that?"

"I didn't know that, no."

"Saint Barnabas told me."


# 5


The headline said,


## TIMOTHY J. O'FAY
## MONSIGNOR WAS 104


No known kin. Oldest priest in the archdiocese. Ordained in 1894. Had spent his declining years at Saint Bridget's Retreat in Chatsworth since his retirement from parish duties. That was a laugh.

"You okay, Dad?" It was Em knocking at the bathroom door.

"Just having a laugh, Em," I said. She hated me to lock myself in the bathroom. She thought I'd have a stroke or my heart would go and she'd have to call the fire department to take the door off the hinges and the new paint job would be chipped.

"Reading the funnies then?" Em said. She had this idea that old people had to sneak off to the crapper to read the funnies.

"The obituaries," I said.

Em wouldn't see the humor of Saint Bridget's Retreat in Chatsworth. Saint Bridget's was a nice way of saying the old priests' home. A lot of twinkly-eyed nuns laughing at some old boy's jokes about Fat Phil Doolin. Father's got such a sense of humor, they would say. He laughs so hard the tears come to his eyes. And the drool leaks out of his mouth, is what they usually forget to say.

The thing about Tim O'Fay was that before he was at Saint Bridget's, he was in the old priests' home at Saint Margaret's in Oxnard and before that at Saint Stephen's in Chula Vista. Eighty years a priest, Tim, and sixty-one of them he had spent in some old priests' home. Which is one way of saying that Tim O'Fay was nutty as a fruitcake from the day he was ordained, although it took twenty years for the archbishop to figure it out, the archbishop never being known for being quick on the trigger. You can say that sort of thing now, but when Des and me were growing up, if you even hinted that the archbishop was a little short upstairs you'd get a cuff on the ear for your trouble. Nowadays, with Phil Berrigan and that crowd, all of them showing up on "The David Susskind Show" with the boots and the blue jeans and the turtleneck sweaters and the kids and the wife, who was the former Sister Theodosius, you can say that the archbishop is banging his housekeeper and the nuns will smile their twinkly little smiles and say, "A living saint, His Excellency," probably because they've got a little going on the side with some curate who wears a gold chain around his neck.

"Monsignor O'Fay was well-known throughout the archdiocese for his musical endeavors." I wonder where the paper dug that one up. The truth of the matter was that Tim O'Fay had one of the most beautiful tenors you ever heard. It used to be said around the archdiocese that Tim was the only tenor ever made John McCormack envious. Except he used to sing at odd times. I got that from my brother Des. My brother Des was Tim O'Fay's curate. That was right after Des was ordained and long before he became famous in his own right as the "Parachuting Padre." Des would call and say the monsignor was going to sing the solemn high on Sunday and not to miss it. Des had a little Berrigan in him, even then. So I'd drive out to Saint Malachy's to hear the monsignor. He said a good mass, no flourishes, and with that voice and all it was a treat, like watching Charley Gehringer hit. Except that every once in a while, instead of singing the *Sanctus* or the *Agnus Dei,* the monsignor would wing into "My Old Kentucky Home," or "Marching Through Georgia." Of course there were people over to Saint Malachy's didn't appreciate the old Civil War standards, and they would complain and the archbishop would come out, but then Tim would just croon the best *Agnus Dei* you ever heard. Old Tim was shrewd and he had already served a stretch at Saint Stephen's in Chula Vista, and with the archbishop there he wasn't about to break parole. Until that last time at Morty Moran's funeral, Morty being an old pal of the archbishop's, what with him donating a new Packard every year, and Tim thought it would be a nice touch at Morty's requiem mass if instead of the *Credo* he slipped into "Carry Me Back to Old Virginny," since Morty was born in Roanoke and all. Right after which the archbishop shipped Tim back to the old priests' home. For keeps.

"Telephone, Dad," Em said later that day. "It's Uncle Des."

18

"How are you, Des?" I said.

"Carry me back to old Virginny," Des said. "That's where this old darky's heart am long'd to go."

"I figured you'd be calling, Des."

# 6

My brother Des. The Right Reverend Monsignor Desmond Spellacy. Once regarded as a comer, a future Prince of the Church. Once upon a time. Domestic prelate before thirty years of age. Former chancellor of the archdiocese. Toastmaster and scratch golfer. A regular at Del Mar and the Thursday night fights at the Olympic. Friend of Sam Goldwyn and Stan Musial. Spiritual advisor to Willie Pep, as well as Shake Hands McCarthy and Dan T. Campion and all those other papal knights who held the paper on the archdiocese. The man who introduced Brandt coin collectors and Record-O-Lopes to the Sunday collection. For the past twenty-eight years, pastor of Saint Mary's of the Desert in Twenty-nine Palms. I guess that's my fault, Des being in Twenty-nine all these years. That's what they call Twenty-nine Palms. Twenty-nine. Imagine being in exile in a place where they've got to count the palm trees to give it a name. And make no mistake about it, Des was in exile and I was responsible.

Me and Des. Des and I. Des and me.

Des said there was something he wanted to talk to me about, so the following weekend I drove out to Twenty-nine Palms. There's nothing much to say about Twenty-nine except there's a lot of sand. And old people. From Chicago, Detroit, places like that. Guys retired off the assembly line at Magnavox or Chrysler and they moved to the desert on their UAW pension to take the waters and ease the arthritis. Old guys whose tattoos are all faded and whose wives wear hair-

19

nets and whose children don't call much anymore. People from tough mick and Polack neighborhoods where old Monsignor Bukich would let them use the parish hall for their meetings on how to keep niggers out of the neighborhood. Some of them live in trailers now and some in cinderblock houses with tin foil crimped in the windows to keep out the heat. I used to wonder how Des got along with them. It was such a long way from the Cardinal's three-story mansion on Fremont Place where Des had lived in the old days. The good days.

Saint Mary's of the Desert was a falling-down wood and cinderblock building with an imitation-gold cross rising out of what passed for the steeple on the roof. At one point it had been white-washed, but the sun and sandstorms had stripped it down to nothing in particular. Stuck in the sand in front of the church was a wooden sign on which was painted a fund-raising thermometer, the faded reminder of a building fund drive for a new church that had failed more years ago than I care to remember.

In the gravel driveway next to the rectory was an old two-tone Chrysler with the hood up, and under the hood, tinkering with the engine, I could see a man in blue jogging pants with red-and-white stripes down the seam to the ankle. I rang the rectory doorbell.

"The bell doesn't work," the jogger-mechanic said. "May I help you? I'm Father Duarte, the assistant pastor."

He seemed to be a new addition since I was last there. He was a young Mexican with curly black hair and over his jogging pants he wore a grease-stained T-shirt lettered "Chicano Power." Just the thing, I thought, for a parish full of retired Polacks.

"I'm here to see my brother."

"You're the monsignor's brother. It's a very great

20

honor." He wiped his hands on the T-shirt. "Eduardo Duarte."

We shook hands.

"I'm helping the monsignor out until he's a hundred percent." I hadn't realized that Des wasn't a hundred percent. "It's a pleasure working for such a totally dedicated priest, Mr. Spellacy. Aware of the winds of change in our Church and yet a real Catholic of the old school." I had never quite thought of Des in those terms, and I'm sure he hadn't either. "Once I fix the carburetor on the car here, I'm going to repaint the thermometer. We're going to get the building drive underway again. The new Saint Mary's will be the flower of the desert, you mark my words."

The new Saint Mary's. The flower of the desert.

"I see an old Spanish mission of the type built by the late Father Junipero Serra. You are familiar with the late Father Serra, Mr. Spellacy?"

It was like referring to the late Abe Lincoln. I nodded.

"I think of him as the first Chicano."

I kept nodding.

"I am taking your time, Mr. Spellacy, I am sorry. But when I think of the mission we will have here, I sometimes get carried away. The cactus flowers will be in bloom. We will have benediction in the sunset. A desert showplace for Catholics from the colder climes. And we must recognize the spirit of ecumenicism. We will have tours come up from Palm Springs. Are you aware of the Bob Hope Desert Classic?"

"The golf tournament?" I wondered how it fit into Father Duarte's plans.

"In Palm Springs, yes. I plan to speak to Mr. Hope. I know I could convince him that the fans at his tournament would love to see the new Saint Mary's. I'm sure he'd do a benefit. His wife's a Catholic, you know. And one of my classmates at the seminary, Father

Fabian Mancuso, is a curate at Saint Philip Neri in Palm Springs. Mrs. Hope's church. You may have heard of Fabian Mancuso?"

I shook my head.

"He was on television in San Francisco. 'Father Fabe, The Narco Priest.' He worked wonders combatting the drug problem."

There was something mesmerizing about listening to Father Eduardo. I am sure that was what he would want to be called. Father Eduardo. Father Fabe. It was like listening to a murderer confess. You couldn't break into the spiel. No wonder Des wasn't a hundred percent. This mad Mexican was driving him crazy.

"Tommy."

It was Des standing in the doorway of the rectory. He was holding a cigar and wearing a white polo shirt with a little blue alligator on the breast pocket. I left Father Eduardo to his faulty carburetor, the first step in the resurgence of the new Saint Mary's, and went inside with Des.

"Does he always talk like that?" I said. We were in what passed for Des's study. An old desk, a few books, that morning's newspaper folded to the obituary pages. It was cool in the study and so dark with the curtains drawn against the sun that I couldn't get a good look at him.

"It's actually quite restful when you get used to it," Des said. "Like tuning in to an FM station. You don't have to listen very hard. Conversation to think by."

"Father Fabe . . ."

"Oh, yes." The old smile, softening his face. Des always could find a certain amount of levity in the priesthood, which I guess was a drawback in a priest. "He's a good priest, Tommy. Doesn't look upon the convent as a dating bureau, like some. Dedicated."

It was what Father Eduardo had said about Des. "How do the harps like him?"

"Not much. He's a Mexican. 'It's a well-known fact,' Mrs. Gilhooley told me, 'that Mexicans have more hemorrhoids than other people.' As if I should prepare a lethal dose of Preparation H for the poor man. But then when Father Stephanowski was my curate, Mrs. Gilhooley told me it was a well-known fact that the Polish had more midgets than other people. And if I ever have an Eskimo curate, she'd no doubt tell me that Eskimos get more blisters than other people. All that slipping around on the ice with their bare feet."

He always was good value, Des. The words came easy. "How are you, Des?" I said.

The smile again. Which meant he wasn't going to answer.

"Let me see," Des said. He pulled on his cigar. "This morning after mass, Mr. McHugh stopped in to see me. A nice man, Mr. McHugh, once you get past the palsy. But one thing you learn about being a pastor, Tommy, and that's that no one ever rings your doorbell, even if it works, unlike mine, to tell you the whole family's working and John's on the wagon and the little ones are getting nothing but the highest marks in parochial school and so much money is rolling in they've got to stuff it in a mattress and they all received Holy Communion at the nine last Sunday. No. Nothing like that. If it's not that Aunt Min wets her bed, it's that Uncle Jim broke parole or that Little Jim, the famous used-car man, got a Catholic girl in trouble.

"So when Mr. McHugh stopped by, I knew it wasn't to tell me that he wants to be finance chairman of Father Eduardo's building drive and that he knows Bing Crosby and Bing's dying to lend a hand. Uh, uh. Mr. McHugh tells me that his niece, the Carmelite nun, is leaving the convent to become a professional bowler. Think of it. *A professional bowler.* I didn't even know they had alleys in the convents these days. 'Would you talk to her, Monsignor, please?' What am I supposed to say to the poor girl? Give her advice on how to drill the holes in the balls for her fingers? So I told him I'd say a mass for her. Maybe it will help her bowl a perfect string.

"And after Mr. McHugh, there was Pinky Heffernan with the latest status report on his bowels. He beat cancer of the rectum twenty years ago, Pinky, and now every time he flushes the toilet he's on the phone calling me. Every movement a miracle. Do you remember when Eisenhower was in the hospital and you couldn't pick up a newspaper that didn't tell you how many times he went to the bathroom? Well, Pinky kept me filled in every day. 'Himself had an enema today, Monsignor, did you see? In the Los Angeles *Times*. Ain't that grand? He'll soon be fit as a fiddle and ready for love. An enema a day keeps the cancer away.' "

The effort of speaking had tired him out and all of a sudden I realized that Des had grown old. He was four years younger than me, and with all that tennis and golf he had played in his younger days as chancellor, always leaner and in better shape. But now he was slumped in his chair in this ruin of a parish and I knew why he had called me out to Twenty-nine Palms.

"How are you, Des?" I said.

"I'm going to die, Tommy," my brother Des said.

# One

What Tom Spellacy remembered later was that it began
as just another 187. One of 212 that year. One of 19
that month. One of two that day in April. The other
homicide, the one that nobody ever remembered, was a
shine killing over on Central Avenue. The newspapers,
however, never bothered with dinge 187s. A colored
girl, even one cut in two, the first thing the papers
would say was, "A hooker," and the second thing was,
"Forget her." The *Express,* especially. If it were only
a shine, fuck her. Stick with the important things. Like,
2D MICKEY ROONEY MARRIAGE HITS ROCKS. If you were
a smoke, the only way you'd ever make the *Express*
was the day you celebrated your 142nd birthday. SAW
A. LINCOLN, LOCAL MAN CLAIMS, was the way the *Express* would put it. Just underneath, BABY THRIVES ON
SIX CUPS OF COFFEE A DAY.

But he didn't get the dinge.

He got the other one.

It was the day he won the office pool. In fact, the
only good thing that happened that day was that he had
the Dodgers and five runs in the Robbery-Homicide
pool and Ed Head pitched a 5–0 no-hitter against the
Boston Bees that was good for fifteen clams. That was
it. The rest of the day was shit. He was tired and
Fuqua was on his ass and he had ten investigations and
Crotty was off buying a motel in Culver City. Cleaning

up the fine print, Crotty said. He didn't ask where Crotty got the down payment. I got Chinese partners, was all that Crotty would volunteer. Which meant as deputy watch commander he had to cover for Crotty while Frank was off with his Chinks in Culver City. On all ten investigations. The queer in Echo Park who had screwed a 300-watt light bulb up his boyfriend's behind. The drunk off-duty patrolman from the Traffic Division who had tried to shoot a cockroach on the wall of his bedroom and killed an old lady walking her dog by his window. A triple homicide in Japan Town they wouldn't crack in a million years. A funny suicide in North Hollywood. A ginney hit in Silver Lake. That one he didn't like to think about. Memories. They had the hooker who had set it up. Here was one ginney getting his glass blown in the Silver Lake Motel and another ginney comes in and gives him three in the pump, a nice neat little triangle, and the girl doesn't even get a powder burn. She's got the john's joint in her tonsils and she doesn't remember a thing. Not the trick's name. Not what the shooter looked like. Listen, Tom, I was occupied, I wasn't looking at the door.

It made him uncomfortable, the way she called him "Tom." He knew she knew it would. They knew each other from the old days. In Wilshire Vice.

And then there was Fuqua.

Captain Fuqua.

And his coffee pot.

An ass-kissing clerk, Fuqua. Just the qualifications for chief of homicide. He had this way of doing things. The systems approach. The definite-patterns approach. Like the definite pattern in the absentee rate. That was Fuqua's big score in the department, investigating the absentee pattern of the uniformed squad when he was in Personnel. He got all the rosters and broke them down. There was the Monday pattern and the post-payday pattern and the Christmas pattern. That was

28

how he nailed Jim Quinn, with the Christmas pattern, and got the homicide job. Seven Christmases out of nine, Jim Quinn had turned in sick before the holiday. First it was the kidneys and then it was the ankle and then the kidneys again and then the gallbladder. The bad back was a favorite. What Jim Quinn was doing, it turned out, was running a Christmas-tree lot out in Inglewood. The Christmas pattern. And so Jim Quinn got suspended and then someone got the bright idea of applying the definite-pattern approach to the homicide detail. Probably Fuqua himself. And now he was chief of homicide and guardian of the coffee pot.

"You been using my coffee pot, Spellacy," Fuqua said on the morning of the 187 at 39th and Norton.

"The plug on mine's all fucked up, Fred."

"Regulations say you shouldn't even have a coffee pot. The watch commander has a coffee pot and I got a coffee pot and those are the only two coffee pots we're allowed."

"Says who?"

"The TO&E, that's who."

"I'm sorry, Fred."

"You want some jake, you use Crotty's coffee pot."

"His office was locked, Fred, it was a long night with that hooker from Silver Lake there and we wanted some coffee."

"You want coffee so bad, you go to the cafeteria and get it, it's open all night."

"It's on First and Temple, the cafeteria, for Chrissake."

"You're not in Vice anymore, Lieutenant, you're in my division, and in my division, we go by the book."

"So I used your coffee pot, Captain, I'm sorry. I don't see the harm in it, but I'm sorry."

"The harm is, you left it on all night and you burned a hole in my desk and the desk is city property and I got to make a report on how a desk that belongs to the taxpayers is all fucked up because an officer in my division used my coffee pot without my authorization. Is that clear enough for you?"

"All that typing, Captain, you can get off on that, I bet. In triplicate."

"I'm putting you on report, Spellacy."

"For drinking coffee? I had a couple of sinkers, too, you want to throw the book at me."

"For gambling."

"When?"

"You think I'm deaf, dumb and blind, I don't know about you making book on the ball games."

"Making book? It's a fucking baseball pool."

"This isn't Wilshire Vice, Spellacy. I'm watching you. The way they should've in Wilshire Vice."

Wilshire Vice. There was always someone ready to bring up Wilshire Vice. Even though he had been on his best behavior since he came downtown to Robbery-Homicide from Wilshire Vice. It would be a long time before people forgot his tour as a nightwatch lieutenant in Wilshire Vice. Especially the night he shot a hood named Lenny Lewis who had tried to stick him up when he was sitting in a parked car on Normandie. The problem was the car was registered to a woman named Brenda Samuels and Brenda Samuels ran three houses in his division and Lenny Lewis was making off with his wallet and eleven hundred dollars when Tom Spellacy dropped him. There were all sorts of questions about what he was doing in a car with Brenda Samuels and eleven hundred dollars in his wallet and the questions were complicated by Lenny Lewis's testimony that the girl in the car was giving the guy in the car a blow job when he stuck it up. Not that anyone took Lenny Lewis's word over Tom Spellacy's. Him with a daughter in the novitiate and a wife in Camarillo talking to the saints. The only rap against Tom Spellacy was that he was such a lousy shot. He was going to use his piece, he should've dropped Lenny Lewis for keeps. It would have saved a lot of trouble. Brenda didn't say anything. She had too much to lose, with the girls and the tables and the private games. Tom Spellacy was the problem. Better to cool him off. Move him out of Wilshire Vice into Robbery-Homicide downtown. Forget the eleven hundred in his wallet, he had a good day at Del Mar, maybe. Give him a citation for stopping Lenny Lewis's 211—armed robbery. Everybody was happy that way. Except Brenda, who lost everything, even though she kept her mouth shut. And except Lenny Lewis. He got three to eight in Q. Where a fairy cut off his dick and he hung himself with a wet bedsheet.

Tom Spellacy thought, It was funny Lenny Lewis knowing that a wet bedsheet doesn't tear. It was the sort of thing you picked up in the joint. A lot of things were funny. If Lenny Lewis hadn't decided to stick up a parked car, he would still be in Wilshire Vice. The good life. No coffee pot. No Fuqua.

No Code 3 from Bingo McInerney and Lorenzo Jones: a possible 187 at 39th and Norton.

# 2

"The butler did it," Crotty said at 39th and Norton.

Which means now we can get down to business, Tom Spellacy thought. Two years he had cased stiffs with Crotty and it was always the same from Frank: "The butler did it." Even if it was an old lush with his throat cut in a mission downtown.

"What a sweet piece of ass she must've been," Crotty said. "What a nice pair of titties. She was alive, I'd get a hard-on, I think."

He started to sing. The tune was "Finiculi, Finicula." The words weren't.

> *"Last night,*
> *I stayed up late*
> *To masturbate.*
> *It was so nice,*
> *I did it twice."*

All the time looking, Frank, picking up things and bagging them, never missing a trick. A button. A little piece of glass. A piece of thread. The chewed-out stub of a pencil. An old tennis ball. A fat man in a white suit that used to belong to Sydney Greenstreet, singing dirty songs and saying the butler did it and what do we have here. It was shit, more than likely, but you never could tell, one thing might lead to something else, so you tracked everything down.

An empty matchbook.

"McGovern's," Crotty said, reading the matchbook cover. "You know McGovern's?"

"The one in Lincoln Heights, the one at the beach?" Tom Spellacy said.

"A fag place, the one at the beach," Crotty said. "A swell joint. They do it in the gents', is where they do it. I busted a guy in there once, I was in Venice Vice. A big red-headed guy, he had so much vaseline up his asshole I thought it was the fucking Panama Canal, every battlewagon in that joint'd been up it, I bet. They practically fucked him to death. So I says to this little fairy I say 'You ever fucked this guy?' And he says to me, so help me, God, Tom, this is what he says, 'Are you kidding?' One of those prissy little fairy voices. 'I'd rather fuck a girl than a red-headed guy.' "

Crotty laughed and stuck the matchbook in his pocket. "Not the one at the beach. The other one, McGovern's. The one in Lincoln Heights."

"I know it, I never been there," Tom Spellacy said.

"Harp place," Crotty said. "All the harp wise guys go there, tell each other how long their thing is and who they been sticking it into. And drink beer, the cheap bastards. I bet McGovern doesn't sell seven bucks' worth of booze a year. Drink beer and eat the free pickles and the hard-boiled eggs for five cents an egg. Fucking place smells like a sewer, all the guys cheesing on the beer and the eggs and the pickles. Go into the can there, McGovern's, smells like they been piping in every fart since Jay Cee was a little kid there."

"I never been there," Tom Spellacy said. "Somebody has, though. It's something to check out, that matchbook."

"That's what I was thinking," Crotty said.

A police photographer began snapping pictures of the upper half of the dead woman's torso. Her features were beaten and slashed beyond recognition. Bingo McInerney's vomit had congealed on her chest.

"Fucking Stars lost again last night," Crotty said. He never missed a night at the ball game, Crotty, when the Stars were at home. On the cuff, of course. A seat in the press box at Gilmore and all the beer and hot dogs he could stuff into himself.

"Six–one, I heard it on the radio," Tom Spellacy said. He reached under the torso and with his handkerchief extricated a pair of battered eyeglasses. Crotty whistled and put the glasses in his bag. They moved across the lot toward the severed lower torso of the victim's body.

"You should've seen that sonofabitch, Zernial," Crotty said. "Two hundred thirty-five pounds, all muscle including his brains, and he bunts. Runs the hundred in nine years, Zernial, and he bunts. My sister, the nun, with the club foot, she could beat him to first base, especially she knew there was going to be a saint standing on it. I mean, the day they start canon-

33

izing first basemen, she's a threat, my sister, a definite threat." Crotty shook his head. "Five runs down, he bunts."

The policemen around the lower half of the body parted to let them through. They knelt beside the severed torso and removed the sheet covering it. Tom Spellacy sucked in his breath. A votive candle was stuck obscenely into the woman's vagina.

"Jesus Christ."

"It's a nice touch, I got to admit that," Crotty said. "You ought to check your brother the monsignor out on that one. What it means in canon law, a votive candle up the joy trail."

Tom Spellacy nodded. There was also a tattoo of a rose disappearing into the victim's pubic hair.

"That's the other touch I thought you'd like, Tom," Crotty said. "It makes you think maybe she liked to fuck. Unless they're tattooing pussy in the convents these days, is what I mean. That's another thing you can check the monsignor out on. He'd know, I think."

Tom Spellacy stood up. "That's our little secret, I think, the tattoo."

"And the candle. Don't forget the candle."

"The mystery clue is what they call it, Howard Terkel and them."

Crotty whistled through his teeth at the police photographer. "Hey, Berman, a lot of pussy shots, we want." The photographer grunted that he would be right over. "Jew," Crotty said, nodding toward Berman. "Ever notice, the guys with the cushy jobs, they're all lox jocks. Show me a job you run into a bad person sometime, I'll show you a bagel bender doesn't want it."

They walked to the curb. There was a pattern of skid marks on the road.

"Left a lot of rubber," Tom Spellacy said.

"What I'd like to know is where he got the tires, leave rubber like that," Crotty said. "There's more rubber on the street there than I got on my DeSoto. Retreads is what I got."

"Chewing gum is better," Tom Spellacy said. "The guy who stopped here stopped awful quick, it looks like. Why do you think he did that?"

"The girl he was with, she might have put her hand where she's not supposed to," Crotty said. "Where it's a mortal sin to put it. It would make you stop awful quick, she put her hand there. On the other hand, it could have been a bad person. He sees the empty lot and jams on the brakes."

"That's what I was thinking."

"We'll get the bagel to take a few pictures. Then all we got to do is find the car to match the tire marks to."

"You're going to miss a few ball games on this one," Tom Spellacy said.

"You know Phil Spitalny?"

"The All-Girl Orchestra Guy."

"He was at the ball game last night, Phil," Crotty said. "And I says to him, I says, he was in the press box there, I says, 'Phil, you tell that Evelyn she can play my magic violin anytime.' He nearly pissed his pants, Phil, he laughed so hard."

"She's got two left tits, Evelyn, is what I hear."

"Two left tits," Crotty said. "Jesus, Tom, I got to tell Phil that, next time I see him. He'll roar." And then Crotty began to sing again:

> "Won't you tell me, dear,
> The size of your brassiere,
> Twenty, thirty or forty.
> If it's a forty-five,
> I'll be at your side,
> Sunday, Monday and always."

He took getting used to, Frank, but Tom Spellacy liked the chat. Black, white, young, old, male, female, tall, short, fat, skinny, always the constant chatter from Crotty. It made a stiff just another stiff, Crotty's steady chat. Even a stiff like this one, stuck under two different bushes, maybe fifty feet apart, with the toenails painted brown and the face worked into pulp and the candle in the twat and the nice little rose tattooed over her pussy.

"You better talk to Bingo and the other one," Crotty said. "I hate to say it, Tom, but the other one is the one with the brains. He was standing in the back of the church, Bingo the day they was handing out the smarts. He must've thought it was the ten o'clock mass down to Saint Luke's there."

Bingo McInerney and Lorenzo Jones. You don't see many stiffs cut in two when you're riding around in a prowl car, so the first thing Bingo did when he saw the body was chuck his Wheaties. He was a little green after throwing up, Bingo, but Tom Spellacy was certain that what bothered him most was that Lorenzo Jones had kept his breakfast. You couldn't be around the locker room without hearing how Bingo felt about Lorenzo. It wasn't bad enough Bingo was stuck riding with some jungle bunny. The department wanted to experiment, that was okay with Bingo, he said so himself. But a jungle bunny going to law school at night, that was too much. One thing Bingo didn't want to depend on was an uppity dinge. Lorenzo called Bingo "Bingo," but Bingo was goddamned he was ever going to call Lorenzo "Lorenzo," no matter how long he rode with him. In fact, Bingo had never known how to address a colored. "Hey," he would say sometime, or "Hey, you," if he was pissed off, or "Boy," when he was busting one. Sometimes all three when he was busting one: "Hey, hey, you, boy, don't give me no shit." None of the three would work with Lorenzo. So when Bingo had something to say to him, he would touch him on the shoulder. More than a touch actually, but not quite a jab. Forefinger into the shoulder: "Hang a right on Alhambra there." Into the arm: "There's a place up here we can get some coffee and tacos." Sharp into the shoulder again: "Listen, you hear how the Mexicans won the Battle of the Alamo? They thought it was the welfare office and it was the first of the month." Fucking coon never laughs, Bingo was always saying.

Bingo was standing next to his black-and-white, pulling rapidly on a cigarette. His fingers were stained yellow with nicotine. Lorenzo Jones leaned against the car, hands in his pockets. Bingo ignored him.

Tom Spellacy took his notebook and a pencil from his shirt pocket. The point on his pencil was broken.

"Use mine," Lorenzo Jones said. "I always use a Scripto."

Tom Spellacy nodded and took the pencil. I bet he has extra lead, too, he thought.

"Keep it," Lorenzo said. "I have an extra."

Bingo McInerney stirred himself. "He's always got lead in his pencil," he smirked at Tom Spellacy. "One of them, anyway. Get it, Champ?"

Bingo had once seen Tom Spellacy fight at Legion Stadium, and when he thought he could get away with being familiar, called him Champ. Tom Spellacy stared coolly at Bingo until the latter averted his eyes.

"What happened?"

"It must've been 6:30 we got the call—" Bingo said.

"6:43," Lorenzo said, checking his clipboard.

"We were over on Western," Bingo said.

"Normandie," Lorenzo said.

"Five minutes it took us to get here, at the most," Bingo said.

"Seven minutes exactly," Lorenzo said.

He must drive Bingo nuts, Tom Spellacy thought. But at least you could trust him. Lorenzo had nothing to add to what was already known. The woman who found the body was hysterical. The nearest bungalow was half a block away. The bungalow was uninhabited. There were no known witnesses. No one in the neighborhood had noticed anything out of the ordinary during the night. No loiterers. No noises. No strange cars.

"Anything unusual the rest of your tour?" Tom Spellacy said.

"Nothing like this, Champ . . . Lieutenant," Bingo said. "All my years in the department, I ain't never seen anything like this. Somebody must've really got pissed off at her, is what I think. Lipping off is probably what she was doing. They do that, broads . . ."

"We had a 902," Lorenzo said. "Fatal."

"Whyn't you learn to speak fucking English?" Bingo said. "A 9-0-fucking-2. Guy pisses in a sink, you'll say it's a 219, something like that."

Lorenzo looked at his partner for a moment and then said quietly, "That'd be a 415. Disturbance of the peace."

"Yeah, well, this one here, it still takes the cake," Bingo said. "The other guy, the 902, he wants to call it that, Tom, he runs into a telephone pole over on Vermont there."

"Hoover," Lorenzo said.

"Jesus Fucking Christ, will you stop correcting me like that," Bingo said. "A guy can get sick and tired of that. Like you're the only one ever went to night school, correcting all the time like that. A real pain in the ass you can be, you know that?"

"Knock it off," Tom Spellacy said.

"Northbound on Hoover," Lorenzo said, reading from his notebook.

". . . the fuck cares, northbound or southbound?" Bingo said. "You know what's eastbound, Lieutenant? Africa's eastbound is what they tell me."

"5:07, the call comes in," Lorenzo said. He never

38

raised his voice. It was as if Bingo were not even there and he was making a report into a dictaphone. "A 902, the call said, 2600 block on Hoover. 5:13. We arrive on the scene."

"Think the lieutenant cares some juiced-up clown runs his Plymouth into a pole?" Bingo said.

"1936 Ford V-8," Lorenzo said. "Totaled. Driver appeared to be deceased."

" 'Driver appeared to be deceased,' " Bingo mimicked. "Halfway through the fucking windshield, don't have to go to some night school, know he was dead. Right, Lieutenant?"

Tom Spellacy ignored his wink.

"Dispatched the coroner," Lorenzo said. You could light matches under the balls of his feet, Tom Spellacy thought, and he'd finish the report before stamping them out. With all the proper codings from the dispatcher's code. His voice droned on, oblivious to an argument in the background between the medical examiner and the ambulance crew over whether to put the body on one stretcher or two.

Crotty came up. He was holding the empty matchbook from McGovern's Bar & Grill in his hand.

"Lorenzo Jones," Crotty said. "How's your wife, Belle, Lorenzo?"

"Oh, shit, that's rich," Bingo McInerney said.

"You guys can go now," Crotty said to Bingo and Lorenzo. "Something just came over the radio. Possible 187, Avalon and 43rd Place. Across from Wrigley Field there."

"187's a homicide," Lorenzo said to Bingo. The toneless sarcasm escaped Bingo. Or maybe Lorenzo's just trying to help him out, Tom Spellacy thought. As you would your moron kid brother.

"Colored lady whacked out her husband," Crotty said. "Dropped a fifty-pound watermelon on his head, I bet."

"Oh, shit, that's rich," Bingo said.

" 'That's rich, *Lieutenant,*' " Crotty said.

Bingo flushed, "Sorry, Lieutenant."

"You know McGovern's?" Crotty said.

A chance to recover for Bingo. A knowing grin. "The Pope a ginney?"

"Matches must be yours then," Crotty said, handing the empty matchbook to Bingo. "Not enough you puked on the victim, like you never seen a pair of charlies before, but you drop your fucking matches, too. Ten days I could've spent checking these out, I didn't know McGovern's was where all the dumb harps hang out. Only one of which is in the vicinity. Keep your hands in your fucking pockets, the scene of a crime. Like your buddy, Lorenzo, here."

The rebuke drained the color from Bingo McInerney's face. Tom Spellacy thought he was going to get sick again. Lorenzo Jones moved discreetly out of range.

"Let's go," Crotty said to Tom Spellacy.

3

They drove to Chinatown. It was always the same after Crotty saw a stiff. Day or night, the upstairs room at Wo Fat's was always open for Crotty after he saw a stiff. Some egg rolls, a little cashew chicken, a plate of sweet-and-sour pork, a dish of steamed Chaio-Tzu and Crotty began to feel better. He ate and rolled dice and read the comics. He was always wondering if anyone was getting into Ella Cinders, Frank. It gave him time to collect his thoughts and not have to worry about Fuqua and his definite patterns. The obituaries, too. A page of death by natural causes had a soothing effect on Crotty.

"Chet Hanrahan's funeral's tomorrow," Crotty said.

Tom Spellacy nodded. His mind was elsewhere. The girl must have been brought to 39th and Norton from somewhere else. Where there's an awful mess, he thought. Unless she was sliced up in a bathtub. Which meant the house had to have running water. A house, not an apartment. The screams would have attracted attention in an apartment. And the house must have been in a remote area for the same reason. The remote-area approach, Fuqua would call it.

"The monsignor going to be on the altar?" Crotty said.

"I would guess," Tom Spellacy said, forcing himself back to Wo Fat's. He knew it was impossible to rush Crotty. Yes, Des would be on the altar. Chet Hanrahan was, or had been, chairman of the Building Fund for the archdiocese. Des never missed the important funerals.

"A grand man, the monsignor," Crotty said. Tom Spellacy smiled to himself. Crotty always called Des "the monsignor." And referred to all priests by their titles. The Monsignor. His Excellency. His Eminence. Father. You went to confession to Father. You heard Father say mass. You never argued with Father. And you never bothered Father with your business dealings in Culver City with a bunch of Chinamen. Father was for sins. Nothing else.

"I asked the grand Chester Hanrahan to put money into my motel," Crotty said. "All I got out of him was a lot of mumbo jumbo about inflation and rising unemployment and the high cost of building materials. Well, he'll be saying no to the worms from now on, is who he'll be saying no to, the pious harp bastard. Doing business with the likes of Jack Amsterdam and not with me. He must've had a full-time job looking the other way, the way Jack was steal—"

Crotty stopped in mid-sentence. He avoided Tom Spellacy's eye and poured them both some green tea.

Jack Amsterdam.

The name hung there between them.

Jack Amsterdam.

Jack A.

Chief construction contractor for the archdiocese and pillar of the community. Building gymnasiums and giving new altars to the Church. Invited to civic dinners for visiting Mexican dignitaries. Recipient of autographed photographs from the governor of Baja California and the archbishop of Vera Cruz. Friend of the Right Reverend Monsignor Desmond Spellacy. It troubled Tom Spellacy that he never knew how much Des knew. About Jack A. and himself. And Wilshire Vice. He was sure Jack A. still had a piece of Wilshire Vice. It was probably what he donated to the Building Fund. Brenda had worked for Jack A. There were those in the department who thought the eleven hundred he had in his wallet the night he shot Lenny Lewis had come from Jack A. He supposed a strict definition of the eleven hundred made him a bagman. The word made him wince.

"Down to business," Crotty said. A good way to change the subject, Tom Spellacy thought. That was one nice thing about Frank. He was a good cop, but he didn't believe in strict definitions. "What do you think?"

"Offhand I'd say a nut," Tom Spellacy said.

"You sound like fucking Mary Worth in the funny papers," Crotty said. "When Jim is banging Susan and his wife Alice is home crying with the kids. 'Offhand I think Jim is jumping Susan,' is what Mary is telling Alice. Like Alice is a dummy or something. Of course it's a nut."

Jack Amsterdam had been dispelled.

"No ID, no clothes," Tom Spellacy said. "The way her face is worked over, it's going to be tough to get a make on her teeth."

42

"It's the no blood anyplace that bothers me," Crotty said. "Which means someone had to bring her there."

"Which means she was dead six, seven hours when that someone dumped her."

"The skid marks are our best bet," Crotty said.

"Which means we don't have much."

"Which means we got nothing," Crotty said.

Tom Spellacy opened his notebook. "We need a list of sex crimes with the same M.O."

"A check of all known sex offenders."

"And their cars for bloodstains."

"Put the word out to the garages and the wrecking yards for anything that comes in with blood on the seats."

"Or in the trunk."

"We should probably check the joint, see if any sex offenders went over the wall recently."

"The funny farms, too," Tom Spellacy said.

Crotty sipped his tea. "Fuqua will love it. The systems approach. You know what we'll come up with, don't you?"

"Shit," Tom Spellacy said. "Shit for the newspapers."

"Weeny flashers," Crotty said. "Guys who shit on the sidewalk. Panty sniffers. Guys who fall in love with their shoes. The guy who belts his hog on the Number 43 bus there. People like that. The kind you want to invite home at Christmastime there to meet the old lady and give them a missal for a present. Nice people to have in the house, you got a pair of gloves to wear when you shake hands with them. And what are we going to be pulling them in for? To find a guy, sliced up a girl who's got a rose tattooed on her pussy. Like my old mother there. We never could keep Ma out of the tattoo parlor. The flower on her twat, the cock on her tits, those were Ma's favorites. A big nigger cock, a foot long, Ma was crazy about that one. She was always flashing it at Doc Daugherty's wife Sadie at the Stations of the Cross there."

Tom Spellacy finished his beer.

"I got a motel to run is all I'm telling you," Crotty said. "You think I'm going to lose any sleep over who took this dame out, you're shitting strawberries and whipped cream, is what you're shitting, you think that. Fuck her, is what I say. And you should say, too. You know how we're going to break this one. Couple of years from now, they'll bring in a guy ran a red light. 'I did it,' he'll say. 'Did what?' we'll say. 'Killed the girl with the rose tattooed on her twat,' he'll say. 'Which fucking one was that?' we'll say. That's how we're going to break this one."

"Don't tell Fuqua that," Tom Spellacy said. "It'd give him acid indigestion, I think."

Crotty called for the check. Wo Fat said it would dishonor his house if Lieutenant Crotty paid. Crotty bowed.

When they reached the street, Crotty said, "Listen, Tom, I think I did a little talking out of turn about Jack A. up there. I mean, I know how tight the monsignor is with him."

"Fuck him," Tom Spellacy said.

"The monsignor?"

"Him, too."

# *Two*

The Right Reverend Monsignor Desmond Spellacy counted the mink.

Enid Fallon had a mink. Theresa Dowd and Mary Devlin had minks. Regina Gaffney's mink had horizontal pelts and Helen Donahoe's vertical pelts. Verna Boylan had a champagne mink, Edna Whalen a silver mink.

Mrs. Chester Hanrahan was weeping into her mink jacket.

Desmond Spellacy shifted his weight on the prie-dieu. It was quite a send-off for Chet. The vicar general saying the solemn high-requiem mass, thirty priests and monsignors on the altar, all the ladies from the League of Catholic Women in their mink. He searched for Monica Gargan. It wouldn't be a funeral without Monica. There she was in the second pew, matching Mrs. Chester Hanrahan tear for tear. "Two hundred and eleven spiritual bouquets Chet's got so far," Monica had whispered to him at the rosary. "Do you think that's a record, Monsignor? I know for a fact that Andrew Costigan only got 194." Trust Monica to know that. And the make and year of all the cars in the funeral procession. Quentin Houlihan had the record for Cadillacs. She knew the number of wreaths, too, and whether they had come from Jim Daley's or Harry McAuliffe's. "You get your bargains from Jim," Monica Gargan said. "Harry gives you a quality wreath.

Colorado carnations and a grand piece of silk ribbon with the gold lettering. It's the day-old salmon glads from Jim, and the cheap satin doesn't hold the printing." One last dismissal of Jim Daley. "The Polish all use Jim. And the Italians."

"*Credo in unum Deum . . .*" Augustine O'Dea sang. The vicar general's rich bass rolled through the cathedral. Desmond Spellacy was originally supposed to sing the funeral mass, but Mrs. Chester Hanrahan had vetoed that. "All he's done for Holy Mother the Church," she had sobbed after the coronary, "Chet deserves a bishop at least." It was the Cardinal she wanted, but His Eminence was indisposed. A touch of the flu. Although Desmond Spellacy suspected that the real reason His Eminence was absent was because he had never been able to stand Chester Hanrahan.

"*Patrem omnipotentem . . .*" The men's choir took up the refrain.

Doris Doyle's mink had a full collar and Sadie Cormier's cuffs big enough to be muffs. Dolores Kearney wore a red mink and Vitaline Dowdy a black mink. Dan T. Campion had a mink collar on his Chesterfield.

Desmond Spellacy noticed that Dan T. Campion was sitting with the delegation from the police department. Good. Dan was keeping on top of that situation. He made a mental note to suggest to His Eminence that he attend the Policemen's Ball. If only to give his blessing. In and out in five minutes, that was all it would take. One picture in the newspapers would do it. The Cardinal in purple and ermine showing his solidarity with the department. At a time when the department desperately needed a vote of confidence. The vice scandal had almost wrecked it. The mayor recalled, the chief indicted, seven senior officers resigned. One suicide, God rest his soul.

"*Oremus . . .*"

He thanked God Tommy had never been indicted.

46

He knew it wasn't a coincidence, Tommy being transferred out of Wilshire Vice when he was. But that was all he knew and all he wanted to know. He blotted Tommy from his mind. The immediate problem was getting the Cardinal to the ball. His Eminence deplored the appearance of opportunism, although not opportunism itself. It would not do to argue that the new police chief, soon to be selected, would appreciate the favor and that it never hurt to have a friend in the department. Something more high-minded was in order. A scholarship, perhaps. He ran over the possibilities. A college education sponsored by the archdiocese. Four years at Loyola. He knew he could get the Jesuits to agree. The jebbies wanted the Cardinal's approval on that new dormitory. A Loyola education, but for whom?

The son of a policeman killed in the line of duty.

That would do it. His Eminence could announce the scholarship at the Policemen's Ball. Not that the Cardinal would be fooled, but appearances would be satisfied.

*"Lavabo inter innocentes . . ."* Bishop O'Dea intoned.

Appearances. They were very much on Desmond Spellacy's mind today. Augustine O'Dea, for example. Tall, in his late fifties, with massive shoulders and the mane of snow-white hair. The very picture of a bishop. He had only one drawback: he was a boob. A view, Desmond Spellacy knew, that was shared by the Cardinal. That big, booming voice always ready to discourse on Saint Patrick and the snakes or the day Babe Ruth said hello to him at Comiskey Park. Two favorite topics. (Desmond Spellacy had once pressed him on the Babe and what the Babe had actually said was, "Hiya, keed.") But. . . . Always the *but*. There was something about Augustine O'Dea that seemed to amuse the

47

Cardinal. With rapt attention, Hugh Danaher listened to the endless monologues about the day little Bernadette met Our Lady at Lourdes or the absence of snakes on the Emerald Isle. Is that right, Augustine? I didn't know that, Augustine. It was as if the vicar general provided the Cardinal with his only relief from the byzantine tedium of running the archdiocese.

It could have been a situation with Augustine O'Dea. Desmond Spellacy was certain of that, but the Cardinal had handled it perfectly. It was a matter of turning a sow's ear into a silk purse. Hugh Danaher was, after all, only an obscure coadjutor archbishop in Boston when he succeeded Daniel Shortell, who had died quietly in his ninety-first year, leaving the archdiocese, in a word, broke. It was easy to get rid of most of the deadwood that had accumulated around Archbishop Shortell, but Augustine O'Dea was vicar general, second in command in the archdiocese, and he had expected to be Daniel Shortell's successor. The simplicity of Hugh Danaher's solution was exquisite: he just took advantage of the vicar general's imposing good looks. If there was a ribbon to be cut or a communion breakfast to attend, there was Augustine O'Dea posing for the photographers, telling of his plan to send a Christmas card to every Catholic in the American League. Because of his long friendship with the Babe, of course. Title after title was piled onto his broad shoulders, each more meaningless than the last. Director of the Apostleship of Prayer. Chairman of the Sodalities of Our Lady. Director of the Priests' Eucharistic Congress. Spiritual Director of the League of the Hard of Hearing.

Vintage Hugh Danaher, Desmond Spellacy thought. He had a gift for turning a liability into an advantage. A complex man. Desmond Spellacy doubted that he would ever really understand the Cardinal. Except for one thing. He would never try to pull a fast one on him. Even now, nearing eighty, in the twelfth year of what had appeared, when he was named archbishop, only a caretaker appointment, the Cardinal could still be ruthless. Desmond Spellacy shivered. He had seen the Cardinal in action too often. That cold stare. Where the seconds seemed like hours. He had seen priests crumble under that stare. John Tracy, sixty-eight years old, who had asked His Eminence why he had never been named a pastor. The stare. Until poor John Tracy wept. The Cardinal never had to give the answer John Tracy had dreaded: because you're a homosexual.

It was that kind of ruthlessness which had helped him pay off the debt of five million dollars left by Daniel Shortell. And create twenty new parishes, eighteen new high schools, sixty-four new parochial schools. Desmond Spellacy knew how the rich laity quaked when Hugh Danaher put on the squeeze. "When Mary O'Brien, a chambermaid, can give seventy-five cents to the Building Fund, I expect Randle J. Toomey, who would like to be a Grand Knight of Malta, to give seventy-five hundred dollars." Not *in camera*. At the annual luncheon of The Holy Name Society. It got the job done. The Pope rewarded Hugh Danaher with a red hat. Spiritual leader of a flock numbering 1,250,000 people. A bookkeeper in ermine was more like it, the Cardinal said. Interest rates and construction costs and real-estate values. These were the problems that filled his days. The application of marriage laws and the businesslike operation of hospitals, orphanages and cemeteries.

Appearances, Desmond Spellacy thought. A sow's ear. A spiritual leader. He wondered if Augustine O'Dea knew about the polyp on the Cardinal's prostate. He thought not. Augustine O'Dea's latest enthusiasm was trying to perfect his Al Smith imitation. Best not to trouble him. Get Chet Hanrahan into the ground. A new chairman of the Building Fund, that was the immediate concern. Not whether Desmond Spellacy was going to succeed Hugh Danaher.

*"Orate fratres . . ."*

In the front pew, Mrs. Chester Hanrahan leaned toward her husband's casket and keened loudly. The organist from Immaculate Conception High School began to play "Lovely Lady Dressed in Blue." It was Chet's favorite "number," according to Mrs. Chester Hanrahan. As Immaculate Conception was his favorite high, because it was there that he had his first fund-raising success, putting the drive for the new gymnasium over the top with six "Put-A-Pool-in-A-Catholic-School" Sunday collections.

The volume of Mrs. Chester Hanrahan's sobbing seemed to embarrass her two children, Brother Bede Hanrahan of the Athanasians and Sister Mary Peter Hanrahan of the Salesian Sisters of Saint John Bosco. What a windfall for the Salesians and the Athanasians, Desmond Spellacy thought. One thing Chet Hanrahan had never figured on was both his children going into the religious. And now the Athanasians and the Salesians would someday be carving up the Hanrahan Development Corporation.

"It's a goddamn shame, Des," Chester Hanrahan had said after his son had entered the Athanasians, "that boy not having more respect for his mother."

If there was one subject Desmond Spellacy had not wished to discuss with Chester Hanrahan, it was his son's vocation. The Athanasians were a mendicant order who devoted their lives to menial service. "He heard the call, Chet," he answered deliberately.

"To clean up the shithouse in some old people's home?" Chester Hanrahan said.

"If he's happy, Chet."

"Up to his elbows in piss, he calls that being happy?" Chester Hanrahan said. "What about his mother? If

50

he had to go in, why didn't he become a priest then, instead of some goddamn brother. At least his mother could watch him say mass then, he was a priest, or give a retreat. She could buy him a car. What is she supposed to do now? Give him a can of Ajax and watch him swab bedpans?"

You work your ass off, Chester Hanrahan had said bitterly. And he had. A pioneer in subdivisions. Del Cerro Heights. Fairway Estates. Rancho Rio. Wishing Well Meadows. Each new tract announced with billboards off every major artery. "Will There Be Underground Utilities in Del Cerro Heights?" " 'YES!' Says Chester Hanrahan." "Will There Be City Water in Fairway Estates?" " 'YES!' Says Chester Hanrahan." "Will There Be Neighborhood Schools in Rancho Rio?" " 'YES!' Says Chester Hanrahan."

It was over the question of neighborhood schools in Rancho Rio, in fact, that Chester Hanrahan had first come officially to the attention of Desmond Spellacy. That day seven years before when he was in the steam room of Knollwood Country Club with Dan T. Campion, the lawyer for the archdiocese.

"I was talking to Chet Hanrahan the other day," Dan T. Campion said. The sweat poured off his bantam-rooster frame. "He's got this grand new development. Rancho Rio, I think it's called. He'd like to give a little piece to His Eminence for a school. Isn't that a grand thing for him to do, Des?"

Desmond Spellacy nodded noncommittally. The little lawyer could sleep behind a corkscrew. He could imagine Dan T. Campion's conversation with Chester Hanrahan. "Let me bounce it off Des Spellacy, Chet. He's just a lad with the dew behind his ears. Hardly thirty, if he's a day. Learned his numbers at the seminary. Where they teach them to count in one-dollar bills." There was a fee in it for Dan T. Campion, along with his retainer from the archdiocese, if he was passing along an offer from Chester Hanrahan. Of that Desmond Spellacy was certain.

"He's having trouble getting rid of his lots then, Dan?"

"My God, you're a suspicious one, Des," Dan T. Campion said.

"It's not selling, Dan," Desmond Spellacy said. "He needs something to make it go. And the city won't put in a school or the county a golf course. On that very same land he offered both of them before his generous offer to us." He'll wonder how I knew that, Desmond Spellacy thought. And he'll figure out its Sonny McDonough. The only Catholic on the board of supervisors. "I hear he's overextended, Chester Hanrahan. The banks want to call in his paper."

"You're a smooth number, Des, that's exactly what I told Chet. No fast ones on Des Spellacy, I said. His Eminence knew his buttons when he made you chancellor. Though there was some that thought the poor man was in his dotage when he made a boy like yourself such a high monkey-monk. Not me, though. 'Never underestimate Des Spellacy,' is what I said. 'A very cool article,' is what I said. 'Looks like a leprechaun, thinks like an Arab.' My very words." The thick frosting of blarney with the brain clicking away under it. "It was Sonny told you, then?"

"A little bird."

"It's still a grand offer, Des," Dan T. Campion said. "What if Chet were to throw in ten thousand dollars for the Building Fund."

"I'd have to catch it on the bounce, is what I hear."

"You have a grand wit, Des," Dan T. Campion said. "Not like most priests, I hate to say. You say hello to some of them fellows and all they got to talk about is how Genial Jimmy Dahill was dancing the jig at his hundredth birthday party in the parish hall. And wasn't it grand the way that Tommy Lawler, the famous bail bondsman, passed away saying the rosary." He wrapped himself tightly in the Turkish towel. "I think I could persuade Chet to let his construction company build the school at cost."

"Which set of books do I get to see, Dan?"

"It's not every father has such a grand head for business, Des," Dan T. Campion said. "You could get blood out of a stone, is what I like about you. And what Chet likes about you, too."

"And let's say you throw your fee from Chet into the Building Fund," Desmond Spellacy said. "Or else it's the receivers for Chester Hanrahan."

Which was how Saint Eugene's got built in Rancho Rio. And Chester Hanrahan got the sash of a Knight of Malta. And accepted the Cardinal's offer to become chairman of the Building Fund. All because of a conversation in the steam room at Knollwood Country Club.

*"Domine, non sum dignus . . ."*

A new chairman of the Building Fund. It was his choice, he knew that. Subject only to the cardinal's veto. "Get the feel of the situation," the Cardinal said the morning after Chester Hanrahan died. "Play a few rounds of tennis, a few sets of golf." The advice nagged. The Cardinal knew the correct terms as well as he did; he wondered why His Eminence had slipped in the needle. Perhaps it was the Cardinal's way of suggesting that there had been complaints about the chancellor from the clergy. Complaints about the amount of time the chancellor spent in country-club locker rooms buttering up the fat cats of the archdiocese. Desmond Spellacy had heard the whispers. And the pastors didn't like the way he nosed around in parish affairs, either. If there was one thing a pastor guarded jealously, it was the freedom to run his parish as he saw fit. The cost of a new boiler was none of the chancery's business. Desmond Spellacy did not operate that way. No, he had said to the new Carrara marble altar at Saint Dominick's. Too expensive. No to the new baseball diamond at Holy Redeemer. Not unless you're thinking of celebrating high mass at third base, Father. Pay off the debt on your church first. And speaking of your church, Father, it smells like a locker room. Tact never had been his long suit. And so the pastors complained.

They criticized him, Desmond Spellacy knew, because they didn't dare criticize the Cardinal. What they didn't know was that the plan to curb their independence had come from the Cardinal himself. Centralization, the Cardinal said—it was the only way to cut costs and melt the deficits. If the pastors didn't like it. . . . That was where he came in. Desmond Spellacy had no illusions about where he fit into the Cardinal's scheme. He was a combination lightning rod, hatchet man and accountant. Someone to fend off the pastors and take the heat off the Cardinal. Young enough not to be infected with old ideas about how to run a parish or to have formed friendships that could not be broken. If necessary. Ruthless enough to sack an old monsignor. If necessary. Tough enough to talk decimal points with a Protestant banker or lean on a contractor. If necessary. In other words, a man to do the dirty work. "A few rounds of tennis, a few sets of golf." Desmond Spellacy knew now what the Cardinal meant: watch your step. One false move and you become an expensive luxury. Off the plank goes Desmond Spellacy.

Not if I can help it, he thought.

*"In principio erat verbum . . ."*
He heard the cough. That one-of-a-kind cough. Desmond Spellacy searched the cathedral. That awful, racking cough meant that Jack Amsterdam was there. He thought, It's only natural. Jack had done business with Chet Hanrahan. And Jack would have a rooting

54

interest in whoever was the new chairman of the Building Fund. Because the new chairman of the Building Fund would have to do business with Jack. Because in the interest of central financing, Desmond Spellacy had let seventeen million dollars in building contracts to Jack Amsterdam. Schools, hospitals, convents, churches, rectories. There was nothing to be alarmed about. The concrete was good. Nothing had fallen down yet.

*Nothing had fallen down yet.* That's a grisly goddamn thought. Desmond Spellacy crossed himself quickly and asked forgiveness for taking the Lord's name in vain.

It was just that there was something about Jack that encouraged thoughts like that. What happened to Ferdinand Coppola when he made the bid on the new Saint Columbkille's Hospital contract was a case in point. The night before the bids were unsealed, two of Ferdie's big rigs were tipped over into the Los Angeles River. "A high Santa Ana wind condition" blew his rigs over, Ferdie said. And withdrew his bid. Six tons each, those rigs were, and they had never taken a dive to a wind before. "It's a rough business, boyo," Dan T. Campion told him. "Stay out of it." And so Jack Amsterdam got the contract to build Saint Columbkille's.

"So Jack's gone legit," Tommy had said when he heard about the contract.

"What's that supposed to mean?" Desmond Spellacy said.

"It means you're doing business with a real sweetheart there," Tom Spellacy said. "Him and His Eminence will get along good. You ever hear his confession, give me a call. That's one I'd like to sit in on. He swears a lot, I bet. And I bet he's missed his Easter Duty."

Desmond Spellacy chose his words carefully. He wanted to know about Jack, but he wasn't sure he wanted to hear it from Tommy.

"You've been checking up, then?"

"There's nothing to check. He's clean."

"So there you are."

"Listen, Des, Mary Magdalene was clean, too. But she used to be a hooker, someone told me once. And the day she signed on with Jay Cee there, someone pulled her rap sheet."

"That's vivid," Desmond Spellacy said. "And what does this someone tell you about Jack?"

"The ginneys leave him alone is one thing they tell me. They tried to move in on him a few years back, the ginneys. And the story is, Jack took this ginzo from Detroit and dried him out. Dominic. Dominic LoPresti. That was this ginzo's name. Jack took Dominic and stuck him in this dryer in a laundry over to Lincoln Heights there. Shrunk the poor bastard down to twenty-one pounds."

It was Tommy's kind of story. Tommy liked to tell stories about the lowest kind of human behavior. Stories Desmond Spellacy was not likely to hear in confession. This time, however, the story seemed to hold an implicit warning. Desmond Spellacy erased the suggestion.

"You know that for a fact?"

"Des, let me tell you something. I don't know the Holy Ghost for a fact. But you're in the Holy Ghost business. So when you tell me about the Holy Ghost, I believe it."

"Meaning I should believe you."

"Meaning you want to roll around in the shit and think it's clover, then you're not going to believe me, I tell you this is a bad guy to be in the kip with. So let's change the subject. I'm sorry I ever brought it up."

The construction of Saint Columbkille's Hospital was the beginning of a long and profitable relationship between the archdiocese and Jack Amsterdam. None of the other contractors ever bid against him. Perhaps because the cost of cranes was so high. But now there

56

was the story of the asphalt. Chet Hanrahan had mentioned it before he died. Ten tons of asphalt, Jack's invoices said. But the word was nine tons of asphalt and one ton of sand. Which meant that the Cardinal was getting stiffed for a ton of asphalt.

"I don't believe it," Dan T. Campion said. "It's Ferdie Coppola putting out that story, and everyone knows Ferdie's a sorehead."

"Twenty-five grand each those cranes of his cost, is what I hear," Desmond Spellacy said. "Maybe that's why he's such a sorehead."

"The insurance covered it," Dan T. Campion said. "I had Phil Leahy look at the policies for me. Wind damage was one thing Ferdie was specifically covered for."

"I think maybe we better ask Phil Leahy if we've got a policy on someone making a chump out of His Eminence. I keep hearing stories."

"From your brother, the policeman," Dan T. Campion said. "Always thinking the worst, a policeman. Old stories, Des, never proven. He's getting on, Jack, he wants to make amends."

"For what?" Desmond Spellacy said.

"For any mistakes he might have made," Dan T. Campion said.

"Conscience money is what you mean," Desmond Spellacy said.

"It's all still green, the last time I looked, anyway," Dan T. Campion said. "You've got to take the long view, Des. Anyone who gives $75,000 to the Building Fund, we've got to trust him for a ton of asphalt. Assuming, which I don't, Ferdie's story is true."

"There's a word for that seventy-five," Desmond Spellacy said. "Kickback is the one I had in mind."

"Insurance," Dan T. Campion said. "Insurance is the word I would use. Jesus Mary and Joseph, Des, it goes with the franchise. He builds a nice hospital,

Jack. He builds a nice school, too. But you ask a contractor to be in a state of grace all the time, you'd be saying mass in a wigwam. His Eminence, too. He'd catch cold, I think, an old man like that."

"I'll tell His Eminence that," Desmond Spellacy said. "I'll tell him you're worried about his nose getting all stopped up from saying mass in a tepee. I'll tell him you think the best way to get rid of a cold like that is not to sniff around any asphalt. He'll appreciate the diagnosis, His Eminence."

"You do that, Des," Dan T. Campion said. "You take your bathroom scales out to Jack's place there, and you weigh ten tons of asphalt. It's messy is what they tell me, but you do it. Then you tell His Eminence and His Eminence will find you a nice little parish in the middle of Nebraska. It's nice in Nebraska, I hear. You get the change of seasons. A hundred above in the summer, a hundred below in the winter."

"There's one thing I wonder about you, Dan. When was the last time your right hand knew what your left hand was doing?"

"1908," Dan T. Campion said, pronouncing it nineteen ought eight, and punctuating it with the loud laugh, the slap on the back.

*"Et verbum caro factum est . . ."*
There were times, Desmond Spellacy thought, when Dan T. Campion worried him more than Jack Amsterdam. Not that Dan didn't have his uses. The Cardinal sneezed and Dan T. Campion reached for his handkerchief. It was the other noses that he was cleaning that bothered Desmond Spellacy. Give him ten hands and he'd be picking pockets with nine of them and making the sign of the cross with the tenth, Chet Hanrahan had said. And Chet was no altar boy. Which was why the new chairman of the Building Fund was so important. He needed his own man. Someone, to put it

bluntly, who belonged to him. Someone to keep tabs on Dan T. Campion. Someone to pass the word to Neddy Flynn and Emmett Flaherty and the other Catholic contractors (were there any non-Catholic contractors, he suddenly wondered) that they should bid against Jack Amsterdam on any new construction projects. There was one thing you could say about Neddy and Emmett. You wouldn't pick up the newspaper in the morning and read that they'd stuck somebody in a dryer. No old stories, never proven. At least no old stories he couldn't live with.

The new chairman. Someone who would help him unload Jack. When the time came.

Who?

Phil Leahy had all he could handle with the diocesan insurance programs. Ed Ginty would have been perfect, if he weren't in the penetentiary for embezzling that ninety-three thousand dollars. Devlin Perkins, but he was a convert and his wife was president of the Guild for Episcopalian Charities. A Protestant prune, Dan T. Campion called Adela Perkins. Take a bite out of her and she'd flush you out like a physic. Putting on airs and calling herself an Episcopalian, Dan said, when she was just another Prod. Fernando Figueroa? Not with Tony Garcia already the lay director of the Welfare Bureau. The rich laity wouldn't like two Mexicans. . . .

Who then. . . .

The vicar general was anointing the casket with incense and reciting the prayers for the dead. Why do people buy caskets like that, Desmond Spellacy wondered. All teak with silver handles. A banquet for the termites and the weevils. A send-off you could be proud of. The superdeluxe McDonough & McCarthy send-off. . . .

Sonny McDonough.

That was a possibility. A real possibility. Member of

the county Board of Supervisors. President of the Planning Commission, too. Which was always useful in condemnation proceedings. Dedicating his life to public service now after making his pile in funeral homes and cemeteries. He was letting Shake Hands McCarthy run the business. John McCarthy, Desmond Spellacy thought. He must remember that. Ever since Shake Hands became a Knight of Saint Gregory, he insisted on being called John.

Desmond Spellacy noted Sonny McDonough's liabilities. Sonny sang "Tantum Ergo" in the shower. Or to be specific, Sonny sang "Tantum Ergo" in the shower after playing golf with Desmond Spellacy. You couldn't outwait Sonny. You couldn't stay in the locker room until he finished his shower. Not if you minded catching a cold or smelling bad. So into the shower. And there would be Sonny, all lathered up. "Tantum ergo, Sacramentum, Veneremur cernui; et antiquum documentum . . ." The memory made Desmond Spellacy flinch. "A grand number, isn't it, Des?" Sonny McDonough would always say. And sing another hymn: "Heads lifted high, Catholic action our cry, And the Cross our only sword." A number made for that voice. When Sonny was feeling like a tenor, he would sing "Lovely Lady Dressed in Blue." Another grand number. "About Our Blessed Virgin," Sonny McDonough had informed him the first time he rendered "Lovely Lady" in the shower.

He was an idiot, Sonny. An idiot who thought there was an advantage in singing hymns in front of a priest in a locker room. But a definite possibility nonetheless. And one way to bring Sonny around to discounting the funeral costs of all the nuns and priests who died each year in the archdiocese. An idea Sonny wasn't too keen on, but if he were chairman, he couldn't very well turn it down. Tommy would be a help. Tommy would know if there were any little colored boy in Sonny Mc-

Donough's woodpile. Besides that raffle that was fixed at Our Lady Help of Christians. The memory was painful for Desmond Spellacy. Not one of my finer moments. Although it did get the property condemned. It would be a help knowing that Sonny was shifty going in. The question was, how shifty.

Sonny McDonough . . .

There was a sudden stir at the rear of the sanctuary. And then His Eminence Hugh Cardinal Danaher appeared on the altar. He must have thought better of his flu bug, Desmond Spellacy thought. Put-A-Pool-In-A-Catholic-School. The Cardinal blessed the casket and then stood at the foot of the altar steps until the bustle in the cathedral quieted down.

"It is not the custom in this archdiocese," the Cardinal began, "to deliver a eulogy at the funeral of a layman. But I would be derelict if I did not acknowledge in some way the passing of Chester Hanrahan and pay my respects to his godly wife and his two children, Brother Bede and Sister Mary Peter, whom he gave to his Father Almighty." There was absolute silence in the cathedral. "I remember that day so many years ago, the nation coming from depression into war, when I asked Chester Hanrahan if he would take over the Building Fund. I think you all know what he answered. 'YES!' said Chester Hanrahan. And over the years, everything I ever asked of him, a new boiler for Saint Malachy's, new classrooms for Our Lady of the Assumption, a new hospital for the Sisters of Saint Joseph, you know the answer I always received. 'YES!' said Chester Hanrahan. . . ."

# Three

Tom Spellacy chewed on a hangnail and waited for the pain in his stomach to pass. Gas, probably. In the three days since the discovery of the body at 39th and Norton, he had eaten nothing but donuts and hamburgers from the cafeteria at the corner of First and Temple. All those hours and nothing to show but BO and constipation. No fingerprints, no identification. No friends, no neighbors, no employer, no acquaintances. The girl at 39th and Norton seemed not to exist before her murder as she did not exist now. He picked up the report from the night watch. Five witnesses heard a woman scream the night of the murder two blocks from where the body was found. A house-to-house investigation. The screamer was a young woman whose husband had returned that day from service in the Pacific with the marines. It was the first day she had had sexual intercourse in three years, four months and two days. He wondered who had computed the days, the woman or the night watch.

The cream in his coffee had curdled. Flecks floated on the surface of the olive-colored liquid and the soggy paper cup had begun to leak. He watched the stain widen on his desk blotter. Corinne used chicory in her coffee. She also put a bay leaf in her spaghetti. There was a spice rack in her tiny kitchen, and when she cooked, he handed her the bottles of dill weed and thyme and tarragon and oregano and sweet basil. Mary

62

Margaret did not use herbs or spices. Spices caused diarrhea, Mary Margaret said. Mary Margaret also did not do the things to him in bed that Corinne did.

He made a note to call Corinne.

Mary Margaret had Saint Barnabas.

He had Corinne.

"Are you going to book me or not?" Tommy Diamond said.

He had forgotten that Tommy Diamond was sitting there. Tommy Diamond was fingering the papers in his out box.

"Hands off," Tom Spellacy said. Tommy Diamond was the only person he knew who parted his hair in the middle.

"I did it." Tommy Diamond had a disability pension from Water & Power. He had slipped in a puddle of spilled Jello in the company cafeteria. His back was bent and he could not clerk and now he had time on his hands.

"You ever get tired of confessing, Tommy?"

"I did it."

"You queer?"

"My back was okay, I'd throw you out the window, saying that."

"This is the sixteenth homicide you confessed to since I been downtown. What else am I supposed to think? You want to go to the joint and be someone's sweetheart." He leaned across the desk. "You pitch or catch?"

Tommy Diamond smiled. "Anyone else confess?"

Better to talk to Tommy Diamond than to think dirty thoughts about Corinne. "Two marines from Pendleton."

"Shipping out, I bet. Didn't want to go fight for Aunt Sam. Fuck the red, white and blue."

"You understand confessing, Tommy."

"Who else? There's always a lot of nuts in a case like this."

He laughed. "A drunk from the Lincoln Heights tank."

Tommy Diamond shook his hand. "I've been in there. You can't turn around without someone pissing in your face. I'd say I had a contract to hit the Pope if it got me out of there."

The end of the comedy hour. "Get out of here, Tommy."

"You're going to be sorry, Lieutenant. One of these days I'm going to kill somebody and no one's going to believe me."

They're coming out of the woodwork, Tom Spellacy thought. Take yesterday. An astrologer in Altadena asked the exact time of death and promised to deliver the murderer's name in five days, fourteen hours and twelve minutes. A man who said he was a Ph.D. in extrasensory perception asked to photograph the dead girl's eyeball; the final image in it, he said, would be the face of the killer. A woman in Covina said her husband did it. She wanted grounds for divorce. A landlord in Studio City said his tenant did it. He wanted to evict the tenant and double the rent.

The telephone rang. Tom Spellacy held the receiver to his ear and took a sip of the cold coffee. It tasted worse than it looked.

"So your daughter's name is Mary Lou," he said after a moment. "And the last time you saw Mary Lou was the middle of January."

"The sixteenth," the woman said.

"January sixteenth." He took a pencil and wrote the date down.

"1943."

"1943," he repeated. "You didn't say that before."

"I was going to bring it up."

"Right," he said. "She went out to get a package of cigarettes."

"She always smoked Philip Morris. I got to think it was Philip Morris she went out to get. The girl you found, she smoked Philip Morris, she could be my daughter."

"That's the last time you saw her, January sixteenth, 1943."

"Right with Eversharp."

"And you never reported her missing before."

"She moved around a lot. 1939 was the last time I saw her before that. She was on her way to Seattle. Going to work for Boeing, she said. She was punching a keyhole press before that, I think. In Tulsa. Maybe it was Oklahoma City. She lost a couple of fingers in the keyhole press. That's what she told me, at least."

"This one we got," Tom Spellacy said, "she's got all her fingers."

"I figured that," the woman on the telephone said. "Actually, she had a face like a horse, Mary Lou, you want to know the truth, so I had a feeling she couldn't be this Mystery Beauty that they're calling her in the newspapers."

"Yeah."

"Say, listen," the woman said after a moment, "I get downtown a lot."

"That's nice," Tom Spellacy said.

"I take the bus," the woman said. "I get off at Figueroa and Olympic, the weather's nice, and I walk. It's raining, I take the trolley on Sixth Street. I could stop in and see you sometime. Your name is?"

"Diamond," Tom Spellacy said. "Tommy Diamond."

"I'll call you sometime, Tommy," the woman said. "Maybe we can have a drink. Woman of fifty-two, I don't look bad, I say so myself. You know how to play carnival?"

"I don't know that one, no."

"I sit on your face and you try to guess my weight," the woman said. "That's a swell one, isn't it?"

Tom Spellacy hung up and swore to himself. Mystery Beauty. Beauty only because Crotty had told reporters she had nice tits and a nice bush. Mystery because there was still no ID. There was nothing to go on, not even a dental profile because her face was so smashed up. Unless you counted the clothes. There were a lot of clothes, actually, if you believed all the breathers calling in. Four pair of silk hose, corner of Pico and Vermont. A pair of red sandals, size seven, 3400 block of Slauson. A black high-heel patent-leather pump, six triple A, back of a coon whorehouse on West Adams. A red halter. A green wool knit skirt. A leather handbag with a Kotex in it. A plaid purse with a package of Trojans inside. Listen, I found a brassiere. Size 34, C-cup. Black lace. She was the type wore black lace, I bet. Nice ones, Jeez, I bet she had nice ones. Pointy, you know what I mean. And a pair of panties I found, too. With a blond pussy hair in it. The hair between her legs is blond, these are her pants, I bet.

Tom Spellacy swiveled in his metal chair and put his feet up on the desk. His office was a cubicle separated from the Robbery-Homicide bullpen by a flimsy wooden partition topped by a section of frosted glass; the whole divider was less than six feet high. Through the open door he could watch the detectives in the long, green bullpen. The ringing of telephones caused a constant din. He had assigned Masaryk and Bass to check up on the breathers. Bass made the calls and Masaryk typed up the reports. Never mind that Masaryk was a moron, a forty-watt bulb in a hundred-watt socket. He typed fast, which was why Fuqua plucked him out of Admin and made him a detective in Robbery-Homicide. He was a real asset when you got behind on your reports. Always willing to help out.

Ninety words a minute and never a mistake. Then there was Bass. Thirty-five years in the department and no one could make him turn in his papers. Where am I going to go, he said. I got no family. 1911, he joined up. 1911. When it was the fucking Pony Express, Crotty said. And always the lessons from Ben Bass. You want to break up a card game, Ben Bass said, you knock on the door and ask for a guy named Slim. There's always a guy named Slim in a card game. Or else you piss under the doorway and they'll think it's a drunk and open up. Piss under the door and ask for a guy named Slim. Thirty-five years in the department and that was what Ben Bass had picked up.

Masaryk and Bass. The Lone Ranger and Tonto.

He picked up the telephone and dialed the Jury Commission. "Mrs. Morris," he said.

"Mrs. Morris," Corinne said when she answered the phone.

"I'll be by tonight," Tom Spellacy said.

"For a change," Corinne said.

He lowered his voice and watched the door in case someone walked in. "We can play carnival."

"I know how to play carnival."

"You do?" The answer dampened his enthusiasm for her. She took bed for granted, knew more about it, in fact, than he could concoct in his wildest dreams.

"I sit on your—"

"Never mind," he interrupted. "I've got a call on the other line. I'll see you around seven."

And she never felt guilty about it.

Masaryk stood in his open doorway. His hair was clipped to the skull and his face wore its perpetual look of surprise. Tell Masaryk that the sky was blue or the ocean deep and he would treat the information as he would have the Resurrection the first Easter.

"Fuqua called when you were on the phone. He wants to see you and Crotty."

"Where's Crotty?"

"Interrogation room 3." Masaryk remained in the doorway. "Tom . . ."

Tom Spellacy waited.

"I think that's a swell Mystery Clue. I mean, I couldn't even tell my wife." Masaryk put up his hand to shield his mouth and whispered, "And she's Italian."

Interrogation room 3 was down the corridor past the bunco bullpen. Tom Spellacy told Crotty that Fuqua wanted to see them and then looked through the two-way mirror at the man sitting at the table in the room. The man's hands were shaking and he was weeping uncontrollably.

"Who?"

"Leland K. Standard, family man," Crotty said. "Wife named Maureen and three little ones named Mary, Dorothy and Theresa. Little Theresa's mental. One of them mongolian idiots there, I think they call them. His wife's brother's a Dominican priest. He has a cocker spaniel named Lester and he makes $4,500 a year as a draftsman for Pacific Telephone."

"Alibi?"

"Tight as a popcorn fart," Crotty said. "Drove the parish chorale up to Ventura County. The K of C sing-along at Saint Boniface's in Santa Paula there. Stayed the night in the parish hall. Got back in the morning."

Tom Spellacy lost interest. "Let him go, Frank."

"Fuck him," Crotty said. "Let him sweat. He didn't want to be here, he shouldn't make a habit of flashing his weenie." He waved a manila folder. "It's in the file. 'Shake hands with this, little girl,' he says to one of them. 'Liquid candy, little girl,' he says to another. Dad and Mom there pressed charges, he'd be waving it around in Folsom, is where he'd be waving it. Know why they didn't press charges? The Dominican brother-in-law is why. He goes to see Dad and Mom, promises them two box seats in heaven. He also tells them Leland K.'s lawyer's going to put their little girl on the stand, let her tell the jury how big it looked, and wouldn't that be a terrible thing. Big deal he's married and got a family. It's only a matter of time he does it again."

Through the mirror Tom Spellacy watched Leland K. Standard slump forward on the table and cradle his head in his arms. It always surprised him how few suspects realized that the mirror was two-way and that they were always under surveillance even when they were alone.

"One thing I should tell you is I checked out that chorale group there," Crotty said. "Twelve girls and the guy driving the bus and we know who the guy driving the bus was. Our friend, the candy man. Fourteen and under the little girls are. He's got something on his mind, I think, and it's not the four-part harmony, I bet."

"We got enough troubles, Frank, without a Dominican on our ass."

"There's nothing to worry about is what I'm trying to tell you," Crotty said. "The wife and kids are out of town, visiting grandma and granddad at the farm, milking a cow, I think. What's he going to do? Call the Dominican, swear to God his fly's been zipped ever since he pissed in Little Nancy's belly button? Don't you believe it."

2

Fuqua stood framed by the window in his office as the photographer moved a chair to get into better position. His suit jacket was buttoned, all three buttons, and stays held the collar points on his white shirt firmly in place. The fan had been shut off so as not to rustle the papers on his desk. The heat was stifling. Fuqua told the photographer to include the picture of his wife and two children in the shot. Tom Spellacy looked at the photograph. Both little boys wore braces. On the wall behind Fuqua's desk there was a framed certificate attesting to his successful completion of the Police Management Course at the Roger J. Minihan School of Penology and another certificate noting that he had passed the marksman's course on the department range. Tom Spellacy could feel the half-moons of sweat spreading down the side of his shirt. The photographer asked for one more picture. Fuqua put on his glasses and stared at the report in his hand. Crotty jumped when the flashbulb exploded.

"That's it," Fuqua said, and waved the photographer out of his office. He took off his jacket, loosened his tie and switched on the desk fan. He stood in front of the fan for a moment, shaking his damp shirt away from his armpits.

"I wanted you two in the picture," Fuqua said as he took his seat, "but Benny Carmody at the *Times* said that the *Express* had already run a shot of the three of us and he wanted something different."

Tom Spellacy nodded. "I like you better without the glasses, Fred. You get a glare with the glasses."

"It might mess up the shot, the glare," Crotty said.

"I can get him back, you want," Tom Spellacy said.

Fuqua stared from one to the other, then slowly reknotted his tie, straightening it from the reflection in his desk glass.

"I been to see the commission is the reason I got you up here," Fuqua said. The Select Commission had been appointed by the Board of Supervisors to run the department until it picked the new chief. Without a chief, every division in the department was in effect a private army run by its division commander. "I told them this one was a major crime."

"The major-crime approach," Tom Spellacy said.

"Right," Fuqua said. He either did not notice or had decided to overlook the sarcasm in Tom Spellacy's remark. "Right," he repeated. "And I told them that for major crimes we ought to have a major-crime section."

"That's a hell of an idea, Fred," Tom Spellacy said. It was well known in the department that Fuqua was bucking for chief, but he could not believe that the commission would be stupid enough to pick him.

"And I told them that the officers in the major-crime section should have no other duties. . . ."

"Except major crimes," Crotty said.

"Right," Fuqua said. "That's how to be on top of things, Crotty. Which is why I want you to head up the Major Crime Section."

Tom Spellacy looked at Crotty and then at Fuqua. "You mean, the commission said all right?"

"As you said, it's a hell of an idea," Fuqua said. There was a smirk on his face. "I'll be in operational control and Crotty will run things day to day. You'll be his deputy."

"What about Chief Davis?" Morty Davis was the deputy chief for internal affairs, and since the indictment and resignation of the former chief, had overseen the affairs of Robbery-Homicide.

"What about him?" Fuqua said. "You got no cause to love Chief Davis."

Crotty kicked Tom Spellacy in the foot. A warning to keep his mouth shut. No, he had no cause to love Morty Davis. Morty Davis had wanted to fire him when he got caught with the eleven hundred in his pocket. The funny thing was, he liked Morty Davis. He was smart. And honest. The first was rare in the department, the second rarer still.

"Well, then, we'll be working together," Fuqua said.

This dumb son of a bitch thinks I'm going to owe him, Tom Spellacy thought. The Major Crime Section.

A way to get Fuqua ink, that was all it was. A way to make him chief. Not with my help.

Fuqua reached into his desk drawer and pulled out three tie-pins. He gave one each to Crotty and Tom Spellacy and put the third on his own tie. The tiepins bore the legend H-187—the designation for homicide in the state penal code.

"Every man in the section will get one of these," Fuqua said. "It'll be like a second badge. We wear our tiepins, the press will know we're not in Traffic when we show up at the scene of a major crime."

Tom Spellacy looked at Crotty to make sure he was hearing correctly.

"It's a grand idea, Fred," Crotty said. He kicked Tom Spellacy in the foot a second time.

"And this being the first major crime the Major Crime Section has investigated," Fuqua said, "I asked the commission to put up a reward."

"How much?" Tom Spellacy said.

"$10.000."

"They said yes?"

"Of course."

Tom Spellacy whistled tonelessly. Crotty took a cigar from his pocket and rolled it around his mouth.

"You don't think much of that idea," Fuqua said.

Crotty held a match to the end of his cigar and drew on it until it was lit. He made no attempt to answer.

"Not much," Tom Spellacy said finally.

"That's all you've got to say?" Fuqua said.

"What Tom means," Crotty said, exhaling a stream of cigar smoke, "is that we've got creeps crawling out from under every rock in town as it is. You put up ten grand. . . ." He shrugged and fished a snapshot from his pocket. It was a picture of a young Mexican. He handed the snap across the desk to Fuqua. "I got this in the mail yesterday."

Fuqua examined the photograph. "So?"

72

"There was a piece of paper with it. 'THIS IS YOUR MURDERER,' someone's written on the paper. I give it to SID, see if they can lift a print. I sent the picture over to Hollenbeck, let them run it through their mug file. Yesterday afternoon, SID comes up with a print. Armadelia Luna."

Tom Spellacy started to laugh.

"I don't see what's so funny," Fuqua said.

"The Flower of Figueroa Street," Crotty said. "Fourteen arrests. Shoplifting. Lewd conduct. Public drunkenness. . . ."

"I nailed her once on grand theft auto," Tom Spellacy said.

"She's got a boyfriend," Crotty said. "Rafael Saldivar." He pointed at the photograph in Fuqua's hand. "Guess who?"

Fuqua handed him back the snapshot.

"He was fucking around," Crotty said. "Which is why she sent us the picture. Now she's sorry she did it. . . ."

"I don't see the point," Fuqua said.

"The point is, Fred, there must've been eight cops working on this yesterday, maybe sixty man-hours in all."

"You put up a $10,000 reward," Tom Spellacy said, "we're going to be chasing even more of these than we're doing now."

"I don't think it's a way to get the Major Crime Section off to a terrific start," Crotty said. "We need to crack this one quick." He drew on the cigar for a moment. "You have to think beyond the Major Crime Section, Fred."

# Four

"A tiepin," Tom Spellacy said when they left Fuqua's office. "A fucking tiepin." He held the H-187 pin between his thumb and forefinger and dropped it deliberately into the ashtray by the elevator.

"He wants to be chief," Crotty said. He extracted the tiepin from the sand in the ashtray, shook it off and put it into his pocket.

"He's a horse's ass," Tom Spellacy said. "The worst kind of horse's ass. The kind that likes to see his name in the papers."

"So who says a horse's ass can't be chief," Crotty said. "That's why he fucked Morty Davis. That's why he dreamed up this Major Crime Section. He cracks this one, he thinks he's got a chance."

"*He* cracks it," Tom Spellacy said sharply. "He's got trouble cracking a can of beer. They're making morons chief this year, *then* he's got a chance."

"He never stuck his mitts in the poorbox that I heard," Crotty said. "And he scores good on the chief tests they give, too, Fred does. 'You come to a four-way stop sign, who's got the right of way,' Fred's always got the answer."

"Which he probably picked up at the Roger J. Minihan School of Penology," Tom Spellacy said.

"And he speaks nice, too," Crotty said. "Roomful of niggers over on Central Avenue, they come out thinking he's a mulatto or something, the coon mumbo

74

jumbo he gives them. It's Fred, we don't screw it up for him, is what I think."

"Then we ought to stop looking for the son of a bitch took this girl out then," Tom Spellacy said. "Better him on the bricks than Fuqua chief is the way I look at it."

Crotty checked his watch. "Woody said he'd have the autopsy report before lunch."

"Then we better go look at it before that asshole sees it and starts reading it over KFIM."

The County Medical Examiner's Office was in the basement of the Hall of Justice. In the spring heat the corridors were thick with the smell of formaldehyde. They walked through a cavernous autopsy room painted a weak green and then past the refrigerated compartments where the day's catch of corpses was kept. Woodrow Wilson Wong's private office was in the far corner of the basement. His walls were covered with enlarged photographs of battered babies and bashed-in skulls and mutilated breasts and patterns of stab wounds. The pictures drove Fuqua's stupidity from Tom Spellacy's mind.

"You ever get the idea that Woody likes this job a little too much?" he said, examining the photographs.

"Twelve thousand stiffs a year," Crotty said. "Lose your sense of humor here and the coroner's job could get to be a pain in the ass."

"They say he likes to go shopping at the May Company weekends," Tom Spellacy said. "He never buys anything. Just checks out lamps and tennis rackets and chairs and toys, stuff like that. He wants to find out what kind of marks they'd make, somebody gets the bright idea to kill you with one of them."

"What else am I supposed to do?" Woodrow Wilson Wong said as he hurried into the room. He was smoking a large black cigar and the ashes had splattered over his white medical coat. "The supervisors don't give me any money. This is a nickel-and-dime operation. 'You teach those stiffs how to vote, we'll give you more money.' That's how the supervisors look at it."

Woody's being a Chink wasn't much of a help either, Tom Spellacy thought. That was another theory of the board of supervisors: only a Chinaman would want a job like this. The supervisors saw the coroner's office as a skid row for doctors and out-of-work embalmers. A place for medical students to practice and pick up extra money. Twenty bucks an autopsy and bring your own microscope and knife sharpener. All appendages that drop off the deceased belong to the county. That was how Woody's predecessor lost his job. He had used a skull as a paperweight, and the paperweight turned out to have a brother and the brother raised a stink. Give the job to Charlie Chan, the supervisors said. No more paperweights, the supervisors also said.

Woodrow Wong handed them each a copy of the autopsy report. A complete set of photographs was attached to both files. There was an autopsy slab in the center of Woody's office that he used as a conference table. The ME's idea of a joke, Tom Spellacy thought. He and Crotty sat on either side of the table and read. Woodrow Wong turned the pages along with them.

Name: unknown. Address: unknown. Female, adult, Caucasian, the autopsy report read, 20-to-30 years old, 110 lbs., 64 inches (approx.). Blood type: O. Appendectomy scar, old fracture of right forearm. Wax fillings in third and fourth molars, rest of teeth smashed and broken.

"What kind of dentist puts in wax fillings?" Tom Spellacy said.

"It's something you do when you can't afford a dentist," Woodrow Wong said. "You melt down some wax and pack it in where it hurts."

Tom Spellacy looked across the autopsy table at

Crotty. "The candle up her cunt. It must've been for her teeth."

"And whoever did it found another use for it," Crotty said.

Wood splinters in facial lacerations, indicating victim probably beaten with a blunt wooden instrument, possibly a two-by-four. Cause of death: knife wounds, hemorrhage and shock. Face slashed from ear to ear. Severing clean, one inch above the navel, probably accomplished with sharp surgical instrument or a butcher's knife. Blade sharp on both sides. Depth of wounds in excess of five inches. Width of wounds between 1-and-1½ inches. Thickness of wounds ⅛-to-¼ inch. Rope or wire wounds on wrists and ankles. Phosphorescent dye right thumbnail.

"She was selling her blood," Tom Spellacy said. "That's what the dye's for. The blood banks put a spot on the thumbnail so you don't come back too soon."

"The drunks would come in five times a week if you let them," Woodrow Wong said. "The law says eight weeks between visits."

"They rub it off with battery acid, the drunks," Tom Spellacy said. "It buys a lot of Sterno, a pint of blood."

Crotty scratched a match along the autopsy table and held it to his cigar. "It's a good bet she was broke," he said. "She can't afford a dentist and she's selling her blood. She's also got a rose on her pussy, so let's assume she was peddling that, too."

"We should get Vice on it," Tom Spellacy said. "See if any of the girls knew her. Or if they know anyone likes to cut."

They'd check Brenda, he thought suddenly. Brenda Samuels. She was working out of a hotel off Alvarado now. An escort service. Brenda's Personal Services, Ltd. Making ends meet. Yes, they'd check Brenda. She always had her ear to the ground. Anything that was happening with the girls, Brenda would know about it.

Fine. As long as I don't have to see her. For a moment he wondered what Corinne would say if she knew he was the bagman Brenda had paid off.

The smell of formaldehyde filled his nostrils and he gagged.

"Howard Terkel says we should look for a 'well of loneliness type,'" Crotty said. "A female pervert." He puffed on his cigar to keep it lit. "Jerry Troy had one of them once when he was in the department. Remember Jerry?"

"Jerry Bang Bang," Tom Spellacy said. "He was a shooter."

"Fucking card is what he was," Crotty said. "Competitive fucker on a case, though. Always wanted the collar by himself." He spat a piece of cigar wrapping from his mouth. "Finish first and third in a five-man jackoff contest, you give him the chance."

A little like Des, Tom Spellacy thought. "I know the type."

"Anyway, he collars this les, Jerry," Crotty said. "She sliced up her girl friend there, then tried to flush her down the toilet. There she is telling Jerry how she couldn't fit the head down the crapper and she begins to cry. Really bawl. 'There, there,' Jerry says. With that brogue you could cut. 'There, there, it's the sort of thing that could happen to any one of us.'" Crotty exploded into laughter. "Isn't that a grand story, though? God, I love a good story, Tom. I roar every time I remember that one."

"He shot somebody at the ball game, didn't he?" Tom Spellacy said.

"It was a joke was all it was," Crotty said. "He had the DTs, Jerry. He got drunk one night, the Stars were playing Seattle at Gilmore, and he tried to shoot that big Polack pitched for Seattle, used to pitch for the White Sox, Hriniak, I think his name was. He loved the Stars, Jerry, and they weren't doing anything against

78

this guy, and Jerry says, 'I'll fix that Polack fuck,' and takes out his Special. Except he was so pissed he couldn't hold it and it dropped and went off. It was Nuns' Night and he shot a Sister of Mercy in the toe. Fucking shame they let him go, Jerry."

No semen in vagina or mouth. Large number of bristles around all wounds. Bristles probably from a coconut-fiber brush used to clean wounds. Undigested food in stomach.

"Egg rolls," Woodrow Wong said.

"Go fuck somebody sideways," Crotty said.

"I analyzed the food," Woodrow Wong said. "Egg rolls."

"Maybe Woody's got something, Frank." Tom Spellacy straightened the pages of the autopsy report and placed it in the folder on top of the photographs of the victim's bifurcated body. "The undigested food means she ate not long before she was killed. But she's got burns on her wrists and ankles. Rope burns or wire burns."

"She was tied up," Crotty said. He worked each sentence over carefully. "She was a captive. She had to eat." He tapped his fingers on the autopsy table. "She had to be fed. Nobody cooks Chinese except a Chink and let's say for the moment it wasn't a Chink, the bad person." He looked back and forth between Tom Spellacy and Woodrow Wong. "Takeout food. The son of a bitch was stuffing her with takeout egg rolls."

Woodrow Wilson Wong laughed.

"I guess we don't eat Chinese today," Tom Spellacy said.

2

The corridor outside Robbery-Homicide was crowded with parents and pederasts, lesbians and whores, cab drivers and bus drivers, bartenders and waitresses, pimps and policemen and children with stray articles of clothing, all claiming some knowledge of the unidentified woman from the corner of 39th and Norton. Crotty ignored the din.

"We check out every Chink restaurant between Oxnard and San Diego."

"The cutlery shops," Tom Spellacy said. "Surgical-equipment houses. Butcher supplies."

"Barber wholesalers," Crotty said. "He could've used a razor."

"Blood banks."

"Religious-supply houses. I guess that's where you get votive candles."

"You think it would make it any easier, Frank, there was a $10,000 reward?"

Crotty laughed. "Lunch later."

In his office in-box, Tom Spellacy found a report from SID on the eyeglasses found under the victim's body. Negative. There was nothing yet on sex offenders and nothing from the body shops, no cars reported with suspicious bloodstains. He told Bass to check the knife outlets and Masaryk the Chinese restaurants.

"We're looking for egg rolls," Masaryk said.

"Takeout egg rolls."

"Takeout egg rolls," Masaryk repeated. "On the night of the incident."

"Incident?"

"Until we have a conviction, Tom, we have to call it an incident."

"You go to night school, Masaryk?"

"Yes, sir."

"The Roger J. Minihan School?"

"Yes, sir. It was highly recommended by Captain Fuqua."

"I thought so."

"How many egg rolls are we looking for, Lieutenant?"

Tom Spellacy closed the door of his cubicle and spread the photographs of the victim over his desk. The dark patch between her legs made him think of Corinne. He shook the thought away. In one series of pictures, Woody had tried to piece the body back together again. Looking at her that way, it was hard to think of her as the woman the newspapers called Mystery Beauty. He tried not to think of all the parents, brothers and sisters of the missing Mystery Beauties he had seen since the morning of the murder. Mary Jane sang in the choir. Lucy was the class valedictorian. Edna never looked at another man in her life. They all belong in the convent is what I think, Crotty had said.

The telephone rang. The woman said her name was Mabel Leigh Horton. Mabel. Leigh. Leigh like in Vivien. *L-e-i-g-h.* From Guin, Alabama, Mabel Leigh Horton said. That's *G-u-i-n,* capital *A-l-a-b-a-m-a.* Now residing in Culver City.

"What can I do for you, Mabel?" Tom Spellacy said.

"Mabel *Leigh,*" Mabel Leigh Horton said.

"Sorry."

"First you hard-boil an egg," she said.

"Hard-boil an egg," he said.

"Then you put it in the young lady's right hand."

"Then I put it in the right hand," he said. "Got it."

"Then you close the casket," Mabel Leigh Horton said.

"Close the casket," Tom Spellacy said. "Right." He waited. "Then what?"

"Why in seven days the murderer will confess," Mabel Leigh Horton said. "It's something we do in Guin."

"Right."

"What do you think of that?"

"I think you and my wife would get along good," Tom Spellacy said.

He checked the teletype in the bullpen, and when he got back to his cubicle, Howard Terkel was standing over his desk, rifling through the photographs of the victim.

"You think there's a werewolf angle on this one, Tom?"

Tom Spellacy gathered the pictures in a pile, put them in an envelope and locked them in a desk drawer.

"It's been a while since they had a werewolf, the zoo tells me, Howard."

"You think it was a fiend, then."

"Eliminate the Cardinal, a fiend's a good bet."

"You've definitely eliminated the Cardinal as a suspect, then?"

"It was only a figure of speech, Howard."

"Your brother carries a lot of weight with His Eminence, they tell me," Howard Terkel said. "You might mention to him it would be a wonderful story if His Eminence was to say the funeral mass. Let me know what he says, your brother, and I can arrange it so His Eminence gets an exclusive on what it all means, the death of this cunt."

"We don't have an ID yet, Howard," Tom Spellacy said. "So we don't even know she's a Catholic cunt or not."

"We can work that out later," Howard Terkel said.

Tom Spellacy stood up. "It'll be a factor, Howard. A definite factor."

Crotty's office was on the other side of the bullpen. As watch commander, his wall partition ran all the way to the ceiling. There was a middle-aged couple sitting in the office. They looked worn and tear-stained. The man had not shaved and there was a hole in the woman's hair net. The man was holding a dog-eared

82

graduation photograph of a young girl in a white cap and gown.

"Mr. and Mrs. Constantine," Crotty said.

"Konstanty," the man said.

"Let's eat Mexican," Crotty said.

"I didn't mean to interrupt," Tom Spellacy said.

"Casa del Sol," Crotty said.

The father handed the photograph to Tom Spellacy. "She wore braces until she was seventeen."

"She loved Bing Crosby," the mother said.

"And a retainer after that," the father said.

"Gee, I wish the press would stop predicting trouble between Bing and Dixie," the mother said.

"Only at night, the retainer, never on dates," the father said. "Ten o'clock she had to be home on date nights, and then she'd pop the retainer in."

"We want Bing and Dixie to stay together," the mother said. She started to cry. "That's what my baby wanted, too."

"Your baby ever been tattooed?" Crotty said.


3


"*Dos cervezas*," Crotty said to the waiter. "The oysters good?"

"*Sí, señor.*"

"I had a dozen in here the other night and only one of them worked."

The restaurant was crowded. Once La Casa del Sol had been a Mexican bar with live mariachi music. The narcotics squad had kept it under close surveillance but no arrests were ever made. Now it was populated by policemen and politicians and assistant water commissioners and deputy tax inspectors all kneeing their secretaries under the tables. Crotty and Tom Spellacy sat against the wall under a bullfight poster. Crotty tucked a napkin under his chin and drank half a glass of Carta Blanca.

"This used to be a swell place when I was in Narcotics," he said. "I was making a buy in here one time from this pretty little *chiquita,* and she says to me, 'Why don't we take a fuck before we do it?' And I says to her, I didn't want to lose the collar and I had to think fast, I says, 'I'd love to, *querida,* but I got a bad dose of the clap.' And she says to me, 'That's okay, *muchacho,* so do I.' " He laughed until he began to choke and people at the adjoining tables turned to stare. "Isn't that a bastard of a story, Tom?"

Crotty's laughter was interrupted by a hand that gripped his shoulder like a vise.

"Monsignor McGrath," Crotty said.

"I missed you at the seven last Sunday, Frank."

"I went to the ten at Immaculate, Monsignor."

"Is that so, Frank?"

"A big investigation, Monsignor. It went late."

"And you slept in?"

"I'll be at the seven next Sunday, Monsignor."

"That's grand, Frank. I heard you speaking Mexican. You speak it, do you?"

"I do, Monsignor."

"Then I wonder if you'd ask the waiter to send over some buns. I don't speak the lingo and I'm over there with Supervisor McDonough and we'd like a few buns."

*"Muchacho, un poco de pan para el padre."*

Monsignor McGrath clapped Crotty on the shoulder and went back to his table with Sonny McDonough.

"Of all the fucking nerve," Crotty said.

"You should've told him you were investigating Father Dicky Donohue's drunk-driving charge, is the reason you missed mass," Tom Spellacy said.

"I bet he's hitting up Sonny there for a new car," Crotty said. "You should've seen him last year, his fiftieth birthday party in the parish hall. A trip to

84

Hawaii he got. A set of matched luggage. A year's free haircuts. A bagful of golf sticks. A season's pass to Santa Anita. And he was mad. He had his heart set on an Oldsmobile. A Hydra-matic. I thought he was going to excommunicate Jack Walker, the car dealer."

Sonny McDonough broke a piece of bread. He was wearing a dark suit and a black tie with a pearl stickpin.

"You know Sonny's on the Select Commission picking the new chief?" Crotty said.

Tom Spellacy nodded. The selection of the new chief was a subject he did not wish to consider. The last chief had gone before the grand jury and shortly after that he was indicted and then John Dempsey, the chief of detectives and Fuqua's predecessor, had blown out his brains and the whole period brought back memories of Wilshire Vice.

"Who do you think it's going to be, it's not Fuqua?" Crotty said.

String Frank along. He wondered sometimes why he had never been indicted. He could make an educated guess that Des being his brother had something to do with it. The Cardinal carried a lot of weight downtown.

"Kenny Meyer, I suppose," Tom Spellacy said. The deputy chief of administration. Gray and colorless.

"You seen him lately?" Crotty said. "He looks two hundred, Kenny, and he can't be more than forty-nine. It's the wife. Two tits she's lost already, and a kidney's coming out next week. The liver's not too sharp either, is what I hear. It ages a guy, looking for spare parts like that. They don't have Father Time in mind, I think, the commissioners."

"Harvey Zim, then," Tom Spellacy said. He really didn't care which of the front runners or dark horses replaced the former chief.

"J-E-W," Crotty said. "Nothing wrong with being a Jew, you like wearing a beanie, but hot fudge sundaes

85

in the gas chamber, that's a better bet than putting your money on a Hebe."

So much for Harvey Zim, chief inspector, uniform police. Anyway, he thought, the last chief had beaten the rap. The indictment didn't stick.

"He's got a place in Balboa now, I hear, the last guy."

"And one in Ensenada," Crotty said. "He come out of it all right. Two houses and he beats the rap. Tears the shit out of being chief, though, getting indicted like that, even you beat it."

The waiter brought two more Carta Blancas. Crotty ordered chiles rellenos and enchiladas verdes for the two of them. When the waiter left, he leaned across the table and said softly, almost as if he were afraid of being heard, "What do you think of Morty Davis's chances?"

He thinks I'm afraid Morty's going to get rid of me, Tom Spellacy thought suddenly. He doesn't know it's no worse than Des saving my ass.

"He's a saint, actually," Tom Spellacy said. "Twenty-two cents he's got in the bank, Morty, and a hole in his shoes. He's either dumb or honest, he's so poor, and honest is the one I'd pick. And he never looked the other way when the last guy had both his dukes in the tambourine."

Crotty leaned back and smiled. That reassuring conspiratorial smile. That you've-got-nothing-to-worry-about-Morty-Davis smile.

"Not a chance. He blew the whistle on the last guy. The last time they rewarded a guy for blowing the whistle, they had white blackbirds. The sun rose in the west that day, too. Sure they want somebody honest, but they want somebody knows how to play ball, too, the commissioners."

He knew that Crotty was right. Morty Davis never looked the other way. That could be dangerous. He was suddenly angry. The last guy indicted, poor John Demp-

86

sey's brains splashed all over a wall, Morty Davis out in the cold because he was honest. And not a finger laid on Jack Amsterdam. The paymaster. Now the civic benefactor. And Des Spellacy's golf partner. Not a man to point the finger at. There were just too many layers between Jack and the street. And there was always Brenda to take the fall for him.

"So that's why I'm putting my money on Fuqua," Crotty said. He mixed the rice and the refried beans together with his fork and lowered his voice, as if what he had to say embarrassed him. "Don't give him any static, Tom." He kept stirring the food, avoiding Tom Spellacy's eyes. "Keep your trap shut. I got enough trouble with my Chinamen without worrying about you giving Fuqua shit. I just don't want my life complicated."

Tom Spellacy nodded, but he was not listening. Maybe I'm dreaming, he thought. Maybe Des didn't have anything to do with it after all. Maybe once the chief was indicted and John Dempsey put his service revolver in his mouth, maybe then the grand jury said enough's enough, we made our point, the department's as clean as a whistle. He signaled for two more beers.

Anything to change the subject.

"Those glasses under her tits," he said. "SID checked them out with an optical house." He took the SID report from his pocket. "Standard frame, stock lenses, didn't have to be ground to order. 'The owner is probably a man,' " he read, " 'with a small volleyball-shaped head. His eyes are far apart, his left ear is approximately ¼-to-½ inch higher than his right and he is extremely myopic.' "

"Did they belong to our guy?"

"Probably not." Tom Spellacy watched Sonny McDonough prepare to leave the restaurant. Bills disappeared into the hands of waiters. Sonny McDonough shook hands at every table. The two-handed shake.

Along with the sincere smile reserved for the loved ones of the faithfully departed. "SID says the way the screws are rusted, the glasses probably been there for a long time."

"No reason you got to mention that," Crotty said. He raised the napkin to his lips and burped. "We should give it to the papers, that report, except the last part. Make them think we're on top of things. Nothing Howard Terkel would like better than looking for a guy with a volleyball-shaped head. Put an ad in the *Eye, Ear, Nose & Throat Monthly,* let Howard check out the replies."

Sonny McDonough stood over the table. He grasped Crotty's hand, but Tom Spellacy kept his under the table.

Sonny McDonough slapped Tom Spellacy on the back.

"I got a grand story for your brother," Sonny McDonough said. "I was telling Charley Moylan last week, I said, 'Ben Hogan's helping Des Spellacy with his golf swing, did you know that, Charley?' Pulling his leg, you know, you can appreciate that, a well-known leg puller like yourself." Tom Spellacy wondered where Sonny McDonough had ever dreamed up the notion that he was a well-known leg puller. "And Charley says to me, 'He a Catholic, Ben?' And I said to him, 'Never heard of any Jew Hogans, Charley.' And Charley says, 'I knew a Methodist named Hogan once.' And I said to him, 'He must've fallen away from the Church.'" Sonny McDonough pounded him on the back again. "Isn't that a swell story? You got to tell it to Des."

"I can't wait," Tom Spellacy said.

# Five

Tom Spellacy dreamed.

He was stealing a car. Pry open the window with a screwdriver. Pull up the lock with a coat hanger. Hot-wire the ignition and drive off. Simple.

He awoke.

The portable radio was playing softly on the bedside table. From the mountains to the desert, from the desert to the sea, here's the news, all the news. Washington. Elliot Roosevelt. Johnny Pick-Up-The-Check Meyer. Chicago. Pickle packers puzzle picking name for pickle. Locally. Police still sifting clues brutal slaying unidentified victim. Search for man with volleyball-shaped head.

Rain beat against the window.

He knew why he had been dreaming of stealing cars. It was raining. His ass always hurt when it rained. Ever since a dog took a chunk out of it when he was stealing a car in 1933.

He dug the sleep from his eyes.

He had stolen 319 cars in 1933. Legally. Five dollars a car. Less expenses. There were rules. Never break into a locked garage, even if there was a car inside. That was B & E and a one-to-three pop if you got caught. Never break into a garage attached to a house. That made the garage part of the house and the owner could shoot you. Otherwise his kind of car theft was legitimate. He did it for a finance company. Repossession was the fancy word for it. The finance company looked at it this way: the guy who wasn't making the payments on his car was stealing it from the bank. If you took him to court, it would cost you money, even if you could find him, which wasn't easy, because guys who didn't keep up their loan payments generally moved around a lot. Proving they were good at ducking out on their rent, too. And if you did find the guy and slap a piece of paper on him, he would probably tell you to go fuck yourself. After he worked you over. Because a guy who was out of a job didn't usually like some fairy in a coat and tie telling him he had to show up in court a week from next Tuesday. So the finance company hired someone to steal the car from the guy who was stealing the car from the bank which hired the finance company to steal the car back. Because Mr. Giannini at the Bank of America didn't want to get in the hot-car racket, legal though it was.

He rubbed his ass.

The dog who bit him in 1933 was named Wolf and Wolf had taken thirty-seven stitches worth out of his ass when he was trying to lift a black Packard with nine thousand miles on it. Crotty was the cop on the beat and when Tom Spellacy screamed, Crotty showed up and drilled Wolf with one shot. You dumb fuck, Tom Spellacy had said, you could've got me. Not a chance, Crotty had said. He blasted Wolf once more for good measure. You ought to think about joining the department, Crotty said. It beats hot cars and you can shoot the fucking dogs. It was the first time he had ever laid eyes on Crotty.

Tom Spellacy lit a cigarette.

Corinne was singing in the bathroom. Mary Margaret always called the bathroom "the toilet." 6:30 A.M. The voice speaking on the radio seemed familiar. Oh, shit. "If you have any information on this case, call this special number and ask for me, Detective Captain Fred Fuqua, that's F-U-Q-U-A, Fuqua."

The bathroom door opened.

"That's all you need, a special number," Corinne said. "You're going to hear from a lot of swell people you might've missed otherwise."

She had a towel wrapped around her wet hair, otherwise she was naked.

"That asshole," Tom Spellacy said. He tried not to look at her breasts. Don't point them at me, he thought, they might go off. "He wants to be chief."

"Everyone in town doesn't like his brother-in-law's going to get in touch with you."

"Not with me. With F-U-Q-U-A. Serve that fuckhead right."

She stood by the radio, legs astraddle, hands on hips, belligerent. He could count on the fingers of one hand the number of times he had seen Mary Margaret naked. Always the locked door when she took a bath. Always the darkened bedroom and the fumbling under the rough flannel nightgown. It could be a hundred degrees with a hot dry wind off the desert and still she would wear the flannel, and the only light in the bedroom would be the flickering votive candle on the dresser in front of the statue of the Immaculate Heart of Mary.

Corinne sat on the bed and began to paint her toenails.

"There was a guy called yesterday, wanted to know if she was having her period."

"He was belting it, I bet. And saying ooohhh and ahhhhhh on the telephone."

Mary Margaret had never talked about his work. Meat loaf, she talked about, and whether it was too expensive to put a strip of bacon on top for flavor. Or whether she should put the skim milk in the macaroni and cheese. Or whether his socks needed darning or whether Father Plunkett would hear confessions Saturday with Father Sheed in the hospital with cancer of the bowels. It was useless telling her that Johnny

Kinsella got seven-to-ten. Sand dabs is good for Fridays, she would say. Or that Brian Manners who used to be an altar boy over to Saint Anatole's was shot in the head by the Jew fag he was living with. Kev got a C in catechism, she would say. It's Sister Felita teaching catechism this year and she's a much tougher teacher than Sister Geraldine. They call it Christian Doctrine in the sixth grade, not catechism. CD is the nickname for it, all the kids use.

The radio announcer said that hundreds of suspects were being questioned.

"Fuck her," Tom Spellacy said suddenly. "She's not worth worrying about."

Corinne stopped working on her toenails. "What do you mean, 'Fuck her'?"

He swung his legs out of the bed. Change the subject fast. "You've got nice tits, Corinne."

"Don't talk about my tits. Tell me what you mean, 'Fuck her.'"

"Your tits are nice to talk about."

"My tits are for later."

Tits. Ass. Belly button. He moved his eyes away. He wished he had never brought up the girl. Maybe it was better talking about Sister Geraldine. Or sand dabs.

"Why 'Fuck her'?" she repeated. "Come on, I'm interested. The only thing she did wrong was get hacked up."

"She fucked the world, Corinne." He knew that was his second mistake. He headed toward the bathroom. Buddy Clark was singing "It's A Big, Wide Wonderful World" on the portable radio.

"So that's it. She was in a state of mortal sin and it offends all you harp cops cheating on your wives." He stopped in his tracks. "Look at me," she said. "Somebody hacks me up, you going to say, 'Fuck her, she fucked the world'?"

He tried to imagine having this conversation with

92

Mary Margaret. Mary Margaret who was probably even now having breakfast with Saint Barnabas of Luca.

"You haven't."

"That's right. Nothing much past the county line."

He tried not to look at her breasts.

"Jesus Christ, Corinne, you know what I mean. You think you can swim in shit and come out smelling like chocolate ice cream."

"How about the guy who nailed her? What's he swimming in?"

"You sure it's a guy? How about a girl? A girl friend, maybe?"

"She a dyke?" Corinne asked quickly.

"It makes a difference then?"

"No."

She returned to her toenails. Lesbians made her uncomfortable. He had saved her life once by suggesting she might be a lesbian and she had never really forgiven him for it. He knew he was in control now.

"That's a mortal sin you're not too crazy about."

"Was she?"

He suddenly felt very tired. It was a stupid argument, made more so when conducted stark naked. "We don't even know her name yet, Corinne. It's just something we've got to consider, is all."

"That's really swell. How about dogs? You considering dogs, too?"

"It's cold, Corinne. I'm going to freeze it off, standing here."

"You might as well freeze it, all the use it gets," Corinne said.

He closed the bathroom door. Buddy Clark was still singing. ". . . A Nero, Apollo, the Wizard of Oz." Her cosmetics were lined up on the sink. Her diaphragm was in its pouch, neatly dusted with cornstarch. She never seemed to wear it anymore. He wondered if she had left it out on purpose. As a reminder. He remembered that night six months ago when he had first come to this apartment, searching the medicine cabinet for a diaphragm or contraceptive jelly. It embarrassed him to admit it, but looking for things like that made him horny. And he had never expected to meet her again, not after telling Turd Turner she was butch.

It was funny how much he liked Turd Turner. He was strictly bush league, Turd. He couldn't even stick up a candy store without fucking up. Eighteen years in the joint, eighteen months outside since he was seventeen years old. When he got a contract, he hit the wrong guy. When he ran a string of girls, he got the syph. Turd's luck. When he got drunk, he pulled a kidnap. And ended up in the gas chamber.

Tom Spellacy lathered his face. He tried not to catch his eye in the mirror. All the use it gets, Corinne had said. She was like Brenda in that one way. She used her box as if it were a weapon.

Better to think of Turd Turner.

It wasn't as if Turd were a Bruno Hauptmann, pulling a kidnap for the potatoes. He was just dumb and lonely was the reason he did it. It was V-J Night and everyone was celebrating in the streets and getting laid and Turd was two weeks out of the can and broke and only wanted to be a part of the celebration. So he stuck up a liquor store and got drunk and feeling good and when he ran out of booze he decided to stick up a bar-and-grill, even though he still had the money from the first job. Thinking never was Turd's long suit, especially when he was on the juice. But something went wrong in the bar-and-grill and he had to take a customer hostage and he holed up in an apartment on Bunker Hill with three guns and two bottles of rye and a broad who was scared out of her skin. The mayor was there and the chief of police and Fuqua and searchlights and Crowd Control and enough hardware to invade Japan.

Tom Spellacy couldn't quite remember a scene like it.

"Why the fuck are all these people here?" he had said when he arrived.

"They think it's a hell of a way to end the war," Crotty had said. Tom Spellacy could not ever recall seeing Crotty rattled. Whatever happened, it was always one big joke to Frank. "You seen the mayor yet? He's wearing his National Guard uniform. 'Let's go in and take him, boys,' he says. I swear to Christ, Tom, he said that."

"I'd like to send that fuck in first," Tom Spellacy had said. "I know Turd. I collared him twice. He's not going back inside. He'll shoot it out."

"You can bet your sweet ass he will with a 207," Crotty said. "That's a gas-chamber bounce."

Just like Turd. No luck. Never. Not even with his nickname. He had picked it up at Joliet when he was seventeen and in for armed robbery. His first time inside. Cherry. ("Except for one time with my sister," he had told Tom Spellacy once. "My half-sister, so it was okay.") He was Horace Turner then, with a fourth-grade education and an IQ of 86. An old bull, a lifer, had tried to ram him in the ass and Horace Turner was so scared he crapped all over the lifer's pecker. He had been Turd ever since.

"Who's the hostage?" Tom Spellacy had said.

"Her name is Corinne Morris," Crotty said. "Works in the County Courthouse. Assistant Jury Commissioner. War widow. Her old man was killed at Pearl Harbor." Crotty lowered his voice so the reporters gathered at the barricade could not hear. "She fucks like a bunny rabbit, they tell me."

"Is the mayor getting any?"

"Not that I heard."

"Why's he so steamed up then? The Turd's a loser."

"The shit he's in, the mayor, he's looking for all the

95

ink he can get. Anything to make him look good. The chief, too."

Tom Spellacy shook his head in disgust. "There a phone in there?"

"Madison 5244."

"Let me see what I can do."

He pushed his way through the crowd until he found a public telephone booth at the foot of Bunker Hill. A sailor was passed out inside the booth. Tom Spellacy hauled him outside and dropped him on the sidewalk. Then he fished a nickel from the sailor's jumper and dialed Madison 5244. The telephone rang six times.

"Turd, Tom Spellacy, how they hanging?"

"You're going to have to come in and get me, Tom. I'm not going back inside."

"Listen, I understand, it's no country club, the joint."

"All I want's a car and enough gas to get across the border."

"Jesus, that's a tough one, Turd. We got the mayor here, and the chief. And with all that grand jury shit about corruption in the department, they want to hang you out to dry, get their names in the paper."

"I got the girl."

"They don't give a shit about the girl," Tom Spellacy said. His voice was matter-of-fact. "She's a dyke."

"What do you mean, she's a dyke?"

"Been sniffing pussy for years."

"You kidding me, Tom?"

"We got a yellow sheet on her, Turd."

"Jesus, one thing I could never stand, it's a dyke. All those years in the joint, dreaming about pussy, and I got to snatch a les. It's unnatural, being a dyke."

Tom Spellacy wondered if Mrs. Morris of the Jury Commission was listening to the conversation. He hoped she would keep her mouth shut. Her one real chance was to go along with the story. Keep Turd talking, that was what he had to do.

96

"I'll buy that," he said to Turd Turner.

"You know what the story of my life is, Tom?"

"It's shit," Tom Spellacy said. He hoped he sounded sympathetic. He felt in his pocket for some change. If the time ran out, the girl was done for. He placed a dime and three nickels on the metal counter in the booth.

"Even the booze I steal is shit," Turd Turner said. "Four Roses."

Tom Spellacy could hear him noisily take a drink at the other end of the telephone. He pumped a nickel into the coin slot and hoped Turd was too busy to hear it.

"I wish you'd think it over," he said.

"You think I should, Tom?"

"They're not giving you a rain check on this one. They're coming in after you, like in the movies. The chief's got a tommy gun, for Chrissake. They'll get you and the dyke. And blame her on you. That is no shit."

"Those assholes."

"They'll give that dyke a funeral like you never saw. A city holiday. The mayor. The chief. She's worth a lot to them dead. The Cardinal. A big municipal funeral, all the pictures in the paper, and no one will ever know she's a dyke except you and me, and you're dead and I got a pension I got to worry about. You give them a big funeral and that's going to take a lot of that grand jury heat off their ass."

"You crapping me, Tom?"

"How long have I known you?"

"I'd hate to help those assholes out of the shit."

"For a dyke."


Tom Spellacy cleaned the lather off his face and stepped into the shower. The hot water made him feel better. It was funny how things turned out. The Turd was convicted, the mayor recalled, the chief indicted. And Crotty was right. Corinne was a great fuck.

"How did you talk him out of there?" she would say.
"We were old friends."

He had never expected to run into Corinne again. It was eight months after he had talked Turd Turner into letting her go. He and Crotty had stopped at an all-night drugstore off the Strip that did most of its after-midnight business with the girls who worked in the line at the Mocambo and the Troc. Tampax and douche bags and rubbers. The walls were decorated with a dozen eight-by-ten glossies of dance teams, the man in each picture in tails, the girl hanging backward over his arm, her tits all flattened out, with inscriptions like, "Thanks, Bernie, from Lurene and Ned, The Fox Trotters." He was drinking a cup of coffee when he recognized her. She was buying a package of tampons.

"Not Kotex," Crotty said. "They wear tampons, then they must fuck. Crotty's law."

He got up and walked back to the feminine hygiene counter. "Hi," he said.

"Beat it," she said.

"Sorry."

He went back to the table and ordered another cup of coffee.

"You're a lost cause," Crotty said. "I'm going home."

He watched her buy some tooth powder and aspirin and lipstick. Dr. Lyons, Bayer and Helena Rubinstein. Noticing brand names was like remembering license plates, something he did. All part of being a cop. Like watching a Mexican wearing sneakers in a bus line. Snatch and run, it was quicker in sneakers. Or going down to the basement and turning off the water before a drug arrest. The stuff couldn't be flushed down the crapper if the water was off.

Then she was standing at the table.

"Listen," she said, "I'm sorry, I didn't recognize you, I mean, I don't think I ever thanked you. . . ." She seemed to falter. "And I guess you saved my life. That night, I mean."

"Some coffee?" he said.

She wanted a drink. Her apartment was only a couple of blocks away. One large room and a Murphy bed. She had half a pint of rye and no ice. The refrigerator was defrosting. The mattress on the Murphy bed was soft and the frame unsteady. The center of the mattress caved in and in effect she slept in a trench. His knees could not get purchase and his elbows slid and he kept slipping out of her. Finally she had him lie beneath her and she got on top of him. The veins in her arm stood out and there were beads of sweat on the down on her lip and she told him what to do and at last he did it.

"Sometimes I think my brains are in my cunt," Corinne Morris said.

Cunt. C-U-N-T. It was a word Brenda used, or one of her girls. Not the girls in Boyle Heights. Not Mary Margaret. "Down there," Mary Margaret said, and she meant down there on him as well as down there on her. He wondered if she talked about down there with Saint Barnabas of Luca.

"I'm sorry the way I was in the drugstore," Corinne said. "You know the kind of guys they get in there, the way they come on. They got a rubber rolled up in their wallet, so you can't miss it, and then they flash it at you and ask you for a date. Assholes." She threw her leg over him. "I hate assholes like that."

"There's a lot of them like that," he had said. He couldn't think what else to say. It was easier talking to Brenda. The take, the payoff, who was in on the action, things that were useful. Maybe if he had talked to Mary Margaret about assholes with rolled-up rubbers in their wallets instead of wishing that her period lasted for a long time, maybe she wouldn't be in Camarillo at that very moment.

99

"My husband was one."

He remembered her husband was killed at Pearl Harbor. Making her a gold-star widow.

"The war hero."

"That was my second husband. Homer Morris. Charlie Quinlan was my first husband. Both assholes. They always seem to find me, the assholes."

"Thanks."

She ran a finger down his face. "Not you. None of the creeps I know would have saved my life." She raised herself on an elbow. "You know where I was on December 7th?"

He shook his head.

"The about-to-be war widow was grieving in Reno, getting a divorce."

"Fucking a cowboy, too, I bet." He was getting more comfortable with her. He seldom indulged in bed talk. Mary Margaret called it talking dirty. She would not permit it.

"How'd you guess?" She seemed pleased that he would reach that conclusion.

"I'm a cop."

"Kiss my brains, copper," Corinne said. "Eat my brains."

He went down on her and even as he did he let his eyes roam the apartment. Her pussy's in my face, he thought, and I'm still casing the layout. Her thighs held his face in a vise and he checked where the door was, one thing a cop should always know and that's where the door is, and how many steps to his piece, he should have put his piece under the pillow and not on the couch, what if someone came through the door, his piece was too far away. Then she moaned and as she came he took in the old Victorian wicker chair and the monogrammed bill box and the pewter candlesticks and the faded Christmas cards still stuck in the book-

case and he made a note to ask her about them sometime.

That was the first time he had come to her apartment.
He never had asked her about the Christmas cards.

They never went to his place. "The Essence of Valley Living," the late Chester Hanrahan called his place.
Three bedroom. two baths, one family room. That was
a joke, family room. He had bought the house for
Mary Margaret the last time she got out of Camarillo.
"A home environment is what she needs," the psychiatrist had said. "No stress." No fucking around is
what he meant. It was funny the way Mary Margaret
could always sense it. There was never any evidence,
he was careful about that. He slept with her once
every menstrual period, he had made a point of it for
ten, fifteen years, he couldn't recall exactly how long.
The definite-patterns approach. But she still sensed it.
A Brenda, a Corinne. And she began to talk to Saint
Barnabas of Luca. "Involutional melancholia," the
psychiatrist called it. Back to Camarillo. She seemed
to like Camarillo. Except for Father Cruz, the chaplain
who gave her communion once a week. Why isn't he
down in the missions of Bolivia, she would say, working with the Mexicans? To Mary Margaret, everyone
who lived between San Diego and Tierra del Fuego was
a Mexican.

Maybe Des can arrange it, he would say.

Or Saint Barnabas, she would say.

And so he never brought Corinne to the Chester
Hanrahan Development. Never volunteered, never
asked. There were too many questions there. It was
always her place and the Murphy bed with the trench
in it.

The Murphy bed was made when he went back into
the living room. Corinne was wearing a half-slip and
nylons and shoes. Nothing else. Half-naked. A nun's

101

phrase, "half-naked." ("No playing ball half-naked in the schoolyard, Thomas Spellacy. *Put your undershirt back on.*") He noticed that she had laid out some fresh clothes for him on the bed.

"I bought you a couple of shirts yesterday," Corinne said. It was as if the argument had never happened. "And some Jockey shorts."

"I don't like Jockey shorts usually," Tom Spellacy said. "They bind is what I don't like about them."

"They bind so nice," Corinne said.

"How'd you happen to get them?" he said. It had always been understood before. She didn't come to the house in the Valley, he didn't leave any clothes in her apartment. Something like that you shouldn't have to spell out.

"I cleared out a drawer," she said. She lit a cigarette and began to puff on it nervously. "I had these old winter things I got rid of and the drawer was empty."

"Oh."

"You put on the same shirt, the same socks every time you leave here, it's got to be grubby."

"You got some socks, too, then?"

"At Bullock's. The mid-month sale. Men's furnishings." She crushed her cigarette into the ashtray at the side of the bed. "I'll blow you, you want."

What I want is what she's doing now, he thought. What she's so good at. What I don't want are the shirts and the socks and the Jockey shorts. It'll be the sport coat next and buying the brisket at the Safeway and a bigger apartment and the movie at Grauman's Tuesday and Saturday and the occasional sneak preview in Glendale. Jesus, she's good at this. A Catholic girl, that's the funny part of it. Makes you wonder what the nuns are teaching over to Holy Resurrection there. Funny thinking of the sisters teaching her this. Cop the old joint, Corinne, when the conversation gets a little nervous. They must pass out A's when you learn that at Holy Resurrection.

The telephone was ringing. On the eleventh ring, she rose and picked up the receiver.

"It's Crotty," she said. She was suddenly furious. "I thought you were never going to give this number to any of your scummy cop friends."

"I thought you were never going to buy me any Jockey shorts."

She glared at him as he took the phone.

"Tom," Crotty said, "I know I shouldn't call that number . . ."

"That's okay, Frank."

Corinne rose from the edge of the bed. She came to the telephone table and knelt in front of him.

"We've got this little problem, is why I called."

"Jesus," he said. "Can't it wait?"

"Not really."

"Sweet Mother of God . . ."

"You all right, Tom?"

". . . the fuck is it, it can't wait?"

"It's something the monsignor might be interested in, is the reason I don't want to talk about it on the phone, if you get my meaning."

"Des."

"That's the one."

"Son of a bitch."

"The Alvarado Arms Hotel."

"Oh, Jesus, on 11th Place."

"Step on it."

"Jesus."

# *Six*

He drove slowly past the Alvarado Arms once, turned around at the end of the block and parked down the street from the hotel in front of a dried-out frame house with a faded "Rooms to Let" sign stuck crookedly into the tiny, scorched lawn. The trash barrel by the door of his car was filled with broken liquor bottles. He lit a cigarette. The smoke filled the car. Through the rain-washed windshield, he occasionally saw curtains move in the unkempt houses lining the street. Checking me out, he thought. And checking out the prowl car in front of the hotel. It was a dumb place to park the black-and-white. Whoever was driving should have pulled it into the alley leading to the garage. There was no point in making the people behind the curtains curious. They weren't bad people. Just too-little, too-late people. Has-beens, never-weres, never-will-bes.

He opened the car door and dropped his cigarette into a rain puddle. The broken palm trees along the street all looked as if they had curvature of the spine. Even with the rain now beginning to pelt down, he walked slowly reluctantly across the street toward the hotel. The Alvarado Arms was a dilapidated five-story building with chipped masonry cornices and a fire escape grafted on the front to hide the cracks and scars of the 1933 earthquake. The gilt lettering in the ground-floor windows was starting to peel: BRENDA'S 24-HOUR

COURIER SERVICE. BRENDA'S 24-HOUR CHAUFFEUR SERVICE. BRENDA'S PERSONAL SERVICES, LTD.

It's been a long time, Tom Spellacy thought as he stared at the windows. You put me in the shit, Tom, Brenda Samuels had said. I don't need that. Stay away. So he had stayed away. While Brenda took the heat. First from the grand jury, then from the military. It was a funny thing about the army. They passed out rubbers to the GIs going on pass, then they closed down the whorehouses. Join the army and jerk off in a Rameses. Not that it stopped Brenda for long. She was nothing if not resourceful, Brenda. He had followed her career in the Yellow Pages. BRENDA'S PERSONAL SERVICES, LTD. Nothing fancy. Nothing like the old days. Mobile screwing. Enough to get by. And Vice let her alone. Vice always liked Brenda. Especially after she kept her mouth shut when she testified to the grand jury. It wasn't much, but it was a living.

That fucking Lenny Lewis, he thought.

The linoleum in the lobby of the Alvarado Arms was worn through to the floor. Crotty was standing by the desk. The desk clerk was a frightened old man with one opaque lens in his eyeglasses.

"Second time in six months a guy checked out in this fleabag, he was in the saddle," Crotty said.

"I wasn't on that time either, Lieutenant," the desk clerk said. His shirt was frayed, he needed a shave and he was beginning to snivel. A comic book was open on the desk in front of him. "It was the night man that time, too. It's a swell place in the daytime, I make sure of that. Very quiet."

"That's why the Shore Patrol was bitching last week about sailors catching the clap in here," Crotty said.

"Not to me," the old man said. "It must've been the night guy again."

"You ever done time?"

"Not that I can remember."

105

"What were you in for?"

"Exposure."

"I figured you had to have references, get a nice job like this," Crotty said. He turned and pointed Tom Spellacy toward the stairs. There was no elevator in the Alvarado Arms. They did not speak until they reached the first landing.

"What the hell is this all about?" Tom Spellacy said. "I don't have enough troubles, I got to see Brenda?"

"That just happened, Tom, it's one of those things," Crotty said.

"She here?"

"Third floor."

"She say hello?"

"She told me to go fuck myself."

"She hasn't changed then."

"Forget Brenda, Tom, she's not the problem. It's the stiff in 514 that's going to upset the monsignor."

"What's it got to do with Des?"

"You'll see." The exertion of the climb was making Crotty sweat. On the fourth landing he had to pause to catch his breath. "Vice was checking out the girls like you said, to see if anyone knew someone liked to cut. Or a girl with a rose tattooed on her pussy. They don't like to roust Brenda, Vice, so they got the beat cops to do it. Bingo and the jig."

"Oh, shit."

"A good fucking thing, Tom. Bingo recognized the stiff and called me."

Bingo McInerney and Lorenzo Jones were standing in the corridor outside Room 514. Crotty told them to go to the landing and not let anyone up to the fifth floor. Bingo winked at Tom Spellacy.

"Of all the guys to be dipping it . . ." Bingo said.

"Shut the fuck up," Crotty said.

The body in Room 514 was naked under a sheet on the bed. His clothes were folded neatly over the back

106

of a chair. His socks were balled inside his wing-tip shoes, which were lined up even with the bedpost. On the bureau were his keys, wallet and a handkerchief monogrammed with the letters *MG*. There was no money in the wallet. Tom Spellacy checked the identification.

"Shit," he said.

"Mickey Gagnon," Crotty said.

"Monsignor Mickey," Tom Spellacy said.

"He used to be a curate at Saint Luke's there, was the reason Bingo recognized him."

Tom Spellacy looked at the ID again. "Saint Lawrence the Martyr in Redondo Beach, it says."

"He's the pastor there now," Crotty said. He blew his nose in the handkerchief monogrammed *MG*, then put it in his pocket. "The girl must've crapped her pants, she laughed so hard when she saw the ID."

"Not so hard she forgot to clean out his wallet," Tom Spellacy said. "She got a name?"

"Claudine Smith. A shine."

"Swell."

"We can pick her up."

"Forget her," Tom Spellacy said. "That's all we need on this caper is a blabbermouth fifteen-dollar hooker."

"Ten," Crotty said.

Tom Spellacy turned to the body again. The pleasant look on Monsignor Gagnon's face embarrassed him.

"Heart attack?" he said, wrenching his eyes away.

"Looks that way," Crotty said. "Come to think of it, it's not a bad way to go, the heart-attack hump, you don't mind going in a state of mortal sin. I'd take my chances, I think."

"It's going to look swell in the newspapers," Tom Spellacy said. "MANHUNT TURNS UP MONSIGNOR IN CATHOUSE."

"That's why I called you," Crotty said. "I thought you might like to give your brother a little warning."

He took a toothpick from his pocket and put it in his mouth. "What do we do with the monsignor here?"

"The first thing we do is get him dressed," Tom Spellacy said.

It took them ten minutes to put the clothes on Mickey Gagnon. When they finally double-knotted his shoes, they propped him up against the headboard and folded his hands in his lap. He looked as if he were on the first day of a vacation.

"What the fuck were you doing here?" Tom Spellacy asked the corpse suddenly.

"Getting his ashes hauled is a good bet, I think," Crotty said. "You figured out yet how we keep the coroner out of this?"

Tom Spellacy picked up the car keys from the bureau.

"He's got a car around here someplace," he said. "A black Buick, I bet. Parked on the street. We send Bingo and Lorenzo out to find it. They bring it back here, they park it out back in the alley."

"Then what?"

Tom Spellacy stared at the body on the bed. "He's wearing those duds, then he must've been taking the day off or something. What do you do, you take a day off."

"Go to the track."

"He's a priest, for Chrissake, Frank."

"Then what the fuck's he doing here, he's such a terrific priest?" Crotty said. "He'd've been better off at Santa Anita, I think."

"Jesus, you're a help."

"Go to the beach then."

"It's raining."

"Go shopping."

Tom Spellacy snapped his fingers. "That May Company over on Pico."

"The new one."

"It's got a parking lot a mile long."

"We get Bingo and Lorenzo to leave him in the lot."

"The way it's raining, nobody's going to pay any attention to them."

"Somebody's bound to find him sooner or later."

"Coronary in the car."

"Happens all the time," Crotty said. "What do you tell the monsignor, is what I want to know."

"I tell him not to get too curious how Mickey checked out, is one thing I tell him," Tom Spellacy said. "No autopsy is another thing I tell him."

"You're not going to say anything, I'm not going to say anything, nobody in this joint's going to say anything," Crotty said. He dug at his teeth with the toothpick. "The coon's a tomb. Which leaves Bingo."

"I'll take care of Bingo."

Tom Spellacy opened the door of Room 514 and called Bingo McInerney inside. Bingo closed the door behind him and whistled when he saw the corpse propped up on the bed.

"Jesus, you did a hell of a job is all I got to say," Bingo said. "I nearly shit, I saw who it was. A real pain in the ass in confession. You told him you picked your nose, he'd give you a rosary." He began to smirk. "When my old lady was president of the Altar Society at Saint Luke's there, it was always Father Gagnon this and Father Gagnon that. She'd crap her pants, she knew he was a tail chaser."

"How about the boys at McGovern's?" Tom Spellacy said.

"They'll cream."

"You like a transfer to 77th Street?" Tom Spellacy said.

"You got to be kidding," Bingo said.

"Wall-to-wall nigger in 77th Street," Crotty said.

"It's a fucking jungle, 77th Street Division," Bingo said. "What'd I do, deserve 77th Street?"

109

"You open your face about this, McGovern's or any other place, you'll be walking the bricks out of 77th Street," Tom Spellacy said.

"Jesus, Tom, you can trust me," Bingo said. He jerked his thumb toward the door. "It's the coon you got to worry about."

"No, we don't," Crotty said. "It's you." He smiled pleasantly. "Tom's brother, the monsignor, he's got a special mass he says for them cops been blown away in the 77th. They play the fucking tom-tom."

"Jesus," Bingo McInerney said.


2


Bingo McInerney and Lorenzo Jones found the black Buick parked across from MacArthur Park. There was an illegal parking ticket stuck under the windshield wiper. When Lorenzo Jones drove the car into the alley behind the Alvarado Arms, Crotty tore the ticket up. He and Tom Spellacy placed the body, which they had carried four flights down the back stairs of the hotel, in the middle of the front seat. The body immediately collapsed toward the passenger door. It looked like a drunk who had passed out. Crotty told Lorenzo to park the Buick in an empty section of the May Company lot and to leave the glove compartment open with the keys in the lock to make it look as if Mickey Gagnon had been searching for something when he was stricken. He was then to walk through the store and out the front door. Bingo would be parked in the black-and-white two blocks away. They were then to resume their watch and not mention the incident in their report.

"Any questions?" Crotty said.

"No," Lorenzo Jones said.

# THEN

"It's too early in the morning and its raining too hard for anyone to be around," Crotty said.

"I know," Lorenzo Jones said. He eased the Buick out the alley.

"He thinks this is something white folks do," Tom Spellacy said.

"I got a question," Bingo McInerney said. "How come the coon drives Mickey?"

"He's got a natural sense of rhythm, it comes to driving a Buick," Crotty said.

"I could've done that," Bingo said.

"You could end up in 77th Street, you don't shut up," Tom Spellacy said.

3

"Who was that you were sneaking out of here?" Brenda Samuels said.

"The mayor," Tom Spellacy said.

Brenda poured two cups of tea and placed the kettle back on the hot plate. Her rooms smelled of cats. There was a pan of kitty litter in one corner of the sitting room and saucers of soured milk in the other three. Through the open door, he could see a rust-colored cat asleep in the unmade bed in the bedroom and a mangy Persian chewing on a curtain it had torn loose from the curtain rod. He remembered that she had always had cats. They just never smelled before.

"You always were a talkative bastard," Brenda said. "Where's your friend, does all the business with the Chinks?"

So she knows about Crotty's motel, he thought. He wasn't surprised. Brenda always liked to know what was going on. Even in a dump like this, she would be plugged into what was happening. It always helped.

111

Especially in a dump like this. "He went back downtown."

"He used to like dark meat, he ever tell you that?"

Tom Spellacy sipped his tea. That was something that must have slipped Crotty's mind.

"Never took off that white suit when they were doing him. I used to watch him through the peek."

On the cuff, no doubt. He wondered what else Crotty got from Brenda.

"Lenny Lewis hung himself," he said.

"I heard." She poured some cream into a spoon and let the Persian lick it. "Fuck him."

Her hair had grayed and she had gained weight. There was a network of wrinkles under her eyes and her fingers were stained with nicotine. She had started turning out in San Diego at sixteen and she was running her own joint before she was twenty. Now she was a woman in a dirty nightgown going to fat. Except for the nicotine, she reminded him of Mary Margaret. He wondered if that had always been the attraction.

"You look like shit."

She shrugged. "How's the wife? Still in the crazy house?"

There it was, that fuck-you quality he had always liked.

"And the monsignor? I hear him on the radio. 'The Rosary Hour.' KFIM at noon. He loves all that bullshit, I bet. The Latin. The Stations of the Cross. I bet he used to say a novena for you, every time I sucked you off."

The matter-of-fact voice. She didn't scare. Ever. He remembered telling her once he bet that she pissed ice water.

"You haven't changed much," he said.

"What'd you expect, Shirley Temple? I need you like I need another fuck."

112

He said nothing. She would push again, he knew that.

"He plays a nice game of golf, your brother, Jack used to say."

"Fuck you, Brenda."

"You used to like to," she said. She poured herself another cup of tea. "What's this all about? I pay Vice good money not to roust me."

"Murder One."

She stifled a yawn. "Who?"

He told her about the body at 39th and Norton. The story did not seem to impress her.

"What's that got to do with me?"

"She had a rose tattooed on her pussy. That ring any bells?"

"I don't owe you any favors."

"That's it?"

"That's it." The rust-colored cat leaped up on her lap. She stroked its neck until it began to purr. "You got a girl friend, I hear."

"You do keep up."

"She's got a cunt like cashmere, I also hear."

He flicked his hand across the table and hit her in the face. The cat scurried off her lap and hid under the faded brown couch.

"I think you get your cookies off doing that," Brenda Samuels said quietly. There was a red welt growing on her face, but he knew she would never rub it. "I bet it gives you a boner. You got a little fellow, as I remember. I bet the only action it gets is from Five-Finger Mary." She reached for a Camel. He noticed that her hands didn't tremble. Being hit was a professional hazard. "You slap me around, you get a gen-u-ine hard-on, isn't that right?"

"Something like that." He hadn't hit her because of what she had said about Corinne, he knew that. Corinne would know that, too. And Brenda. It was just that she was always in control. And always had been. Like all the women he had ever known. He lit a match with his thumb and held it out to her cigarette. "We need an ID on that girl."

She drew deeply on the Camel. Two puffs and then the cigarette went into her teacup.

"I don't know anyone with a tattoo."

"Ask around."

"Hooking?"

"Possibly," he said. "You know anyone likes to cut?"

"Johnny Levene."

"He's in Folsom. He's got cancer."

"Good," she said. "I'm glad." He knew she meant it. If he thought one of his girls was holding out on him, Johnny, he liked to stick a heated coat hanger up her cunt, just to remind her who she was working for.

"Not a pimp. A john."

"I'll put the word out."

He rose to leave. "Keep in touch."

"Tom?"

He stopped. He knew she was going to ask again about the body on the fifth floor. She never did like loose ends.

"That guy upstairs, he's got something to do with your brother, right?"

"How do you figure that?"

"Come on," she said sharply. "I been running joints for twenty-five years. When four cops sneak a stiff down the back stairs of a whorehouse, you think I don't know something funny's going on? And you, you haven't worked Vice since that night I was blowing you in the front seat of my car."

She didn't beat around the bush. "I told you. Murder One."

"A guy gets a heart attack in the middle of a fuck isn't Murder One. A stiff brings you down here, it's

114

got to have something to do with your brother. It was a bishop at least, I figure, that guy."

There seemed to be no point in denying it. She would not believe him anyway. "A monsignor."

She did not smile. She picked the soggy cigarette butt from the teacup and dropped it in an ashtray.

"Once a bagman, always a bagman." She never raised her voice. "Except now you do it for your brother. He sings a swell mass, I hear. Got a voice like Buddy Clark."

He moved toward her. She didn't flinch.

"You ever wonder why you never got indicted?"

He stopped. So now I'm going to find out, he thought.

"He was doing too much business with your brother, Jack was. All those parochial schools he was building. It wouldn't've looked good, you going on trial. You might've talked." He thought, She's really enjoying this. She's waited a long time to say it. "He put the fix in downtown."

So that was why Jack Amsterdam had thrown Brenda to the wolves. He needed a body. And she had kept her mouth shut. Probably because she didn't want to end up in a dryer, he thought. No copping a plea. No pointing a finger at the chief contractor for the archdiocese. He watched the hard smile on her face. Debt canceled.

"Fuck you," he said.

"I'll keep in touch," Brenda Samuels said.


4


The early-morning rain had stopped. Someone's bound to find Mickey Gagnon soon, he thought. He wasn't ready to call Des. Not just yet. Des, who played such a nice game of golf. According to Jack. Des, who was the reason he wasn't in the cooler. Let Mickey wait. Fuck Des. And Brenda, too.

Once a bagman, always a bagman.

She always could get under his skin. He'd like to try her out with the rubber hose. He was very good with the rubber hose. He never hit anyone with it. At least when anybody was around. Bang it against the table in the interrogation room. And against the back of a suspect's chair. That was usually enough. It scared the piss out of them. Sometimes more. Johnny Levene had crapped his pants. He'd like to try Brenda. Maybe Des, too.

Once a bagman, always a bagman.

Except now he was doing it for Des.

Paying off the debts of a Catholic childhood. He'd helped a lot of priests in the archdiocese out of the shit. Leon Jeanette, drunk driving, seventy miles an hour down Western Avenue, three cars sideswiped, his own totaled. Eddie Kieran, $7,700 of the Peter's Pence Collection at Holy Trinity riding on a pair of treys. A word here, a word there. Charges dropped, case dismissed.

It was the only coin he had to offer.

Once a bagman, always a bagman.

He stopped on Broadway for a shine. Broadway Bates slapped polish on his shoes. Broadway Bates. 36 YEARS SAME LOCATION, BEST SHINE WEST OF CHICAGO. Broadway Bates had a tip.

"I hear she was a whore, Tom." He pronounced it *whooor*.

Brenda's words reverberated in Tom Spellacy's ear. "A cunt like cashmere, I hear," he said.

"That's what I hear, too."

The vendors on Broadway always had tips. The Wig Man. The Flower Man. The Tie Man. There were cops in the department whose only sources were the sidewalk vendors on Broadway. You're a sidewalk

116

vendor, you keep your eyes open, Ben Bass liked to say. A poodle pissed on a tree in Beverly Hills and Ben Bass was out checking The Wig Man, The Flower Man, The Tie Man. Broadway Bates knew a guy with a poodle, had a pair of Scotch-grain Florsheims needed a shine, down at the heels, no cuffs on the pants. From the cuffs down, Broadway Bates never made a mistake.

"Two weeks ago, Tom," Broadway Bates said. He never took his eyes off the shoes. It occurred to Tom Spellacy that although Broadway Bates had been giving him a free shine for years, he probably could not pick him out of a lineup. All he ever saw was the top of his head. "A dame with a scuff mark on a pair of navy blue patent-leather pumps. Imitation-gold buckles, sharkskin heel guards. Sitting in the third chair. She wasn't wearing no pants. It was like cashmere, I swear to God, no shit."

Tom Spellacy buried his face in the *Express*. The headline on Howard Terkel's story said, POLICE SEEK WEREWOLF SLAYER, and the subhead, in smaller type, MYSTERY CLERGYMAN CLEARED.

He swore.

"She's the one, Tom," Broadway Bates whispered. For the first time he noticed there was a knob on the back of Broadway Bates's head.

He read.

"The modern counterpart of a medieval torture chamber," Howard Terkel had written, "in which a slim, unidentified Mystery Beauty writhed for hours before her brutal murder by a maniacal 'werewolf' killer, was still being sought by homicide detectives today.

"An eminent local clergyman has definitely been 'eliminated' as a suspect, a police source also indicated."

Tom Spellacy swore again.

Mystery Beauty. For a sudden, irrational moment,

117

he thought it was all her fault. Brenda. Jack. Des. Once a bagman, always a bagman. A cunt like cashmere. Mickey Gagnon.

Fuck them all.

He dialed Des when he got to headquarters. The nun on the chancery switchboard had a voice like Sister Clarita in the fifth grade at Saint Anatole's. ("Fighting in the toilet again, Thomas Spellacy. It's the rubber hose for you.") She asked who was calling.

"Homicide," he said, remembering Sister Clarita.

"I beg your pardon."

"LAPD."

"For what purpose do you wish to speak to the monsignor?"

"I got a fistful of tickets to the Policemen's Ball I want to get rid of."

"I'm sure Monsignor Spellacy doesn't want to bother himself with that. I'll connect you with Father Barry."

"Blow it out your ass, will you, Sister. Just get me Monsignor Spellacy."

Des picked up the phone a moment later.

"What'd you say to Sister Margaret, got her so upset?" Des said.

"Basically I told her to blow it out her ass," Tom said.

"Basically that'd do it," Des said. "She doesn't hear that much from the Mother Superior, I bet."

"You talk to her next, you tell her I hope all her sons are Jesuits."

He could hear Des breathing on the other end of the telephone. "I've been reading about you in the newspapers," he said finally.

"They miss all the good stuff, the newspapers. All the solid citizens calling in with their clues. There was this guy yesterday, Sister Margaret might like to meet him, I think. He said he was Jay Cee's younger brother Jim."

"The Bible doesn't mention him that I know of."

"That's what I told him was my impression. He had a birth certificate, he said, Jim. March 14, 29 B.C. And that wasn't good enough for me, Jim said, I could go take a flying fuck, you'll excuse the expression, Monsignor."

"Excused," Des said. "I read something about a Mystery Clergyman."

"You think it was one of yours?"

"Just wondering."

"Actually it's your boss."

"The Cardinal?"

"Yeah, you see, Howard Terkel asked me if there was anyone we had definitely crossed off, and I mentioned His Eminence."

"Thanks," Des said drily.

"You'd better watch that Howard, he's an alibi-checking bastard."

"His Eminence was at a dinner for the Italian-American League that night," Desmond Spellacy said.

"Dinner with the ginneys," Tom said. "Nice place to be, you want to get shot." He knew Des was getting irritated. "He got home, Sister Margaret better've tucked him in tight, is all I got to say." He fumbled for a cigarette and lit it. "He'll drop it though, Howard, if the Cardinal says the funeral mass and gives him an exclusive."

"You mean, if he's not in the can," Des said.

"The lawyers you got, Dan Campion and them, they'll get him out on a writ easy."

Des said nothing.

"It ought to be a new experience for him, Dan, going into court. He generally puts the fix in outside."

Des still did not respond.

"Tell him the judge is the one in the black robe."

"If you're finished," Desmond Spellacy said. With that voice I hate, Tom Spellacy thought. The don't-call-

119

me-I'll-call-you voice. Now was the time to spring it on him.

"Listen, Des, before you hang up, I almost forgot the reason I called."

He told Desmond Spellacy about Mickey Gagnon. There was a long silence when he finished.

"She could've been a relative," Desmond Spellacy said finally.

"He's got any nigger relatives, then she could've been a relative."

"Or he might've been making a house call."

"Des, when was the last time you put your pants over the back of a chair when you were making a house call? And wore black-and-white wing-tipped shoes. Pretend he made a perfect Act of Contrition and give him a great send-off."

The call was making him feel immensely better. For the first time that morning, he was beginning to enjoy himself.

"Thanks, Tommy," Desmond Spellacy said after a moment.

"Think nothing of it, Des."

"I've been meaning to call you anyway. There's a couple of things I'd like to talk to you about. You free for lunch?"

If he wants to have lunch, Tom Spellacy thought, it isn't because he forgot to say Happy Easter. Or because he thinks he owes me. He wondered what his brother had on his mind. "Dinner's better."

"No, I've got to go to Camp Roberts this afternoon."

For his National Guard training, Tom Spellacy supposed. Desmond Spellacy had been an army chaplain during the war, and because the Cardinal was vicar general of the armed forces, he was still active in the reserves.

"You're going to be Captain Spellacy this weekend."

"Major Spellacy."

"You've been promoted, then. You got every right to show a little pride. You must've been doing a swell job in plenary indulgences. Or getting the boys to fill their mite boxes."

Desmond Spellacy did not reply.

"The Parachuting Padre," Tom Spellacy said. That was how Dan T. Campion always introduced Des at all those Notre Dame alumni dinners and insurance-industry Catholic-of-the-Week banquets he attended. Because Des had been a paratrooper.

"Are you free for lunch or not?" Desmond Spellacy said with a flash of irritation.

"Oh, I am, Des, I am. Especially if you're going to wear your soldier suit. I like to look at all those pretty ribbons."

"One o'clock then. At the Biltmore." There was an edge in his voice, as if Desmond Spellacy already regretted the invitation.

"Don't forget to tell Sister Margaret I'll be her son's godfather."

# Seven

His Eminence Hugh Cardinal Danaher was in a foul mood. The temper began long before his conversation with Monsignor Spellacy. For nearly sixty years the Cardinal had said mass at five A.M., and for nearly sixty years he had hated it. It was a daily mortification that had never become a habit. The rattle of the alarm at four-thirty. The fetid taste in his mouth. He never

121

brushed his teeth for fear he would swallow some water and break his fast. The altar boys. He often wondered if other princes of the Church detested altar boys as much as he did at five in the morning. Always telling him they were going to the seminary and then going out to work in the missions of China. Or pouring too much wine in his chalice, as if all he wanted first thing in the morning was a stiff wake-me-up. Or else avoiding his eyes when they didn't receive, as if his only concern was the mortal sin committed under the blankets the night before.

Always while saying mass, the Cardinal went over in his mind the agenda for the upcoming day. He was a methodical man and he hated surprises. Problems existed to be anticipated. It was a basic rule. One that Monsignor Spellacy appreciated. Perhaps too well. It often occurred to the Cardinal that in the ten years Monsignor Spellacy had been his chancellor, he had never once called him Desmond. Monsignor Spellacy liked to deal with problems.

Problem: the threatened strike of the lay teachers in the parochial schools for higher wages.

Monsignor Spellacy's solution: threaten to import teaching nuns from Ireland.

Problem: Brendan Keenan, the pastor at Saint Robert's.

Father Keenan had never been one of the Cardinal's favorites. Especially since his discovery of Boys Town. Every time a youngster at Saint Robert's stole a pencil, Father Keenan wanted to send him to Boys Town. "Let Father Flanagan shape him up," Brendan Keenan liked to say. He thinks Boys Town is where you send Mickey Rooney to learn how to milk a cow, the Cardinal thought. Now there were reports about Brendan Keenan. He had taken to weeping in the confessional. But only with women penitents. Telling them how lonely it was being a priest. All the things he was missing.

The little dinners. The mistletoe at Christmas. The last straw was asking Agnes McNulty for a date. In confession. A tennis date. Agnes McNulty with her eleven children. Six nuns and five priests was the way she always described her brood. The Cardinal tried to imagine Agnes McNulty in tennis whites.

Monsignor Spellacy's solution: the CYO needed a new sports director.

Just the thing for Brendan Keenan, the Cardinal thought. A Boys Town all his own. Where he could spend the rest of his priesthood dedicating new ball diamonds and assigning umpires to CYO league games. And in his dotage, be made a papal chamberlain for his services to the youth of the archdiocese.

Problem: Monsignor Gagnon.

Monsignor Spellacy had told him after breakfast. It always gave the Cardinal a start to see Monsignor Spellacy in his uniform. With the neat row of ribbons on his chest topped by the paratrooper's badge. The Parachuting Padre. He was glad he had insisted that the monsignor remain in the reserves. The National Guard was like a touch of parish training, allowing Monsignor Spellacy to brush up against human problems. A little humanity was the only thing the monsignor seemed deficient in.

The Cardinal bestirred himself. He knew his mind was wandering. It was what he hated most about growing old.

Monsignor Gagnon. That was a problem the Cardinal had not anticipated. And the reason he was still in such a bad mood. That damn fool. In a way the Cardinal blamed himself. He should have known there was something amiss. He kept his ears open to every nuance in the archdiocese. But there had never been a whisper about Mickey Gagnon. No family problems, no other signs of stress that might have led him astray. He wondered how long it had been going on. A long time, he imagined. From what Monsignor Spellacy had implied, it was not the sort of place one just stumbled on.

He hoped Mickey had been in a state of grace.

It was an assumption he was prepared to make.

Monsignor Spellacy had been so discreet. He had never mentioned his brother by name when he told the Cardinal about Mickey Gagnon. "A friend in the department," was the way he put it. The Cardinal had never met Lieutenant Spellacy. Not that he was unaware of services rendered. On many occasions. One thing the Cardinal knew about policemen: they accepted as a given the taint on the human condition. The true Calvinists. Monsignor Spellacy was that way, too. Hardly a virtue in a priest. But a flaw I share myself, the Cardinal thought. Perhaps it was the only way to get the job done.

The drone of Augustine O'Dea's conversation interrupted the Cardinal's thoughts. The vicar general sat across from the Cardinal's desk as he did every morning, detailing what he had done yesterday and what he was going to do today. Monsignor Spellacy sat beside him, as always during this daily recitation of events, impassive. He looked uncomfortable in his uniform.

"Poor Mickey," Augustine O'Dea said. "I bet I know what he was doing at the May Company, Your Eminence."

The Cardinal started. "And what would that be, Augustine?"

"He was a grand fisherman, Mickey," the vicar general said. "Always out in Charley Dunn's boat, he was. Judge Dunn. The undertaker's brother. *The Other Half.*"

"The other half of what, Augustine?"

"That's Charley's boat, *The Other Half*," Augustine O'Dea said. "He had all the tackle."

"Charley?" the Cardinal said hesitantly.

"Mickey," Augustine O'Dea said.

"I didn't know that," the Cardinal said.

"If he was at the May Company," Augustine O'Dea said, "I bet they were having a sale on poles. I bet you can check that out, Des, before you go off on your soldier training."

"A sound idea, Bishop," Desmond Spellacy said. "Very sound."

"For the eulogy," Augustine O'Dea said. "With the Twelve Apostles being fishermen and all, it would be a nice point for the eulogy, if Mickey was buying a pole."

The Cardinal abruptly changed the subject. "Tell me, Augustine, how did the Holy Name Society luncheon go yesterday?"

"I heard the grandest story from Lourdes, Your Eminence . . ."

"I could do with a miracle today, Augustine."

"Jack Costello told me."

"Do I know Jack Costello?"

"The famous Coca-Cola bottler."

"Ah, yes," the Cardinal said.

"He got that freezer wholesale for Saint Agnes's Home."

"Ah, yes."

"His sister-in-law, Theresa Curtin. Hasn't walked a step in twenty-five years. Legs as crippled as a Communist's mind."

"A felicitous analogy."

"She goes to Lourdes with that bunch from Saint Lawrence O'Toole's, dips her legs in . . ."

"And now I suppose she's doing the polka," the Cardinal said.

The vicar general beamed. "At Cas Stasiak's reception for his boy's confirmation."

"It's right out of *The Song of Bernadette*," the Cardinal said.

"A grand movie, Your Eminence. I don't know how many times I've seen it."

"Eleven," Desmond Spellacy said.

"At least," Augustine O'Dea said. He paused for a moment. "This Jennifer Jones. Is she a Catholic girl?"

"I believe she is under contract to David Selznick," the Cardinal said.

The vicar general laid out his schedule for the rest of the day. Confirmation at Saint Bernard's. Lunch with the Legion of Decency. The dedication of the new wing at Saint Jude's Hospital. The invocation at a symposium of Catholic college athletic lettermen. Dinner with the Sons of Saint Stephen the Bulgar. The Cardinal was certain that at each event, the vicar general would pick up some new testament to the glory of God. The Miracle Wireless, the Cardinal called it. And the reason Augustine O'Dea was such a source of comfort to Hugh Danaher. The vicar general could make any problem seem trivial. Even Monsignor Gagnon's unfortunate end seemed not only palatable but even ludicrous.

When Augustine O'Dea had departed, the Cardinal said to Desmond Spellacy, "Did your brother mention a sale on fishing poles?"

"No, Your Eminence."

The Cardinal noted that it did not seem to surprise Desmond Spellacy that he knew who his "friend in the department" was.

"Perhaps Augustine should give the eulogy," the Cardinal said. "I'm sure he can work in a reference to The Big Fisherman."

"Yes, Your Eminence." Desmond Spellacy balanced a clipboard on his knee. The Cardinal's ill-humor seemed to be fading. The vicar general always seemed to have that effect on him. Perhaps that was why the Cardinal kept him around.

The Cardinal eyed the clipboard with distaste. "What have you got?"

"First, a possible candidate for the Cardinal's Scholarship. If Your Eminence agrees, you can announce it at the Policemen's Ball."

The Cardinal nodded.

"A student, altar boy, athlete, father a patrolman shot during a holdup—"

The Cardinal waved his hand impatiently. "Name."

"Antonio Biscailuz."

"Good," the Cardinal said. And smart, too, he thought. There had been complaints for some time now that the chancery took the Mexican-American quarter of the archdiocese too much for granted. Very smooth. The Mexicans and the department placated in one stroke. You had to hand it to Monsignor Spellacy. "Next."

"The new nurses' home at Saint John Bosco Hospital."

"What about it?"

"I thought I'd ask Neddy Flynn and Emmett Flaherty to bid on the construction contract."

The Cardinal nodded. "Fine."

So he's finally wised up to Mr. Amsterdam, the Cardinal thought. He must have heard about the ton of sand. And God knows what else. Let Monsignor Spellacy get rid of him himself. And good riddance. "Next."

"I've been thinking of Supervisor McDonough as a possible replacement for Chet Hanrahan."

Another sharp harp, the Cardinal thought. But not as smart as Monsignor Spellacy. Maybe not a bad idea. Let it sit for a while. "Keep me posted."

"Of course," Desmond Spellacy said. Their dialogue was ritual, a search for meanings among the monosyllables. Like smoke blown into the wind, it left no traces if the interpretation was wrong. "Keep me posted" translated into "proceed with caution." He checked the clipboard. "I had the appraiser look at Mabel Higgins's Vermeer."

The Cardinal shuddered. Mabel Higgins was a cross he had to bear. She gave twenty thousand a year to archdiocesan charities. On top of the crisp, new hundred-dollar bill in the collection envelope every Sunday at Saint Vibiana's. "The cancer people are always after me, Your Eminence." Always there was the charity panting to get Mabel Higgins's money. "And there's this grand new one now, multiple sclerosis. The crippler of young adults, they call it. A grand cause. Not that I don't tell them all, 'His Eminence comes first.'" In other words, the archdiocese might get some of her fortune if the Cardinal listened when she pestered him about the possible beatification of Lucille Gorman. A hundred years dead, Lucille Gorman, mother of sixteen children, and then after Mr. Gorman passed to his eternal reward, she had received special dispensation to join the Sisters of Charity. Sister Gorman, she was called in the convent. "California needs a saint, Your Eminence," Mabel Higgins reminded him constantly. "One of our own is what I mean. Not a Mexican, saintly though they may be." The Cardinal had done some checking on Sister Gorman. Mabel Higgins's great-grandaunt by marriage, it turned out. A fact Mabel Higgins had neglected to mention. And Sister Gorman had died of diarrhea not six months after she joined the convent. Apparently convent food did not agree with her. He would like to tell that to Mabel Higgins. Montezuma's revenge, as it were.

"What is it worth?" the Cardinal said. Mabel Higgins had taken to donating the odd painting or piece of sculpture to the archdiocese. When cash was what the Cardinal would rather have.

"It's a fake," Desmond Spellacy said.

"Worthless?"

"Except for the frame."

The Cardinal buried his face in his hands for a moment. "If we say it's worthless, we'll have a lawsuit on our hands. She's a most litigious woman. She sued her plumber last year."

"We let an art scholar see it, he'll probably say it was painted by that plumber."

The Cardinal sighed. "The appraiser—any possibility he made a mistake?"

Desmond Spellacy shook his head. "Jack Tobin. The best on the coast. His sister's a nun. A plus for us."

"We can't hide the painting, not under the terms of the gift. And if we do hang it, the art scholars will hang us."

The grandfather's clock in the Cardinal's study struck the hour.

"I have a suggestion," Desmond Spellacy said when the chimes finished. "The new Felician convent. Suppose you decided to hang it there."

The Cardinal drummed his fingers on his desk and stared at Desmond Spellacy. The chancellor's face was impassive. He could run General Motors, the Cardinal thought. An Irish Medici, that one. Perhaps that's the problem, perhaps I've taught him too well. "A cloistered order," he said finally.

"The only man allowed inside is a priest giving the last rites."

"I don't suppose the Sisters of Saint Felix would know it was a . . . reproduction," the Cardinal said.

He has trouble with the word *fake,* Desmond Spellacy thought.

"Which leaves your friend, Mr. Tobin," the Cardinal said.

"I think he might like to be made a Knight of the Holy Sepulchre."

To keep his mouth shut was left unsaid. That was Monsignor Spellacy's way. Never say more than was

129

necessary. His talk was like a gong. You had to listen for the echoes. He had been that way ever since the Cardinal had first become aware of him as a young curate at Saint Malachy's. Saint Malachy's, the dumping ground for problem pastors. First Tim O'Fay and his Civil War hit parade. Then Monsignor Cosker. Tippling Tommy. A connoisseur of altar wines. Not the spot for a young curate who did not know how to roll with the punches.

"It can be arranged," the Cardinal said. His mind was beginning to wander. The morning had wearied him. Like a bad cold, death, something he could not shake off. With age and the emphysema and the polyp on his prostate, the Cardinal knew he didn't have much time left. A year, possibly two. The succession, that was what mattered. Already he had petitioned Rome for a new auxiliary bishop. Someone who could take over when his time came. Poor Augustine O'Dea. At least that was one thing the Cardinal and the Vatican agreed on. Knowing Babe Ruth wasn't a qualification that carried much weight in Rome. "Anything else?"

"Monsignor Fargo called."

Seamus, the Cardinal thought. An acquaintance for sixty years. Not friend. Acquaintance. He wondered how it was possible for two men to know each other for sixty years and not become friends. "What did he want?"

"To talk about your insurance program."

"Oh, my God," the Cardinal said irritably. That was one reason they had never become friends. Seamus Fargo was impossible. He had tried to thwart the archdiocesan master plan at every turn. He complained about central financing. And about central purchasing. And centralized construction planning. The Cardinal was encroaching on the power of the pastors. A pastor must be lord of his own house. The Cardinal wondered

130

how many times he had heard Seamus's arguments. "What did you tell him?"

"That you were busy, Your Eminence."

"That's never stopped him before."

"He's agreed to see me at eleven instead."

The Cardinal nodded. God, Seamus could make him feel guilty. With good reason. We're both getting old, the Cardinal thought, we have to make way for others. But Seamus wanted to hang onto everything. He wasn't going to like being replaced as chairman of the new fund-raising drive. He had administered these drives for more than a quarter of a century without any help from professional fund raisers. Now the new twenty-million-dollar program that was scheduled to be kicked off in the fall was going to be handled by a professional. Mr. Leo I. Walsh, chairman of the board of Diocesan Giving, Inc.

"Will you mention Mr. Walsh to him?"

"I'll say we're having discussions," Desmond Spellacy said. "I think we should wait until the contracts are signed with Mr. Walsh before we inform the monsignor that it's a . . ." He searched for the precise phrase.

"A *fait accompli?*" the Cardinal said.

"The term has a certain . . . austerity, Your Eminence."

"Austerity," the Cardinal said. "Yes." An austere number himself, Monsignor Spellacy. "I'm told the Aquinas Guild is going to honor Seamus."

"Next month. For his services to the Church."

"He deserves it," the Cardinal said. "I'll write him a note. I think I should attend."

I'm babbling like a guilty old man, the Cardinal thought. And Monsignor Spellacy is taking it all in. It would be a cold meeting between the two monsignors. Seamus could not stand Desmond Spellacy. He had made that clear often enough. My fault, the Cardinal

131

mused. It was to Seamus that he had sent Desmond
Spellacy after Saint Malachy's. Someone had turned
Saint Malachy's around and the Cardinal knew it wasn't
poor Tommy Cosker. All the reports indicated that it
was young Father Spellacy. But perhaps Father Spel-
lacy needed a little more seasoning. A little humility.
A little less hubris. Seamus Fargo, pastor at Saint
Basil's, was just the man to take a young curate down
a peg or three. A martinet of the old school, Monsignor
Fargo. No conversation at dinner unless he initiated it.
No social visits with parishioners without his permis-
sion. Lights out in the rectory at ten o'clock. No good
words for Sigmund Freud, H. G. Wells or F. Scott
Fitzgerald. Desmond Spellacy had spent two years at
Saint Basil's under the thumb of Seamus and he
seemed to wear the experience well. Better than Sea-
mus. He wondered how Seamus would react if Desmond
Spellacy were named the new auxiliary.

"Desmond."

"Your Eminence."

"Tell your brother I'm grateful."

Desmond Spellacy nodded and left the Cardinal's
study.

He knows, the Cardinal thought. He knows I've
suggested his name to the apostolic delegate. For a
moment, the Cardinal felt a spasm of irritation. If he
doesn't know, then I've had a fool as chancellor for
the past ten years. The spasm passed. It was really
guilt, the Cardinal knew. Guilt about his treatment of
Augustine O'Dea. He just had not expected the apostolic delegate to mention Augustine as his successor.
But then the apostolic delegate was a hard one to figure
out. Thirty years a Vatican diplomat in the capitals
of the world had taught him to play his cards close to
the cassock. As with his sudden visit to the archdiocese
the week before. Ostensibly to officiate at the rededi-

cation of the old Spanish mission in Santa Barbara. And then afterward, the long, private dinner with the Cardinal. A dinner during which death was never mentioned. Only eternal rewards. As if the apostolic delegate already had a set of the Cardinal's X-rays in his briefcase.

"A very effective preacher, Bishop O'Dea," the apostolic delegate had said.

"Terribly effective," the Cardinal said. "He has the knack of satisfying everyone." He paused. "And offending no one."

"A gift," the apostolic delegate said. With that wintry Vatican smile. "He is a humble man."

"With a common touch," the Cardinal said. "When he was pastor in San Juan Bautista, he used to dye his hair green on Saint Patrick's Day. Of course, there weren't many Irish in the parish, but it made a great hit with the Mexicans, I'm told. *El padre verde,* they called him."

"I see," the apostolic delegate said.

"I knew you would," the Cardinal said.

*"Bene, bene,"* the apostolic delegate said. "A wonderful endorsement." He patted his lips with the linen napkin. "There are other good men?"

"Monsignor Spellacy."

"Young."

"Thirty-eight."

"No pastoral training."

"A chaplain during the war," the Cardinal said. He enjoyed sparring with the apostolic delegate. "I daresay a chaplain hears things and knows things and does things your average pastor wouldn't hear or know or do in a lifetime."

"Perhaps," the apostolic delegate said. "He is still young."

"Cardinal Gibbon was thirty-four when he was made a bishop."

"In the nineteenth century," the apostolic delegate said. "Cowboys and Indians. A time for a young man."

"You were thirty-seven, I believe," the Cardinal said. "Benedict's secretary."

"Pius XI," the apostolic delegate said. "I am not an antique, *Eminenza.*" His eyes did not blink when he smiled. "Yet."

"Like me, you mean," the Cardinal said. It was Desmond Spellacy who without asking had put the *Vatican Directory* on his desk before the apostolic delegate's arrival.

"Antiques have great value, Your Eminence," the apostolic delegate said.

"Some of them," the Cardinal said.

"Yes." The apostolic delegate drew the word out for several syllables.

"You were in Berne during the war?"

"Ankara."

"I thought Berne," the Cardinal said. He wondered how amused the apostolic delegate would be to know that Desmond Spellacy had brought the *Vatican Directory* to his attention. An instructive volume in which to browse and pick up dates and places.

"Only until 1941," the apostolic delegate said. "Then Ankara."

"A peripatetic life."

"Yes."

"Grand."

The apostolic delegate parted the rice pudding he never ate with a spoon, separating it into quadrants. "Monsignor Spellacy is intelligent?"

"Very."

"A holy man?"

"And a practical one as well." As holy as I myself, the Cardinal thought. As holy as the apostolic delegate himself, he also suspected.

134

"An interesting combination," the apostolic delegate had said.

And that was that. It was always best not to rush Rome on such matters. Not for nothing was it known as the Eternal City. It took an eternity to get anything done there. But the Cardinal was quite sure that the apostolic delegate had already forwarded his recommendation to Rome and that the new auxiliary would be Monsignor Spellacy. As well as his likely successor. He felt another twinge of guilt about Augustine O'Dea. Such a good man. But at sixty-one years of age still to be claiming that his favorite book was the Baltimore Catechism. Because the rules were so clearly laid out. And what was there to say about a man who had seen *The Song of Bernadette* eleven times.

Except that he was a kind, holy man.

A friend.

Betrayed.

Which left Monsignor Spellacy.

He's more like me than I care to admit, the Cardinal thought.

I wonder if he'll feel guilty at eighty.

On a morning as bad as this one.

# Eight

"Monsignor."

"Sister Margaret."

"That crying this morning when the policeman called, I'm very sorry about it."

135

"Nonsense."

"Tell the policeman I'll say a novena for him."

"I will, Sister, he'll appreciate it."

Desmond Spellacy held Mary Margaret's letter in his hands. He wished she hadn't written him. She should have written Tommy. He could guess why she had written him. He put the thought out of his mind. It would be tough enough telling Tommy at lunch. He could imagine the reaction.

Ten minutes to eleven. He knew Monsignor Fargo wouldn't be late. Desmond Spellacy smiled. Seamus wouldn't give him that satisfaction. On the stroke of eleven, he would be announced. He would be civil. He wouldn't shake hands. That was Monsignor Fargo's way.

The fact is, he liked Seamus Fargo.

That flinty intractability.

"The older he gets, the bluer his eyes get," the Cardinal had once said. "They're pale as snow now. And never a twinkle. I've always hated priests whose eyes twinkle. Show me a priest whose eyes twinkle and I'll show you a moron. But I look at Seamus and those cold eyes and sometimes he makes me yearn for some dumb harp twinkler, talking about the leprechauns and Mrs. Teddy Feeney's trip to Donegal and how she picked up a little shamrock belonging to Saint Patrick himself. A thousand years old, the shamrock is, and still as green as the Emerald Isle. You don't get that from Seamus."

"No, Your Eminence."

"We were curates together in Boston. You didn't know that, did you?"

"No, Your Eminence."

"Fifty years ago."

So that was it. That was why Monsignor Fargo was the only priest in the archdiocese who could crack the Cardinal's composure.

"When McKinley was president," the Cardinal had said. "William McKinley. The Spanish-American War. That McKinley."

"Teddy Roosevelt."

"Don't rub it in, Monsignor."

"I'm sorry, Your Eminence."

"Do you know why Seamus was sent out here from Boston?"

"No, Your Eminence."

"Exiled is more like it. He ran afoul of old Cardinal Sheehan. A terror, he was. There was a man who knew how to take care of snippy young priests. As I seem incapable of taking care of snippy old ones. Anyway. Every winter Cardinal Sheehan would go to Nassau. When the frost was on the pumpkin, so to speak, there would be the Cardinal sailing out of Boston harbor, giving his blessing. And an elaborate blessing it was. *'Ben-e-di-cam-us Do-mi-no.'* You could hear him in Worcester. 'Isn't it grand?' the old biddies in the archdiocese would say. They didn't have two lumps of coal to see them through the winter, and there they'd be saying, 'Isn't it grand?' Just like they were sailing right along with His Eminence toward the sun and the sand. 'Ah, yes,' Seamus would say. 'Such a sensitive man, His Eminence. You know why he goes to Nassau, don't you? It just breaks his heart to see the poor shiver in the dead of winter.' " A rumble of a laugh had started in the Cardinal's chest. " 'It breaks his heart to see the poor shiver,' " he repeated almost to himself. The memory of fifty years past seemed to warm him. "Once too often," the Cardinal said, "once too often Seamus said it. The Cardinal got wind of it and Seamus was on the next train west. And lucky not to have been put on a Conestoga wagon."

It pleased Desmond Spellacy that he had liked Seamus Fargo before he heard that story. As it pained him

137

now knowing that Seamus Fargo would disapprove of him being made a bishop.

Oh, yes, that he was going to be a bishop he was certain.

"Desmond," the Cardinal had called him earlier in his study.

After all these years, the Cardinal had called him "Desmond."

That was the clue, the kind of veiled hint the Cardinal specialized in. Familiarity did not come easily to Hugh Danaher, and when he used it, there was usually a point to be read.

He could not explain why the idea so depressed him. Not that he didn't want it. For ten years he had wanted it. Perhaps that was it. Becoming a bishop would only authenticate the work he had been doing for the past ten years. And would continue to do for the next forty, if the Vatican tapped him on the shoulder.

Forty years. Living out his death. What was it the Cardinal called himself? A bookkeeper in ermine. Central financing to improve the care and feeding of souls.

Living out his death.

He supposed the die was cast at Saint Malachy's with Tommy Cosker. It was at Saint Malachy's where he first got to know Dan T. Campion. "Look at it this way, Des," Dan T. Campion had said. "It's an opportunity with Monsignor Cosker the way he is. Twenty-five years old you are, and you're running things. You make it work here and you won't have to wait until you're sixty to get a parish of your own like the rest of the deadbeats." One thing about Dan Campion: he always called a spade a spade. "I did the parish taxes last year, Des," Dan T. Campion said. "It was like doing the books of one of them nigger countries over to Africa there." And so Desmond Spellacy quietly had taken charge of Saint Malachy's. The first thing he did was to liberally spike Tommy Cosker's altar wine with Welch's Grape Juice. The pastor falling down on the altar, that was a bad way to begin the day. Then he got Bucky Conroy to dry-clean all the vestments free for a couple of years. In return for a letter of recommendation to Fordham for Bucky Junior. Who was also known as Bad Bucky. With good reason. Two counts of statutory rape, dismissed, and one pregnant colored girl in South Pasadena. "A high-spirited youth," he wrote in his letter, and asked the forgiveness of God and Fordham. And then hit Bucky Senior up for a new furnace and a year's supply of altar wine.

The envelopes had been his idea. And the listing of contributions in each Sunday's parish newsletter in order of generosity. "They won't like it if you make them look cheap, Des," Dan T. Campion had said, "but they'll give more so they won't." No more nickels, dimes and quarters rattling in the Saint Malachy's collection basket. My Weekly Sacrifice, the envelopes said. Or, This Is for My God and My Parish. Name as well as amount listed on the front of the envelope. So that no one could claim ten outside and only slip a five inside. "You shouldn't embarrass them," Monsignor Cosker had said. The way to raise money was a cake sale in the parish hall, Monsignor Cosker thought. Something more personal, less regimented. "It's an honor being a Catholic," Tommy Cosker liked to say. "It should be fun." Such a dear sweet man. Not that he minded the debt being paid off. If only it were more fun.

Living out his death.

He knew why the Cardinal had sent him to Saint Basil's. Seamus Fargo was a different kind of pastor than Tommy Cosker. "A terrible sermon, Father," Seamus Fargo would say. "We eat everything on our plates in this parish, Father," Seamus Fargo would say. "The new freedom, Father, is the old license," Seamus

139

Fargo would say. In his two years at Saint Basil's, Desmond Spellacy had only two extended conversations with Monsignor Fargo. The first was the day he arrived at the rectory. "You'll find that I'm a different man than Monsignor Cosker, Father," Seamus Fargo said. "Less pliable. Less amenable. I give orders and I expect them to be followed. None of your mailings here, Father. No letters of recommendation for young hoodlums. No grape juice in the altar wine. You're surprised I know that, aren't you, Father? It's a violation of canon law, you know. Perhaps if I were to be your confessor, you might wish to confess it to me." Which Desmond Spellacy did. "Your penance, Father, is to do as you're told. Nothing more, nothing less. With no complaint." And for two years there were no complaints from Desmond Spellacy. He said mass, heard confession, took the census, counted the collection, visited the sick, prayed for the dying and kept his mouth shut.

His second conversation with Monsignor Fargo was on the day he left Saint Basil's to become vice chancellor.

"I'll make myself perfectly clear, Father," Seamus Fargo had said. "I told His Eminence I was against this appointment. You have the makings of a good priest, Father, but you're not one yet. You have a mind like an abacus. You do everything, in fact, but feel. And it's the unfeeling ones that bring the Church into disrepute. That is what I told His Eminence, Father. Apparently he disagreed. Is there anything you wish to say?"

"I would like you to continue as my confessor, Monsignor."

"I think you'd be more comfortable, Father, with one of those priests who read Sigmund Freud."

"I would prefer you, Monsignor."

"There is no edge in it, Father."

A battle of wills. Desmond Spellacy often wondered if he had pushed it because he knew that ultimately Seamus Fargo must yield. That was the edge. A victory for pride. The thought made him uncomfortable. Can a proud man discern pride? It was a sin he never confessed. And for the past ten years, Seamus Fargo had said, "Your penance, Father, is to do one good deed." As if he was incapable of one. Maybe feeling that way was Seamus Fargo's edge. A tough old bird.

Desmond Spellacy ran his finger under the starched khaki collar chafing against his neck. He was certain that Seamus would ignore the uniform. It was just another of Monsignor Spellacy's pretentions. The Parachuting Padre. He tried to imagine the curl of Seamus's lips as he said those words.

If only he knew, Desmond Spellacy thought.

His orders had been to jump into Bastogne with the relief troops. The Catholic chaplain was dead, the troops needed a priest. What the troops needed was food and ammunition, but orders were orders. He had stood in the open doorway of the C-47 with an altar stone in his kit and a package of twenty-four thousand unconsecrated hosts in his arms, and when the green jump light went on, out he went. But when the parachute opened, the hosts were ripped from his arms, and the wind tore the package open and hosts drifted down like snow behind the German lines. It seemed forever before he hit the ground, and when he did, the altar stone broke in two and then the paratrooper on his right blew up and then the one on his left. "Freeze," he heard someone say, and then, "Mine field." Big deal. He had figured that one out already. What he hadn't figured out was how to get out of his parachute harness without moving, and if he didn't, the wind would pick up the chute and drag him across the mine field like a human firecracker. So he said a perfect Act of Contrition and then he rolled over and released the harness. Then he sat in the snow, waiting to be killed, and added up the score. The altar stone was broken and he had lost twenty-four thousand communion wafers and he was trapped in a mine field, but other than that, the mission was a big success. He could not help wondering what the Germans had thought as they picked the hosts out of their hair. It was not exactly the kind of story a priest should have on his mind as he died, but so be it. It took six hours before the mine field was cleared, and by that time his hands and feet were frostbitten. The medics took him to a field hospital, where he spent the rest of the Battle of the Bulge with hot compresses on his fingers and toes. For all of which he was promoted, awarded the Legion of Merit and invalided back to the States for a War Bond tour as the Parachuting Padre.

Eleven o'clock.

Monsignor Fargo got right to the point.

"You mean, Monsignor, that I am no longer free to buy fire insurance for Saint Basil's?"

"His Eminence wishes the chancery in the future to purchase all the insurance for the archdiocese."

"Including my automobile insurance?"

"That is correct."

"Even my own life insurance?"

"Equally correct."

"Am I permitted to ask why?"

"Certainly."

"Why?"

"It will save $241,000 a year in premiums. Two hundred forty-one thousand and change."

"I'm glad you did not forget the change, Monsignor."

"Thank you, Monsignor. The change adds up."

Seamus Fargo surveyed Desmond Spellacy across the desk. "I'm told you're in negotiation with Leo Walsh." He added with ill-disguised contempt, "The fund raiser."

So he's heard, Desmond Spellacy thought. Not that it was surprising. Seamus heard everything. "We're having . . . conversations," he said carefully.

"Conversations," Seamus Fargo said.

"Conversations," Desmond Spellacy repeated.

"Am I to be replaced?"

"Your experience is irreplaceable, Monsignor."

"This is your doing, no doubt."

"There is nothing done yet, Monsignor."

Seamus Fargo rose. "His Eminence approves of your methods, it seems."

"The Vatican approves of His Eminence, Monsignor." Desmond Spellacy stood and faced the old man. "I might add, Monsignor, that I'm pleased that you're being honored by the Aquinas Guild."

Seamus Fargo shook his head almost imperceptibly. "Thank you, Monsignor. Good morning."

"Good morning, Monsignor."

The Parachuting Padre.

Living out his death.

# Nine

Howard Terkel stood at the Biltmore bar and ordered a Scotch mist. He pushed a bowl of peanuts toward Tom Spellacy.

"You're not having lunch with Jack, then?" Howard Terkel said.

"No," Tom Spellacy said.

"He's at the first table inside the door."

"Swell."

"I check out who's having lunch in here every day. You never know when you might pick up something useful."

"I never thought of that, Howard."

"Part of my job," Howard Terkel said. "I said hello to him, Jack, when he came in."

Tom Spellacy ate a peanut.

"He said hi right back. He doesn't high-hat you, Jack, is what I like about him. I know Jack Amsterdam twenty years, he always says hello when you see him. Or hi." Howard Terkel sipped his Scotch mist. "What're you doing here, then?"

"Having a beer."

"You don't see many cops here," Howard Terkel said. "Unless they're on the pad."

"It's nice to know that, Howard. I'll watch out."

Howard Terkel scooped a handful of peanuts and dropped them into his mouth. "I know why you're here, Tom."

"Why's that, Howard?"

"You want to know how I got that autopsy report. I'm not going to tell you, Tom. It's a freedom-of-the-press type thing."

"Shit, I know how you got that report, Howard."

"You do?"

"A little hard-nosed reporting."

"Fucking right."

Plus twenty dollars spread around the coroner's office, Tom Spellacy was sure. He could've bought the body for another ten, the way things were run at the morgue. The morgue had a system and even Woodrow Wong couldn't change it. A deputy medical examiner had told him Howard had the report. A piece of information that cost five dollars. It was probably the same ME who had sold the report to Howard in the first place. Maybe Howard had stiffed him. Maybe it

144

was just free enterprise. Anyway, Fuqua was furious. Tom Spellacy wondered how a man could spend twenty years in the police department and still talk about the Mystery Clue. You're good at sneaking a priest out of a whorehouse, Fuqua had said. What you're shitty at is Mystery Clues.

"Fuqua wants to throw your ass in jail."

"He wants to be chief, too. Although the way he's running this investigation, they should put him the corner of First and Temple, blowing a whistle."

"Personally, Howard, I don't give a fuck, you having that report. But there's a couple of things Fuqua'd rather you didn't print. It'd make my life easier."

"I don't know if I can do that, Tom."

Tom Spellacy leaned toward him and whispered, "It's the Mystery Clue."

Howard Terkel rubbed his stomach thoughtfully. "What is it?"

"I can't tell you, Howard, unless you promise not to print it."

"That's a big order, Tom." Howard Terkel considered the proposal. "I don't print this, what'll you do for me? I went to a lot of trouble getting this. If I'm in the shit with Fuqua, I want something for it."

I've got him, Tom Spellacy thought. "An exclusive with the killer when we catch him."

"Fuqua's already promised that to Benny Carmody at the *Times*," Howard Terkel said.

And to Manny Jacobs at the *Examiner* and to Lou Gore at the *News*, Tom Spellacy thought. That dumb bastard didn't know you didn't pass out exclusives unless you got something in return. He wondered what to offer now.

"Georgie Goldberg's going to the gas chamber next week," Tom Spellacy said. "You want to be a witness?"

"Old news."

"Your case. The Hot-Plate Slayer." Georgie Goldberg had electrocuted his wife by dropping a hot plate into her bathtub. Howard Terkel had named him The Hot-Plate Slayer.

"I don't know, Tom."

"First Jew in the state of California ever to go to the gas chamber," Tom Spellacy said.

Howard Terkel hesitated.

"I'll talk to the warden," Tom Spellacy said quickly. "Maybe he can wear a yarmulke when he goes in, Georgie." He thought, And I'll get the warden to put a propeller on it, too, if that's what he wants, Howard.

"That's a cute angle, Tom."

"A big story on Fairfax Avenue," Tom Spellacy said. He made an imaginary headline in the air. "HEBES WEEP AS HOT-PLATE SLAYER TAKES GAS." Oh, shit, he thought, what if Howard's one. He rephrased the headline. "JEWISH PEOPLE WEEP AS HOT-PLATE SLAYER GOES TO GAS CHAMBER."

"Sensational," Howard Terkel said.

"I'm on?"

"You're on."

"It's the tattoo."

"Jesus, I thought that was it." Howard Terkel chortled and pulled a copy of the autopsy report from his inside jacket pocket. "It's right here," he said, turning the pages. " 'Rose tattooed right quadrant of genital area.' " He tapped the report on Tom Spellacy's chest. "I put one over on you, Tom. There's no way I could get 'genital area' into the paper, no way."

"You could try 'dark triangle,' Howard."

"Shit, Tom, they wouldn't even let me use *mons veneris.*"

He finished his beer at the bar after Howard Terkel left. It would be a swell lunch with Jack Amsterdam at the first table inside the door. Des should like that. Maybe they'll build a convent.

The headwaiter ignored him. He seated John Dever,

the CPA, and Tommy Brady, the bandleader. Tom Spellacy unbuttoned his jacket. He let the headwaiter catch a glimpse of his shoulder holster.

"Do you have a reservation?" the headwaiter said finally.

"Monsignor Spellacy's table."

"I was under the impression that Monsignor Spellacy was lunching with Mr. Amsterdam."

"You made a mistake, fuckhead."

Like a rubber hose on the back of a chair. A small bow, a tight smile and the headwaiter showed him to a table. In the back, next to the kitchen. He bet that Des was usually first table inside the door. Jack Amsterdam didn't look up as he passed. He wondered if Jack even recognized him. They had never met. Brenda had conducted the business. Otherwise Jack was just an old photograph clipped to a rap sheet, a face at ringside at the fights. You read the newspapers, you'd think the only thing Jack ever did besides building hospitals was putting his money into Mexican featherweights. If a fighter's name was José, Angel or Jesus, you could bet he belonged to Jack Amsterdam. Except that Jack would always give him a name like ". . . the two-fisted featherweight champion of the Yucatán Peninsula." Mexican jockeys were another pastime of Jack's. If Manuel or Julio was up, you'd look at the odds and bet the other way, you had any brains at all.

You've got to hand it to him, Tom Spellacy thought. Jack runs a nice operation. He had East LA in his pocket. The ginneys left him alone was the main reason. East LA was tough to crack, you were a ginney. You had to be a Mexican. Which Jack was on his mother's side. And think like a Jew. Which Jack was on his father's side. He had picked East LA clean. The only thing he had ever been busted for was smuggling illegals. To a gringo judge, smuggling illegals was a humanitarian act. Supplying cheap labor, he called it.

It was nothing you went to the joint for. Especially when Brenda was copping the judge's own joint twice a week. Brenda had told him that. That was how she first got tied up with Jack. Case dismissed. And the beginning of a beautiful friendship between Jack and Brenda. Brenda said Jack took a hundred grand a month out of East LA. Part of which went to keep things cooled down. The police department wasn't crazy to know what a bunch of wetbacks were doing anyway, so as long as Jack kept things quiet, the cops stayed out of his hair. For a price. It was just another business expense for Jack.

Like I used to be, Tom Spellacy thought.

For a moment he did not recognize Des when he spotted him at the headwaiter's stand. That goddamn soldier suit. It always irritated Tom Spellacy to see Des in uniform. Not that he had been crazy to go back into the navy. He had an essential job, the draft board had said. He wondered if they meant being a bagman in Wilshire Vice. Maybe Jack fixed that, too.

Des stopped at Jack's table. Jack stood up. A two-handed handshake. Jack didn't look well, Tom Spellacy noticed. His dark complexion was ashen and his suit didn't seem to fit. Something to check on. Des waved at John Dever, the CPA, and Tommy Brady, the bandleader. Working the room, Tom Spellacy thought. The Parachuting Padre.

He remembered being surprised when Des told him the Parachuting Padre story.

"You were born under a lucky star, Des."

"That's what His Eminence said when I told him."

"I wouldn't make it a habit, telling that story."

"I won't."

"And Des . . ."

"Yes."

"Thanks for telling me."

The Cardinal and me, Tom Spellacy mused. A strange parlay. A strange family. He tried to imagine telling Des a similar story. Besides those he told him in confession. About the reason he shot Lenny Lewis, say. Not because Lenny stuck him up. Because Lenny stuck him up when he was getting his glass blown. He would've let Lenny go, he wasn't getting his glass blown. Better to let Lenny get away with the eleven hundred than face all those questions. It was just that he didn't want to get stuck up when his thing was in someone's face. So he let Lenny have it. He didn't think he could tell that story to Des. There were not many things that made him feel guilty. Lenny Lewis hanging himself in Q was one, though. It would be hard to explain to Des.

Desmond Spellacy took his hand. A one-hand handshake. He wondered if Des would try and get the table moved. No. Des was too smart. Never embarrass the policeman.

"Rob Roy, straight up, twist," Desmond Spellacy said to the waiter. "Drink, Tommy?"

"Schlitz." He noticed that Jack Amsterdam was staring at them from across the room. He started to add, "Straight up, no twist," but held up.

"And we'll order." Desmond Spellacy gazed at the menu. He already knew what he was going to have. The usual. Chicken salad, no dark meat, melba toast, tea with lemon. He wondered why it was always so difficult to start a conversation with Tommy, why it was necessary to bury his head in the menu.

"The usual, Monsignor?" the waiter said.

Desmond Spellacy nodded. There was a slight smile on Tommy's face. The usual. That had brought the smile. Advantage Tommy. Better not bring up Mary Margaret's letter yet.

Tom Spellacy ordered a club sandwich. "What's on your mind, Des?" he said after handing the menu to the

149

waiter. "Don't tell me. You want to know if there's any atheists in the foxholes."

"Actually I don't."

"You really believe that shit?"

Desmond Spellacy said nothing.

"No, Des, I'm interested."

He's laying down the ground rules, Desmond Spellacy thought. It was ever thus. "Not really. The nuns believe it, though, and the sisters tell it to the little ones . . ."

"And they're the future of Holy Mother the Church."

"Something like that."

"It's not exactly what Cardinal Spellman had in mind, I think."

"I guess not," Desmond Spellacy said. He folded his hands, as if in prayer, on the table. "His Eminence said to tell you he was grateful."

"How did he know it was me?"

"He's not a fool, Tommy."

Tom Spellacy shrugged. "I hear you're going to be made a bishop."

Desmond Spellacy gazed evenly at his brother. Tommy's capacity to intuit the top secret no longer surprised him. "You've been having drinks with the Cardinal, then."

"Mai tais, his place," Tom said. He noticed there were no denials. "He likes all that fruit shit when he boozes."

Desmond Spellacy smiled, but said nothing.

He's not going to get drawn into that one, Tom Spellacy thought. Smart as a whip, Des. Always calculating the odds. Even as a kid, Des had this flair for numbers. Give him any set of numbers and he could multiply them in his head. Thirty-nine times a hundred twenty-seven. Quick as Jack Flash, Des would be back with the answer: four thousand nine hundred fifty-three. It was a way to make a little extra money back in Boyle Heights. Des winning bets on his multiplication, Tom remembered, me threatening to break a few arms if the bets weren't paid off. A free ride on the merry-go-round, that was the stake.

"Ninety-six times forty-three, Des," Tom said.

The sardonic smile at the corners of the mouth. Thirty-eight years old and not a line on Des's face. It was women who put lines on the face, Tom thought. He wondered if a monsignor ever got a hard-on. Check that. What he wondered was how a monsignor confessed it.

"Four thousand one hundred twenty-eight," Des said.

"You haven't lost the knack."

"Except I do it in millions now, Tommy. Dollars."

"Doesn't give you much time to save souls."

"I didn't know you were interested," Des said. "In souls, I mean." Again the smile. "Actually I save souls every day between 9:15 and 9:45. Unless I'm giving a speech for His Eminence at the Grand Knights of Columbus communion breakfast."

The waiter brought lunch and the drinks. So that's the usual, Tom Spellacy thought, looking at the stringy chicken salad. Des must be keeping in shape for his golf game. It was funny, Des being a golfer. Not many golfers came out of Boyle Heights. His first putter he had stolen when he was caddying. He was always putting rocks, Des. And playing the municipal courses after dark. It was Gene Sarazen he wanted to be. Not Gene Tunney.

"That should give you a lot of time to work on your handicap," Tom said. "Still six, is it?"

"It's down to four at Knollwood."

"I was at Knollwood once. They had this Mexican in the kitchen. And he knifed another one. Mexican, I mean. That's the only time I was there, though."

"I wasn't playing that day."

"Nice kitchen. Nice service entrance, too."

"Cut the crap, Tommy," Des said. "Don't give me

151

that fake proletarian garbage. The harp Benny Leonard, that's what you always wanted to be. The main event at Legion Stadium. A title fight in a ball park. That was going to be you."

You had to hand it to him, Tom Spellacy thought. Take away the manicure and he was still a Boyle Heights mick.

"Glass hands, that was always my problem," Tom said. "Some guys got a glass jaw, I had glass hands. Knuckles like potato chips. Even now, I give a hooker a nice right, they swell up."

"The ladies don't hit back either, they tell me," Des said. "And you've got a rubber hose now, they tell me that, too. Saves wear and tear on the knuckles is what I hear."

"It gives you a little edge. They must've taught you about that at priest school, the edge. Like you want to break up a teachers' strike, what you do is bring over a bunch of nuns from the old country. That's what I mean by an edge."

"I'm glad to know that," Des said. It was odd hearing Tommy talk about the edge. He sounded like Seamus Fargo. And made him feel just as uncomfortable.

"That's just what we need over here, Des. A boatload of harp nuns with their plastic blarney stones and the cowshit still sticking out of their ears."

He never misses a trick, Desmond Spellacy thought. Add a rubber hose and he would be one tough customer. The thought made him shiver.

"And speaking of the edge, I hear you're going to Europe this summer, see the Pope."

"You do keep up on my schedule."

"I try."

"Actually it's a pilgrimage," Des said. "The Dominican sisters. And some of the girls from Holy Rosary. Honor students, I think. You know the kind of trip.

152

Fifteen stops in fourteen days. A night in Shannon to see the old sod. It was two days in London until the Mother Superior got wind of it. All those Protestants scared her, I think. Skip Paris and go directly to Lourdes. If we're lucky, maybe we'll see a deaf mute talk. Or a blind man see. What's a trip like this without a high point? And then overnight in Fatima. It seems we're stopping every place Our Lady touched down. Then a public audience with the Pope in Rome. The girls from Holy Rosary and fifteen thousand of their closest friends. I'm just a chaperone, really."

"Keeping the ginneys out of their knickers is what you mean."

"Somehow, Tommy, I thought you'd say something like that."

Tom Spellacy ignored him. "I knew a girl from Holy Rosary once. Clementina something. A dago name. Clementina Testa. Let her loose in Rome and she'd lead you a merry chase. Maybe teach you a few things you might've missed along the way."

"No doubt," Des said. "You always did favor girls like . . . what's her name? Clementina?"

Tom Spellacy flashed. "Don't give me that pious crap, Des. Not after the way you fixed that raffle at Our Lady Help of Christians." That should stop him, my knowing that, he thought. "No wonder you give the big hello to Tommy Brady over there. You nearly had the city attorney on his ass."

There was not a flicker from Desmond Spellacy. He split a piece of melba toast into quarters and surrounded the chicken salad with them.

"Tommy's brother, John, he's in the department. He was pissing bullets there for a while, Tommy. Jesus, Des, having him palm a ticket so that Sonny McDonough's daughter gets the new Studebaker. You should know better." He took a bite from his sandwich. "One thing I always wondered is what you got out of it."

Desmond Spellacy was matter-of-fact. "Sonny's vote on the Planning Commission." That was one thing about Des, Tom Spellacy thought. There was no bullshit when he was in the corner. "It got the property condemned for the new high school at Our Lady."

"You don't get him for a Studebaker now, Sonny. Or a Cad either. Your pal, Jack Amsterdam, he's probably told you all about it."

"He hasn't mentioned it."

"Yeah, well, Jack hasn't been getting too many reservoir-cleaning contracts since Sonny got on the supervisors."

"I don't know who'd want to clean a reservoir anyway," Des said.

"For six hundred grand I think I'd give it a shot," Tom said. "It seems that Sonny's rent, though, comes a little higher than Jack's been used to paying."

An entry for Sonny's file, Desmond Spellacy thought. He had a feeling that file would be filling up rapidly. Chet Hanrahan had been right. You could get a crick in the neck looking the other way. He wondered what it was about cement that seemed to breed venality.

"That's what you'd call a bribe, isn't it?" Des said, and realized immediately that it had come out wrong.

"There's people who'd call it that," Tom said. "The DA and them. It must make you glad you're a priest, not having to know things like that."

They ate in silence, methodically, not looking at each other. Tom Spellacy wondered when Des was going to get to the point. Des wasn't one just to pass the time of day. He had to have something on his mind. Maybe he already had what he wanted. That was Des's way. If you didn't ask for anything, you didn't owe any favors.

Finally Desmond Spellacy said, "How's Mary Margaret?" He wiped the corners of his mouth with a napkin.

"She thinks it's the catacombs, Camarillo," Tom said. "Eats with her fingers. They didn't have any spoons in the catacombs, she tells me. And I tell her they didn't have Instant Cream of Wheat, either."

"You're a compassionate sort."

"I want to hear your advice on marriage, I'll go to one of those fancy retreats you give. Where is it this year? Santa Anita?"

The amenities, Tom Spellacy thought. He sometimes wondered how much he really liked Des. It was as if he was always waiting for you to stumble, and after you did, it proved some kind of point that only he could understand. Until he found the opportunity to use it. He was like a cop that way. Maybe that was it. They understood each other too well.

"The Malibu Colony." There was a trace of a smile on Des's lips. " 'Contemporary Marriage and the Post-war Industrial Society: The Church's View.' "

That was one thing about Des, Tom Spellacy thought. He was seldom without his sense of humor. And not just about the pretentions of the Church. At times he seemed almost amused by sin. He supposed that made it hard being a priest.

"Ma would like to hear that," Tom said. "She wouldn't understand it, but she would've liked to hear it."

"God rest her soul."

"Shit, Des," Tom said. "She was a lot like Mary Margaret, Ma. Those rosary beads always wrapped around her fingers. I used to think they were a part of her hand, I was a kid. Like the warts."

Trust Tommy to remember the warts that covered Ma's fingers, Desmond Spellacy thought.

"I did some checking up, Des. You know how many people in the history of this city got killed getting hit

155

by a trolley car? Phil Spellacy. The only one. You ever think, that's a hell of a place to sleep one off, on the trolley tracks. He must've thought they were bear tracks, Phil, and the old trapper was checking them out when the trolley hit him."

"He nearly put Ma in the ground with the drinking."

"She was a nut, Ma, anyway. She and Mary Margaret would have gotten along good, yakking it up with all the saints there. No wonder Phil hit the sauce. Purgatory she was always talking about, Ma, remember? And how much time old Phil would have to spend there, she ever stopped saying novenas for him. Me she had down for life plus ninety-nine years. Not you, though, Des. The express. No stops."

Desmond Spellacy thought, It's always been like this. Push. Probe. Find the nerve.

"Tell me something, Des. What're you going to call yourself when you become Pope?"

"Simplicius II, that has a nice ring about it," Des said. "Or Gelasius III. There hasn't been a Gelasius since 1119."

"You been boning up."

"He who is prepared, Tommy, is never surprised," Des said. He squeezed lemon into his tea. "But then, on second thought, Gelasius has the ring of the Dark Ages. Something simpler. More to the common touch." He picked up the teacup. "Thomas. After you. There's never been a Pope Thomas. Thomas the First."

"Thomas the First. I like that." Tom tapped the empty beer bottle. "Nice and common."

"I like it, too," Des said. "A constant reminder to me that the flesh is weak."

Tom Spellacy's smile hardened. He wondered if Des were fishing. Or if he knew about Corinne.

"The first Pope who bought a church with a Studebaker."

"A high school."

156

"I seem to recall something about the end and the means," Tom said. "From Sister Clarita. Remember her? In the fifth grade at Saint Anatole's. It was a no-no, I think is what she said."

"I seem to recall that," Des said.

"She was a pain in the ass, Sister Clarita. The ruler on the knuckles is what she was famous for."

"You were lighting up in class is the way I remember it," Des said. "And smoking in the fifth grade was against the rules, I think. At Saint Anatole's, at least."

"She kept me back was the reason I did it. It was the fifth commandment I was bad in. 'Thou shalt not steal.' 'Like your brother in Folsom,' I told her. You know, as an example of what would happen."

"That would do it, probably," Des said. "She died a couple of months ago, you know. I said the mass."

"I wasn't invited."

"It started me thinking, the funeral. Seven hundred dollars it cost. There's this fund His Eminence pays funeral costs out of. Nuns and priests. So I did a little checking. He paid for 291 funerals last year. Nuns, priests, indigents in the old people's homes."

"Two hundred ninety-one times seven hundred, Des," Tom said.

Desmond Spellacy waited until the waiter cleared away the lunch dishes. "Two hundred three thousand seven hundred dollars, actually," he said finally. "So I went to see Sonny McDonough. To see what he'd say about McDonough & McCarthy handling all the funerals in the archdiocese. Of religious, I mean."

"Wholesale is the word you're looking for, I think," Tom said. "Jesus, no wonder you want those nuns from Ireland. The boat sinks, you can build a cathedral on what you save." He paused to see if Des would react. No. He was good at ignoring remarks like that. "What did Sonny say then?"

"He said he'd think about it."

157

"Mention the name Corky Cronin to him," Tom said. "It might make him think a little harder."

"Oh?"

"Cornelia Cronin. A bookkeeper in one of his stores. She broke her back one weekend. In Catalina. On Sonny's boat. While Mrs. Sonny was off making a retreat. With the Jesuits, I think. He prays better on the boat, Sonny, is what I hear."

"You hear a lot."

"She gets five hundred a month for life, Corky. For the limp, I hear. And to keep her trap shut, too, I bet."

Desmond Spellacy nodded. Sonny seemed to have quite a history. At least he didn't get along well with Jack Amsterdam. That was a plus. He suddenly felt uncomfortable. He always had been able to translate a minus from Tommy into a plus for himself. It was a malignant kind of mathematics. And it was becoming a habit. I'm sure Tommy knows what I'm doing. It probably pleases him. The way a spot on a white coat would probably please him.

He remembered the letter. There was no way to avoid it.

"I got a letter from Mary Margaret."

"She wants you to get rid of that Spic chaplain at Camarillo."

"She did mention that."

"And she wants a parish named after Saint Barnabas."

"Something like that." Don't stall. Get it over with fast. "She said she was coming home soon, Tommy."

Swell, Tom Spellacy thought. Just what I need. He's so good at breaking the news, Des, maybe he'd like to break it to Corinne, too.

"She didn't mention it last time I was up. It must've slipped her mind, I guess."

He had trouble, when Mary Margaret was away, remembering what she looked like. A little like Brenda,

158

that was it. He had taken her picture out of his wallet.
It was not something he wanted Corinne to see. The
photograph was also fifteen years old. Taken when he
was still sleeping with her regularly. If it ever could
have been called regularly.

"A family reunion is what she has in mind, she said,"
Des said. This was going to be more difficult than he
thought.

"It must've slipped her mind I'm a member of the
family, too," Tom said. "The way she didn't write me
first."

Wriggle out of this one, Monsignor. Learn a little
about family life you might have missed in confession.
With your fucking manicure. Pumping me about Sonny
and them, like I'm some sort of harp booby in the Holy
Name Society, I don't know what you're doing.

"Tommy." Des chose his words carefully. "It's for
Kevin when he gets discharged from the army. She
wants Moira there, too, if I can pull some strings and
get her a weekend off from the novitiate."

"Oh," Tom said. "That's swell, Des, you doing a nice
thing like that. I didn't realize that was it."

Desmond Spellacy looked at him warily. He knew
Tommy would not just let the subject drop.

"But one thing I wonder is how she put it to you in
that letter there," Tom said. " 'P.S., tell what's-his-
name to put the crucifix back over the bed?' Or, 'Tell
himself to dust off the statue of the Infant of Prague
I like to kiss when I wake up in the morning.' I don't
know. Maybe it was something about the Sacred Heart
of Jesus calendar she likes to check the date out on. Or
maybe she didn't say anything. You just said to yourself, 'I wonder if good old Tommy knows anything
about this. They get forgetful when they're soft in the
head, so maybe she didn't mention it to him. He's
made a date to go to the ball game that day, Tommy, I

159

could be neck deep in piss, so I better check it out with him first.' "

"Are you finished?" Des said.

"Turkey, we'll have, and stuffing and gravy. You're her pen pal, you can carve. You're good at carving is what I hear, all that roast beef you put away with His Eminence there."

"Tommy, she wrote me because she thought I could do something about Moira."

"She always did like to chat with the priests. All her little secrets, Father got them first. When she was having Kev, the first one she told was Father Dolan there at Holy Martyrs. Remember him, Dummy Dolan? 'So you're going to be a dad,' Dummy says to me one Sunday morning. First I heard of it. 'You know what I'm going to call him, it's a boy?' I says to him. 'What?' he says. 'Dummy,' I say. He didn't like that much, Dummy."

"I can see where he might not."

"He went crackers, the story is," Tom said. "But he left three hundred grand, I hear."

"Three hundred and twenty," Des said. "He bought Coca-Cola when it was first issued. He left every cent to his goddamn cat." Desmond Spellacy sighed. "I had to break his will."

"I wouldn't mention that to your pen pal, I was you. Mary Margaret always had a soft spot for old Dummy."

"She's not my pen pal," Des said. "But I'll remember it anyway."

"She always had a soft spot for you, too, Mary Margaret, now that I think of it. You were the one she always had her eye on, we were kids."

He watched Des signal for the check. The fact of the matter was, Mary Margaret always had been sweet on Des. You might enjoy it more, he had told her early in their marriage, you tried thinking it was Des doing it to you. She had hit him in the mouth with a fistful of

160

rosary beads. Women. Brenda. Mary Margaret. Corinne. He felt hemmed in by them today.

"I don't remember that," Desmond Spellacy said.

" 'Mary and Des,' she used to write in her notebooks over to Saint Anatole's there. You know, she'd draw the little heart with the arrow through it, and inside the heart it would say, 'Mary and Des.' And 'S.W.A.K.' She wrote that, too."

"Sealed with a kiss."

"You do remember."

"You have an overactive imagination, Tommy."

"I bet she put that on her letter, S.W.A.K."

"She didn't."

"It would've saved me a lot of trouble, you and her got together, I think," Tom said. "But the Church would've lost a great golfer."

Des was silent for a moment. It had gone about as well as could be expected. One thing you could never do with Tommy and that was rise to the bait. You never knew when he would erupt.

Jack Amsterdam was approaching the table. He took the check from the waiter's hand and waved him away.

"I'll take care of it, Monsignor."

Desmond Spellacy stood up. "You shouldn't do that, Jack."

"Your money's no good here, Monsignor."

"Do you know my brother Tom?"

"I haven't had the pleasure," Jack Amsterdam said. He spoke with an effort, his voice husky, as if the words were squeezed one by one from his diaphragm. "He's got the family resemblance, Des. Is he older or younger?"

It was as if Tom Spellacy were not even there.

"Older," Des said.

"That's nice," Jack Amsterdam said. "It's nice to have an older brother. I wish I would've had an older brother." He put his hand on Des's arm. "I don't hear from you yet about Saint John Bosco."

"We're doing some new surveys, Jack."

"I see," Jack Amsterdam said. "His Eminence, he got the invitation to my fund raiser at San Conrado's?"

"He did."

"Tell His Eminence I'm counting on him."

"I will."

Jack Amsterdam turned to Tom. "Nice to meet you. He's a winner, your brother."

Tom Spellacy wrapped both hands around his beer glass. "And only the winner goes to dinner."

"I like that," Jack Amsterdam said. "You hear that, Des. Only the winner goes to dinner. It runs in the family, brains."

Tom Spellacy rotated the beer glass between his palms. "I used to work for you," he said quietly.

Both Des and Jack Amsterdam stared at him. "When was that?" Jack Amsterdam said.

"When you were running whores," Tom Spellacy said. "I was your bagman in Wilshire Vice. I did the payoffs."

For a moment, none of the three said anything.

"I got to be going, Des," Jack Amsterdam said finally.

"Sure, Jack."

Jack Amsterdam did not look at Tom Spellacy as he turned and walked out of the dining room. Des sat down and stared across the table.

"Jesus, Tommy, you can be a pain in the ass."

# *Ten*

The morning after Tom and Des Spellacy had lunch at the Biltmore, the *Express,* under Howard Terkel's by-line, printed the full pathological report from the Medical Examiner's office, omitting mention only of the rose tattooed above the victim's pubic region and of the votive candle in her vagina. Two hours after the *Express* hit the streets, a girl who worked in the rouge room at Max Factor called the special telephone number set up by Chief of Detectives Fred Fuqua to receive information on the Mystery Beauty. The girl in the rouge room said that her ex-roommate used to melt down candles in order to put the soft wax into the holes in her teeth where the fillings had fallen out. She said that her ex-roommate's name was Lois Fazenda and that Lois Fazenda had skipped three weeks before, sticking her and her six other roommates with her share of the month's rent. The girl in the rouge room also said that Lois Fazenda stole the candles she melted down into fillings from a religious-supply store on Hollywood Boulevard, and that after she was caught shoplifting, she began blowing the owner of the store to keep out of jail. The caller said her name was Gloria Deane, and for the newspapers not to forget the *e* at the end of Deane.

At the same time that Gloria Deane was calling Fuqua's special number, Tom Spellacy was checking the overnight reports from the Central Division. Fuqua's idea. The systems approach. The votive candle could be a definite pattern. Look for rosary beads in the crotch. Crucifixes. Scapulars. Mite boxes. A definite pattern of Catholic boffing. Tom Spellacy shuffled the reports. 93 thefts. 42 burglaries. 21 robberies. 6 assaults with deadly weapons. 2 morals offenses. One rape. One attempted rape. 32 stolen vehicles. No mite boxes.

He wondered if he should call Des. Maybe an apology was in order. He thought not. He wasn't good at apologies. No better than Des was. They hadn't spoken since lunch. Des didn't say much after calling him a pain in the ass. I wonder if he'll confess that. Don't bet on it. Des always did have a very relaxed idea of what constituted a sin. Even the sixth commandment. He didn't get too choked up about Thou shalt not commit adultery. There were always extenuating circumstances. He was very big on extenuating circumstances. What he needed was one of those tough old ginney pastors who'd chop off your arm you reached for a second piece of pie. Try extenuating circumstances on them and they'd have you walking up Wilshire Boulevard on your knees.

They had walked out the front door of the Biltmore, still not speaking. John Dever, the CPA, and Tommy Brady, the bandleader, were standing by the taxi rack. There were a lot of two-handed handshakes. John Dever said he was doing the books for Our Lady of Good Hope. Cooking the books if I know Monsignor Sagarino, Tommy Brady said. A good laugh was had all around. Tommy Brady said he had played at Vinny Sagarino's twenty-fifth anniversary in the priesthood. He had done a Jew bar mitzvah in the afternoon, then Vinny's shindig in the evening, but that was what made orchestra leading such an interesting business, all the people of different religions you met. John Dever said he'd give Des a ride back to the chancery. Tommy Brady was left alone on the sidewalk with Tom Spellacy. The bandleader didn't quite know what to say. He began tapping his foot.

He runs a grand raffle, your brother. A real wiz at bingo. He could get them Mexicans at Our Lady taking chances on whether Easter fell on a Sunday or not. Where you living? Saint Jude's?

Perpetual Help, Tom Spellacy had said.

Last time I saw you, Tommy Brady had said, you were still living in Saint Jude's.

61 disturbing the peace. 2 arson.

That was real swell of the wiz at bingo, telling him that Mary Margaret was coming home. He still hadn't figured out how to tell Corinne. Maybe she and Mary Margaret could make a novena together, work it all out. You get Sunday mass, I get Friday nights. You get the Stations of the Cross, I get the afternoon matinees. You get Des, I'll take Tom. It was funny about Corinne. She seemed as hipped on Des as Mary Margaret. She went to Saint Vibiana's to watch him say mass. He wears loafers on the altar, she reported. She received Communion from him. His nails are buffed, she said. And he has a razor cut. She wanted to meet him. Why, he had said. Because sometimes I think I'm fucking him, she said.

That was one thing about Corinne. She didn't beat around the bush about the sixth commandment. She was asleep when he returned last night. Don't wait up, he had told her, I'll be working late. Which meant spending half the night listening to Crotty talk about his Chink partners until he was sure she wouldn't be awake. That was one way to avoid mentioning Mary Margaret. He did not turn on the light when he came in. She snored quietly. In the dark, the Murphy bed with the trench in it seemed to fill the entire room. He

165

suddenly realized how small the apartment was. The only place he could be alone was in the bathroom. Not even there, really. The jar of Arrid made the bathroom hers. And the Nair. He had never even heard the word depilatory until he met Corinne. The hair on Mary Margaret's legs was like a beaver compared to hers. Now Corinne was using his Gillette. Every morning her leg stubble pitted his blade. He had tried to get her to wash the blade, but she always forgot. It occurred to him as he was getting undressed how little he knew about Corinne. She knew everything about him except that Mary Margaret was coming home, but he could not recall her ever mentioning friends or family, except her former husbands and the occasional first name at the Jury Commission who had got fired or been promoted or missed her period. He wondered if he had just blotted it out, if fucking women was burden enough without getting to know them. They had no life outside the tiny apartment, yet he found it impossible to call the apartment home.

"How did lunch go?" Corinne's sleepy voice had come from the trench in the bed.

"You've got a cunt like cashmere, I hear," he had answered. What a shitty thing to say. But he didn't want to talk about lunch and he didn't want to talk about Mary Margaret checking herself out of Camarillo.

"Is that what you hear?"

He put his shoes under the bed and his Police Special in one of the shoes, just an arm's length away. As he perched himself between her knees, he wondered who he was going to shoot.

"Do you love me?"

"Yes, of course." He wondered what muff-diving had to do with love.

"You never say it, you know." Her voice had been quiet, matter-of-fact. "I mean, I say, 'Do you love me,' and you say, 'Yes.' But you never say the word itself. It's not a complaint, Tom, it's an observation."

"I do."

All in all a day I'd like to forget, he thought. He thumbed through the remaining reports. Peeping Toms. Vag loitering. Solicitation for the purposes of prostitution. Murder One in the Rampart Division. A husband took out his wife. That's the kind I like. Give the poor bastard a cigarette and he tells you why he did it. His old lady had wax in her ears. Or hair on her tits. Something you could understand, him whacking her out for. Twenty minutes later he's in the gas chamber. There was no crap about definite patterns.

12 bunko.

One suicide. He picked up the report. A jumper. Off the roof of the Bradbury Building. The jumper took the elevator to the top floor, went up the little staircase to the roof, took off his shoes, hat and glasses, put his wallet in the crown of his hat open to his driver's license so that he could be identified, then jumped. He was dead the instant he hit Broadway.

It was the jumper's name that caught his attention. Shit was going to hit the fan. The report was something Crotty should see. This jumper was his problem.

Masaryk was standing by the water cooler in the squad room, practicing quick draws from his shoulder holster.

"Where's Crotty?" Tom Spellacy said.

Masaryk jumped. He quickly began twirling the chambers of his .38 as if he had only been trying to see if it was loaded.

"With a 261 suspect," Masaryk said. He talked very fast. "Name of Rafferty. Raymond F. He's got a sheet fourteen pages long. Caucasian. Five feet eleven and three-quarter inches in height, 147 pounds, thirty-one years of age . . ."

167

If only his draw was as good as his memory, Tom Spellacy thought. Put Masaryk on a tail and he'd tell you exactly how many steps the suspect took before he lost him.

". . . snake tattoo right forearm, no other identifying marks." Masaryk was trying to put his .38 back into its holster. The telephone rang and so startled him that he dropped the gun on the floor.

"The phone," Tom Spellacy said. He put a pencil in the barrel of the revolver, lifted it from the floor and handed it to Masaryk.

"It's X. O'Brien," Masaryk said, giving him the phone.

"Shit." Francis Xavier O'Brien, criminal attorney, was always called X. He weighed 247 pounds, and winter and summer he wore a black FDR cape. His specialty was sex. Pimps. Rapists. Exhibitionists. Smut peddlers. Foot freaks. His only legal strategy was delay. Never give anything away. File enough motions and the judge might have a heart attack. Hope for a mistrial. "What's up, X.?"

"Crotty's got a boy of mine stashed away, Tom," X. O'Brien said. Every client was X. O'Brien's "boy." He loved to listen to the charges against them. A grand story, X. O'Brien would say. A mortal sin if you prove it. Tell it to Father Toby McNamara in confession and his hair would fall out. But he was making a retreat that day, my boy. Thinking about becoming a Catholic. Converts don't shit on your toe.

"What's his name, your boy?"

"That's for me to know and for you to find out."

The only way to deal with X. O'Brien was never to argue with his logic. "He's got a guy named Rafferty. Suspicion of rape."

"My boy never raped anyone in his life."

"He's got a sheet fourteen pages long, X."

"His sister's a postulant."

168

"Then Rafferty is your boy?"

"How do you know his name is Rafferty?"

"He told us."

"On what evidence?"

"Oh, for Chrissake, X. His mother told him."

"That's hearsay."

Making a point like that could keep X. O'Brien happy for a week. Tom Spellacy said he would check with Crotty. He picked up the suicide report and walked down the corridor to the interrogation room.

"A regular sweetheart, our friend Rafferty," Crotty said. "A real addition to X.'s stable. He hops into the lady's car and tells her she doesn't drop her panties, he's going to cut her into veal chops like he cut the Mystery Beauty."

"All it was was a way to get something fast," Raymond Rafferty said. He had watery green eyes and the snake tattooed on his right arm coiled around the letters M-O-T-H-E-R. "I'll take the bounce on this one, but I don't do knife tricks, that's not my M.O."

"He hits the horn on her car when he starts fucking her," Crotty said. "But he's so hot and bothered he doesn't even notice until the black-and-white pulls up."

"She was sixty-one years old," Raymond Rafferty said. "They're all over sixty, that's my M.O., look it up on my sheet. I stay away from tight pussy."

"You know, you really got terrible teeth," Crotty said. "No wonder you're a rapist."

"All that green shit," Tom Spellacy said. "You ever see a dentist?"

Rafferty moved his lips over his teeth. He spoke without moving his mouth. "Fuck the dentist."

"It's a well-known medical fact," Crotty said, "people with clean teeth commit less crime."

"You listen to Bob Hope?" Tom Spellacy said. "That's no shit about Pepsodent. 'You wonder where the yellow went, when you brush your teeth with Pepsodent.' You think Bob would bullshit you?"

"I get plenty," Raymond Rafferty said.

"Like our friend the Mystery Beauty," Crotty said.

"I'm telling you, I stay away from tight pussy," Raymond Rafferty whined. "You know my M.O. Old dolls. I been telling you, I knocked over an old broad on Western and Romaine that night. I don't remember the address, but it was apartment 3B, she must've made a complaint." Crotty nodded at Tom Spellacy. "A nice old broad, about seventy-five, eighty years of age."

"She liked you, too, Raymond," Crotty said. "Especially you coming in her nose. It's something she's been missing the last sixty years."

Crotty knocked on the door of the interrogation room. A uniformed officer came and took Raymond Rafferty back to his cell. Crotty lit a cigar.

"It checks," he said. "He was poking the old broad in the nose from midnight to five in the morning. She's ready for the farm, but she won't file charges."

"X. O'Brien will love that," Tom Spellacy said. He handed Crotty the suicide report. "Leland K. Standard."

"Who the fuck is Leland K. Standard?"

"Jumped off the Bradbury Building last night."

"So what," Crotty said. He opened the report. A round of cigar ash fell on his white vest. He read for a moment, then stared at Tom Spellacy. "His brother's a Dominican."

"Brother-in-law."

"He leave a note?"

Tom Spellacy shook his head.

"His old lady and the kids?"

"Still visiting the grandparents."

Crotty shut the report. "Then fuck him."

"Someone's going to know he was down here, Frank?"

"Not a chance," Crotty said. "I called him at the

office, asked him to come down, nice as pie, there's a couple of things I'd like to ask him. It's not the sort of thing, he goes to the gang at the water cooler and says, 'Lieutenant Crotty wants to know if I been waving my pecker again, so I'm going downtown, see if I can help out our friends in blue.' He didn't say that, I bet. The wife, she's going to think he's been up to old tricks and couldn't live with himself anymore, is what she's going to be thinking. The Dominican's going to be thinking good riddance, and try to fix Sis up with Johnny Cosgrove, the rich widower's been wanting to get in her pants all these years. Me, I got the file in my bottom drawer, where I forgot it's there, anyone asks. 'Oh, that Leland K. Standard,' I'll say, anyone asks. 'The family man.' Don't waste any sleep over it, is what I'm trying to tell you. They happen, these things. It's nobody's fault. He should've kept his pecker in his pants, the first place."

They walked back to the squad room. Masaryk was on the telephone. He cupped his hand over the receiver.

"They think her name's Lois Fazenda," Masaryk said.

Gloria Deane said that the apartment building where Lois Fazenda lived until three weeks before her death was on North Cherokee Avenue in Hollywood. It was a nondescript two-story bungalow turned into a warren of one-room apartments with hotplate privileges. There were eight girls sleeping in four double-decker bunk beds in what used to be Lois Fazenda's apartment. The rent for each girl was a dollar a night. Their bathroom was strung with wet lingerie and the wastepaper baskets were overflowing with balls of split hair, rouged Kleenex and brown paper bags filled with used Kotex. Besides Gloria Deane, the girl from Max Factor, there were three actresses, a model, a singer, a telephone operator and a cocktail-lounge employee living in the

171

one room. A check of police-department records established that two of the girls had records for prostitution, one for shoplifting and a fourth for acting in a stag movie as a minor. Five of the eight had moved into the apartment since Lois Fazenda's departure and only the girl from Max Factor, the singer and the telephone operator remembered her. All three recalled that Lois Fazenda had a rose tattooed on her lower abdomen and that although she claimed not to know a soul in Los Angeles, she had a date nearly every night. Gloria Deane remembered a "tall sinister elderly man" who drove a Packard and sometimes paid her rent. The singer recalled a radio announcer with a British accent named Maurice and the telephone operator a famous prop man at Paramount, Jim, Johnny, a man named Red, a pilot from Chicago, Jack, Lee, an outfielder from the Sacramento Solons and someone named Fred who possibly ran a model agency. The girl from Max Factor said that the telephone operator remembered all these names because she was always eavesdropping on Lois Fazenda's telephone calls. The telephone operator said she was trained to remember names. She also said that the girl from Max Factor had been sweet on Lois Fazenda. Gloria Deane replied that the telephone operator had a nigger pimp.

The building on Cherokee was owned by one Timothy Mallory, who had a record making stag movies going back to 1937 and who called himself an associate producer. Framed on the wall of his apartment was a headline from the June 6, 1944, Los Angeles *Times*: BRUSH FIRE IN HILLS THREATENS HOME OF HOLLYWOOD ASSOCIATE PRODUCER.

"Same day as D-Day," Timothy Mallory said. "No one gave a fig about my house."

"About your alibi, homo," Crotty said.

"It's hard to check."

"Why?" Tom Spellacy said.

"I'm a pimp, that's why. It's not exactly a nunnery I own here. Not very many people, bright eyes, are going to tell you, 'I saw Timmy today and his new find, that twelve-year-old dinge from the Belgian Congo.' "

"You pimp for Lois Fazenda?" Tom Spellacy said.

"Pussy pictures, that's all I did with her," Timothy Mallory said. He adjusted his toupee in the mirror and then pulled a nudist magazine from a drawer. Lois Fazenda was lying in a glade, the sun glinting off her hair. The thrust of her leg elongated and distorted the rose tattooed on her lower abdomen.

"A rock is a rock, a tree is a tree, shoot it in Griffith Park," Timothy Mallory said. "It's an old saying in the Industry. Meaning it's where I shot the picture." He smiled at Tom Spellacy. "I know your murderer."

"It'd be a help if you told us."

"J.H., Columbus, Ohio, that's who you should look for," Timothy Mallory said. "He wrote the magazine and said he had a thing thirteen inches long and where he would like to put it was guess where. J.H., Columbus, Ohio, was the way he signed himself." Timothy Mallory sighed and once again straightened his toupee in the mirror. *Ou sont les* 'J.H.' *d'antan?*

"What the fuck is he talking about?" Crotty said.

During the next forty-eight hours, the Robbery-Homicide Division established the following facts:

Timothy Mallory was clean. On the night Lois Fazenda was killed, he was directing a stag movie in a house out by the airport with the telephone operator, the model, a girl from Bakersfield, two boys, an old man and a horse. The girl from Max Factor had a severe case of menstrual cramps and never left the house on North Cherokee Avenue. The singer attended a sneak preview in Burbank of *They Wouldn't Believe*

*Me* with Robert Young, Jane Greer and Susan Hayward and afterward had her nose broken in a bar on Central Avenue by a unit publicist and spent the evening in the emergency room at Central Receiving Hospital. The prop man at Paramount had an alibi, as did Jim, Johnny, the man named Red, Jack, Lee and Fred, whose model agency was actually an outlet for Timothy Mallory's dirty photographs. The outfielder for the Sacramento Solons was playing in Seattle against the Rainiers and went oh-for-five and dropped a fly ball in the bottom of the tenth to let in the winning run. As it happened, the pilot from Chicago was in Seattle and had seen the game. The pilot said he hoped the outfielder could fuck better than he played ball and then said he was sorry about Lois Fazenda but she wasn't all that great a piece of ass. The owner of the religious-supply store on Hollywood Boulevard was at Saint John of God's Hospital where his wife gave birth to stillborn twins and developed a puerperal infection. Maurice, the radio announcer with the British accent, was actually a Jamaican octoroon and was now an all-night rhythm-and-blues disk jockey at a colored station in Brownsville, Texas. The tall, sinister, elderly man who drove a Packard was in fact short, thirty-seven, drove a La Salle and was Timothy Mallory's trick.

These facts were learned about Lois Fazenda. She was twenty-two years old. She had come west from Medford, Massachusetts, three years before in hopes of becoming a movie star. She worked as a waitress, an usherette in a movie theater, a carhop and a checkout girl in the PX at Fort MacArthur. For two months she was a volunteer at County General Hospital, working for a Catholic charity called the Protectors of the Poor. The volunteers of the Protectors of the Poor worked the emergency rooms and orthopedic wards of County General passing out candy and cigarettes and toothpaste and razor blades and Virgin of Guadalupe medals to indigent accident victims of Mexican descent.

Lois Fazenda also did two days as an Arab extra in *Casablanca* at Warner Brothers. Her only other movie work was being eaten out in a film directed and associate-produced by Timothy Mallory. She lived in a series of boarding houses much like the one on North Cherokee. On West Adams Boulevard she thought she was pregnant. On Camino Palmero she hemorrhaged. On North Orange Drive she was tattooed. The tattoo artist was currently in the federal penitentiary on Terminal Island for violation of the Mann Act. On Linden Drive in Long Beach she left behind a poem that said, "Remember me and keep in mind/A faithful friend is hard to find/But when you are good and true/Trade not the good ones for the new." On K Street in Lancaster there was an unmailed letter to Joe that said Doc was courting her and that unless Joe made his intentions clear, she could not vouch for what Doc would do. There was also a letter from the pilot in Chicago: "You say in your letter you want us to be good friends, but from your telegram you seem to want more than that. Are you really sure just what you want? Why not pause and consider just what your coming out here would amount to. Helen still hasn't agreed to the divorce. I think she has private detectives following me. I care too much for you to subject you to that. Perhaps Matt is your out. In your last letter you mentioned he had sent you a ring. Diamond? Engagement? You gave no explanation. Matt sounds like a big spender and if he wants to make an honest woman out of you (that's a J-O-K-E, ha ha), he might be better for you than me." On Bronson Avenue, there was a newspaper clipping from the Wenatchee, Washington, *Herald:* LOCAL ACE HONORED. The story said that Captain Matthew J. Kronholm, a flight instructor at Peterson Field in Colorado, had recently been promoted to major. "Major Kronholm is the son of Mrs. Matthew J. Kronholm, Sr., and the late Mr. Kronholm, a local pharmacist. Major Kronholm's brother, Samuel, is an actor in Hollywood under the name of Sammy Barron. Major Kronholm is engaged." To whom it did not say, but the word *engaged* on the clipping was circled in lipstick. On Harold Way there was a letter from Mrs. Matthew J. Kronholm, Sr.: "Matt asked me to write you because he said you were a very refined girl. He said you would 'fit right in.'" On Sierra Vista there was a note from Sammy Barron: "The doctor's name is Snyder and he'll do it at his house and not at his office and bring $200." On Formosa Avenue there was a telegram from Mrs. Matthew J. Kronholm, Sr.: "Received word from War Department Matt killed in a crash. Our deepest sympathy is with you. Pray it isn't true." Lois Fazenda had left Formosa Avenue without paying her rent. Nor had she paid her rent on Sierra Vista, Harold Way, Bronson Avenue, K Street in Lancaster, Linden Drive in Long Beach, on North Orange Drive, Poinsettia Avenue, Camino Palmero or West Adams Boulevard.

Lois Fazenda's mother had died of a stroke when her daughter was sixteen. Her father, who had divorced his wife in 1931 and moved west, was a refrigerator repairman in Lompoc. He had not seen his daughter in two years. She had come to live with him in Lompoc when she was out of a job, but he had thrown her out after five weeks. Lewis Fazenda said his daughter would not keep house for him and was only interested in men. She had once wired him for two hundred dollars. He had not sent it. It was his opinion that his daughter was "no damn good." He had a graduation picture of Lois Fazenda wearing a white cap and gown and it was published in the *Express*, the *Times*, the *Herald*, the *Daily News*, the *Examiner* and the Long Beach *Press-*

*Telegraph.* Sammy Barron had a photograph of Lois Fazenda in the Arab costume she wore during her two days of extra work on *Casablanca* at Warner's. It was printed in the *Express,* the *Times,* the *Herald,* the *Daily News,* the *Examiner* and the Long Beach *Press-Telegraph.*

Sammy Barron was a midget. He lived in a trailer park in Glendale.

"She nearly shit, Lois, when she saw I was a little person," Sammy Barron said. "Matt was a tall, blondheaded kid. His prick was bigger than I am. The schlong on him. I mean, you could have put it in costume and given it a lead in *The Wizard of Oz.*"

Sammy Barron puffed on a cigar. He was losing his hair and his legs barely extended to the edge of his chair. Tom Spellacy wondered if it was better to stand or to sit. He slouched down in the chair in Sammy Barron's trailer until he was practically sitting on his shoulder blades.

"Nobody told her I was a little person," Sammy Barron said. "Not that I don't grant you it's a tough subject to ease your way into." He began to speak in a high-pitched falsetto voice. " 'He's not exactly Matt's *big* brother, Lois, he's what you might call an *older* brother.' " Sammy Barron pulled on his cigar. The ash shivered. "My old man used to look at me funny and say, 'Circus work is good, I hear. Steady. Outdoors. Like being a cowboy.' Three foot two, eyes of blue, I was going to sit on the Lone Ranger's lap. The tiny Tonto." He dipped the butt end of his cigar into a beaker of brandy. "So I cut out of Wenatchee when I was twelve. With a circus."

"You kept in touch with Matt?" Tom Spellacy said.

"He looked me up when he joined the Air Corps," Sammy Barron said. "That was the golden age of little people in this business. *The Wizard of Oz* I did, then

*Lady in the Dark*. Speaking parts. You know Ray Bolger? A good pal of mine. Jack Haley. Ginger Rogers."

"Judy Garland?"

"A pain in the ass. And Georgie Jessel, too." Sammy Barron sucked the brandy from the cigar end. "Anyway, Matt comes to see me on the set. I take him to lunch in the commissary and he's looking at all the fluff and he says, 'How long has this been going on?'"

"Did you introduce him to Lois?"

"Quiff is one thing Matt never had any trouble finding. He latched onto her somewhere and then when he's leaving town, he asks me to look out for her."

"They were engaged."

"Shit," Sammy Barron said. "He was dipping it, is all. Knocked her up is what he did. I was doing *Casablanca* at Warner's. No lines, but two close-ups. In that crowd scene outside of Rick's Place where Peter Lorre gets it. I got run over, is how I got the close-ups. Anyway, I talk to this friend of mine and he talks to another guy and this guy talks to Curtiz and Curtiz thinks it's cute, a little person with a girl friend. 'Most guys go down on a girl,' he says. 'You go up.' I give him a big wink and he gives her a job. She didn't have any close-ups, though."

"I got a couple of suits off that picture," Crotty said. Sammy Barron looked perplexed.

"From Sidney Greenstreet," Crotty said. "You remember the white double-breasted one?"

"It had bone buttons," Sammy Barron said.

"That's the one," Crotty said.

"I didn't know you knew Sidney," Sammy Barron said.

"I know somebody who knows him, gets me his suits," Crotty said.

"You're about the same size," Sammy Barron said.

"48 regular," Crotty said.

Tom Spellacy cleared his throat. "You arranged the abortion?"

Sammy Barron looked from one officer to the other.

"You won't get busted," Crotty said.

"I lent her the two hundred," Sammy Barron said. "And gave her the name of the guy does all the major studio scrapes." He chewed on his cigar. "That's the last I saw of her." He grew pensive. "She was very interested in the problems of little people."

"There's a little good in everybody," Tom Spellacy said.

Sammy Barron pulled himself from his chair. "Listen, I could use a little ink if you can see it that way, maybe mention me to the boys in the city room. 'Her friend, Sammy Barron, the actor, wept when he heard the news,' something along that line, and then a couple of credits. I cry on cue, the papers need a picture. It's always been slim pickings in this business for a little person, is why. Stand-in work is all I get now. For screen tots." A look of distaste crossed his features. "Cinemoppets. Roddy McDowall."

*Howard Terkel was being a pest.*
*Think of a nickname, Crotty said.*
*The Virgin Tramp, Tom Spellacy said.*

# *Eleven*

Tom Spellacy stopped at a red light at the corner of Figueroa and Seventh. The motor coughed and died. He held his foot on the accelerator until the engine caught and turned over.

"It idles funny," Corinne Morris said.

"It idles funny because someone pinched the radiator cap and I've got a piece of cloth stuck in there," Tom Spellacy said. "Right in the department parking lot there, they pinched it. They got a regular black-market ring working the lot there, pinching radiator caps from 1937 Plymouths with 110,000 miles on them, they're such a desired item."

"What's it cost, a new one?"

"Nothing, you want to know the truth. I go to an auto-supply store and say I'm a servant of the people, a man in blue, and I hear he's got some swell radiator caps, and it's a shame he could lose them all in a fire, him having those greasy rags in a pail out by the back door and all. And he says take two, they're small, as a matter of fact, take a box, and speaking of caps, here's some distributor caps, I had a cap pistol, you could take one of them, too." The light changed and he made the left turn across Seventh into Figueroa. "It's the principle is all, why I don't get a new one." He shook his head. "The department parking lot."

"Sometimes I think there's more crooks in the department than on the street."

"There's them thinks the same way," Tom Spellacy said. She ought to meet Jack while she's at it, he thought. Brenda, too. It might make it easier to take, Mary Margaret coming home. He shuddered. He was going to have to tell her.

"Actually I meant a new car," Corinne said.

"That's what I thought you meant." The traffic was backing up. Horns hooted. He made only one block on Figueroa before the light changed again. "I got my eye on one, as a matter of fact. An Olds 98. Fully loaded. Hydra-matic."

Corinne smiled. "That's terrific, Tom."

He realized he had made a mistake. Everything he talked to her about carried so much freight, could be interpreted as meaning something else. The Olds 98 had the weight of making plans, looking to the future. Bail out. "And I bought my ticket to the Irish Sweepstakes. My horse comes in, I can make the down. Otherwise I got to hope Santa's going to be good to me this year."

Corinne stubbed her cigarette into the ashtray. "You're always complaining about money."

"You don't have any, you bitch about it, that's the way it works, they tell me." He did not like to talk to Corinne about money. Low down, monthly payments. They hinted at domestic arrangements he was not willing to make. Even if Mary Margaret weren't getting out of Camarillo. Change the subject. A newsboy was working his way through the stalled traffic. Tom Spellacy gave him a nickel and handed the *Express* to Corinne. The headline read: THOUSANDS ATTEND VIRGIN TRAMP'S LAST RITES. He thought, Oh, shit, it never ends. The women in my life.

Corinne read, " 'Thousands of curious mourners backed up downtown traffic for nearly an hour today as funeral services were held for Lois Fazenda, playgirl victim of a werewolf slaying that has shocked the free world.'" Corinne dropped the newspaper on her lap. "That is such shit," she said.

"What else does it say?"

Corinne picked up the paper. "'As reported exclusively in the *Herald-Express,* Miss Fazenda, twenty-two, was known as The Virgin Tramp. . . .'"

"I still don't believe that," Corinne said. "They made it up."

"They'll do anything to sell newspapers, those people," Tom Spellacy said. No need to tell her how Lois Fazenda got the name. No need to complicate my life any further.

Corinne continued reading, "'The last rites were conducted by Evangelist Jack Mayo, who under the name Cap'n Jack is pastor of the evangelical Good Ship Grace. . . .'"

Corinne crumbled the newspaper and threw it on the floor of the car. "Shit, that's all it is," she repeated. "Why not let the poor girl go quietly. Instead of making it a circus."

"Corinne, that dame is out of control," he said quietly. "People are bored. The war's over. They need something, sink their teeth into."

"Forget their own crappy lives," Corinne said.

He started to say, I was there, it was worse than you think, but he held up. He did not want to debate the morality of Lois Fazenda's funeral with Corinne. Especially since his dreaming up the name was one reason it was a circus. For an instant he wondered what they had to talk about outside of bed. It had been that way since Des told him about Mary Margaret. He erased the thought. The funeral. Fuqua's brainstorm. Murderers show up at funerals sometimes. Me, I don't think that's such a hot idea, but Fuqua said it was a definite pattern. The Good Ship Grace was an experience. Des could pick up some pointers, next time he's thinking of building a cathedral. Stained glass portholes instead of windows. The center aisle a fucking gangplank. No murderer showed up. Just a fairy who wanted to get into the casket with her.

"I heard part of it on the radio," Corinne said. "McDonough & McCarthy sponsored it. They had some fucking thing called the Layaway Layaway Plan they were pushing." She mimicked the announcer. " 'Our layaway plan allows you to lay away a loved one.' "

You have to hand it to Sonny, Tom Spellacy thought. "He planted her, Sonny. Free. Cap'n Jack was his idea. He's got a big following on the radio is why he picked him. He'll come out all right, Sonny, doing it for nothing, don't you worry about that."

"I'm surprised he didn't try for the Cardinal," Corinne said.

Tom Spellacy leaned on the horn. The traffic began to untangle. "He did. He was hoping she was a Catholic."

"She would've been better off, the Cardinal said a Solemn High for her. 'Ahoy, all sinners,' Cap'n Jack says. 'All fornicators to the poop deck.' On the radio. Live. 'Let's pipe this virgin into heaven.' "

Tom Spellacy eased by the car causing the tie-up. It was an old Studebaker with a flat tire. A family of frightened Mexican children stared out the windows at the drivers shouting curses at them. Their father was under the car with a jack that did not appear to work. A traffic patrolman was screaming at him to move.

"Forget about it," he said. "That's why we're going out tonight, forget about shit like that. See the fights, have a few drinks, relax. I got to worry about Lois Fazenda in the morning, is why I don't want to think about her tonight. Okay? I'm home from the office, shaved, showered, clean socks, nice Jockey shorts,

183

starched shirt, tie, I don't want to think about her, let's have a nice time, we haven't had one lately. Okay?"

"Okay."


He turned into the lot at the Figueroa Auditorium and parked in a space marked Matchmaker. In the shadows of the parking lot, a raucous crap game was going on. He turned on his headlights to see the game better. A uniformed police officer was standing over the kneeling players with a handful of dollar bills. The policeman told him to turn off his fucking lights.

"You can't park there, buddy." The voice belonged to a thick-set Mexican with balloons of scar tissue over both eyes.

"Fuck off," Tom Spellacy said.

The Mexican circled slowly, moving with difficulty, looking for an opening, his hands in the fighting position. Corinne clung to the automobile, afraid to speak. Tom Spellacy crouched, waiting. Suddenly the Mexican was inside his guard, pummeling him in the stomach. Tom Spellacy tied him up. The Mexican stepped back, a smile on his face.

"You always were a fucking petunia, Tom."

"How's it going, Polo?"

"Good, Tom, good." He motioned toward the crap game. "I got the game. I hear things, I get a little down now and then."

"Who's going in the water tonight, Polo?"

"Anyone goes, it's the *negrito* in the semi." Polo looked at Corinne. She smiled at him tentatively. Tom Spellacy made no effort to introduce them. "You want a ticket? Give you two for a dollar. They're two-fifty each at the box office."

"Swell, Polo," Tom Spellacy said. He gave him a dollar and took the two tickets. Polo limped off toward the crap game.

"He's scalping for less than they cost," Corinne said.

184

"To last week's fight," Tom Spellacy said. He tore up the tickets. "A big night, he gets away with it." He shrugged. "Other nights, his friends help him out."

They walked into the auditorium. It smelled of piss and liniment. The walls of the arena were covered with faded tinted photographs of old-time strongmen and wrestlers and fighters and announcers.

"Then he's a friend of yours," Corinne said.

"In a way," Tom Spellacy said. "He took me out in the fourth round one night at Legion Stadium in El Monte." They stopped in front of a tinted photograph of a welterweight skipping rope in trunks and a tank shirt. The identification marker said, "The Ever Popular Enrique 'Polo' Barbera." There was no scar tissue over his eyes. "He didn't even work up a sweat."

They made their way through the jostling crowd. Their seats were at ringside, on the aisle in the second row. On the other side of the ring, George Brent was signing autographs.

"I thought sure he was going to get the shot in the ball park, Polo, the night he beat that colored guy here. The one it was like punching fog, trying to hit him. Mercury. Mercury Johnson. He punched his ticket, Polo. He was a great fighter that night."

Corinne said, "What happened, he didn't get it?"

"He was supposed to go in the water, it turns out. There was a lot of money riding on it. He just got carried away, Polo. And a lot of people got burned."

"And?"

"They broke his knees with a baseball bat." George Brent was wearing a camel's hair blazer and a white shirt and a yellow ascot. He wondered if he could ever dress that way. "You've got to wait your turn. He should've known that, Polo."

Corinne sucked in her breath. "I'm glad you're out of that," she said.

"You're seven-seven-and-two after sixteen fights, you

don't have much choice, you still got your brains left."
He ordered two beers from a vendor and handed one
to Corinne. "You don't get a main event in Yankee
Stadium with seven-seven-and-two."

The fighters in the first four-round preliminary were
shuffling down the aisle toward the ring. The ropes
parted. They scuffed their feet in the resin. Bantam-
weights. Romero and Napoles. Each seemed lost in his
robe. The gloves dwarfed their caved-in chests. They
met in the center of the ring. The referee gave his
instructions in English, then in Spanish. Romero had a
tattoo of the Sacred Heart of Jesus on his right arm.
Napoles had acne. The pimpled whiteheads spread over
his back. Each fighter crossed himself in his corner.

The bell rang.

He remembered his first fight. A four-rounder at
Ocean Park. He got twenty-five dollars and a pasting
from Jackie Ahearne. He knocked out Jackie two years
later in San Bernardino when the syphilis was eating
away at his brain. The truth of the matter was he
couldn't fight worth a shit. He was always the first to
say it. It made it a little easier. He never laid it on his
bad hands. He just said, I couldn't fight worth a shit,
and let it go at that. It was his cousin Taps Keogh who
put him in the ring. And his mother. He had never told
anyone that. Taps had a grocery store picked out. The
two of us could knock it over easy, Taps said. No job,
no money, why not. He had always wanted to tell the
old lady that God had intervened. In the person of the
old lady herself. Nutty as a fruitcake ever since the
old man went to sleep on the trolley tracks. It was
Holy Thursday and like always she climbed up the
stairs on her knees, saying a rosary every step. Except
this year she fell and broke her hip. He had to take her
to the hospital. Taps went alone. The beat cop caught
him in the cellar. They sent him away for two years.
He had to do something after Taps went away, so he

went in against Jackie Ahearne. No job, no money, the old man dead, the old lady crazy and Des in the sem. He would've murdered Des, Jackie Ahearne, even with the syph.

There were no knockdowns in the first preliminary. When the four rounds were over, he put his arm around Corinne. "Who'd you pick?"

The ring announcer was collecting the judges' cards.

"The Sacred Heart," she said.

"No, it's Pimples easy."

The boy with acne was squeezing a whitehead. The announcer lifted his arm.

"Another beer?"

"I'd love one."

"I like the way you lick the foam."

She stuck her tongue in his ear. The featherweight champion of Yucatán was climbing into the ring. A long wait. Then the two-fisted slugger from Bakersfield was announced. The two-fisted slugger from Bakersfield was wearing a robe lettered The Modesto Kid. The robe made Tom Spellacy smile. The Modesto Kid must have backed out. He ran over the possibilities. Knife fight. Drug overdose. Something like that. The Modesto Kid wouldn't miss a paynight for a cold. Or a broken arm, if he could get away with it. Leave it to Marge. She could always find a replacement. Marge Madragon was the matchmaker at the Figueroa. Large Marge. A 257-pound lesbian. She was too fat to drive, which was why he always took her parking place. Her friend Skinny Minny Esposito had failed her driving test fourteen times. Minny was nervous. Minny was also the bookkeeper at the Figueroa. They always took cabs, Marge and Minny.

The replacement from Bakersfield went down thirty seconds into the first round. He was up at the count of eight, legs wobbly.

"He looks like he's going to die," Corinne said. "He can hardly move. He must be forty years old."

The replacement from Bakersfield began bleeding from a cut over his right eye. He tried to hold on in the corner directly above them. A left and a right splattered blood over the spectators at ringside. The crowd was howling for more. The bell rang and the cut fighter slumped on his stool. Blood spurted from the gash above his eye.

"Why didn't he go down?" Corinne asked.

"He wants his hundred, he's got to go at least three," Tom Spellacy said. "She drives a hard bargain, Marge."

"She must like the sight of blood."

"That's why she cuts the ring." Corinne stared at him for explanation. "It's only eighteen-by-eighteen here. It's twenty-by-twenty normally. She doesn't like to see anybody running from anybody, Marge. She'd put them in a telephone booth, she could."

Corinne clutched his arm through the next two rounds. The replacement from Bakersfield was systematically pounded, but he refused to go down. The beer brightened Corinne's eyes. After every sip, Tom Spellacy erased her foam mustache with his finger.

Twelve seconds into the fourth round, the replacement from Bakersfield was counted out. The Modesto Kid's robe was draped around his shoulders and he danced around the ring as if he had won.

"I'll guess he'll get his hundred now," Corinne said.

"You're learning," Tom Spellacy said. He glanced around the arena. Marge Madragon waved at him from her box in the mezzanine. He waved back. It was Marge who gave him his first job after he quit. Corinne looked at him, then at Marge. At her gym downtown. Stretching people. On a rack. He smiled at the astonished look on Corinne's face. Ten dollars a shot. Four to him, six to Marge. Mainly shorties an inch or two shy of the five-five regulation height required by the police and fire departments. A belt around the ankles, another under the armpits, then crank away until he thought something would break inside. The stretch only lasted an hour. If there was a long line for the department physical, they had to come back the next day and get pulled apart all over again.

"Why did they do it?" Corinne said.

"It was the Depression, Corinne. These guys were pushing pencils on street corners. This was a steady job with a pension at the end of it."

"It's a wonder no one ever died of internal bleeding."

"Marge always said with all the guys I helped get into the department, I was a cinch to beat the sneezer, anyone checked out."

He felt someone tap him on the shoulder. Minny Esposito knelt in the aisle. She was stick thin. There was a pencil stuck in the raggedy bun of her hair. She looked away when he turned around. Minny never looked directly at anyone. "Marge wants to see you."

He looked up. Marge Madragon was beckoning him to the mezzanine. The fighters were being introduced. He shook his head.

"Go on, Tom," Corinne said. "I'll be all right. I'm enjoying myself."

Marge Madragon's box was in the first two rows overlooking the ring. The seats in the first row had been removed for a wooden table on which was an adding machine, a pair of binoculars, a carton of Hershey bars, a box of tacos and a bucket of guacamole. Marge's seat in the second row had been specially molded to fit her huge frame. She motioned Tom Spellacy down next to her, peeled back the wrapping of a candy bar and dipped it into the guacamole.

The two fighters in the ring were feeling each other out.

"Polo said the colored one's going in the tank," Tom Spellacy said.

"Polo should keep his fucking mouth shut, he knows what's good for him," Marge Madragon said. "I give him the game in the lot, I can take it away from him, I want."

"Marge can take it away from him, she wants," Minny Esposito said. Tom Spellacy looked at her quickly, but she was too fast for him. She had already turned away before their eyes could meet. She busied herself with the adding machine.

"It's a gold mine, that game," Marge Madragon said. "I told him I wanted a piece of it. He told me to go fuck myself."

"He told Marge to go fuck herself," Minny Esposito said.

"He told me he'd fuck Minny before he gave me a piece of the game," Marge Madragon said.

"He told Marge he'd fuck me before he gave her a piece," Minny Esposito said.

"Shut up, Minny," Marge Madragon said.

The Negro fighter below was backpedaling fast.

"The ropes weren't there, he'd been on his way to Tijuana," Tom Spellacy said. He looked down at Corinne, chin in her hands, intently watching the action. Marge Madragon was also staring down at Corinne. The thought of Corinne imprisoned between Marge's barge-like thighs made him wince.

"What happened to the Modesto Kid?" he said suddenly, trying to draw Marge away from Corinne.

Her eyes remained fastened on Corinne. "Cut last night at the Casa Mazatlán."

"You kept his robe."

She looked at him. "He's got no use for it. DOA at County General."

Tom Spellacy shrugged. "That was some replacement you got."

"The bartender at Casa Mazatlán."

He laughed. The bell ended the first round. Minny

leaned over the railing and shouted, "Hit him with a coconut."

"Shut up, Minny," Marge Madragon said. "Fucking bartender wanted new gloves. A record of 1-13-1 and he wanted new gloves. Main eventers get new gloves, I tell him, not preliminary boys. He beat a main eventer once, he says. Vinny Avila. I say, You beat him in the parking lot at the Casa Mazatlán. And you hit him with a hammer. And he says Vinny had the hammer, he had a tire iron. So I give him the new gloves."

"You're all heart, Marge."

"Tom says you're all heart, Marge," Minny Esposito said.

Marge Madragon picked up her binoculars and surveyed the house. The second round was beginning in the ring below. Someone shouted, "Hit him, you bum, you got the wind with you." Tom Spellacy knew the fix was in, but still he was absorbed. In his mind, he picked off punches, looked for openings. He wished he had been able to fight better. He could taste the rubber mouthpiece, feel the salve rubbed into the cut above his eye, the balls of cotton pushed into his nose to plug the bleeding, taste the globs of bloody mucus leaking into his throat from the nosebleeds.

"You shouldn't've done that, Tom," Marge Madragon said. Her eyes were still glued to the binoculars. She seemed to be focusing on a refreshment stand across the arena.

Her voice startled him. "What are you talking about?"

The crowd suddenly roared. The Negro was on his back on the canvas. The referee was counting.

"I could hear the splash up here," Minny Esposito said.

The Negro was on his knee, then on his feet. The referee wiped his gloves. The fighters began moving around the ring. He was no longer watching. Marge

191

Madragon avoided his eyes. He knew there was a reason that she wanted to see him. He had a feeling what it was. At least it would get her mind off going down on Corinne.

"You shouldn't fuck around with Jack, Tom. You embarrassed him with your brother. You shouldn't've done that. He did you a big favor once."

He wondered how many other people knew that Jack Amsterdam had paid someone off so that he wouldn't be indicted. Brenda. Marge. He did not really want to know who else. Mary Margaret was the only one he was certain didn't know. He could have diagramed it for her and she still wouldn't have understood it. May Dalton's uncle Slats Shugrue is in the bag business, she would say. At the A&P. A grand bagman he is, May tells me. A regular breadwinner.

Corinne. He did not want to think about that. Better she knew that Mary Margaret was coming home than that he used to work for Jack.

"This your idea, Marge, or his?" He knew that Jack Amsterdam held the mortgage on the Figueroa.

"He deals with important people now, Tom," Marge Madragon said.

"He has a tuxedo," Minny Esposito said.

The crowd was on its feet. The Negro was curled on his side. The referee picked up the count. Eight. Nine. Ten.

"He own that coon?" Tom Spellacy said.

"Sixty percent," Minny Esposito said.

"Him and his tuxedo and his important people, he still tells some jigaboo to take a dive," Tom Spellacy said.

"He's got too much to lose now, Tom. Don't cross him."

"Tell him to go fuck himself, Marge."

"He can be dangerous, Tom."

For an instant the thought crossed his mind that there

192

had to be something else Jack Amsterdam must be worried about. Not just an altercation at lunch. He could not think what it was. Something that would smear shit on his tuxedo.

"Ask Polo," Marge Madragon said.

"So Jack was responsible for his legs being broken," Tom Spellacy said.

Marge Madragon unwrapped another Hershey bar. She did not reply.

"One thing I always wondered, Marge," Tom Spellacy said finally. "You do it to Minny or she do it to you?"

The crap game was still going on in the parking lot when they left the arena. Polo Barbera was nowhere to be seen.

"The white one, got knocked out, the heavyweight, I liked him best," Corinne said hesitantly.

Tom Spellacy kept walking and did not reply. He got into the Plymouth and started the engine and waited until she got into the other side. Even before her door was shut he gunned the Plymouth out into the traffic. He did not look at her nor did he speak.

Two blocks up Figueroa, Corinne said, "Let's get something to eat."

Tom Spellacy scratched a match lit with his thumbnail and put it to the cigarette in his mouth. He exhaled a stream of smoke but said nothing.

Corinne stared out the car window for a moment, then tried again. "We could go to the Trocadero."

"We could go to the Cotton Club, too," Tom Spellacy said. "If I stuck up a gas station along the way, pay the cover charge."

"The Windsor, then."

"Check my gun, see if it's loaded, so when I say, 'Stick 'em up,' they know I mean business."

Corinne leaned her back against the car door so that

193

she was facing him. "Look, Tom, what happened back there."

"Nothing happened back there."

"Okay, have it your way. Nothing happened back there. So let's have some fun. Let's go to the Troc. We can afford it. We've got two incomes."

He braked to a halt in the middle of the block. Cars screeched to a stop behind them and then horns began to scream. Tom Spellacy turned and stared at her, as if oblivious to the jam he was causing. "Next thing you're going to tell me is two can live cheaper than one."

She blurted the words out, so softly that the car horns almost drowned her out.

"Next thing I'm going to tell you is I'm pregnant, I think."

# Twelve

He took it better than she expected. His eyes flickered for a moment and his hands tightened on the steering wheel, but beyond that nothing. She had been waiting for the moment to tell him for three days, but now she wished she could take the words back and lock them in a box along with all her other devils.

The car drifted out toward the center divider. She lifted her hands to ward off the blinding headlights of the oncoming cars, and for an instant, she thought he was trying to kill them both. A horn screeched and he shouted, "Go fuck yourself!" and then he eased back into the center of his lane. He drove out Sixth and then crossed over to Melrose and it wasn't until he stopped at a red light at Highland that he spoke.

"You're sure." It was a statement, flat and unemotional. He tapped his fingers on the wheel waiting for the light to change.

"Pretty sure." She forced herself to look squarely at him. "Very sure. The rabbit died."

The light changed and he turned right and headed toward Fountain. She couldn't tell him it was a matter of self-preservation. She worried, but then she always worried. She was thirty-four years old and a two-time loser. He had called her that one night when she tried to ask him about Mary Margaret. "For a two-time loser," he had said, "you give out an awful lot of advice about other people's marriages." He had tried to laugh it off, but sometimes when he was in bed with her, he would caress her and say, "My little two-time loser." It was Tom's way of keeping her at arm's length, she knew that. And didn't care. That was what she was, there was no getting around it. Not that she wanted to try marriage a third time. But she didn't want to lose Tom either. The question she did not wish to consider was whether it was out of love or fear of being alone.

She hunched against the door of the car and lit a cigarette. The matchbook cover said Hotel Roosevelt. When was it they had been there. A week ago. Two. To hear Frankie Carle. She always kept hotel matchbooks. For memories. She thought of the hotel rooms she had been in. She had always loved hotels. Her father was a pharmacist in Vernon, and when she was a little girl, he occasionally brought drug salesmen home to dinner. After they had eaten, the men would tip back their chairs and talk about the Cornhusker and the Grady and the Tutweiler, and then they would leave, heading on downtown to the drinks they had been denied before dinner. She dreamed then of ordering London broil in the Tutweiler Grill, of knowing how to tip the bellboy and how to call room service for ice, of walking through hotel lobbies and being admired, making friends, a lonely ten-year-old's dream. Then when she was nineteen, one of the salesmen had brought her downtown and fucked her in Room 432 at the Ambassador. It had hurt and she had bled but what troubled her most was that she had become a traveling salesman's story. She knew it when the drummers began to call. It was odd knowing you had a telephone number that was passed around in the Palm Court of the Palace Hotel in San Francisco.

And at the Raddison and the Grady and the Tutweiler.

Tom Spellacy stopped the car in front of her apartment. He crimped the wheels toward the curb, turned off the ignition and made sure the rear doors were locked. So he's going to come in, Corinne thought. To tell me he can't marry me or where I can get a clean scrape. If he says he's only thinking of me, out he goes. She wondered if he would offer money for an abortion.

Tom took her by the arm, and when they got to her apartment, he unlocked the door with his own key. He opened the refrigerator, got out some ice and made them both drinks.

"There's something I have to tell you," he said finally. Corinne braced herself. And then he told her that Mary Margaret was coming home.

When he finished, she took a sip of the rye highball in her hand. It was too strong and she poured some more ginger ale in it.

"Well?"

"It wasn't what I expected."

"What did you expect?"

"It doesn't matter." She couldn't think of an abortion now. Suddenly she exploded. "Why the fuck didn't you tell me she was coming home?"

"She's crazy, Corinne." He knew the answer was not adequate. It was just his standard line on Mary Margaret. "She's always got some scheme. Chatting it up with the priests. Next week she'll say she's going off to work in the missions. Sister Mary Margaret, the Mary-knoll. Raped by a fucking Chinaman."

"When is she coming home?"

"Soon. A couple of weeks." He did not tell her that Mary Margaret had notified Des and not him. Or that Des would try to get Moira a day off from the convent. He tried to change the subject. "When is it due?"

"I have plenty of time to get a scrape, if that's what you're thinking."

"It wasn't what I was thinking."

"I just might keep it."

He stared at her.

"Make your high and mighty brother an uncle again." That should stop him.

"And if I do get an abortion, I won't need your help. I've had one before."

There suddenly was nothing more to say, only one place for it to end. She unhooked the Murphy bed and let it fall into place. It had always been this way. When words failed, when she could not express fear or doubt, sex was the only release, the gateway to the fatigue that killed pain and anxiety. They coupled briefly, violently, clothes on, clothes off. She claimed him with her mouth, searching his face for the signs of guilt, the sense of sin that anything he regarded as unnatural brought to it. Finally he slept and she dozed.

After awhile she woke and looked at the luminous hands of the clock on the bed table. Three-seventeen. The sheet under her was stained with semen. It had always bothered her that after lovemaking it was she who had to lay in the warm viscous pool. She went into the bathroom and dampened a washcloth. Her body was reflected in the full length mirror on the bathroom door. She had never had any feelings of narcissism about her body, and as she stared at herself in the mirror, she thought, Now I'm pregnant, but there was no reaction, neither dread nor fulfillment. With the washcloth, she rubbed at the stain on the sheet. She had often wondered if the chambermaids in the hotels where she fucked were aware of the signs of lovemaking in a deserted bed.

Her laundering did not affect Tom. She picked up his shoes and his socks and hung up the clothes scattered on the floor. He slept on his stomach, his face cradled in his arm, his sleep punctuated by a slight, even snore. She couldn't bear the sound of snoring. It grated on her nerves like the sound of fingernails scraping down a blackboard. Tom groaned and rolled over. She wanted to wake him, to talk to him, but he seemed to resist conversation. It was as if he wanted to protect himself from being told anything more.

She went back into the bathroom, tripping over an ashtray brimming with dead cigarettes. She thought the noise would awaken him. His breath caught for a moment and he coughed, but then the even pattern of his snoring continued. She closed the bathroom door and sat on the toilet seat. She could feel a migraine coming on. When she had a migraine, she thought of sex, not in any lubricious way—she never got wet—but almost as a problem in physics, the interaction of two moving properties. She reduced the act to an equation whereby the circumference of the orifice equaled the circumference of the member plus friction. She wondered how Sister Angelica, her physics teacher at Holy Resurrection, would react to this application of elementary physics; the thought made her laugh. The reduction of the sexual union to a scientific equation seemed to blunt the pain of the headache. Even the aura disappeared. After a few moments, almost out of a sense of duty, she wet a finger and put it between her legs. She could feel the first flickering of response, then she stopped. She never brought herself to orgasm. It was a holdover from her childhood when she believed that masturbation was sinful only if she came. A theory she never tried out on Sister Angelica.

She was wide awake now and in her mind she began to make a list. Corinne always made lists when she couldn't sleep. It was her way of counting sheep. Somewhere in the apartment, there was a list of lines from *Gone With the Wind*. She was always adding to it. "I believe in Rhett Butler—that's the only cause I know." "Some little town in Pennsylvania—called Gettysburg." "If you have enough courage, you can do without a reputation." "She's a pale-faced mealy mouthed ninny and I hate her." Corinne thought: "Fiddledeedee. I get so bored I could scream." She must remember to write that down. What else?

She remembered the books in the cabin at Arrowhead.

The weekend when she got pregnant.

Arrowhead had been her idea. She knew Tom would never go, but she had made the reservation and packed his clothes without telling him and by that time it was too late for him to say no, to invent an excuse. They drove the two hours to the lake in silence. The storekeeper at the combination gas station and general store had the key to the cabin. He wore slippers and a mothy cardigan and he apologized for not having a greater selection of food in stock. "Don't get too many folks out here this time of year," he had said automatically, as if he had seen too many couples out of season and knew they would never complain about the quality of his stock. They bought some bread and milk and bacon and instant coffee and set off down the boardwalk for the house. The houses on the lakefront were gray and weathered, their verandahs bereft of

199

furniture. The loneliness of the lake seemed to Corinne to contain an intangible threat, as if there were no-where deserted enough for the purpose for which they came.

The house was on the hill overlooking the lake. Tom unstacked the upended wicker chairs in the living room and placed them around the straw floor matting. Going into the kitchen, he lit the pilot light under the stove and searched around for ice and glasses. There was no ice, but he finally found two empty peanut butter jars and poured two drinks. The tap water tasted of rust, but Corinne drank gratefully, eager for anything to ease the weight of silence. With her finger, she traced her initials in the dust on the table at her side.

"You didn't find a duster?"

"No."

"I'd better clean up."

She pulled sheets and blankets from a closet and went into the bedroom. As she tucked in the hospital corners on the double bed, she could feel Tom watching her through the open door and knew he was wondering what he was doing there. She placed their suitcase on the bed and unpacked it, hanging her coat and nightgown neatly on hangers, arranging his shaving equipment and her cosmetics carefully on the cigarette-scarred bureau. When she was finished, she picked a book from the cheap stained bookshelves by the bed. The volumes left in a summer house always seemed so sad to her. She examined the titles and wondered who and why in the past had been given or bought *A History of Phelps Dodge* or *Hardy Perennials and Herbaceous Borders* or *Anthony Adverse* or *Harper's Electricity Book for Boys*. Inside *The Collected Poems of Sara Teasdale* was the inscription, "To Betty Howard, with love from Aunt Agnes, March, 1928." Corinne wondered who Aunt Agnes was, and Betty Howard. Where had the young girl gone, what had she become. What tremor of youth had made her underline the words:

> Heart, we will forget him
> You and I tonight.
> You will forget the warmth he gave,
> I will forget the light.

Even now Corinne could remember how the words had touched her.

"Shall we go for a walk?" Tom had said.

"No."

It was a tired summons and she took him by the hand and they lay on the mildewed sheets, more alone than together.

Eleven weeks ago.

Corinne looked at herself in the bathroom mirror. There were tears in her eyes. She dug the heels of her palms into her cheekbones and moved them back toward her ears, then down over her jaw until the pinched pity disappeared from the long, guarded face. She turned out the lights and went into the living room.

It seemed simpler to spend the rest of the night on the couch.


## 2


When Tom Spellacy awoke, she was gone. There was a penciled note on the floor under one of his shoes saying she had gone to mass. Swell. He noticed the pillow and the blanket on the couch and felt a momentary flash of irritation. She was usually as neat as a pin and he suspected that the mess of bedclothes on the divan was her way of telling him she was perfectly capable of going it alone, of taking care of herself. He rolled over and swore. Why had he agreed to go away to Arrowhead? It was the first time he had ever gone away with a woman. A weekend was trouble. A house and keys and groceries and arrangements and excuses to be away from town. Too many people knowing what you were doing, too many opportunities for things to go wrong. A cop's reasoning. That's all right, that's what I am. There was a lot to be said for the anonymity of an automobile, the lack of commitment in a motor court.

He thought, I always seem to fail women, but even as he said it, he knew it was a lie. He never gave enough of himself to women to fail them. He knew it and they knew it. Which made it a self-congratulating lie at that.

He lay back on the pillow, trying to make out objects around the room. It occurred to him suddenly that he had never been alone in the apartment before. Corinne had always been there. He had slept there for months, but to him it was a room like so many others he had known, a room with nothing of himself in it. There were two photographs in a silver frame on the bureau and he assumed they were of her parents, but he had never asked. A Tiffany lamp shade with a crack in it that must have meant something to her, but he did not know what. He got up and walked around the apartment. He was a detective, but he had never paid any attention to the old invitations he found in the desk drawer or the books that said *Ex libris* Homer Morris. They were clues to a mystery he did not want to understand.

He thought of Turd Turner. He supposed it was only natural. Without Turd Turner, there would be no mystery to understand.

He considered the ifs. If Turd Turner had not snatched Corinne, she wouldn't have met me. She wouldn't be pregnant. Turd Turner wouldn't have gone to the gas chamber.

Poor Turd. If. If. If.

A 207 conviction hung on a three-time loser. It didn't matter that Corinne had not been harmed except for a bad case of hysterics. (And meeting a cop who would knock her up, he thought.) The law was the law. A snatch under those circumstances meant the gas chamber.

He did not like to think of his part in it.

Not now.

With Corinne pregnant.

He never told Corinne that he had watched Turd die. The surprise was Turd asking to see him the night before he went to the gas chamber. He could have avoided it. There were any number of excuses. Fuqua didn't want him to go. We're short-handed, Fuqua had said. He's a nobody, Fuqua had also said. Meaning that if Turd Turner had been a somebody, Fuqua would have gone himself. He went anyway. And not just to spite Fuqua. The fact was, he felt a little guilty about his part in sending Turd to the gas chamber. He lied to Corinne to cover his absence. A stakeout. You won't see me for a couple of days. And he went to Q. It was creepy sitting in the holding cell on death row. He thought it wouldn't get to him, but it did.

"I got no family, Tom," Turd Turner had said. "All the times you collared me, I guess you come as close as anyone, being family."

"There's no hard feelings, then?"

"Jesus, Tom, you were just doing your job."

"It's nice you'd think that way," Tom Spellacy said. "You seen the chaplain?"

"Shit," Turd Turner said. "The regular chaplain's sick and they wanted me to hold hands with this nigger minister. I seen him taking a leak in the crapper and he's got this thing, it looks like a Louisville Slugger. 'You got one of them in white, I'll take it,' I says to him. I mean, I'm going out tomorrow, I can use a few laughs. Right?"

203

"Right."

"Laugh, shit, he starts giving me this shine voodoo."

"They do that."

"Fuck him," Turd Turner said. He smiled conspiratorially. "You're the law, Tom, but I bet you got a drink."

Tom Spellacy nodded. A cop could get away with a lot of things on death row. Especially the arresting cop. He took out a flask and poured some rye into a paper cup.

"Jesus, that's good," Turd Turner said. He downed the drink and held the cup out for a refill. "You know they got two chairs in there. Chair A and Chair B. Like in a fucking Chink restaurant. So when the warden comes around to see me this morning, I says to him, I say, 'Chair B, that's for me, with the warden on my knee.' Another fuckin' stoneface. Like he never heard a pome before."

Tom Spellacy poured some more rye into the outstretched cup. Anything to keep Turd Turner talking. The manic conversation was the last line of defense against death.

"You know, Tom, I nearly made the Ten once."

"I didn't know that."

"It's a federal list is the reason you didn't know, probably."

"Probably." Under any other circumstances the idea of Turd Turner being on any Ten Most Wanted list would have made him laugh out loud.

"A lot of my friends in law enforcement told me I was the eleventh most wanted man in the country and that Mr. Hoover was fixing to put my name on the Ten as soon as he had an opening. Mr. Hoover said my nickname was against me or I would have made the Ten a lot sooner. That's what my friends in the FBI tell me. If I had a name like Two-Gun Turner or Machine-Gun Turner, I would have made it easy."

"Tuffy Turner."

"That's a swell name, Tom." He burped and Tom Spellacy filled the cup to the top. The cup was beginning to soften at the sides and the rye was leaking out. Turd Turner held it in both hands and downed it in a gulp. "But all my friends in the press, they all knew my nickname was Turd, and my real name was Horace, and that wasn't good enough, Horace. I mean, there's never been a Horace on the Ten. Ever. Horace Turner. That's not a tough name."

"It's got a nice ring to it, though," Tom Spellacy said carefully. "Horace." It was the only thing he could think to do, calling him Horace. It was bad enough going to the gas chamber without the last person you talked to calling you Turd.

"It was really swell of you coming here, Tom. I mean, how many guys take the deep breath with a hangover, right?" He reached for the flask and put it to his mouth. "And hell, the things I've done, I was going to end up here sooner or later anyway."

They were like that, guys going to the gas chamber, Tom Spellacy knew. When the jig was up, they confessed to a lot of crimes they had nothing to do with. It was the stand-up thing to do. Palship. Taking the heat off someone else in the bunch. Going out doing some other guy a good turn.

Turd Turner mentioned a hit in North Hollywood.

A bank job in Inglewood.

Running forged green cards down to Mexico for Jack Amsterdam.

The flask was empty. Turd Turner stood up unsteadily.

"Well, I guess that's it, Tom."

"I guess it is, Horace."

Turd Turner embraced Tom Spellacy and then sat down heavily on the bunk.

"One thing, Tom . . ."

205

"Sure, Horace." He knew what was coming, knew the reasons he had been summoned to this holding cell on death row.

"Was she really a les?"

"A real bull, Horace."

He didn't tell Corinne that. Nor did he tell her that Turd Turner had held his breath for forty-one seconds. Not good, not bad, the warden had said. The record was two minutes fourteen seconds. A professional life guard from Seal Beach who had taken out his boyfriend. It was like he wanted to get his name into "Believe It Or Not By Ripley."

Tom Spellacy picked up a nicked ashtray. It said The Mocambo, New Year's Eve, 1939.

If it hadn't been for Turd Turner.

If. If. If.

He wondered what Corinne was doing at mass.

# *Thirteen*

"Bless me, Father, I confess to Almighty God and to you, Father, that I have sinned. . . ."

Desmond Spellacy settled back in the confessional and made the sign of the cross. There was one nice thing about hearing confessions at Saint Vibiana's: a kapok cushion covered the hard wooden bench in the priest's cubicle. Leave it to Jamie Marinan to think of his bottom. The pastor at Saint Vibiana's was convinced that priests had a higher incidence of hemorrhoids than other people and that the reason was sitting on a hard bench for hours at a time during confession. It's the priests' disease, Des, Jamie Marinan liked to say. Look at how many of the fellows in the sem with us are all bent over and walking like their legs were stilts. You sit in a confessional long enough and passing gas is like passing razor blades. Terminal piles is what most priests die of, you can look it up.

"I lied four times and I took the name of the Lord in vain seven times. . . ."

"What kind of lies?" Desmond Spellacy said. He leaned close to the mesh screen. He knew that the young boy on the other side of the screen did not expect the question.

"Uh . . ."

"You told your mother you did your homework and you didn't do it, is that it?"

"Yes, Father."

"You said you practiced your violin and you didn't do it."

"Yes, Father."

"Four times."

"Yes, Father."

"You said you took the Lord's name in vain seven times. Not eight. Not six. Not fourteen. You must be a very good bookkeeper."

"Yes, Father."

"What did you say? Goddamn? Jesus Christ? Holy Moses?"

Desmond Spellacy could feel the hot, bad breath of the youth expelled into his face. He knew the boy would check his name card on the confessional door and avoid him like the plague in the future.

"The first two, Father."

He was tempted to ask the boy if he had said anything scatalogical. Or sexual. Shit? Fuck? No. Better to save that. Wait for the proper time and place. Drop

207

it on someone like Dan Campion. Swearing was the kind of sin Dan confessed. Except he called it cursing. Or Agnes McNulty. Always congratulating herself on being such a good Catholic. He savored the fantasy: Shit. Fuck. Are they the cursewords you said, Agnes?

The boy was waiting for his penance. Desmond Spellacy gave him five Our Fathers and five Hail Marys and told him to make a good Act of Contrition.

*"Ego te absolvo . . ."*

It was odd how the mind wandered during confession. He wondered why people like Dan and Agnes even bothered to go to confession. They were such ignoramuses. They had no concept of sin. Nor did they comprehend that the calibration of sin was the essential element of his trade. Confessors sin, he thought. I sin. Mary Ginty. He remembered those nights after Ed Ginty first went to prison. Poor Ed. Embezzling that money to bail himself out of the market. He made a mental note to speak to the Cardinal about Ed Ginty's situation. Ed would be out on parole soon and perhaps they could find an opening at the Society for the Propagation of the Faith. It needed a lay administrator, and Ed had always been a conscientious executive before the trouble. At Ginty & Klein's, the accountants. Maybe the job would make up for his dreams about Mary when Ed went away. She always kept up appearances. There wasn't a charity she didn't volunteer for, a wake she didn't attend. He was always running into her. It was her courage he admired. A stranger would ask about her husband and Mary would say, Ed's in the penitentiary. And never flinch. He dreamed about her. That was all. He would awake in a state of arousal, his bedding wet from the nocturnal emission. "State of arousal," he thought. "Nocturnal emission." Wet dream, he had always called it in Boyle Heights. Boner. He always was fluent in the argot of the streets. He knew all the anatomical words. And how they applied to the girls in the Heights. Tommy was right about one thing. He had wondered about Mary Margaret when they were young. What she looked like. How it would feel. He had a good idea how it would feel. From Clementina Testa at Holy Rosary. What was it Tommy had said about her? "She could teach you a few things you might have missed along the way." She had. Once at fourteen, once at sixteen. His only two ventures with the flesh. He suspected that Tommy knew. The impulses of the flesh were the darkest sins in Tommy's canon. How wrong he was. Those impulses could be sublimated. Pride was a substitute. Power. The urge to manipulate. Vices that I possess in abundance, Desmond Spellacy thought. That at least was Seamus Fargo's opinion, intoned from the darkened confessional at Saint Basil's. The mental liaisons with Mary Ginty had not impressed Seamus Fargo. They were dreams and dreams would pass. Hubris was the constant . . .

Three Hail Marys to the boy who stole a baseball. A decade of the rosary for the woman who admitted pleasure in her neighbor's rejection by the Junior League.

Calibration . . .

He did not have to hear regular confessions, but he liked to help out. It made him feel more like a priest. Perhaps it was his one good deed. He heard every morning before mass at Saint Vibiana's, and on Saturdays and the nights before Holy Days of Obligations, he would volunteer at other places around the archdiocese. Sometimes at a convent, sometimes a hospital, sometimes a colored or a Mexican parish; never the same place twice in a row. This is Monsignor Spellacy, Father, I know Father Garcia is on vacation and I wonder if I might help you out hearing confessions Saturday. He knew what Seamus Fargo said to that: "As if any pastor would say no to the chancellor of the archdiocese. When all he wants is flush toilets in the rectory and the chancellor is saying they're too expensive." Leave it to Seamus to know everything he turned down. Flush toilets or pew cushions, his grapevine was infallible. He doubted he would ever be able to please Monsignor Fargo. Too bad. At least dealing with Seamus was character-building. The thought made him smile. He wondered what Monsignor Fargo would say to that.

"I was late for mass once, Father, the car broke down and I had to walk and I didn't get here until the *Confiteor.* . . ."

Good, solid, safe Saint Vibiana's. Upper-middle-class sin. Nothing Latin or Slavic. Not like last Saturday at Santa Teresita. First the nun in the convent. An Irish sister from Cork sent to a Mexican parochial school in East Los Angeles, where almost no one spoke English. Perfect planning. Hands across the sea.

"Bless me, Father, I'm going to have a baby."

The nun's brogue was thick with tears.

"How old are you, Sister?"

"Fifty-one years of age, Father."

"I don't think you're going to have a little one, Sister."

In the convent for thirty-five years with no idea how babies were made, let alone where they came from. Something they did not bother to teach the postulants in Cork. Going through menopause and thinking she was pregnant. An immaculate conception at the convent of Santa Teresita.

Then there was the twelve-year-old Mexican boy.

*"Válgame Dios, mi padre, porque he pecado. Yo puse un* cherry bomb *en el* asshole *di mi hermano. El tiene seis años. El es retardo."*

He did not understand much Spanish, but he got the gist. *Hermano.* What did it mean? *Hermano.* Brother. That was it. The brother was six, the brother was retarded . . . Oh, my God. *"Su hermano,"* he had said carefully, *"está muerto?"*

210

*"Yo no sé,"* the boy had said. *"Yo tengo un problema pequeño, no?"*

*Un problema pequeño,* he thought. A little problem. A cherry bomb stuck up his retarded six-year-old brother's asshole. That was only *un problema pequeño?* He wondered what the parishioners at Santa Teresita would consider a big problem.

Certainly not the confessions of conspicuous consumption at Saint Vibiana's. Sons who wrestled with themselves beneath the sheets. And thought they were going to become midgets if they didn't stop. Mothers who cheated at bridge. Fathers who had lewd thoughts about their neighbors' wives. Five Our Father, five Hail Mary confessions. He hardly had to listen, only raise his hand periodically in absolution. It gave him time to figure out how to negotiate with the Community Chest over the start of its fund-raising drive, which was scheduled to start the same day as the Catholic Charities drive. Both wanted May. April was out. It was only a month after taxes. Give the Chest May, Desmond Spellacy decided suddenly, we'll take June. Protestants worry about summer camp for their children, but the drive to a tennis camp in Monterey was not generally a Catholic concern. Or a Catholic summer expense. Desmond Spellacy smiled bleakly to himself. Of the ability to make such distinctions were bishops made.

The litany of venial sins slackened. Desmond Spellacy turned on the light in the confessional and began to read his office. The words were automatic; his attention began to wander. He took a pencil and made a note to ask Devlin Perkins and Phil Leahy about the Protectors of the Poor. The banker and the insurance man were both connected downtown, but he still wished he could get Tommy to do the checking. He was a tomb of secrets, Tommy. He wondered if Tommy kept a ledger on favors done the archdiocese. It was like a

211

mortgage long past due. Although he suspected that Tommy's payment was in discovering yet another example of human frailty. No. Tommy was out of the question. They hadn't spoken since lunch that day at the Biltmore. The memory pained Desmond Spellacy. Goddamn Jack. No more stalling. He had to take care of that situation. But first the Protectors of the Poor. The newspapers said that girl was a volunteer of the Protectors. The girl with the ugly nickname. Whose murder Tommy was investigating. Lois Fazenda. There was something hauntingly familiar about her. Desmond Spellacy wished he could put his finger on it. Perhaps she just reminded him of those wayward girls whose confessions he heard at the House of the Good Shepherd.

That must be it.

Get Dev and Phil on the case. Find out what the hell the Protectors were up to. All I need is a headline that says, THE VIRGIN TRAMP AND HIS EMINENCE'S FAVORITE CHARITY, Desmond Spellacy thought. He tried to imagine explaining that one to the Cardinal.

No, thank you.

Enough of that. Desmond Spellacy closed his breviary and switched off the light in the confessional. In the aisle he saw that Jamie Marinan was still hearing. He wondered if Jamie logged his thoughts. Probably not. Jamie thought too much thinking was bad for the character.

He knelt at the altar rail for a moment. A short prayer to erase the debris from his mind. It was not a particularly holy use of prayer, but it was an orderly one.

"Monsignor."

The woman was handsome. Mid-thirties. Hair wrapped in a scarf. A fine network of lines around the eyes. No perfume. No lipstick. Level gaze. He wondered if it were proper taking all this in.

212

"Yes."

"Would you hear my confession?"

"Monsignor Marinan is still hearing."

"I'd prefer to go to you, Monsignor."

He nodded and pointed her toward the confessional. There was something about the woman that was distinctly not Saint Vibiana's. In the cubicle, he kissed his stole and opened the screen.

There was no preamble. "I have committed adultery."

Not impure actions. He liked that. Simple and to the point. "And that's all."

"All that's important."

"I see. Are you married?"

"No."

"Then you . . ." He had trouble saying "committed adultery." Here was a time when it would have been useful to say "fucked," but the word stuck.

"With a married man, yes."

He realized he had not asked how often the adultery was committed, but then thought, It's not like stealing a Mars Bar. The number did not increase or diminish the importance of the act.

"Will you stop?"

"I don't know."

"Are you sorry?"

"No."

The woman was a refreshing experience. She seemed to know the unequivocal weight of every word.

"Do you think it's a sin?" He knew that already he was falling into her diction. Not the absolute, Are you sorry for your sin? Instead the less certain, Do you think it's a sin?

"No."

The answer was not unexpected. Desmond Spellacy knew she was not to be trifled with. The sham brimstone would not work nor the coded pieties. The torpor of the morning evaporated. He felt suddenly stimulated, as he always did when absolutes were challenged. It occurred to him that he had no real interest in right or wrong, only in the ambiguities and ambivalences of any moral question. A strange attitude for a priest.

"Then why are you here?"

"To talk."

"Ah," Desmond Spellacy said. He waited for her to speak and when she did not, he asked, "Do you believe in God?"

"No."

"And you think He cares?"

"Doesn't He?"

"I would think He had more pressing concerns."

The woman said, "I bet you're proud of that answer."

"You think it's cheap."

"Debating club."

Desmond Spellacy smiled. "The point is taken."

"You're different."

"How?"

"I thought you were like . . ."

"Who?"

"It doesn't matter. The reason I came here was to tell you . . ."

"What?"

"How? Who? What?" the woman taunted.

"What?" Desmond Spellacy repeated.

"To go fuck yourself," the woman blurted.

"And you think now I should ask why?" The woman was silent. "It's every child's wish. A show of bravado. 'I hate God.' I've thought it myself."

"You?"

"Of course. More recently than you think, probably."

"Why?"

"There are times when even a priest feels irrelevant. Useless."

"That's a sin of pride."

"Hubris, actually. And even priests sin."

214

The woman was silent. For a moment Desmond Spellacy thought she was going to leave the confessional. He realized he did not want to discontinue the discussion.

"I'm pregnant," the woman said quietly.

"What are you going to do?"

"Abort."

Desmond Spellacy said nothing. This was not a woman to argue with. The wrong word and she would flee.

"You're not surprised?" she said.

"No."

"You don't talk about murder like other priests."

Desmond Spellacy collected his thoughts. "I think you are aware of what you are considering and also of its consequences."

"Goddamn you, you talk less about sin than any priest I've ever met."

"I'm here to let you consider the possibilities."

"And that's all."

"You came to tell me to go fuck myself. I can't believe now you want my advice."

"No."

He could hear her rustling around the booth, making ready to leave. He knew he had to make an overture, some holding out of hope.

"Would you like absolution?"

"I didn't confess. I'm not sorry."

"You're here."

"Is that enough?"

"Yes."

"Are you sure?"

Desmond Spellacy laughed. "I have to act on that assumption."

"Thank you, Monsignor."

*"Ego te absolvo . . ."*

When he finished, she said, "My penance?"

215

Without hesitation, Desmond Spellacy said, "Do the right thing."

"If that's your idea of an easy penance, I'd rather have a rosary."

"I never give them." A thought formed in his mind. "Did you wish to see a priest—or me specifically?"

The woman was silent.

"You don't have to answer that," Desmond Spellacy said.

"I won't."

Then she was gone. Desmond Spellacy sat back on the kapok cushion and considered one word.

Tommy.

# Fourteen

That was Thursday.

Friday marked the beginning of the third week after the two halves of Lois Fazenda's body were discovered at the corner of 39th and Norton. In the third week the following things happened:

Gloria Deane, the woman who worked in the rouge room at Max Factor, was telephoned at three in the morning and told, "You're next, you whore."

An unemployed actress named Betty Faith wept as she told reporters and photographers that her real name was Elisabeth Fazenda, although she was not in fact related to the victim.

The manager of the PX at Fort MacArthur told Howard Terkel of the *Express,* "I first met Lois in

1943 when she arrived in San Pedro from her home in New England. I was won over at once by her childlike charm and beauty. She was one of the loveliest girls I have ever known, and the most shy. She never visited over the counter with any of the boys and always refused to date them."

The assistant manager of the PX at Fort MacArthur told Howard Terkel that Lois Fazenda blew the manager's crippled husband every day in the storeroom at the rear of the Post Exchange.

A practical joker sent the morgue wagon to Gloria Deane's new address with instructions to pick up her body.

The police department received a message glued together from newspaper lettering that said, "Don't try to find the Fazenda girl's murderer, because you won't."

Two hotel keepers in San Pedro reported that on the night of the murder, a young man with "dirty blond hair" tried to rent a room with a bath.

A waitress at the Dew Drop Inn at Broadway and Ninth reported a man who dropped a fourteen-inch butcher knife and said, "I don't feel like eating, would you feel like eating if you just cut a woman in half?" The man was arrested, questioned and returned to the mental hospital he had been released from two days before.

The police department received another message glued together from newspaper lettering. This one said, "Had my fun. Turning in Monday. Virgin Tramp's Killer." No one turned himself in. A police-lab analysis showed that the hairs on the Scotch tape sticking the letters to the paper were different in both messages. The first message came from a man with red hair on the back of his hands, the second from a man with black.

Fourteen more people confessed to the murder of Lois Fazenda.

* * *

Tom Spellacy asked the landlady of the rooming house on Sierra Vista if she had a Bromo Seltzer. His head pounded. Legwork, Fuqua had told the Major Crime Section. Legwork is how we're going to crack this thing. Masaryk was the perfect partner for legwork. He didn't have a brain in his head, but he wrote everything down. And never interrupted his train of thought. And typed a beautiful, neat report. With every fact in place. The fact was, Tom Spellacy liked legwork. Check and recheck. A teletype to all divisions ordering them to report any unusual disturbances the night of the murder. Check the baggage-claim areas at the railroad and bus stations and at the airport. Lois Fazenda must have left a suitcase somewhere. Check the cab companies. Show her picture. Check the funeral parlors. See if the morticians had anything funny to report. Go over old ground. Such as the rooming houses where Lois Fazenda had once lived. Which is what brought Masaryk and Tom Spellacy to the living room on Sierra Vista.

The landlady said she did not have any Bromo. "I'm Christian Science," she said. "That's what first attracted me to Lois."

"She didn't like Bromo either?" Masaryk said.

"She was Christian Science, too," the landlady said. Her name was Mrs. Parnell and she was wearing a faded violet housecoat which she nervously pinched between her thumb and forefinger to wipe an imaginary smudge from her rimless glasses.

"What's that got to do with Bromo?" Masaryk said. His notebook was out and his pencil poised. He thinks Bromo's the breakthrough, Tom Spellacy thought.

"Forget it," he said.

"It could be important," Masaryk said.

"It's not." His shirt clung to his back. It was the second day on the shirt and he knew he was beginning to smell. Corinne's fault. She wanted to think about

218

things, she said. Meaning she wanted to be alone. Meaning he was back in the Chester Hanrahan Development in the Valley. Where the sheets were gray and there was no clean laundry.

"She didn't have good Christian Science habits," Mrs. Parnell said. She avoided looking at both policemen, smoothing an antimacassar on the back of an overstuffed chair, crumbling a paper doily on an armrest. Tom Spellacy knew the type. A widow come upon hard times, forced to take in boarders she resented. There were neatly lettered signs in the hallway by the pay telephone. No Food. Do Not Put Your Juice in the Refrigerator. She was too refined ever to complain openly about Kotex flushed down the toilet or the lipstick staining the toothbrush glass or the menstrual leakage on the sheets. Just signs. My Castle Is Your Home.

"In what way?" Tom Spellacy said. The only thing he knew about Christian Scientists was that there was some crazy woman who wouldn't let them see doctors. Or use Bromo. He remembered a drugstore at the corner. He could get relief there. He cursed Corinne. Thinking about the abortion gave him the headache. Abortions. Brenda knew where to get one. And Jack. Maybe it wouldn't be a bad idea getting them all together. Corinne, this is Brenda. Jack, this is Corinne. It was the way everyone knew everyone else, the way that everything was coming together that made his head feel that it was going to blow out, like a tire.

"She cheated the telephone company," Mrs. Parnell said. "You cheat the telephone company, you're cheating yourself."

A perplexed look passed over Masaryk's face. "I think I missed something."

Tom Spellacy smiled at the landlady. "How is that?" He wondered who had made Corinne pregnant the first time. Her other abortion. Or if it was only the first time.

219

Mrs. Parnell opened a drawer in a side table. She took out two rolls of coins and held them in her hands. "I didn't want to say anything when the policeman came the first time. She'd just passed to the other side . . ."

Masaryk lifted his pencil. "Where?"

". . . and I didn't want to say anything that would reflect on her." Mrs. Parnell's face hardened. "Even though she never did pay me her last week's rent. And the week before that."

Tom Spellacy took the coin rolls and opened one. Nickel slugs fell into his hand.

"But now from all the things I read about her in the newspapers . . ." Mrs. Parnell shook her head. "All those people she didn't pay the rent to. People like me. With no other income but our rents. It's not right."

Tom Spellacy held up a slug. "Your phone?"

"No, never my telephone."

Of course not. Too easy to trace.

"Mr. Melnicker at the drugstore used to complain. I never made the connection until . . ." Mrs. Parnell pointed to the coin rolls and suddenly she began to chatter, as if Tom Spellacy were going to ask why a Christian Scientist would talk to a druggist. "I only buy my toothpaste at the drugstore. And dental floss. A home perm now and then. Toni. No Bromo."

Out on the sidewalk, the palm trees offered no protection from the sun that blasted down on Tom Spellacy's head. With his thumbs, he massaged the veins in his temples. For a moment the sun made him lightheaded. The headache had been constant since he left Corinne's. Or had she thrown him out? He wasn't clear on that. A mutual leave-taking. Room to breathe. Except he hated his breathing room. You get used to a woman. You get used to their doing the little things. The socks, the Jockey shorts he had not wanted her to buy. It was the same thing with Mary Margaret's meat

220

loaf. It was there, he expected it. Fucking was extra. He wondered if the nuns at the chancery took care of Des. It was funny, it had never occurred to him before that someone must buy Des's underwear, someone must order a dozen boxer shorts, size-32 waist, to cover the priestly basket.

Masaryk coughed discreetly, awaiting instructions.

He stood on the sidewalk with pencil and notebook ready. Tom Spellacy knew that Masaryk still did not understand about the slugs. He was still trying to figure out the Bromo Seltzer. Nor had Masaryk been able to understand checking out the funeral parlors either. He took down the dimensions of the morticians' tables and the manufacturers' names, but only when Tom Spellacy explained did Masaryk realize that a slab with gutters on the side to catch the blood was a perfect place to dissect a body and not leave a mess. Another possible Mystery Clue. Now he waited patiently for Tom Spellacy to draw in the lines between Christian Science and antacids and Pacific Telephone. It would all be in his notebook. He took perfect notes. He never missed an address or was wrong about the make or caliber of a weapon or the label in a hat or the color of a pair of shoes. It was the connections he was bad at.

"She was pumping slugs into the pay phone at the drugstore," Tom Spellacy said. He spoke slowly so that Masaryk could take it all down. "You go to the telephone company and get a record of all the calls made from that phone during the time she was living here. She was probably using other pay phones around here, too. Just so nobody would get too suspicious. A gas station, maybe, a grocery store. So find out from the phone company if any other telephones in the neighborhood were turning up a large number of slugs in that same period. Get the records from those phones, too. Then start comparing numbers, see if the same ones show up."

221

"On all the phones," Masaryk said.

Tom Spellacy nodded. The movement hurt his head. "Then we might find someone she knew."

"Right," Tom Spellacy said. He patted Masaryk on the shoulder. "We do the same thing, every place she's lived the past three years."

"I knew she had to use those slugs for something," Masaryk said. "I thought it was for Hershey bars."

Tom Spellacy reflected for a moment on Masaryk's remark. "Why not Milky Ways?"

"No, I lost a filling once to a Milky Way. A frozen Milky Way. I had to have a root canal. Hurt like a bastard." Masaryk opened his mouth, pointed to a tooth and then imitated a dentist's drill. "Bzzzzzzz. And cigs. She could've used the slugs for cigarettes. Tough to trace, though. And I don't know how much good it would do, tracing cigs."

Tom Spellacy had had enough of Masaryk for the morning. At the drugstore he called in. There was a message to call Brenda's 24-Hour Courier Service. That was something Brenda never used to do, call him at headquarters. The voice on the line at the 24-Hour Courier Service said he was to meet her in MacArthur Park at noon. The third bench west of the boathouse. Leave it to Brenda to remember the bench. It was where she used to pay him off. Sometimes at night she brought a blanket and they fucked on a knoll above the lake. It would be her idea of a joke to meet him there.

He dropped Masaryk off at Pacific Telephone. How do I get back, Masaryk said. Walk, Tom Spellacy said. Or call a cab. Or go over two blocks and take the Number 7 bus. Masaryk nodded and wrote it down in his notebook. It was still early. Tom Spellacy drove around MacArthur Park checking out the cars. Force of habit. Whether you were being paid off or going through a barricaded door, the M.O. was always the same. Know the turf, never be surprised. He was not certain of many things anymore, but he was sure of one thing: he was a very good cop. Maybe not always honest, but always thorough. He liked the trivial detail work of an investigation. Especially now. It gave an order and purpose to his days and kept his mind off Corinne. He liked cataloging the women's clothes that were reported found and interrogating hotel keepers in San Pedro and talking to the waitresses and widows who reported seeing the victim before she died and he liked going through unclaimed luggage at the railroad station and listening to the crazies who confessed. He even liked tracing the false teeth. A newspaper delivery boy had reported picking them up a block from the murder site and Tom Spellacy had followed that old and badly constructed plate through the dental-supply houses and the union medical plans and the records of the VA hospitals. It was the VA who told him that the owner of the plate had died of malnutrition two days before Lois Fazenda's murder.

And it kept his mind off Corinne.

"I went to confession."

"Swell."

"To your brother."

"You've got a real gift for doing the smart thing."

"He didn't know I had anything to do with you."

"He's a lot of things, Des, but dumb isn't one of them."

"I just wanted to talk to him."

"He must've got an earful."

"I had a longer conversation with him than any I've ever had with you."

"He's a terrific talker, Des. He doesn't have a fucking clue what life is all about, but he's got all the answers. He works them out somewhere between the fairway and the green."

223

"He told me to do the right thing."

"His idea of the right thing is not to get a bogie on a par-five hole."

"He's just like you."

"Well, you got all the breaks then, don't you?"

"All I know is that you're afraid of fucking and dying and feeling guilty and doing the wrong thing and even doing the right thing."

"What the fuck you want me to do? Go see Des? 'Corinne says we're so much alike, I thought I'd stop by, find out what the fuck the right thing to do is.' "

"I want to think about things, Tom. Alone."

So he left. And tracked down false teeth. And tried not to think about her.

It was harder than he thought.

He parked two blocks from MacArthur Park. Not that anyone would be poking around. It was just force of habit again. There was still half an hour. He bought an Orange Julius and a newspaper and waited in the car. As always, he read the sports pages first. Ike Williams and Bob Montgomery signed for a rematch in Philly. Sonny Shaw, the jockey, lost a paternity suit. Bill Tilden was in trouble again. Dick Wakefield was 0 for 37. He turned the pages. A chicken in Auburn, New York, had laid an egg nine inches long and nine inches in circumference, with three yolks. The president was in Key West. Hedda Hopper said that Rita Hayworth was involved with an Arab prince. He wondered what it would be like going to bed with an actress. He thought she would always be talking about the set and how Franchot Tone kissed. Fuck her. Britain was balking on the Red pact and the King of Denmark was better and the suicide of banker C. K. Dodge had nothing to do with the slaying of Lois Fazenda, according to Chief of Detectives Fred Fuqua. "Darling," C. K. Dodge's suicide note had read,

224

We could have been so happy if you had continued to have me. I have your picture in front of me. I will look at it for the last time. I love you so much. To think you are in the arms of a clarinet player is more than I can bear. I love you.

Sincerely,

C. K. DODGE

On the front page, three women mystery writers discussed the murder of the Virgin Tramp. Ngaio Marsh said the murderer was a foreigner, Craig Rice said it was a transient pickup and Mignon G. Eberhart said the killer knew his victim. An editor's note announced that the murder would be discussed the next day by Ben Hecht and on succeeding days by Steve Fisher, Rex Stout, Adela Rogers St. John and by the handwriting expert who was a prosecution witness at both the Lindbergh and the Aimee Semple MacPherson trials.

At five minutes to noon, Tom Spellacy walked into the park. He stood for a moment on the knoll above the boathouse. Below he could see Brenda feeding the pigeons. She was wearing a large floppy hat to shield her face from the sun. It had always been a house rule never to let her girls take much sun. The tricks didn't like tan markings. Or stretch marks. Or appendicitis scars or Caesarian scars. There was a time when he knew all of Brenda's house rules. How different his life would have been if he had never met her. It was just chance. That great fucker-up of lives. The memory was like a dream. He was a beat cop. Alone. His partner was sick. An ambulance barreled up Sunset. No siren. No lights. He followed. The ambulance pulled into a house in the hills. He was no dummy. He knew the address. Brenda was polite. There had been an altercation. First between a gentleman and a lady, then between the bouncer and the gentleman. It was always

225

best to handle these things quietly. That was why the police had not been called. Although Officer Spellacy would always be welcome. The gentleman for whom the ambulance was summoned was a pillar of the community. A city councilman, in fact. Not one to complain about his internal bleeding. As the lady would never complain about the cigarette burns on her bosom. There was an envelope in the city councilman's jacket. There appears to be money in it, Brenda said. Count it. I don't wish to be responsible. It must contain five hundred dollars. He stopped counting at two thousand. He knew the drill. Leave the five hundred dollars, keep the rest. He asked to use the telephone. Brenda brought him into her office. The telephone was in a cabinet in the desk. There was also a miniature deputy chief's badge in the cabinet and a paper on which were typed the home telephone numbers of a captain and a watch lieutenant in Central Vice. Brenda smiled at him. In case he did not get the picture that she was well wired. A nice smile. If you want to make it a three-horse parlay, Brenda said, we could fuck.

Brenda.

She knew her man.

She did not look up when he sat down on the bench beside her. A cat crouched on her lap, ready to pounce on any bird that dared to pick up the bread she was throwing.

"You feeding the pigeons or your cat?" Tom Spellacy said.

Brenda laughed. "Day-old bread. There's a bakery down the street that gives it to me." She crumbled a piece between her fingers and lobbed it into the water. The cat watched a duck gobble it up. Tom Spellacy knew enough not to rush her. She would say what she had to say when she wanted to say it. No sooner. He checked the other benches around the lake. No one there but old people feeding the birds. He knew the

226

type. They would strike up a conversation with the mother of a young child and say the baby was the picture of Ginger Rogers or the image of Clark Gable. And then almost without pausing for breath they would begin talking about *Kitty Foyle* or *Mutiny on the Bounty* and after that Carole Lombard and *Nothing Sacred* and wasn't it a shame the way poor Carole went, what it must have done to Clark, but at least he knew she died selling war bonds for her country, that must have been a comfort.

The scene vaguely depressed Tom Spellacy and then he understood why. The projection of an old and lonely Brenda sitting by the lake feeding the pigeons was not one he wished to contemplate. It was too much a coded portrait of his own life.

"Where's your other cat?"

The question sounded strange and forced, and he realized suddenly it was because in all the years he had known Brenda, they had never really communicated except in sexual reference points. Hustling and the payoff were the perimeters of their knowledge of each other. She knew everything there was to know about coming, and as a matter of course she told him about the number of free fucks it took to buy a grand-jury transcript and the cost of a deputy chief and about the triple-decker sandwich the lieutenant governor liked to watch. But that was all. It was a slum of a relationship surrounded by acres of indifference.

"It died."

"I'm sorry."

"It got run over by a car. A blue Packard. The bastard didn't even stop."

"If you know the license, I'll try to do something."

"It won't bring the cat back."

Tom Spellacy watched the ducks swimming in the lake. Except for Corinne, he had only one reference point with all the women in his life. It made them easy to ignore. Religion with Mary Margaret. Sex with Brenda. That was the trouble with Corinne. She was too complicated to ignore. There were too many reference points.

"You asked about a cutter," Brenda said.

He tried to remember when. That morning when Mickey Gagnon died, that was it. Check around, he had said, see if any of the girls know anyone likes to cut. He did not like to remember that morning. He thought that life would be a lot simpler if it hadn't been for Mickey Gagnon. If Mickey hadn't decided to get his ashes hauled, he wouldn't have run into Brenda again. And she wouldn't have told him why he never got indicted. There were so many ifs. And so many things you were better off not knowing.

"Find anything?" The cutter. Mickey. Brenda. Des. Corinne. Jack. Lois Fazenda. He had a feeling that everything was connecting in some way he did not understand. Except that it was a maze and he was in the middle and he had a feeling he was not going to get out.

"It's hard to find a whore hasn't been cut. It's a risk they take."

"That's swell, Brenda. That's why I came all the way over here for, to hear a lot of deep shit about how tough it is being a hooker."

Brenda picked up the cat and put it in her lap. She fed it a piece of bread and began stroking its back.

"There was a guy, a couple of the girls ran into him, three, four maybe, the word is out, everyone on the bricks seems to have heard about him. Bald, fifty, a Rotary button in his lapel. Elks, Kiwanis, I don't know that shit. He picks them up in his car."

"What kind of car?"

"Old. Before the war."

"License?"

Brenda shook her head. "Some kind of sticker in the window. Palm Springs, San Diego Zoo, something like that. Maybe a high school, I don't know. Everyone, the girls, they all got a different story."

"What's his number?"

"He likes to shave the girl's bush. He's a walking fucking barber's college, the word is. Scissors, razors, lather, the works."

"What if the girls don't play?"

"He says he'll cut their tits off."

"Fair enough," Tom Spellacy said.

"She still have her bush, your girl?"

"She still had her bush."

"Then that's the best I got," Brenda said. "Nobody's seen him for a while, this guy, the girls say."

"Thanks, Brenda." Tom Spellacy got up to leave. A pigeon swooped down on a piece of bread and escaped a split second before Brenda's cat struck.

"I'm leaving town, Tom."

He sat back down on the bench and took a piece of bread from her bag. "Why?"

"Change my luck. I don't have any leverage anymore."

He shredded the bread and threw the pieces into the water. "You in the shit?"

Brenda shook her head. "I did a scrape a couple of days ago. I made a mistake. I nicked something. She hemorrhaged."

"Die?" For an instant he wondered what he would do if she said yes.

"No." Brenda did not look at him. "It was one of my old girls. Lucille Cotter. She'll keep her mouth shut. It was one of those things."

"Lucille Cotter." The name was familiar. "Silver Tongue?"

Brenda nodded. Lucille Cotter was called Silver Tongue for obvious reasons. A real pump primer. She had been one of the leading attractions at the house on Sunset. There was a peek into her room so that other customers could watch her work. She never turned out in the line. You had to book Silver Tongue in advance.

"She works lower Sunset now," Brenda said. "She's one of the ones ran into the barber."

"Lower Sunset," Tom Spellacy said. "On the bricks?"

Brenda said yes.

"That's a long drop."

"She got old, Tom," Brenda said. "It happens."

He considered the answer. "You never used to do scrapes."

"That happens, too."

Tom Spellacy watched the ducks swimming in the lake. In the old days with Brenda there had never been young couples in paddleboats floating in the water.

"Where you going?" he said.

"A place in Reno, maybe. And there's a joint in Vegas I can run."

He spoke before thinking. "You want a reference."

Brenda looked directly at him for the first time. "I never had any trouble buying cops," she said evenly. "If you remember."

I deserved that, he thought. I sound like the resentful bagman.

"You know what Jack used to say about you?"

"I don't really care."

"No discipline, he used to say. He used to see you fight. You had trouble making the weight. No discipline."

"He's a real judge of character, Jack," Tom Spellacy said. He wondered how Jack judged Des.

Brenda threw a crust into the lake. Two ducks fought over the piece, pecking at each other with their bills.

"That girl," she said, "the one who was cut."

"What about her?"

"She worked for the Protectors of the Poor, didn't she?"

230

Tom Spellacy nodded. He and Masaryk had checked out the charity at County General. He hated hospitals. The smell of antiseptic and starch reminded him of his mother. She had lingered in a charity ward for seven months before she died. He brought her magazines and she demanded holy pictures and asked him to say a novena and to make the nine first Fridays and the Stations of the Cross. Fuck it, he finally told Des, this is your racket, you see her. The hospital superintendent said she did not remember Lois Fazenda. There were so many charities. And so many volunteers. They come and they go. A bad apple was bound to creep in. You can't blame the hospital for that. The Protectors specialized in Mexicans. Accident victims, mainly. The volunteers passed out candy and cigarettes. The superintendent had smiled. And Roman Catholic doodads, she said.

"Passing out rosary beads," Tom Spellacy said.

"Virgin of Guadalupe medals, too," Brenda said. "Some of my girls used to work for the Protectors."

He stared sharply at her, wondering what whores were doing working for a Catholic charity. "Doing mission work?"

"Rubbing up against guys. Flashing their tits, too, you want to know the honest truth. I bet she was very good rubbing up against guys, that girl."

"Why would she want to do that?"

"To make the guy feel good, I guess. You're all broken up, it must make you feel good, looking down a girl's dress."

"I bet it would at that."

"That's when she flashes the insurance form at him, Tom. 'Sign this, I'll get you a lawyer who'll sue the bastard who hit you.' "

It was slowly beginning to come clear. No wonder whores were volunteers. "I bet there's lawyers who'd pay for a form like that."

"Fifty bucks each, I hear," Brenda said. "Maybe more."

"And the wetback, I bet he never sees the insurance settlement."

"There's a lot of expenses involved, Tom."

"Ambulance chasing is what you'd call it, you want to put a dirty name to it."

"If you want to put a dirty name to it," Brenda said. The cat was licking her hand. "It's worth a fortune. They can't complain, the wetbacks, they don't get their money, because they're illegals, most of them."

"And if they do bitch . . ."

"They can always get hit by another car." Brenda concentrated on the cat. It was almost as if she were speaking to it and not to Tom Spellacy. "When's the last time Robbery-Homicide broke its hump for a dead Mex?"

Tom Spellacy ignored the question. "I wonder who dreamed this one up?"

"I bet you could guess."

Of course I can, he thought. Jack Amsterdam. Every time I turn around, there's Jack. Lois Fazenda does a good deed and it's one of Jack's rackets. That goddamn maze.

"So he knew her."

"He was fucking her."

"He cut her?"

"He's clean."

"So what's his worry?"

Brenda looked at him, a hard smile on her face. "He thinks you're crazy. He's old, Jack, he's going to die. He likes to think he was born at sixty, building cathedrals. And there's this nut cop reminding people when he was a pimp and stuffing people into laundry dryers. He wishes he never heard of you."

"The feeling is mutual."

"He thinks you're going to pull him in."

Tom Spellacy suddenly remembered the warning from Marge Madragon. It was all beginning to come clear. He could imagine the raised eyebrows in the department if he pulled in Jack. That would get a few laughs. He tried not to think of Jack's lawyer telling a judge what old pals they were, Tom and Jack.

"He thinks you're going to drop this girl on him," Brenda said. "And embarrass him. He's had a private audience with the Pope. How many pimps can say that?"

Tom Spellacy wondered if Des had arranged the private audience. "He won't like it, you telling me this."

"Fuck him," Brenda said. "I took the fall for you, Tom. But he's the one made me do it." She picked cat hairs from her dress. "This is my going-away present."

"I don't know if I can do anything with it."

"That's up to you." Brenda held the cat and emptied the rest of the bread bag onto the ground. "Anyway I wanted to say good-bye."

"Why?"

"It's nice to have somebody to say good-bye to, is all. Who do I have? The lieutenant governor? You think I can call him up and say remember me, we used to fuck?"

Tom Spellacy did not say anything. All around the bench, birds and ducks were gobbling up the last of the bread.

"All I've got are old whores and people I bought," Brenda said.

Tom Spellacy stood up. No one paid any attention to them. We're just another middle-aged couple, he thought.

"So long, Brenda."

# Fifteen

Sonny McDonough marked his putt and surveyed the green. "You're away, Des."

"You make that one, Des, they'll give you a gold putter in heaven," Dan T. Campion said.

"That's grand, Dan," Sonny McDonough said. "A gold putter in heaven. Frank Leary would give up being pastor at Saint Jude's, he had one of them."

"He went over the top, I hear, Frank," Dan T. Campion said.

"Most successful fund raiser in the archdiocese," Sonny McDonough said. "It's made of money, Saint Jude's."

"There's not a better pastor than Frank," Dan T. Campion said. "And a nicer man."

"And a worse golfer," Sonny McDonough said.

"Is that a fact?" Dan T. Campion said.

"I was playing with him the other day," Sonny McDonough said. "And he misses a tap-in. 'Jesus, Mary and Joseph,' he says. And I says, 'Taking the Lord's name in vain, Monsignor. You're going to have to confess that.' And you know what he says?"

"No," Dan T. Campion said.

"He says, 'Damn right,'" Sonny McDonough said. "Isn't that grand?"

"A grand story," Dan T. Campion said.

"You got to tell it to His Eminence, Des," Sonny McDonough said.

Who'll think I've taken leave of my senses, Desmond Spellacy thought. He contemplated his putt. A twelve-footer with a slight break to the right. This was one he wanted to sink. Just to show his killer instinct. The killer instinct was something Sonny McDonough would respect. If Sonny's going to be a successful chairman of the Building Fund, he'd better learn right now he's not going to gull me with stories about Frank Leary's golf game.

"You're blocking my view, Sonny. Your shadow's on the cup."

"Oh, I'm sorry, Des," Sonny McDonough said. He scurried out of range.

"Now it's your dime, Sonny," Desmond Spellacy said. "Where you marked your ball. The sun's glinting off it."

"I'll put a penny down, Des."

Desmond Spellacy bent over and addressed his ball. "You know Cornelia Cronin, don't you, Sonny? Corky, they call her."

Desmond Spellacy straightened up. The color had drained from Sonny McDonough's face. Dan T. Campion glanced back and forth between the two men. He's heard about Sonny and Corky, too, Desmond Spellacy thought. Although he wasn't surprised. There wasn't much about deviant behavior that Dan Campion didn't know.

"I do indeed, Monsignor," Sonny McDonough said. So it's "Monsignor" now, Desmond Spellacy thought. "Why do you ask?"

"She ran the Altar Society when I was at Saint Basil's. She used to work for you."

"As a bookkeeper, Monsignor."

"Then she had an accident."

"She broke her back, didn't she, Sonny?" Dan T. Campion said.

He'd kill Dan right now if he could get away with it, Desmond Spellacy thought.

"Something like that," Sonny McDonough said.

"You pensioned her off nicely, I hear," Desmond Spellacy said. "Five hundred dollars a month, I'm told."

"For life, Des," Dan T. Campion said.

"You better putt, Monsignor," Sonny McDonough said.

Desmond Spellacy stroked the ball evenly. It broke to the right a yard from the hole and dipped into the cup. He gave his putter to his caddy and turned his back on Dan Campion and Sonny McDonough. He could hear Dan chortle and knew that Sonny had missed his putt. He turned around just as Sonny putted a second time. The ball rimmed the cup and rolled to a stop a yard away.

"We'll give you that one, Sonny, won't we, Dan?"

"It's you that's giving it to him, Des, not me," Dan T. Campion said. Giving Sonny the business is what he means, Desmond Spellacy thought. First the stick, now the carrot. He put his arm around Sonny McDonough as they walked to the next tee.

"That was a Christian thing you did for Corky, the pension," Desmond Spellacy said. "There's not many employers would do that."

"Thank you, Monsignor."

"It's one of the reasons I told the Cardinal you should be chairman."

"You told His Eminence about—"

"I told His Eminence you were one in a million."

"What a grand thing for you to tell His Eminence, Des," Sonny McDonough said. He seemed ready to collapse with relief. The killer instinct, Desmond Spellacy thought. He patted Sonny on the arm and walked to the next tee. A par-five, 565-yard hole. Desmond Spellacy put his ball on the tee and whacked it down the fairway. His lie was a good forty yards past Sonny and Dan. Plenty of time to be alone. Away from the chatter of the other two. They'd have a lot to talk about. Both wondering how he knew about Corky Cronin. That was one he owed Tommy. For a moment he thought about the girl in the confessional, then put her out of his mind. There were more immediate things to worry about. He knew Sonny was no longer a problem. No fast ones there. Sonny would do as he was told. There would not be much static from Sonny about getting rid of Jack Amsterdam.

God, I'm sick of Jack, Desmond Spellacy said to himself as he approached his ball. You can't look around without seeing him getting his hands dirty. He almost wished now that he had not asked Phil Leahy and Devlin Perkins to check up on the Protectors of the Poor. There was only one thing you could say for Jack: his brain was always working. It was not everyone who would know that Monsignor Aguilar was money in the bank. Ruben Aguilar, the pastor at San Conrado's. Jack's parish. Seventy-nine years old and an IQ to match. He wondered when it had occurred to Jack just how dumb Ruben Aguilar really was. Probably listening to him preach every Sunday. Imagine getting a priest to front for you. He wondered how Jack first put the bug in Ruben Aguilar's ear. A charity. A charity for the Mexicans at County General. Candy and rosary beads and someone to talk to them in Spanish. The Anglos won't do it. The Anglos don't care about Mexicans. If there was one way to get Ruben Aguilar's attention, that was it. Anglos not caring about Mexicans. A tax-exempt charity. Just the thing. You head the charity, Monsignor, I'll get the tax exemption. That was the way Jack operated. The Protectors of the Poor. It would take Ruben Aguilar to come up with a name like that. Or Monsignor Amigo, as the newspapers called him. What a shill. All the volunteers were Jack's people. And the towing companies and ambulance services and body shops and auto-wrecking yards that supplied the Protectors with the names of Mexican accident victims were all paid off by Jack for just that information. In the spirit of Christian charity. And brotherhood.

Desmond Spellacy cursed himself. I should have known. That's what rankles. Every time I saw Ruben Aguilar's picture in the paper shaking hands with the Mexican consul. Monsignor Amigo. I should have known that moron was being had.

Desmond Spellacy was on the green in three.

"It's a terrible thing," Sonny McDonough said as he and Dan T. Campion came onto the green.

"Giving them names like that to sell their newspapers," Dan T. Campion said.

"The Virgin Tramp," Sonny McDonough said. He seemed to have recovered from the Corky Cronin conversation. "If you'll excuse the expression, Des."

"It's the Virgin Mary they should be reading about, not the Virgin Tramp," Dan T. Campion said. "You never get a chance to read your newspaper these days, you spend so much time hiding it from the little ones."

"She worked for the Protectors," Sonny McDonough said. "You knew that, didn't you, Des?"

Desmond Spellacy nodded.

"The one grand thing the poor girl did was help the poor Mexicans," Sonny McDonough said. "Giving them jumping beans, which is what they like."

"Why don't you pipe down and let me putt," Dan T. Campion said. His face was flushed with irritation. "She would've made Mary Magdalene blush with shame, that one."

Dan T. Campion hunched over his putt and holed out.

"You've got to look for the beauty in everyone is what I always say," Sonny McDonough said.

Annoyance still mottled Dan T. Campion's face. "You never planted anyone wasn't a grand girl, Sonny."

"You sound like a coon, saying planted," Sonny McDonough said. He would never stand for any aspersions cast on his profession. "I put the poor child in her final resting place is what I did."

"If you planted killer Stalin, you'd make him sound like one of them elves which kissed the Blarney Stone," Dan T. Campion said. "Because his loved ones had the foresight to pick McDonough & McCarthy, the General Motors of the planting industry."

Desmond Spellacy let the conversation wash over him. It was always this way with Dan and Sonny. First one, then the other pressing the advantage. There was no need to bring up Jack until an opening was presented. He sank his putt, then watched Sonny three-putt for a bogie six. A bad two holes for Sonny.

Dan T. Campion was still chattering. There was something on Dan Campion's mind, Desmond Spellacy was sure of that. When Dan Campion babbled, there was something he did not want anyone to know. That was one thing Desmond Spellacy had picked up in the years he and Dan had worked together. And Dan was babbling like a brook lately. Especially about Tommy. And what a fine detective he was. Such a grand Catholic. A credit to the force. A credit to the Church. A credit to Ireland. When the fact was, Dan T. Campion could not stand Tommy and Tommy returned the compliment.

Desmond Spellacy wondered what was on Dan's mind. As long as it doesn't concern me, he thought, I don't really care.

"G'wan, Sonny," Dan T. Campion said. He was sitting in the shadow of a shade tree, fanning his face with a white straw hat. " 'I planted Carole Lombard,' is probably what you told them. Listing your credits, that's your best sales pitch. Isn't that right, Des? Fatty

239

Arbuckle. Rin Tin Tin of the canine family. All the stars of the animal kingdom. Black Beauty. My Friend Flicka. Nanook of the North."

"That's an eskimo, you dumbbell," Sonny McDonough said. He was washing the dirt from his golf balls, not looking at Dan Campion.

"Buy by the acre, sell by the foot," Dan T. Campion said. "I know the rules of your business."

"The only rule of my business is I'd like to put you in the ground right now," Sonny McDonough said. He turned to Desmond Spellacy and with an elaborate pretense of ignoring Dan Campion, said, "I keep reading about your brother the policeman."

"And doing a grand job he is," Dan T. Campion said. He rose from the bench and took a club from his bag. "The backbone of the city, our policemen. You'd have to agree to that, Sonny. You, too, Des. If we didn't have any policemen, we'd have a lot more crime than we have now. And that's a well-known fact."

"There's always the types likes to run them down," Sonny McDonough said.

"The Mexicans, usually, and the colored," Dan T. Campion said.

"I seen him fight once, your brother," Sonny McDonough said. "Over to the Legion Stadium in El Monte there. Eight-round semifinal. He was fighting a colored boy."

"He won, did he?" Dan T. Campion said.

"Lost," Sonny McDonough said. "Split decision. A dirty fight it was, too. Lots of rabbit punches."

"They're good at the rabbit punches, the colored," Dan T. Campion said.

"Tommy Jefferson," Desmond Spellacy said. "That was the name of the boy that beat him."

It was the only time he had ever seen Tommy fight.

"A terrible thing the way they take the names of our presidents," Dan T. Campion said. "Eye-talian names,

240

they should take, the colored. Or Polish." He turned to Desmond Spellacy. "That fellow Jefferson ever sticks up a bank, he won't try the rabbit punches on your brother if he's there."

"What'd he be doing there in the first place?" Sonny McDonough said. "He's not a bank guard."

"Using his noggin is what he'd be doing there," Dan T. Campion said. "It's why he's such a grand detective, the way he uses his bean. There'd be no bank stickups from this Jefferson with Tom Spellacy on the job."

"You make him sound like Sherlock Holmes," Desmond Spellacy said.

"Oh, that's grand, Des, grand," Dan T. Campion said. "A grand policeman, Sherlock Holmes, and that's a well-known fact."

Desmond Spellacy parred the ninth and tenth holes, double-bogied the eleventh and birdied the twelfth. On the thirteenth tee, he was a hole up on Sonny McDonough and even with Dan Campion. Over the previous four holes, the two men seemed to have reached an accord about the mortuary business.

"I did her for free, you know," Sonny McDonough said. "One of your beautiful thirty-footers."

"How did you get that one past Shake Hands?" Dan T. Campion said. "A tight man with a dollar, Shake Hands McCarthy."

"The argument we had," Sonny McDonough said. " 'You give away a thirty-footer here and a thirty-footer there,' Shake Hands said, 'pretty soon you got an acre full of nothing but deadbeats.' 'Just one plot,' I says. 'A twenty-seven footer,' he says."

"That's what he'll be remembered for, Shake Hands, the twenty-seven footers," Dan T. Campion said.

"Them three square feet give you twenty more plots to the acre," Sonny McDonough said.

"A revolutionary idea," Dan T. Campion said.

"A great man, Shake Hands," Sonny McDonough

said. "For a bookkeeper. It's the long-range planning he has trouble with. 'Think of the publicity,' I says to him. 'Twenty thousand new people moving here every month. This is where they're going to stay until they pass away. What a way to introduce them to Mc-Donough & McCarthy, giving this poor girl a free send-off.'"

"I give you that, Sonny," Dan T. Campion said. "You got to think of the population trends these days. Isn't that right, Des? You got to think of the population trends."

"There's something else we've got to think of," Desmond Spellacy said. His voice was so soft the other two men had to strain to hear. "We've got to think of a way to cut Jack Amsterdam loose."

"Jesus, Mary and Joseph," Dan T. Campion said.

"Holy Mother of God," Sonny McDonough said.

There did not seem much point in continuing the game. They left their clubs with the caddies and walked back to the clubhouse. By the time they reached the pro shop, Desmond Spellacy had filled them in on the Protectors of the Poor. In the bar they ordered beer and sandwiches.

"We could let it go is my advice," Dan T. Campion said.

"It's not as if he done anything illegal," Sonny Mc-Donough said.

"Only profitable," Desmond Spellacy said. His sarcasm seemed to escape them.

"He's done a lot of good works, Jack," Dan T. Campion said.

"That sheeny halfback, it was Jack got him to transfer to Notre Dame," Sonny McDonough said.

"He was going to go to SC is what I hear," Dan T. Campion said.

242

"Then Jack bought him a car," Sonny McDonough said.

"A convertible Studebaker," Dan T. Campion said.

"I thought a Jew would want a Cadillac at least," Sonny McDonough said. "A Jew canoe, that's what they call a Cadillac, you know."

"Oh, that's grand, Sonny," Dan T. Campion said. "A Jew canoe."

"It'll be a coon quarterback next," Sonny McDonough said. "You mark my words. There's eleven Protestants on the team already. I did a check."

"What's Frank Leahy thinking of," Dan T. Campion said.

Desmond Spellacy took the toothpick from his club sandwich and placed it carefully on the side of the plate. He knew that Dan and Sonny would do anything to avoid the issue.

"He still goes."

"You've thought about it then, Des," Dan T. Campion said.

"I've thought about the headlines. MORON PASTOR. AMBULANCE CHASER CARDINAL'S PAL."

"I think you're a little overwrought about this, Des," Sonny McDonough said.

"It was sound business practice is what it was," Dan T. Campion said.

"Like Ferdie Coppola's cranes," Desmond Spellacy said. "And the ton of asphalt."

"Was it your brother the policeman told you this?" Sonny McDonough said.

"No."

"I hear there was a run-in between Jack and your brother the policeman not long ago," Dan T. Campion said.

"You were calling him Sherlock Holmes on the eighth hole," Desmond Spellacy said. It was time to

243

get rough. "When we were talking to Sonny there about Corky Cronin."

The point was made. Sonny and Dan each picked at their sandwiches in silence.

"What's he got outstanding?" Sonny McDonough said finally.

"He's supposed to finish San Pedro Klaber in July," Desmond Spellacy said. "He'd better. His Eminence dedicates the seventeenth and holds confirmations the eighteenth. And he's the only bid on Saint John Bosco."

"Can you extend the bids?"

"Yes."

"Good," Sonny McDonough said. "I can get Neddy Flynn to put one in. You work on Emmett Flaherty, Dan."

"He likes living too much, Emmett," Dan T. Campion said. "He hates getting his bones broke, I hear."

Sonny McDonough ignored him. "You know a lot of people in the police department, Dan. Maybe you can put in a word, tell them not to mention the Protectors. His Eminence wouldn't want to be embarrassed, you tell them."

"I know what to tell them," Dan T. Campion said. He was suddenly furious. "I was telling them when you were still planting poor people."

A look of hurt crossed Sonny McDonough's face. "There's no reason to get personal."

"There's no chief is the problem," Dan T. Campion said. His voice was so loud that people were looking at him. "There's no one to talk to."

Sonny McDonough leaned across the table. "This fellow Fuqua's a comer, I hear. I'm on the Select Commission picking the new chief and he's impressed me." He lowered his voice to a whisper. "That's confidential, of course."

"Meaning I should mention it," Dan T. Campion said. Sour resignation seemed to have replaced his

244

fury. "Meaning I should tell him Sonny McDonough, the famous harp undertaker, says you're a hot prospect, you learn how to keep your lip buttoned."

Sonny McDonough pretended not to hear. He turned to Desmond Spellacy. "Maybe we don't have a problem. He was in to see me the other day, Jack. He wanted a plot for himself."

"He must expect some shooting," Dan T. Campion said.

"Not for him and the Mrs.," Sonny McDonough said. "Just for himself. In the Celebrity Circle, that's where he wanted it. Under a palm tree. Can you beat that? Like he was Al Capone."

Desmond Spellacy wiped the beer foam from his lips. "I don't think we should count on Jack using the Celebrity Circle right away." Although he knew that nothing would make Dan and Sonny happier. Divine intervention. The sure hand of God. There would be no volunteering from those two to tell Jack the archdiocese didn't want his business anymore. "I'll talk to him."

"That's grand, Des," Sonny McDonough said. His relief was almost visible. "There's a lot of grand ways to handle it. So his feelings won't be hurt is what I mean. We can give him a dinner."

"Catholic Layman of the Year," Desmond Spellacy said drily.

"A grand idea, Des," Sonny McDonough said. "His Eminence can give him a sash. Something green. Or purple. Or we can name a wing at Saint John Bosco after him. The Amsterdam Orthopedic Wing."

"For all them bones he broke in the old days," Dan T. Campion said.

A lot of grand ways to handle it, Desmond Spellacy thought. Sonny had the chairman's mentality already.

Dan T. Campion pushed away his sandwich. "I'd like to know who named that girl that."

There's where the trouble began all right, Desmond Spellacy thought.

"I'd like to know who got her into the Protectors is what I'd like to know," Sonny McDonough said.

# *Sixteen*

The roller coaster hung for a moment at the top of its climb, hung as if it were going to slide back, and then with a sudden lurch, plummeted over and down the gorge. Nuns screamed. Black veils snapped straight back, the wind tore at white cowls.

"They got ears," Crotty said. He was eating a hot dog and leaning against the vendor's stand, watching the roller coaster. "I was a kid, over to Saint Patricia's there, I always used to wonder, you know, if they got ears. Like other people. And hair. I always heard they had to shave it off, when they become sisters. They're all bald-headed, nuns, I hear. And another thing I hear—"

"I know what you hear," Tom Spellacy said. The roller coaster had momentarily disappeared down a gulley. The normal noises of the arcade level at Ocean Park replaced the roar of the train. Hawkers, drummers, vendors, tattooed men, mustachioed ladies, hot-dog stands and shooting galleries filled for the silence until the roller coaster drowned them all out once again. "You hear, they got to wrap something around themselves, the sisters, when they take a bath."

"You ever want to check that out with the monsignor, Tom, don't let me stop you. I'd take the mortal sin, I could find that out, and go right to confession afterwards."

"As a matter of fact, it did come up," Tom Spellacy said.

Crotty was incredulous. "You asked your brother, Tom?"

"He said most convents don't let the priests watch the nuns take a bath," Tom Spellacy said. "Most of them got rules about that. He said if he ever found one that didn't, though, he'd let me know."

"Shit." Crotty's huge hand speared a drop of mustard before it lighted on his white suit. He licked the mustard from his finger and then swallowed the last half of the frankfurter. "I heard him speak last night, your brother. At the Catholic War Veterans Dinner. I roared. Every time he jumped out of the airplane, he said, he landed in the water. And this Protestant says to him, he says, 'From the frequency of your immersions, Father, you must be a Baptist.' " Crotty started to laugh and nearly lost part of the hot dog. Tom Spellacy pounded him on the back. "Isn't that a grand story, Tom?" Crotty said when he caught his breath. "He tells a grand story, your brother."

"He tells it often enough."

"You must roar every time."

Tom Spellacy nodded. He wasn't up to discussing Des with Crotty. Or Corinne, either. Especially Corinne. Not after last night. She was such a goddamn fool. He wondered if he would ever understand women. He checked his watch. The puppet maker was late. The puppet maker was someone Crotty had dug up. Name of Shopping Cart Johnson. He carved and sold puppets to the shooting galleries at Ocean Park. Tom Spellacy suspected that Crotty just wanted to spend half a day at the beach. It was all right with him. He watched a pyramid of cotton candy melt in the sun.

"What were you doing at Catholic War Veterans?"

"It was honoring Cosmo Gentile."

"The labor statesman," Tom Spellacy said sarcastically. Cosmo Gentile ran the building trades. "Kickback Cosmo."

Crotty ignored him. "His union built all them barracks during the war."

"And that makes him a Catholic war veteran."

"He did a grand job."

"He got indicted."

"He might've got indicted," Crotty said. "But he never did anything wrong."

Tom Spellacy lit a cigarette. You want to build a motel, he thought, you go watch Cosmo Gentile named Catholic war hero of the year. He wondered what excuse Des had.

"He gave himself a dinner, Cosmo, is all he did," Crotty said.

"The Builders Association gave it to him, you want to be acurate about it," Tom Spellacy said. "A hundred a plate, 340 guests. Extortion I think the DA called it."

"It was a Welcome Home Dinner, Tom."

"He'd only been to Yellowstone Park."

"There's a lot of bears in Yellowstone Park," Crotty said. "Man-eaters is what they tell me."

"Five days. That's all he was gone."

"You go to Catalina for the day, boyo, and I'll toss you a Welcome Home Dinner, too," Crotty said. "They'll be glad to see you home safe and sound, your many friends in the community, and not a victim of the Pacific winds and those terrible ocean tides they have over there. Sweet Mother of God, Tom, it's like the China Sea and the Mindanao Deep and awful places like that, is what I hear about the boat trip to Catalina there."

The roller coaster suddenly careened around a bend not thirty feet from where they were standing. Over the din, Crotty yelled into his ear, "It keeps the labor costs from going up."

Tom Spellacy nodded and smiled, all the while watching the nuns clutch the safety bars of the roller coaster. They seemed terror-stricken. It gave him a small sense of satisfaction. They had never been that way giving him the rubber hose at Saint Anatole's.

When the roller coaster had passed, he said, "Where's this puppet maker?"

"Don't worry, he'll show up," Crotty said. He was watching a girl in a two-piece bathing suit on the beach. "You ever see a nun didn't have a mole on her nose?"

"My daughter."

"Jesus, Tom, I forgot about Moira and her being a nun. Sister Angelo, isn't it."

"Sister Angelina."

"She's a perfect nun type, Moira. She must be very happy."

He knew Crotty meant that Moira was fat. A light heavyweight.

"Listen, I got this letter yesterday." Crotty was trying to change the subject. "Green ink. Pink stationery with little red curlicues all over it. 'Dear Frank,' it says. Personal. Like I know someone uses pink paper. 'I killed the V-dash-dash-dash-dash-dash Tramp.' Can you beat that? Can't even bear to spell the word. Even the nuns don't say The Blessed V-dash-dash-dash-dash-dash. They say it right out. The Blessed Virgin."

"Priests, too," Tom Spellacy said. He liked to give Crotty the needle.

"His Eminence."

"What else did he say?"

"The Cardinal?"

"The letter-writer."

"Oh," Crotty said. " 'Stop me before I kill again.'

249

It was a fairy, I figure. So I bring it down to handwriting. I get the analysis this morning."

Crotty patted his pockets until he found a piece of paper. " 'The fluctuating baseline of the writing reveals the writer to be affected by extreme fluctuations of mood, dropping to melancholy,' " he read. "Blah, blah, blah, blah. Here it is. 'Because the last letters of many words are larger, it reveals extreme frankness. There is a fine sense of rhythm present, showing the penman to be either a musician or possibly a dancer.' "

Crotty put the handwriting analysis back into his pocket. "Not just a fairy," he said. "A fairy who plays the clarinet and dances a nice waltz."

"You should let them analyze your handwriting, Frank."

"Not a chance," Crotty said. "They got it down to such a science, they'll look at the shape of my O's and tell me I'm building a motel with a bunch of Chinamen who got me paying off Cosmo Gentile."

Tom Spellacy thought, She's a gold mine, this Lois Fazenda. A magnet for every two-bit swami and shrink and expert, handwriting and otherwise. Not to mention the newspapers. The life story of Lois Fazenda with photographs of Lois Fazenda in a bathing suit. Somebody was turning a nice piece of change on Lois Fazenda in a bathing suit, he was sure of that. It was hard to pick up a newspaper without finding resurrected an old unsolved murder of some girl, along with a picture of Lois Fazenda in a bathing suit and the headline: WHERE IS THE MISSING LINK? Tits and ass were the missing link, that was simple. He wondered how many little boys were beating their meat into the *Express*. At least they were getting something out of it. There didn't seem to be anything but dead ends. He supposed that was a good thing. Dead ends meant more work, and the more work there was, the less time to worry about Corinne. And Mary Margaret. Mustn't forget Mary Margaret. There was no point in rousting Jack Amsterdam. He could account for every minute the day of the murder. Save that one for a rainy day. When I don't give a shit and it might be nice watching Jack sweat. He had checked the M. O. file after seeing Brenda. For a barber who liked to shave pussy hair. One name. Harold Pugh. Questioned 1944, not charged. Harold Pugh was listed in the northwestern directory. Harold Pugh was also dead. Automobile accident. He had spent the better part of a morning listening to Harold Pugh's widow keening on the telephone. On Harold, the father. And Harold, the husband. And Harold, the provider. There were no complaints about Harold. Good Harold.

The morning hadn't been wasted. He did not think about Corinne once.

The roller coaster pulled to a stop. The nuns got out and surrounded an elderly priest in a black homburg.

"It's His Eminence," Crotty said. He was so surprised that he did not notice the ice cream dripping from his cone onto his suit. "What's an old number like that doing on a roller coaster?"

"Not paying for it, I bet," Tom Spellacy said. He had never seen the Cardinal in person before, and he was surprised at how old he looked. There must be nothing like a roller coaster full of nuns to make him doubt his vocation, he thought. What was he now? Eighty? He looked every minute of it. He's going to conk out soon. Des better get bishop nailed down quick.

"I bet he stiffs that guy for all the nuns, too," Crotty said. He began trailing after the Cardinal's caravan. "I'll go look for the puppet guy."

"His Eminence isn't investing in motels this year, Frank."

"The credit rating he's got, maybe he can pass me a couple of secrets," Crotty said.

Tom Spellacy took off his hat and sat in the sun. I notice Des isn't here, he thought. Him and Dan T. Campion are probably trying to make Cosmo Gentile the next Pope. He watched the nuns lead the Cardinal down the boardwalk, buying sandwiches and soft drinks at the vending stands. No money ever seemed to change hands. He wondered who was going to get stuck with the tab. Probably somebody wants to become a papal knight. The soda pop was just the down payment. There'd be a new kitchen range for the convent and a furnace and insulation for the attic and probably a paint job, too. All in all an expensive afternoon, but then getting to be a papal knight was an expensive proposition. He thought of Moira. He could never think of her as Sister Angelina. He wondered if Des had sprung her for Mary Margaret's homecoming. Moira ought to be here. All that ice cream and cake was like sanctifying grace to Moira. If you got a plenary indulgence for food, Moira would be Mother Cabrini by now.

One of the sisters scooped up a small dog and handed it to the Cardinal. Tom Spellacy saw a look of displeasure flash over his face. Then the Cardinal smiled. Sourly. A nun fastened a leash to the dog's collar and gave it to the Cardinal. He held the leash as if it were a stick with something bad on the end of it.

Tom Spellacy turned away. He was irritated at himself for paying so much attention to the Cardinal. I've got problems enough of my own without worrying if a dog's going to piss on his shoe. He watched the ocean wash against the beach. Six years in the navy and a lifetime in the city and he bet he could count on the fingers of one hand the number of times he had been swimming. It was just a waste of time sitting on the sand. A place to get sunburned. His shoulders always blistered. And then the skin peeled off in sheets and the freckles plastered his back. He had tried to fuck Mary

252

Margaret one night on the beach. Early in their marriage. It was the last time she ever asked about romance. The moon. The stars. And the sand that got in everyplace. Everyplace. It was like doing it with sandpaper. She had cried. But then Mary Margaret cried in the bedroom. Not so Corinne. Corinne got tan. Corinne said she liked to fuck at the beach. There were a lot of things that Corinne liked to do that he guessed he would never get to try.

Not after last night.


It was his idea to have dinner. "The Windsor," he had said over the telephone.

"For old times' sake," Corinne said.

He did not like the sound of that, but he let it pass. "A lot of things have happened."

"Like what?"

"Like Chuckie Quinn's name turned up as a suspect."

"Who's Chuckie Quinn?"

"Isn't that your first husband's name?"

"Charlie Quinlan."

"Oh."

"Close, though." She added, not unkindly, "I can see someone making that mistake."

"He was clean anyway, Chuckie." A stupid mistake. And unnecessary. There was no Chuckie Quinn picked up. It was just that he always needed an opening to talk to her. And so he grabbed a name. The wrong name. Stupid. Her second husband, the one who was killed, what was his name? "At least I didn't say we picked up Homer Morris."

"No."

"You were married to him, too, right?"

"Yes."

"The one who was killed."

"Yes."

"At Pearl."

253

"Tom, you don't get any points for remembering the names of my ex-husbands."

She was like Des that way. Very free with the lessons.

"I'll pick you up."

"I'll meet you. In my own car."

And that was that. She showed up at the Windsor five minutes late. In her own car. He was already working on his second drink.

"I know you got a car," Tom Spellacy had said. "As a matter of fact, I like your car better than I like my car. If the fanbelt works, I got to like any car better than I like my car, you want to know the honest truth. But the way it works, they tell me, if you go out with me, I pick you up in my car. I park the car in front of your house, and if there's a lot of niggers in the neighborhood, I lock it, because cars have a way of disappearing in that kind of neighborhood, is what they tell me. And I ring the doorbell and you say, 'In a minute,' and then you open the door and say, 'Hi, my name is Corinne, would you like a drink,' and I say, 'Thanks, no, I've got a table at the Windsor at eight, we're running a little late,' and you say, 'Swell, I'll get my coat,' and we go downstairs to my car. If I'm lucky, I still got all my hubcaps, and if I catch any little bastard stealing them, I'll break his toe. That's how it works. 'I'll meet you there,' that's a new one on me. 'I'll take my own car,' that's another one I never hear. I figure dinner's thirty bucks and before I even get here, I'm hit with a couple of surprises, and that doesn't include the check."

Corinne put her purse on the table and kept the scarf around her shoulders. She looked as if she were ready to run. "There's a reason I brought my own car."

"I'd like to hear that, I really would."

"I don't want to fuck you."

"That's nice talk. I was in Wilshire Vice there, I didn't have to pay a cover charge to hear talk like that.

254

They talked about that a lot, the people you met in Vice. Sucking, too, you get right down to it. Eating out is what they call it in Vice."

Corinne put her hands on her pocketbook. "You're drinking that stuff like it's water."

"Well, I been drinking it since four o'clock this afternoon, which is four hours and ten minutes ago, the way I figure. You know something? You're not very funny. On my own personal laugh meter, I figure you about a two-and-a-half. You don't even get a box of Mars Bars."

"That's 'Dr. I.Q.,' Mars Bars. The laugh meter's 'Can You Top This.'"

"You know something, you're a pain in the ass."

"I'm leaving," Corinne said.

"And I'll break your arm, you do," Tom Spellacy said. They stared at each other across the table. The waiter came and he ordered another rye and water. Corinne asked for a daiquiri and a menu. She buried her head in the menu until the waiter returned with the drinks.

"I'll have the Salisbury steak."

"That's a four-dollar-and-fifty-cent name for a hamburger," Tom Spellacy said. He asked the waiter how the trout amandine was cooked and the beef Wellington and the breast of capon in white wine sauce and the rognons de veau and the salmon mousse and the chicken tetrazini and he finally ordered Salisbury steak and another rye and water for himself and another daiquiri for Corinne.

Corinne had not touched her first drink.

"You want to start over again?" she said when the waiter left.

"Sure."

She took off her scarf and placed her pocketbook by the leg of her chair. "When you were pulling that act with the waiter . . ." He started to protest but she

255

kept on talking, ". . . I kept thinking about Charlie Quinlan. About after I was married to him, I mean. I don't think I thought of him in years until you mentioned him yesterday."

"I'm sorry I thought his name was Chuckie Quinn, if that's what's giving you the hard-on."

"It doesn't make any difference. I wouldn't recognize him if he was the waiter."

"You were married to him, for Christ's sake."

"For three years. I probably fucked him seven hundred times. I still wouldn't recognize him." She lifted the daiquiri and over the raised glass, she said, "I cut my losses, Tom."

"Always?"

"Always."

"And that's what you were thinking."

"No," she said. "I was thinking that after the divorce, I wore dirty underwear the first couple of years, I guess on the grounds that anything that made me keep my clothes on was all to the good."

"That's swell," Tom Spellacy said. "Really swell. It makes a lot of sense, that does."

She watched a waiter wheel a meat trolley through the room and then looked him in the eye. "It means," she said finally, "I wasn't listening to you. All that time you were doing that number with the waiter about the menu, I wasn't listening to you. I wasn't embarrassed you were trying to cause a scene, I was somewhere else."

"Thinking about your fucking underwear."

"Dirty underwear," she said quietly.

"It's so important, your dirty drawers."

"No," she said, "it was not listening to you that was so important."

The wine steward asked if they wished some wine. Corinne shook her head and Tom Spellacy ordered another drink. The waiter took away the service plates, gave them each a new napkin, switched knives and served the meal. They did not speak until the waiter had departed.

"It's very good," Corinne said after taking a bite.

"Tasty," Tom Spellacy said. His meal was still untouched.

"I have only one rule about restaurants."

"I'd like to hear that."

"You never eat fish in a restaurant where the menu says, 'From Neptune's Locker.' You know, with drawings of mermaids."

"Why's that?"

She looked surprised. "That's what somebody told me once."

"You don't have much gift for small talk, you're not talking about fucking."

Corinne smiled brightly, as if he had just told a joke. She took a drink of water and then leaned across the table, still smiling. "I've moved out of the apartment. That's another reason I brought my car."

"You'll be easy to find."

"I left your things in a box inside the door. You can pick them up and leave the key with the super."

"Fuck the Jockey shorts."

The smile on her face did not waver. She propped her chin on her finger and she was utterly calm and he realized suddenly that she was serious and that he could not make her back down. I always cut my losses. It didn't do much for the pride, but in ways he would not wish to admit, it was a relief. He picked up his knife and fork and began to eat.

"You're going to get the scrape." It was a statement, not a question.

She nodded.

He thought of Brenda nicking Lucille Cotter and he wondered if he should give her the name of a good man. A safe man. When he was in Wilshire Vice, he knew the names of all the safe men, the gynecologists who had lost their licenses for selling morphine or over a woman and who weren't on the bottle. The good men used by city hall and the department and the DA's office. A little scrape to help you out of a scrape. . . .

"Tom," Corinne said.

His smile felt foolish and he wondered if the liquor was beginning to hit him.

"Nothing's changed except it's finished, and you're relieved."

"We could always . . ." He could not continue. Could always what? He did not know what to say.

They ate in silence.

"Don't worry," she said after a while. It had not occurred to him to worry. She caught the surprised look on his face and said, "Not that I think you were consumed by it."

"You know all the answers," he said.

"That's always been my problem. By the time I know all the answers, it's all over." She folded her napkin into a neat triangle. "Right now, for example, you're embarrassed. You think your relief is showing."

He did not answer.

"Have a chocolate eclair," she said. "A second cup of coffee. Change the subject. What shall we talk about?"

He carefully removed the paper from a cube of sugar, avoiding her eyes.

"Your brother," she suggested.

"My brother hasn't got anything to do with this."

"Oh, yes, he does. You don't know why, but you always blame your brother."

"Give it a rest, Corinne." Finish the coffee, pay the check, tip the parking boy. He wondered if he had enough change for both cars. He wondered if they would shake hands or if he should kiss her on the cheek. He felt in his pocket. He had two quarters.

"You give him a rest. You want to make him just like you. You want to prove he's just like you. That's what you don't understand. He is. Just like you. He's your brother."

It always came down to Des.

She shook out her napkin and dropped it on the table.

"Be like me," she said, and then she smiled. "Always hopeful. I've cut my losses so often, I'd better be."

The nuns were herding onto the merry-go-round. Tom Spellacy could see some of them trying to induce the Cardinal to go on the ride. The Cardinal raised his hands and kept shaking his head no. He was holding a bag of peanuts in one hand and there were fragments of peanut shells clinging to his black suit. The merry-go-round started, and as it picked up speed, the Cardinal waved wearily at the nuns. Then he turned and walked slowly to a bench. He seemed to sit down in sections. He dismissed his attendants and took off his homburg. His skin was white and already turning pink in the sun. From the shadow of a hot-dog stand the Mother Superior and a young priest and two middle-aged laymen watched him with the same intensity as nurses watching a patient in an oxygen tent. One of the laymen tried to approach and the Cardinal irritably brushed him away. The tiny terrier arranged itself at the Cardinal's feet. For a moment Tom Spellacy thought he was going to kick it.

The old bastard likes to be alone, he thought. It was an appealing notion. He tried to imagine the Cardinal giving Des the brush. No. It would never happen. Des would anticipate.

I don't anticipate, that's my problem. With me, people cut their losses. Corinne. Brenda. Even Mary Margaret. In and out of Camarillo without so much as a by-your-leave. In the parking lot at the Windsor, Corinne had put her arms around him and held him

259

for a moment. Then she had tipped the parking boy herself.

A half-dollar.

He watched Crotty approach down the boardwalk, leading an old man who looked as if he had not taken a bath in a month. The old man was pushing a grocery shopping cart filled with carved shooting-gallery targets. The Cardinal stared at the spectacle of the old man and for a moment Tom Spellacy thought that Crotty was going to stop and introduce them. A little different from Dan T. Campion and Cosmo Gentile and the other leading Catholic laymen he gets to see, that's for sure. All he knew about the old man was that he carved puppets and pushed his shopping cart around the state, one end to the other, and that his name was Shopping Cart Johnson and that he had left a message for Crotty that he knew the murderer of Lois Fazenda and that he would be at Ocean Park today selling puppets to the target galleries. Crotty had run into him before. He must be a hundred years old, Crotty had said, and he smells like he uses dog shit for shaving lotion. A junk man, we used to call a guy like that, or a bum, maybe, we weren't feeling too good that day, but he picks up things, being on the go all the time, and sometimes he's useful.

Shopping Cart Johnson took a Camel from the package Tom Spellacy offered. He lit the cigarette, inhaled deeply, blew out the match and then put the package into his shirt pocket.

"I'm about as well off as a man can get," Shopping Cart Johnson said without being asked. "Ain't got no rent. I sleep in my pup tent off the road. Do my own cooking, my own laundry. Carve my targets and wash my own clothes every Saturday."

"Today must be Friday then," Tom Spellacy said.

"So it is," Shopping Cart Johnson said. "No bills, no taxes, no worries. Need a little money, can always sell a pint of blood. AB negative. Always in demand. Knew a fellow once, had a bleeding ulcer, wanted to keep me around. Hundred a week, three hots and a cot, and a shot at the nigger maid. 'No, sir,' I said, 'don't appeal to me. I like the wide open spaces.' "

Tom Spellacy had heard worse routines. It had been polished by constant repetition and he was sure that Shopping Cart Johnson could recite it at the first hint of a hot meal. It was the routine of a man used to paying for his supper by chopping wood or doing the chores or washing dishes.

"Always on the go, seeing new spots, meeting new people," Shopping Cart Johnson said. "People know me from Crescent City to Calexico. Knew a fellow in Crescent City, drives a Studebaker, XYL 468, ninety-one years young, married a pretty little thing, fourteen years old. Can't keep a good man down, as the saying goes."

"Or up, as the saying also goes," Tom Spellacy said. He knew it was no use pushing Shopping Cart Johnson. He would get to the point in his own time. In the meantime, enjoy the sun. It was a useless venture anyway.

"So it does," Shopping Cart Johnson said. "What more can a man ask? Only expense is shoes. I go through a pair every two, three weeks. Only bother is ants and flies. But hell, everybody gets flies sometimes."

Tom Spellacy took a notebook from his pocket. "I better get this down, Frank. Fuqua's the one I want to read it to." He wrote the date and "Ocean Park" and "Shopping Cart Johnson" and "Crescent City to Calexico" and out loud he repeated, " 'But hell, everybody gets flies sometimes.' "

"Right," Shopping Cart Johnson said.

"Right," Crotty said.

"Saw your murderer," Shopping Cart Johnson said.

"That'd be a big help," Tom Spellacy said.

"Don't want no reward," Shopping Cart Johnson

261

said. "Got a reward, maybe I wouldn't want to lead the outdoor life. The open road, that's for me. No automobile. Had a Reo once. YNJ 021. I had a little trouble with the Mann Act in that automobile. Gave it up. The open road, the outdoor life. Hadn't been living the outdoor life, wouldn't've found your killer, right?"

"Right," Tom Spellacy said.

"Out to the El Segundo Barracks there," Shopping Cart Johnson said.

"They're abandoned," Tom Spellacy said.

"Since 19 and 44," Shopping Cart Johnson said. "First time I been that way since they had the antiaircraft stationed there. Nice boys. Used to give me their extra condoms. Sold them in a house down in Calexico. Used one myself. Sweet little Mexican thing with a gold tooth. Had a flivver, NDS 465. Imagine a Mexican whore with a car." He shook his head vigorously and grinned. The teeth that weren't missing were green with decay. "Goddamn. That was the last time. Don't get much opportunity on the open road. My age, don't get the urge much anyway, you get my meaning."

"Fuqua won't," Crotty said.

"I was nosing around the ash barrels out in El Segundo there, like I do, looking for salvage. There's them that'd call it garbage, but I call it salvage. Never know what you're going to find. Not that there was anything worth all that much. A teakettle with a hole in it, a Bible with all the pages tored out, for smokes, I guess, couple of burned-down candles, some empty cans the dogs already licked clean, a mousetrap with a little fella in it, neck snapped clean as a whistle. Nothing much more. I was just nosing around and this fella comes up so quiet I don't hear him and he says to me, 'Move it.' I liked to jump out of my skin. And I move around and I see he's got a flat tire on his car, a shiny little '36 Ford, VOM 399, and I says to him,

262

'I can patch tires like a son of a bitch, let me help you out, Pilgrim, with your flat.' "

Shopping Cart Johnson scratched vigorously at his shoulder, then reached inside his shirt and extracted a small insect that he held between two dirty fingers. "You know what he said?"

Crotty shook his head, his eyes on the bug.

" 'Move it.' "

Tom Spellacy tapped his pencil against his palm. "That's it?"

"That's it," Shopping Cart Johnson said, flipping the insect with his forefinger. "I bet I walked a hundred thousand miles in my life, and that's the first man I ever met didn't want help with his flat. You're a judge of human nature like I am, you know a fellow like that's got to be bad."

Tom Spellacy folded his notebook and clipped the pencil into his shirt pocket. "I ever get a flat, Shopping, I hope you're in the neighborhood."

Shopping Cart Johnson said, "You wouldn't have a smoke."

"Your shirt pocket," Tom Spellacy said.

"Right," Shopping Cart Johnson said. "You want to buy some targets? You boys must have a range down at the police department."

Crotty handed him a five-dollar bill. "Stay downwind, Shopping."

Shopping Cart Johnson stuffed the bill into an old paper bag and began pushing his shopping cart down the boardwalk. Crotty watched him go. "What the hell," he said finally, "a fellow doesn't want his tire patched could be bad."

"You tell that to Fuqua, Frank, when you put in for the five."

Crotty shrugged. "As long as I'm out this way, I've got some business I should look into in Culver City."

Tom Spellacy wondered if Crotty's Chinese partners

263

were as suspicious of him as he was of them. He knew that Crotty went out to check the construction invoices at the motel every day. He would not have been surprised if Crotty had Shopping Cart Johnson snooping around Culver City, keeping an eye on the Chinese. That was one way to explain this useless trek.

No. Probably not. They had not been getting anyplace and Shopping was as good as any lead they had. It would look good in the newspapers and that's what Fuqua was interested in. 137 people questioned, 612 telephone leads followed up, 91 articles of clothing itemized and God knows how many thousands of man-hours put in. The numbers were what mattered, not that the leads led nowhere and the people questioned were all like Shopping Cart Johnson.

Worthless.

He walked out to the end of the pier. Crotty's right, he thought. It's no skin off my ass who took this girl out. Some nut. And one nut more or less isn't going to make that much difference. There's always someone standing in line to take the nut's place.

He wondered who to have dinner with. Even Des would be a good bet. Better than puttering around the Chester Hanrahan kitchen. With all the appliances I don't know how to use.

Des would beat being alone.

He suddenly felt his pant leg becoming wet and looked down and saw the Cardinal's tiny terrier pissing on his leg. Quickly he stamped on the dog's trailing leash so that he could not get away. He picked it up and for a moment, he thought of throwing it into the ocean. The dog started to yelp and he clamped its muzzle shut and looked at the name tag on its collar. Trigger. What a stupid goddamn name for a dog.

The Cardinal was still sitting alone on the bench. "Needless to say," Hugh Danaher said, holding the dog's leash at arm's length, "I didn't expect to meet you this way, Lieutenant." He looked at Tom Spellacy's damp trouser leg, and in spite of himself, began to laugh. "I don't expect you meet many people who laugh at policemen."

Tom Spellacy shook his head.

"It's the privilege of great age and a red hat." The Cardinal's laugh rumbled into a cough that bent him over. Immediately the Mother Superior was at his side and she asked Tom Spellacy to leave. Hugh Danaher waved her away. "Mother Bernadette is a good woman," he said when he regained his composure. "But she thinks that if I died on the annual outing of the Sisters of Mercy, the Pope would excommunicate her." He wiped his eyes with a handkerchief. "It takes a certain self-absorption to be in the convent."

"My daughter is a nun."

"Your brother has never mentioned that. I hope you don't take offense."

"No." How could I. Moira always thought that when she received, the world was in a state of sanctifying grace.

"It was indiscreet. The sort of remark I make to Monsignor Spellacy." He stared at Tom Spellacy. "Which must mean you're very much alike."

"I keep hearing that." Altogether too fucking much.

"Oddly enough, I like these outings. I like being with the nuns. They're simple souls, but they're enthusiastic Catholics. In a way, a day like this is like running a parish again. The barter system operates, not high finance. The sisters have a good time and I'm able to persuade our more fortunate lay brethren to . . . retire the mortgage, say."

"You got to scratch their back, too, I bet."

The Cardinal was silent for a moment. "You're more unambiguous than your brother."

"It's the way of the world."

"But you both arrive at the same conclusions." The

Cardinal gingerly touched the sunburned area of his forehead. "Do you play golf?"

"No."

"A strange game. Those that want something playing with those that have something."

He wasn't talking about par or putting, that was one thing Tom Spellacy was sure of. He wondered what the Cardinal was getting at.

"He plays that game good, Des."

"Yes."

Tom Spellacy took a deep breath. "I imagine you do, too."

Hugh Danaher smiled. "I don't play."

"Not with the golf sticks, maybe." He returned the Cardinal's stare. It was as if Hugh Danaher was daring him to continue. "But the other game you play."

The Cardinal surveyed him for a long time before he spoke. "Perhaps not as well as your brother."

"Your Eminence, you've never drawn a breath when you believed that."

The Cardinal threw back his head and laughed. "You're more impertinent than Monsignor Spellacy. I suppose I'll have to put up with it, seeing as my dog made a display on your trousers."

The terrier was licking the Cardinal's shoes.

"He's a present from the priests in the archdiocese," Hugh Danaher said. "On the occasion of my fiftieth anniversary in the priesthood."

In other words the subject of Des is closed, Tom Spellacy thought. "I'd kick anyone gave me a dog."

"Ahh," the Cardinal said. "Unfortunately a solution not feasible for a man of my age or station." He made a pass at tickling the dog with his foot. "His name is Trigger. Like Roy Rogers's horse."

"Yes, Your Eminence."

"A revolting name."

Tom Spellacy nodded.

"Leo Sweeney named him. Father Sweeney. The pastor at Church of the Redeemer. He knows Roy, apparently." The Cardinal turned the dog over with his toe. "And Dale."

Trigger sniffed at the cuff of the Cardinal's pants. "Leo Sweeney once wanted to parachute the Baltimore Catechism into Russia, like leaflets. 'For the peasants,' he said. 'Do they read English?' I said. 'Almighty God will find a way,' he said. 'Perhaps with a Berlitz course,' I said. 'We can parachute the records in with the catechisms.' 'A grand idea,' Leo said. 'I'll pray to Saint Leo every night.'" The Cardinal regarded his pet with distaste. "Apparently Saint Leo told him to turn his attention to dogs. Trigger was the name of Saint Leo's cocker spaniel, I am told."

No wonder he comes out to Ocean Park, Tom Spellacy thought. He's got the dummies on the one hand and the operators playing golf on the other. They give him a little peace, the sisters. They never heard of par and they don't know Roy Rogers, and Dale.

"I have a confession to make," the Cardinal said. "Murder is a secret vice of mine. It's one of the reasons I've wanted to meet you. Do you read Chesterton?"

Tom Spellacy shook his head. The Cardinal was full of surprises.

"The Father Brown stories, not the theology. His theology is unreadable." The Cardinal fanned himself with his homburg. "Indeed I think if I had my life to live over, I'd still devote it to the Church. But I'd gladly give up my red hat to be Father Brown." He turned to Tom Spellacy. "He's a detective."

"So am I. I figured that out."

"I'm sorry, that was patronizing."

Tom Spellacy smiled. He liked the old bastard. And he was sure he could be a bastard. But all in all better him as a boss than Fuqua. "Why do you want to be a detective?"

267

"A priest-detective," the Cardinal corrected. "Sleuthing after vespers. Sex and money, the human frailties denied a priest, but open, vicariously at least, to the priest-detective."

"It's not like real life, detective stories," Tom Spellacy said. He doubted that Father Brown would ever meet anyone like Shopping Cart Johnson. Or run into a victim with a votive candle shoved up her vagina. "I don't run into many stiffs in the rectory."

"And Father Brown never calls a body a stiff."

"So there you are."

A group of nuns hurried down the boardwalk toward the Cardinal. He sighed and placed his homburg firmly on his head.

"I have a feeling you'd be impertinent, Lieutenant Spellacy, even if Trigger hadn't misbehaved."

"I'm glad he did, Your Eminence."

The Cardinal stood up. The nuns held back, not wanting to interrupt. The two men shook hands. "May I ask what you were doing here today?" the Cardinal said.

Tom Spellacy told him.

"That poor girl," the Cardinal said. "I read in the newspaper that she was eating Chinese food before she died."

"Egg rolls."

"Father Brown would appreciate that."

"It's about the only thing he would in this one."

"It's a clue, then."

"So far, the best we've got."

When Hugh Danaher left, Tom Spellacy realized that he had not knelt and kissed his ring.

Nor had the Cardinal held it out.

# *Seventeen*

Hugh Danaher settled into the back seat of his car and closed his eyes. He was glad to be alone. The ride in the roller coaster had nearly killed him. He placed his hand over his heart. It had actually stopped beating for several seconds during the ride. A smile spread slowly across his long thin face as he tried to imagine the apostolic delegate explaining to the Holy Father how he had died. All those years in the Vatican's service would not have prepared the apostolic delegate to diagram a roller coaster. For a fleeting second, the Cardinal visualized the Pope and the apostolic delegate in a loop-the-loop. The Danaher Heresy, he thought, banish it from the mind.

Think croquet. A sedentary game. He played it once a week with Samuel Goldwyn. A quiet game, just the two of them. The big games, the money games with David Niven and Gary Cooper, Goldwyn held on Sunday, but the Cardinal usually had an ordination on Sunday, or a confirmation. In any case, he was never quite sure who David Niven was. *"The Scarlet Pimpernel,* Danaher, *The Scarlet Pimpernel,"* Samuel Goldwyn said, "four million domestic, that's who David Niven is." It amused the Cardinal that the two men called each other Goldwyn and Danaher. No one had called him Danaher to his face in nearly sixty years, and he was damned if he was going to put a Mister before Goldwyn's name. Especially seeing as he could beat Goldwyn regularly at croquet. A silly game, the golf that Monsignor Spellacy played. A game for the shifty elements. Not so croquet. A prince of the Church head to head with a pharaoh of film. Krakow to croquet in two generations. Kerry to croquet, for that matter. That was one way of looking at it. Two old men at ease in the sun was another. And increasingly the way the Cardinal felt. Old friends dead and dying, the next generation obsequious before the red hat. The prince and the pharaoh. Two old men playing croquet.

"I've registered 'The Virgin Tramp' as a title," Samuel Goldwyn had said the week before. "What do you think of that, Danaher?"

"I'll have the Legion of Decency on you," the Cardinal said.

"'The Innocent Tramp,' I've registered that, too," Samuel Goldwyn said. "And 'Innocence.'"

"Better, Goldwyn, better," the Cardinal said. "The names these days. It's the war that did it, I think. You can't pick up a newspaper today without reading about a 'sexpot.'"

"'Mexican Spitfire,' that's another type you're always reading about," Samuel Goldwyn said.

The Cardinal stared out the car window at an office building under construction on Olympic Boulevard. Another ugly box. There were so many changes to assimilate. Ugly buildings, ugly cars, ugly people. He picked up the newspaper his driver had neatly folded for him on the back seat. More changes. The *Express* was even advertising "HORMONES—Male and Female—Genuine Testosterone—Free Literature—THE HORMONE PHARMACY." My God, what sort of person would go to the Hormone Pharmacy.

The Fazenda story was still on the front page.

Sources close to the investigation revealed exclusively to the *Herald-Express* that Miss Fazenda

270

was a "romance seeker" who used her innocent beauty to drive her dozens of men friends into what the sources called "a frenzy."

Not the sort of thing Father Brown would run up against. In a happier time the poor girl would have been called something like The Lilac Delilah. The Virgin Tramp. The name made him shudder. As did her description. Every mole. Every scar. Every wart. "One large wart center of back of neck about even with shoulder line, two small warts one inch to the right of this, one small wart to right of above about one-half inch higher, two warts to left of midline of neck on shoulder, one wart on back about one inch to right of medial line." The Cardinal wondered who would notice or remember or even care about the pattern of the warts. He crossed himself quickly. One of the men driven into a frenzy, of course. Who would also remember, "Hair shaved on legs below knees. Hair shaved under arms. All fingernails chewed down to quick."

It was the fingernail biting that made Lois Fazenda seem so appealing. A Lilac Delilah would have been perfect, and it was hard to feel pity for perfection. He tried to guess what nervous fear made her chew her fingernails. His own were manicured. A small vanity picked up at the age of seventy-two when he was in Rome for his investiture into the College of Cardinals.

He made a vow. No more manicures. And a mass for the repose of the girl's soul. And an extra rosary every day for the hours he had lost getting his own nails clipped and buffed and shaped.

The Cardinal flinched involuntarily. He could imagine Lieutenant Spellacy's reaction to that vow. No more manicures indeed. They were very much alike, those two brothers. They each had the ability to make other men feel small, even cheap. It was not so much that the Spellacys saw themselves as superior. It was rather that their instinct for what was inferior was unerring. And each in his own way knew that what was inferior was often useful. The Cardinal was sure they did not like each other. People without illusions rarely did.

He wished he had talked to Lieutenant Spellacy more about Lois Fazenda. That girl made him feel so uneasy. She was like a dark cloud that seemed ready to rain at any moment on the archdiocese. First the Protectors of the Poor. That stupid Ruben Aguilar. Well, he wouldn't do anyone any harm at the Inter-American Catholic Council in Mexico City. Desmond Spellacy was right. He said that Monsignor Aguilar would think it was a promotion. And Jack Amsterdam. The Cardinal could not bear Jack Amsterdam. And never had. But I can't blame him on Monsignor Spellacy, he thought. We all knew what he was. But he offered such a good deal it was easy to believe in the infinite power of repentance. Maybe that was why Desmond was having such difficulty getting rid of him. Because I was so acquiescent about using him in the first place.

Still it was unlike Monsignor Spellacy to be so delicate. He could be absolutely ruthless. Any number of erring pastors could attest to that. And even one visiting prelate. His Eminence, Miljenko Cardinal Caratan, formerly ordinary of Belgrade, purged by Tito and run out of Yugoslavia by the Reds. He had come to America for a cross-country lecture tour to raise money to fight the Communists. Seamus Fargo had invited him to speak at Saint Basil's. Absolutely, categorically, unequivocally no, said Monsignor Spellacy. The Cardinal smiled as he remembered Seamus's visit about that. Naturally Seamus accused Monsignor Spellacy of being a muddle-headed dupe. It was a shame seeing Seamus getting in over his head. But Monsignor Fargo needed to be taken down a peg or two. He needed to be reminded who was running the archdiocese. Poor Seamus.

That frozen look on his face as he examined the documentation Monsignor Spellacy had requested and received from the OSS showing how cozy Cardinal Caratan had been with the Nazis before Tito took over. How Cardinal Caratan liked to have his picture taken. At a candlelit dinner with Eva Braun. Standing alongside Heydrich in a reviewing stand while the *gauleiter* gave the Nazi salute. Of course Seamus backed down. He went on a retreat with Cardinal Caratan instead. He won't forgive Monsignor Spellacy for that, the Cardinal thought. He knows that it was I who sprung the trap, but he suspects that it was Desmond who fed him so much rope. He prefers to think that I had to be talked into it. We're both too old, Seamus and I. Two devious old men. Who didn't like to be crossed.

Not that Desmond minded helping me put Seamus in his place. He always has had a gift for making enemies. Sometimes I think he hangs them up like trophies. Which is why there had to be a reason he was moving so slowly on the Amsterdam situation. It should be such a simple matter. There have to be connecting wires somewhere, the Cardinal thought. He wondered if Lieutenant Spellacy might have some information he would be willing to impart. No. Not the type. Unless there was something to gain.

The Cardinal's car turned into Fremont Place. For an instant Hugh Danaher wondered if Lieutenant Spellacy might be a connecting wire.

He picked up the newspaper and looked at the photograph of Lois Fazenda in her Arab extra's costume. Such an unlikely source of trouble.

The Cardinal felt every second of his eighty years. I wonder if I have the strength to be ruthless, he thought. Or if I'll live long enough.

# *Eighteen*

That same night, at Dan T. Campion's house in Hancock Park, Peg Campion served corned beef and cabbage for dinner.

"Dan's favorite, Monsignor," Peg Campion said. She was a thin, nervous woman who always seemed to have a cold. She was never without a sweater around her shoulders and a handkerchief balled in her hand. Desmond Spellacy suspected that Peg Campion cried a great deal. "Every Wednesday he wants his corned beef and cabbage."

"Friday's Boston cream pie day," Dan T. Campion said.

"Because the tuna fish casserole's not very fattening," Peg Campion said. She blew her nose and through the handkerchief added, "That's Friday's dish."

"She's a grand girl, Des," Dan T. Campion said. He had scarcely opened his mouth since they sat down to dinner. He had just stared into space and left Desmond Spellacy to talk to his wife. They had discussed the Holy Days of Obligation one by one. Peg Campion said that her favorite was the Feast of the Assumption because it was the only one in the summer. "A creature of habit," Dan T. Campion added, "just like me."

"Twenty-nine years come May thirty-first, Monsignor," Peg Campion said. "I've been thinking of a prime rib."

"Birthdays and anniversaries, it's always the prime

274

rib," Dan T. Campion said. "When Peg says she's having the prime rib, I know I better get a present."

Dan Campion's laugh competed with Peg Campion's blowing of her nose.

"You said you wanted to be alone with the monsignor," Peg Campion said.

"A grand idea," Dan T. Campion said. "In the study, Des."

The study. Desmond Spellacy had bad memories of the study. The study was where Dan T. Campion got down to brass tacks. Coffee and brandy in the study meant that Dan T. Campion had something on his mind. The last time Desmond Spellacy had gone into that study, Peg Campion had been crying. It was before their daughter Maureen was married. Maureen was Peg and Dan Campion's only child. Pale was the only way Desmond Spellacy could think of describing Maureen Campion. Pale eyes, pale hair, pale complexion. She didn't leave much of an impression. She was like a very large Boston cream pie. Pale and two months pregnant. Which was why Peg Campion was weeping in the hallway outside the study.

"It's not her being in a family way I mind," Dan T. Campion had said. "It's a harsh thing to say about your own daughter, Des, but the only way she was ever going to get married was to get in a family way first. She might look like a jelly donut, Maureen, but she's no dummy."

"No," Desmond Spellacy had said. He had not been quite sure exactly where he fit in, and under the circumstances no seemed the safest thing to say. Until he got the lay of the land. Which considering why he was there was perhaps an unfortunate cliché.

"She gets married, she knows I'll take care of her," Dan T. Campion said. "Her and that numbskull which got her this way. He's a pump jockey."

"A what?"

"A pump jockey. In a gas station. Signal Oil. He doesn't even own the goddamn thing. The guy who wipes the bird shit off your windshield, that's him." Dan T. Campion had slammed his fist down on his desk. "You'll have to excuse me, Des, I'm upset."

"Yes." Another perfect answer. He had said no and he had said yes. He had maybe left.

"I need your help, Des."

Not on annulment procedures. Nor on the logistics of placing the child out for adoption in a Catholic agency. The marriage would take place. Dan T. Campion would see to that. And the marriage would survive, if the numbskull knew what was good for him. It was how to announce the marriage in the newspapers that worried Dan T. Campion. What was the best way to proclaim the son-in-law of Dan T. Campion, Knight of Malta, noted counselor-at-law, civic leader, chairman of commissions, advisor to bishops.

"You got to think of something to call him, Des. Besides dumbbell. Besides Signal Oil pump jockey."

"Something that'll look good on the society page is what you mean," Desmond Spellacy said.

The irony in his voice had escaped Dan T. Campion. "That's it," he had said.

The awful thing is, Desmond Spellacy thought, Dan knows his man. He'd never ask my opinion on a matter of dogma or an interpretation of papal encyclicals. The very thought struck him funny. If Dan T. Campion had been at the Council of Trent, his only interest would have been who got the building contracts.

"I think I have it," Desmond Spellacy had said. "A franchised retail representative for the Signal Oil Company."

"What the hell does it mean?"

"It's a fancy way of saying he pumps gas."

"Jesus, that's a grand help, Des."

The study.

The study meant trouble.

Dan T. Campion poured two brandies. Desmond Spellacy noticed that he spilled some on the silver tray.

"I been thinking about Jack," Dan T. Campion said. "It's a terrible thing, his using the Protectors like that." Beads of perspiration were forming on his forehead. "You got it on good authority, did you?"

Desmond Spellacy nodded.

"Your brother, the policeman, I suppose."

Desmond Spellacy sipped his brandy.

"It's grand the way he looks out for the Church, your brother, the policeman. He's a grand Catholic, I'm sure. Where is he now, Perpetual Help?"

Desmond Spellacy nodded again.

"A grand parish. And a grand pastor in Vinny Pellegrini. It was a grand thing, His Eminence giving a parish to an Italian type. They need someone to look up to, your Italians."

Desmond Spellacy said nothing.

"She's mental, his wife, isn't she?"

Sometimes I think Mary Margaret is saner than anyone, Desmond Spellacy thought.

"In Camarillo, I'm told."

"Yes."

"They do a grand job taking care of the fruitcakes, is what I hear," Dan T. Campion said. "In Camarillo." And then suddenly he blurted out, "I know your brother's friend. Mrs. Morris. At the Jury Commission. She does a grand job with the venire."

Desmond Spellacy warmed the brandy in his palms, holding it up so that he would not have to look Dan Campion in the eye. He stared at the mahogany-colored liquid until his anger abated. So that was her name. Mrs. Morris. He was sure it was Mrs. Morris whose confession he had heard. Scared, pregnant, ready to abort. He had tried not to push her over the edge. I should have gone after her. I could have done more.

Even talk to her about Tommy. Tommy would have loved that. No wonder he was upset about Mary Margaret getting out. I wonder how he's going to manage that with Mrs. Morris. And I wonder how Dan Campion knows about her. Dan has to be desperate about something, even to mention Mrs. Morris at the Jury Commission. He can't really expect to pressure the department about Tommy and Mrs. Morris. The last I heard adultery wasn't a felony. If they started firing policemen for adultery, you could fit the whole force into a telephone booth. That's one thing you learn hearing confessions before the department's annual Communion Breakfast. There wasn't any edge, Dan's mentioning Mrs. Morris at the Jury Commission.

Dan T. Campion's hands were shaking.

"You're spilling your brandy, Dan."

Dan T. Campion wiped his hand off on his pant leg. "I did a little checking for you, Des. With the DA. They'll keep the Monsignor Aguilar thing under wraps, I'll promise you that. A solemn promise. They don't want to embarrass His Eminence, you can count on that."

Too many promises, too much fast talk. Get on with it.

"That's swell, Dan. His Eminence will appreciate it."

"And you don't have to worry much about them Mexicans the Protectors were involved with." Dan T. Campion splashed some more brandy into Desmond Spellacy's glass. "They don't snitch much, the Mexicans. It's part of their nature. It's why they're so good in the house. You won't find a better maid than a Mexican, Des. They don't snitch. Your average jungle bunny is a snitch."

"That's nice to know," Desmond Spellacy said. He wondered why Dan Campion was pretending to be drunk.

"Keep it in mind when you get to be bishop."

278

That has to be one of the worst-kept secrets in the world, Desmond Spellacy thought.

"Are they still checking out how she got into the Protectors?" Dan T. Campion said.

"Who?"

"What's-her-name."

"I would guess they are."

Dan T. Campion sucked in his breath. Then the words tumbled out. "You remember her, don't you, Des? Coming up from Del Mar?"

"Who, Dan?"

"Last summer. She was hitchhiking. We picked her up."

"I took the plane up last summer. I had to speak at the Junior Chamber of Commerce's annual dinner. So I took the plane up. And you drove."

"No, the time before that. She was hitchhiking. Around San Juan there. We picked her up. She was Christian Science, she said. You asked her about it, remember?"

Desmond Spellacy remembered. There was no surprise. He thought, I've lost my capacity for surprise. Tommy. Jack. The Protectors. Now Dan. Now me. Even that thought did not startle him. He wondered if anything ever would again. He felt trapped in a web of circumstance. One thing was clear. It explained why her photograph in the newspaper had always seemed so familiar. Like the picture of a girl whose confession he would hear at the House of the Good Shepherd. "I've read a lot about Mary Baker Eddy," he remembered telling her. "Who?" she had said. Which ended that discussion. It was easier talking to Dan about Chet Hanrahan. He had no other memory of the girl. Just the voice saying, "Who?" Was the voice as blank and empty as he remembered?

"We were friends, her and me," Dan T. Campion said.

279

It suddenly occurred to Desmond Spellacy that Dan Campion's grammar was shaky only when he wanted it to be, when he wanted to appear one of the boys. It was impeccable when he was talking to the Cardinal. Who was in a position to do him a favor. Or Devlin Perkins. Or Norman Chandler. Ten years it's taken me to figure that out. He raged in silence: you patronizing hypocritical bastard.

"And who would you be talking about now, Dan?" With just a hint of a brogue. Sink it in and give it a little twist. See how much he likes that leprechaun crap.

"Herself, Des."

He can't even bring himself to say her name.

"Peg, you mean then." Still with the brogue, as if he had just stepped off the boat. "The corned beef was swell. And the boiled potatoes, too. A Jew dish like that. It's not every girl from Kildare can cook the Jew food. Unless it's the Mexican in the kitchen which done the cooking. She don't snitch and she cooks grand."

Dan T. Campion stared levelly at him. His hand had stopped shaking. No more blarney, Desmond Spellacy thought. He knows the jig is up. I wonder how much Peg Campion knows.

"Lois Fazenda."

"I know who you mean."

"I got her into the Protectors," Dan T. Campion said. "She needed a job. I called Jack." He kept rubbing a finger around the rim of his brandy snifter, causing a weird, echoing sound, but he seemed oblivious to the noise. "I was in San Diego the night she was killed."

Desmond Spellacy did not say anything.

"With Peg," Dan T. Campion said. "We were at the western regional meeting of the K of C, Peg and me."

Poor dumb Peg Campion. Kept around for the K of C conventions and the Altar Society communion breakfasts. The perfect alibi for the prominent Catholic layman with the wandering eye. Sweet Mother of God, the Knights of Columbus convention. Where in the name of Christ will it ever end.

"It happens, Des." There was a note of pleading in Dan T. Campion's voice. "I'm sixty-six years of age, a girl like her—"

Desmond Spellacy cut him off abruptly. "This isn't confession, Dan." He was barely able to keep his voice under control. "I'm not interested in any squalid little stories about life passing you by and how you get Boston cream pie every Friday."

Dan T. Campion looked away from him. After a moment, barely audibly, he said, "I'm clean, Des."

"After a fashion."

"I'm sorry, Des. I didn't mean it that way. I don't want to see Peg hurt, is all."

"I don't believe you. It's your own picture you don't want to see in the papers. Holding a hat over your face, when they bring you in for questioning."

Dan T. Campion seemed to shrink in his chair. "If it comes out . . ."

"You should've thought of that."

"If you could talk to your brother, the policeman . . ."

Desmond Spellacy slammed the brandy down so hard on the side table that the glass broke. "Don't you ever call Tommy 'your brother, the policeman.' " His hand was bleeding and the brandy was spilling onto the carpet. "Ever. Again."

"You were with me, Des, remember, the day we met her?"

Desmond Spellacy paused at the door of the study. "We met her, Dan," he said. "You fucked her."

A touch of Boyle Heights. Dan T. Campion shud-

281

dered. He thinks it's worse my saying it than his doing it, Desmond Spellacy thought.

"Des." Dan T. Campion almost shouted the name. "It's Jack I'm worried about."

Desmond Spellacy turned away from the door. He pulled a handkerchief from his pocket and wrapped it around his hand.

"We talked, him and me. When it came out she was in the Protectors."

It was so clear now. Dan's opposition to letting Jack go and his obsessive interest in Tommy.

"And I suppose you told him I was a warm personal friend of Miss Fazenda's."

"I didn't put it that way, Des."

"Of course not." Jack must think the Spellacy family is his insurance policy, Desmond Spellacy thought. Tommy was his bagman and I knew, God help me, the Virgin Tramp.

"He thinks your bro . . . Lieutenant Spellacy is crazy."

"He probably is."

"You got to do something, Des."

"For whom, Dan?"

"For all of us."

Desmond Spellacy stared at the spreading brandy stain on the carpet. "Tell Peg I'm sorry I spilled the drink."

"Des . . ."

"I'll see what I can do, Dan."

For His Eminence, he thought as he drove back to Fremont Place. For the archdiocese. Not to mention myself. Coming up from Del Mar with a winning exacta in his pocket and the Virgin Tramp in the back seat. A Christian Scientist who had never heard of Mary Baker Eddy. There was no face. Just the photograph in the newspapers of the girl in the Arab costume. It would make a nice triptych in the papers.

That photograph flanked by one of me and one of Dan T. Campion. Or one of me and one of Jack. Or just the three of us: Dan, Jack and me. The Three Musketeers. One for all and all for one. A $612 exacta, he remembered. He had given it all to the Athanasians. Because of Chet Hanrahan's son. Brother Bede Hanrahan, who was soliciting for his mendicant order. The cuffs on Brother Bede's habit had needed mending. He remembered that now, too. And the look on Bede Hanrahan's face when he gave him the six hundreds, a ten and two singles. His own cuffs didn't need mending. Chet Hanrahan had bought the suit. Not off the rack. Custom-made. Three fittings. And the black Scotch-grain Lobb shoes as well. You need a last in London, Chet Hanrahan had said. It was a long step from Thom McAn to a last in London. All things considered, a step I would just as soon never have taken. A nice little parish would be just the thing now. Confessions from three to five and seven to eight. Two masses on Sunday, benediction and the Stations of the Cross. Mrs. Rodano would run the Legion of Mary and Jimbo Lenihan the Holy Name Society. Cake sales and bingo. To pay for the new altar linen. He would get Tommy to receive regularly. Every Sunday. That would be the first order of business. Although Mrs. Morris at the Jury Commission might pose a small problem. Necessitating a little marriage counseling. Perhaps it wasn't such a hot idea after all. Tommy never did think much of my expertise on nuptial matters. Or any priest's, for that matter. When I want swimming lessons, Des, I'll go to someone who knows how to swim. Simple and to the point.

Tommy.

My brother, the policeman.

He turned his car into the driveway of the Cardinal's residence on Fremont Place. It was at the Cardinal's request that he lived at the residence. In the past chancellors lived in the rectory at Saint Vibiana's or had rooms at Saint Philip's Hospital. It was not that the Cardinal wanted company. Desmond Spellacy never saw him except officially. The residence was simply too big, His Eminence said. It was wasteful not to live there. He wondered if the Cardinal knew how much he disliked living there. It was like a tomb. The perfect place to live out his death.

Ahhh.

That was it. That was what he was doing.

Living out my death.

He turned off the car engine and sat in the front seat. The headlights were still on. It was like a numbered drawing. Connect the consecutive numbers with lines and a picture began to emerge. A girl was murdered. Mary Margaret wrote him a letter. Mickey Gagnon committed a mortal sin. Dan Campion went to Del Mar. Jack Amsterdam had lunch at the Biltmore. Ruben Aguilar was a moron. Mrs. Morris at the Jury Commission went to confession. The Cardinal was short a ton of asphalt. I win an exacta. The archdiocese needs an auxiliary. Chet Hanrahan has a coronary. Tommy was a bagman.

He thought, I was always the one who connected the lines before. Not now. The pencil had a power of its own. No one had any control over it.

He thought, I am losing my nerve. I have surrendered to fate. Which is another way of saying, I am living out my death.

A flashlight shone into his face. He shielded his eyes from the glare and saw a policeman staring into the car at him.

"Your lights are on, Father."

"I'm sorry, Officer, I must have dozed off."

"It's only nine-thirty."

"I get up at six."

"You're all right?"

284

"Yes."

"I thought you were . . ."

"No, Officer."

"You're all right?"

"Thank you, Officer."

He parked the car in the garage and locked the garage door. He turned off the lights and climbed the stairs to his third-floor bedroom. There was not a sound in the residence.

My God, Desmond Spellacy thought, I'm tired of fixing things.

# Nineteen

"There's a bug in the tomato," Seamus Fargo said. "And sand in the salad. The chicken is underdone, the peas are hard and the ice cream is melted. The coffee is cold and the waiter needs to blow his nose. He will probably pinch a nostril and sneeze into the jellied consommé. I have no doubt that Bishop O'Dea will think it's a caper and recall how Babe Ruth had capers with every meal. And if he is let near the microphone, he will do his Al Smith imitation and talk about Tiny Hennessy's cousin, the Sister of Charity, who was supposed to have had the stigmata in Indianapolis." Seamus Fargo paused for breath. "I have been to lunches like that, Your Eminence."

"So I gather," the Cardinal said.

The curtains in the Cardinal's study were drawn. Another indication of His Eminence's failing health,

Desmond Spellacy thought. The bright sun seemed to make him doze. With the drapes closed, it was easier for him to see, but it lent the study an air of gloom and foreboding. There was only one advantage. In the darkened room, his attention could now wander without coming under the Cardinal's piercing scrutiny. He surreptitiously checked his watch. He was meeting Tommy at eleven in the employees' cafeteria at KFIM. "Homicide Hotline" was the name of the program Tommy was scheduled to be on. About the Fazenda murder, he supposed. A show I very much want to miss. Not that his own schedule was much more edifying. First he would transcribe "The Rosary Hour." Then negotiate the terms for the Cardinal's Christmas Eve midnight mass broadcast. And then try to negotiate Dan T. Campion out of the clutches of the police department. He tried not to think of the girl or of the rage he had directed at Dan Campion the past week.

"I spoke to your Mr. Walsh, Your Eminence." Seamus Fargo's voice interrupted Desmond Spellacy's reverie. "He wore French cuffs."

"Surely no reason to disqualify him," the Cardinal said. He glanced at his manicure and dropped his hands into the folds of his cassock.

"I do not like fund raisers."

And that is too goddamn bad, Desmond Spellacy exploded under his breath. Because Leo I. Walsh of Diocesan Giving, Inc., is going to administer the archdiocese's new $20 million fund-raising program whether you like it or not. He felt suddenly ashamed. He knew his anger was not caused by Seamus Fargo. Dan Campion rather, and "Homicide Hotline." Poor Seamus. For nearly thirty years Monsignor Fargo had chaired all the fund drives in the archdiocese and now the Cardinal was relieving him of that position. At my instigation. No. One thing Monsignor Fargo doesn't want is my pity.

286

"I want you to go to that lunch, Seamus," the Cardinal said.

"He'll have a thermometer in the lobby," Seamus Fargo said. "With a drawing of the Sacred Heart of Jesus. And cheap leather luggage as a door prize. Donated by Timsy Rooney, the merchant, who hasn't been able to get rid of it in twelve years. In memory of his grand Irish mother who lived to be 111 and had all her teeth, and let's hear it for Timsy." Seamus Fargo spoke precisely. "I have seen this man's letterhead, Your Eminence. There is a design of a stained-glass window on it."

"I am aware of that, Monsignor." It seemed an effort for the Cardinal to speak. Desmond Spellacy wondered if Monsignor Fargo was aware of how much the Cardinal had declined. Fatigue overtook him often now before noon. His conversation sometimes tended to drift. "Mr. Walsh went to Fordham."

"A school for Polish football players," Seamus Fargo said.

The Cardinal flushed with anger, but kept silent, as if realizing the irrelevance of his remark.

"Where they evidently did not bother to teach him English," Seamus Fargo continued. "He spoke to me about upgrading the giving habits of prospects. He proposed breaking donors down into lists of advanced, intermediate, and general prospects. The problem is one of salesmanship, he said." Seamus Fargo stared at the Cardinal. It was a constant source of amazement to Desmond Spellacy that no matter how intensely Monsignor Fargo felt, he never raised his voice. "That man proposes to turn the archdiocese into a salesman's territory, Your Eminence. You might as well make Timsy Rooney a bishop and his grand old ma a mother superior."

The Cardinal studied Monsignor Fargo. He was wide awake once again, and brooding. He was at his most

287

dangerous, Desmond Spellacy knew, when he had been caught napping. "Mr. Walsh comes highly recommended, Monsignor."

Seamus Fargo swiveled in his chair and looked across the room at Desmond Spellacy. "By Monsignor Spellacy, no doubt."

Desmond Spellacy rose and opened the briefcase on the Cardinal's desk. One thing about Seamus, he thought, he makes the adrenalin pump. You can't think about Dan Campion and your other problems when he's in the room. "These are the figures of our last drive."

"An eminently successful drive, Monsignor," Seamus Fargo said coldly. He did not open the folder he had been handed. The figures were on the tip of his tongue. "The goal was $6 million. I raised $6 million. It took me two years, I collected on seventy-nine percent of my pledges and it only cost me four percent in campaign expenses."

"You did well, Seamus," the Cardinal said.

"Very well indeed, Monsignor," Desmond Spellacy said.

"For a nonprofessional," the Cardinal said. Quietly. With no flourishes. Seamus Fargo looked back at the Cardinal. He knows he's had it, Desmond Spellacy thought. He knew it when he walked into this room, but Seamus would never go down without a fight.

Desmond Spellacy handed another folder to Monsignor Fargo. "Two years ago, Mr. Walsh designed a drive to raise $5 million for the archdiocese of San Francisco." He could recite the figures by rote. Each decimal point was like a nail in Seamus's coffin. "In eighteen months, he raised nearly nine million dollars. He collected on ninety-two percent of his pledges and the total cost was only two percent." He pointed to the folder in Monsignor Fargo's hand. "The figures have been authenticated by an independent certified public accountant."

He waited by the Cardinal's desk while Monsignor Fargo thumbed through the papers. I have become so familiar with such sums, he thought, even contemptuous of them.

Seamus Fargo handed the folder back to Desmond Spellacy. "A very thorough job," he said carefully. He settled back into his chair, his long, bony fingers drumming against the leather arm-rests. His thin lips parted in a small smile.

"I would hope that in the future, Monsignor," Seamus Fargo said, "you will have Mr. Amsterdam's books authenticated by the same accountants."

The drawn curtains enhanced the silence in the study. The Cardinal glanced back and forth between the two men. Neither spoke, nor did they break off staring at each other.

The clock struck the half-hour.

"Mr. Amsterdam's services to the archdiocese have been discontinued," Desmond Spellacy said finally. The Cardinal was right: Seamus never blinked. His eyes seemed to be held open by icicles. He was not surprised that it was Seamus rather than the Cardinal who had forced his hand. Monsignor Fargo had always been the most implacable of men. God knows, there had been enough rumors over the years about Jack and short-changing. Both Neddy Flynn and Emmett Flaherty were in Saint Basil's and they must have repeated a story or two to Seamus.

"I am delighted to hear that, Monsignor," Seamus Fargo said, "as I am sure His Eminence is, too."

So. He had cut Jack Amsterdam loose. There was nothing to do now but let events run their course. The lines would be connected, the picture would appear. In an odd way Desmond Spellacy felt relieved. He controlled an impulse to snap back at Monsignor

289

Fargo. It would serve no purpose. Seamus had been stripped of one title, and if he did not watch out, he stood to lose another. Words were cheap.

Though wounding.

And sometimes truthful.

"That's settled then, Seamus," the Cardinal said. Desmond Spellacy had almost forgotten he was in the room. That was a mistake. The Cardinal may have been inconspicuous, but he had been keeping score. "The luncheon is on Thursday. I would appreciate it if you introduced Mr. Walsh."

Monsignor Fargo made no effort to hide the sarcasm in his voice. "And say grace, too, Your Eminence?"

"You will pour the coffee, Monsignor, if I tell you to," the Cardinal said coldly.

"As you wish, *Eminenza*," Seamus Fargo said. He made ready to leave. He knelt and kissed the Cardinal's ring and nodded curtly at Desmond Spellacy.

"There is one other thing, Monsignor," the Cardinal said. "Our Lady of Lourdes parish."

"It is badly run, the plant is a firetrap and there are not enough parishioners," Seamus Fargo said.

"Well put," the Cardinal said. "Unlike Saint Basil's. You have the highest credit rating in the archdiocese."

"I am aware of that, Your Eminence."

"I thought you would be," the Cardinal said. He did not ask Monsignor Fargo to retake his chair. He's good at using the little things like that to put someone at a disadvantage, Desmond Spellacy thought. "I feel it incumbent on the more fortunately endowed parishes to help out those less . . . advantaged."

Seamus Fargo shifted his hat and briefcase from one hand to the other. "Lending them money would be a more precise way of putting it, I would think."

"If you wish," the Cardinal said. "I would of course pay interest. Two percent."

"I could do better with pencils and a tin cup,"

290

Seamus Fargo said. "It systematically undermines the authority of every pastor in the archdiocese."

"It is Christian charity," the Cardinal said.

"I believe Monsignor Spellacy would call it central financing." Monsignor Fargo ignored Desmond Spellacy. "This is his concept, is it not?"

The Cardinal spread his hands on his desk, then slowly clasped them. He would never speak until he was in total control. "It would behoove you to remember, Monsignor," he said finally, "that I run this archdiocese, not Monsignor Spellacy."

"As you wish, *Eminenza.*" Seamus Fargo steadied himself on the back of a chair. The strain of standing was beginning to take its toll. He was starting to show his age. "It is still bolshevism by any other name. I would prefer to take over Our Lady of Lourdes myself. Given five years, I could turn it around."

"Seamus, you're eighty-one years of age."

"In perfect health."

"I want the money."

"Is that an order?"

"It is."

Seamus Fargo straightened from behind the chair and bowed. "As you wish, *Eminenza.*"

The Cardinal did not speak for several moments after Monsignor Fargo departed. His head was bowed on his chest, almost as if he were asleep. Desmond Spellacy did not move.

The Cardinal looked up. "I've known that man for sixty years. And not once in those sixty years has he ever called me Hugh." The Cardinal snorted. "*Eminenza.* He spent six months in Rome at the seminary sixty years ago, and now whenever he wants to get snippy, he lapses into that high-falutin' Italian. *Eminenza.* I don't think he knows another word."

Desmond Spellacy said nothing. He had seen the Cardinal this way before about Monsignor Fargo. There was not another person alive who could so crack his glacial reserve.

"He has to go."

"Your Eminence?"

"I mean he has to be fired, Monsignor. Don't act as if you've never heard the word before."

"I'm sorry, Your Eminence."

"Find out what his needs are."

"Your Eminence?"

The Cardinal coldly emphasized every word. "Find a place for him, Monsignor."

"Saint Francis Hospital needs a chaplain." Desmond Spellacy wondered if he had been too quick to answer. It was as if he had just been waiting to drop Monsignor Fargo into the vacancy at Saint Francis.

The Cardinal stared at him without comment. "Perfect," he said finally.

The irony of the situation left a metallic taste in Desmond Spellacy's mouth. In less than an hour he was going to try to keep Dan Campion out of jail and now he was being ordered to fire Seamus Fargo. Another two numbers connected, another line drawn in. The outline was taking shape.

The Cardinal was still talking.

"And not because he looks at me as if I belong in a home for senile priests. . . ."

"Yes, Your Eminence." Who? Seamus. He still must be talking about Monsignor Fargo. The second number . . .

"We need younger pastors, that's the long and the short of it. Men who will do what they are told. Without all that arguing and complaining and obstruction. Getting rid of Monsignor Fargo should make the others fall back into line." The Cardinal paused. "What do you think of that?"

"As you wish, Your Eminence."

"My God," the Cardinal said irritably, "you sound just like him."

Desmond Spellacy's eyes flickered, but he did not move.

"You might as well learn now that you will have to do some unpleasant things," the Cardinal said. "If you become a bishop, perhaps you can find an ambitious young monsignor to do them for you."

The words burned, like a drop of acid. He's a tired, dying old man, Desmond Spellacy thought, but he hasn't lost the knack of putting people in their place.

"I hope you're right about Mr. Walsh, Monsignor. As I hope you've been right about Mr. Amsterdam." There was a rattle of phlegm in the Cardinal's throat. "I've had to get rid of a number of old friends to make things easy." His voice dropped and his breathing became labored. "For you."

"Yes, Your Eminence."

"I hope I've made the right decision."

I don't know if you have, Desmond Spellacy thought.

The Cardinal seemed not to notice he was still there. He stared into the gloom of the room and said, "He hated to see the poor shiver."

# Twenty

"Shit, Des, we know he's clean," Tom Spellacy said.

That word again, Desmond Spellacy thought. *Clean.* Dan Campion and Tommy both seemed to define it the same way. He watched Tommy pour sugar onto a spoon. The crystals cascaded off the spoon into his coffee cup. Tommy always did like sweets. No wonder he had trouble with his weight. No discipline. A fast welterweight grew into a slow middleweight. He must be a lightheavy by now. His neck bulged at the collar. A sudden irrational thought sprang to mind. Someone whose neck bulged at the collar would of course define *clean* in the same way as Dan T. Campion.

"She used to live in Hollywood, your pal's lady friend," Tom Spellacy said. He surveyed his brother over the coffee cup he held in both hands. Looking to see if he scored a point, Desmond Spellacy thought.

"A place on Sierra Vista. When she took off, the only thing she left behind was a roll of nickel slugs. The kind you pump into a candy machine, you don't want to pay for your Oh Henry. They must've rolled under the bed, the slugs, she was in such a hurry to get out. She wasn't much on paying her rent, is the reason she left in such a hurry." Tom Spellacy handed a menu across the table. "You want some French toast? It's very good here, the French toast."

Desmond Spellacy shook his head.

"I saw your picture upstairs this morning. Outside the station manager's office. A nice glossy, hanging on the wall. Next to Edgar Bergen, and Charlie. 'The Rosary Hour,' it says underneath. 'The Right Reverend Desmond Spellacy.' Ed Gardner's hanging on the other side of you. You like Duffy's Tavern?"

"It's all right," Desmond Spellacy said. "I don't hear it that much."

Tom Spellacy picked up an imaginary telephone and spoke into it. " 'Duffy's Tavern, where the elite meet to eat, Archie the manager speaking, Duffy ain't here . . . Oh, hello, Duffy.' "

Desmond Spellacy wondered what Mrs. Morris at the Jury Commission saw in Tommy. It must be his child she was carrying. He supposed it would grow up to be a bad mimic with a thick neck.

"Tommy, you're a swell mimic, but that's not what I came here for, to hear you audition."

"Sorry, Des." Tom Spellacy smiled. "We were talking about your pal . . ."

"And the slugs, Tommy." Desmond Spellacy suddenly felt ashamed. Mrs. Morris at the Jury Commission had obviously made a greater effort to understand Tommy than he ever had. He wanted to ask Tommy about her, but there was no way. He hoped she was all right.

"The landlady found the slugs and kept them. She was one of those nosy numbers, you know what I mean? You pinch a pair of shoelaces, she's the first to know. A real pain in the ass. But she had these slugs and so we checked the telephone company. To see if any booths in that part of town were getting a lot of slugs when she was living there, the girl."

Tom Spellacy brushed the sugar he had spilled on the table into his hand with a paper napkin.

"To make a long story short, there were three pay phones getting stiffed regular, just a couple of blocks from where she lived. Two things the phones had in common. The first was the slugs stopped just around the time she took off."

Tom Spellacy paused and shook the sugar off his hand onto the floor.

Desmond Spellacy waited for him to continue. I wonder how Tommy would react if he knew that I had checked the Jury Commission. "And the second?"

"A grand total of fifty-seven calls to Counselor Campion, Attorney-at-Law. Your pal. Your former pal, I guess I should say now, him being in a state of mortal sin and all. Although that's just a guess, him being in a state of mortal sin. An educated guess."

"He has an alibi, Tommy." But he was thinking of

Mrs. Morris. Corinne. She was no longer working at the Jury Commission. I hope she has not aborted. What would I have said to her? Words. Things will be better. Bullshit.

My God, I am a terrible priest.

"And a swell one, too, Des. A K of C meeting. Two hundred harps all claiming they heard him sing, 'Mother Dear, Oh Pray for Me.' Just about the time his old girl friend there was getting cut."

Desmond Spellacy shuddered. That disembodied voice in the back seat of Dan Campion's Fleetwood. Now she was an "old girl friend." Now she was "cut."

"She got around the archdiocese, that girl," Tom Spellacy said. "She was mixed up with your other pal, too."

Desmond Spellacy did not have to ask who. Jack, of course. Why not? There were no more surprises.

"I met her," he said quietly.

"You what?" Tom said sharply.

"I was with Dan the day they met." She got around the archdiocese. A nice turn of phrase. With my pals. Even Sonny was involved. Sonny turned a dollar, burying her. A nice piece of change in the long run, that free thirty-footer.

"What happened?"

Desmond Spellacy explained. Del Mar. The Fleetwood. The hitchhiker. Tom Spellacy kept stirring his coffee, never taking his eyes off the milky-gray liquid. He did not look up until Desmond Spellacy finished.

"Jack know you met her?"

"I suppose."

"I bet I know what Dan Campion said to you. 'Go down and see your brother the policeman,' I bet he said."

Tommy never lacked shrewdness, Desmond Spellacy thought. Maybe that was one thing Mrs. Morris found appealing.

"And I bet he never came right out and said he was going to spring it. That you were with him, I mean. If he was picked up, I mean. And he had to start talking fast."

"That's not why I'm here, Tommy."

"Sure, Des."

"I can't remember what she looked like, Tommy."

"Swell, Des."

"Or anything about her. What she was wearing. Or if I even noticed."

"I'm glad to hear that, Des." Tom Spellacy folded his arms and pushed the chair back, scraping the polished aggregate floor of the cafeteria. "It was your pals that did the noticing."

Desmond Spellacy sucked in his breath. I can't let him get to me. I have to explain.

"Remember when the Cardinal got his red hat?"

"I don't remember that, no," Tom Spellacy said.

"Mabel Higgins gave him a reception."

"I wasn't invited."

"Eight years ago. And I can tell you what she was wearing. It had cabbage roses printed all over it. And she was wearing blue shoes with silver buckles. And the jewelry. Up and down both those skinny little arms. You know what Chet Hanrahan whispered to me? 'She'll be good for a million easy, when she kicks off.' For the archdiocese is what he meant, Chet. But she's still around. Not 'cut.' Not 'an old girl friend.' It's Chet who's gone, not Mabel Higgins. It was Chet I was talking to Dan about, all the time that girl was in the back seat. You remember, 'Put-A-Pool-In-A-Catholic-School'? That was Chet's slogan for the new gym at Immaculate Conception High. That's what I was talking to Dan about. He asked her didn't she think it was a grand slogan. She was Christian Science, she said." Desmond Spellacy looked at Tom. "But I don't remember what she looked like."

He's not buying, Desmond Spellacy thought. He thinks I'm pulling his chain.

"That's a swell story, Des. When you start feeling sorry for yourself, you can really bring a tear to the eye."

Maybe he's right, Desmond Spellacy thought. Maybe that's all it amounts to.

"Don't worry though," Tom said. "It won't get into the newspapers, your pal not being able to keep his pecker in his pants."

"That's not why I told you, Tommy, to keep it out of the papers."

"He's too useful, your pal."

It was Desmond Spellacy's turn to be surprised. "Dan?"

"To Fuqua," Tom Spellacy said. "They're tight as ticks, those two. Men of the world. Men of the world make mistakes, and it's not for the likes of me to work them over, if it's only a mistake and not Murder One."

"I still don't understand."

"It's simple, Des. When your pal's alibi checked out, he was pleased as punch, Fuqua. He takes him to lunch over to the Windsor there, a little Salisbury steak with some of that swell mustard dip on the side. And the au gratin potatoes and the Dutch apple pie. They're calling each other Dan and Fred by the time the bill comes. 'I'll take it, Dan.' 'No, I insist, Fred.' 'I'll get it next time then, Dan.' 'Grand,' says your old pal there. There'll be a nigger Pope before he ever lets Fuqua spring for his lunch."

"Why?" Because someone wanted something, he was certain of that. It was the way things worked. George Quinn wanted his son assigned to be a curate at Saint Basil's, so George Quinn volunteered his insurance agency to sponsor the Cardinal's Christmas mass. Why should it be any different in the police department?

"Because Fuqua wants to be chief. And your pal

knows all the members of the police commission. Sonny McDonough and them. A word here, a word there about what a swell job his new buddy Fred is doing. A grand policeman, and that's the truth. Fred knows how to keep his trap shut, is what he means, your pal."

"I didn't know that, Tommy."

"Sure, Des." Tom Spellacy stood up. "You wasted a swell story. It was all taken care of already."

There was nothing to say. Desmond Spellacy picked up the check and dropped a quarter tip on the table.

"You don't tip in cafeterias, Des," Tom Spellacy said. "And by the way, I heard from Mary Margaret."

# Twenty-one

"Hi, this is Barry Backer, 'Homicide Hotline,' KFIM, 1090 on your AM radio dial, 50,000 watts direct from our studios at the corner of Franklin and Cahuenga, who am I talking to?"

"Linda."

"Where you from, Linda?"

"Monterey Park."

"No kidding," Barry Becker said. He winked across the turntables at his guests. "We got a gang of biggies here today, Linda. First, Captain Fred Fuqua, chief of detectives in the greatest police department in the world. I guess you agree with that, right?"

"Right," Linda said.

"Then from the major crime section, Detective Lieutenant Thomas Spellacy, and he and Captain Fuqua will talk about, you guessed it, the Fazenda case . . ."

"Oh, that's swell, Barry," Linda said.

"May she rest in peace, right, Linda, right, gang?"

"Right," Linda said.

"RIP," Barry Backer said. "The saddest combination of letters in any alphabet I know of." He whistled mournfully, then said brightly, "Listen, enough of that deep stuff, this is Backer, and we're going to gab about clues, so you got some heavy listening coming your way the next hour . . . no, check that . . . the next fifty-seven-and-one-half-minutes, exactly. You still there, Linda?"

Linda laughed nervously into her telephone.

"Who do you want to talk to, hon?" Barry Backer said.

"Captain Fuqua," Linda said tentatively.

"They must teach you to pick the heavyweights out there in Monterey Park," Barry Backer said. He pointed to Fuqua. "Say hi to Linda, Fred."

Fuqua fingered his H-187 tiepin and cleared his throat. "Hi, Linda."

Barry Backer hit the cutoff button. "Don't clear your fucking throat on the air. You'll get your snot all over the mike." He winked at Fuqua, made a circle with his thumb and forefinger and went back live. "Shoot, Linda, one of those Monterey Park heavy questions."

"Well, Captain, I went to the dump out here in Monterey Park to get rid of my trash," Linda said. "The pickups are awful expensive, is the reason why—"

"Get to it, hon," Barry Backer said.

"Well, I found some . . . dainties . . . in a paper bag at the dump . . ."

"Ladies' personals is what you mean," Barry Backer said.

"That's right, Barry. And I was just wondering if . . . if . . . they might belong to . . . you know . . . and if

300

you ever thought the killer might come from Monterey Park . . ."

"Chamber of Commerce out there wouldn't like that, Linda," Barry Backer said. "Wow. Fred, what do you think?"

"I think I'll have Lieutenant Spellacy or one of his men check out the, uh . . . personals . . . to see if they might have belonged to the, uh . . . unfortunate victim . . ."

Swell, Tom Spellacy thought. Just what I want to do. Grab a few drinks with Linda and check some underwear she found in the dump. Sweet Jesus, call-in clues on a radio show.

". . . and as for the murderer coming from Monterey Park . . .", Fuqua struggled for an answer.

Barry Backer smoothly interrupted. "It's a possibility, Linda. A definite possibility. Hey, we got to go now, you leave your name and number and you will be hearing from . . . 'Homicide Hotline.'" He cut off Linda from Monterey Park and said, "Hey, gang, call in your clues, Madison 6433, we're going to a commercial now and when we get back, I want your calls stacked up, Madison 6433, remember that, Madison 6433, and now, see the USA in a Chevrolet from that smiling Irishman, Charlie Faye . . ."

Barry Backer ran a finger across his neck and the transcribed commercial for Faye Chevrolet went on the air.

"Pep it up a little, Fred. It's like your train's pulling out and you only got fifteen seconds to give her a hump. Wham, bam, thank you, ma'am, get it?"

Fuqua's face was crimson with embarrassment. "I'd like to make a personal appeal to the killer, Barry."

"Hey, swell, Fred," Barry Backer said. "After the calls, we're going to do it." He made a circle with his thumb and forefinger and smiled broadly. Fuqua beamed.

Barry Backer turned to Tom Spellacy. "I met your brother this morning. A real swell guy. And a swell priest. I'm going to broadcast the Cardinal's midnight mass at Christmas. Is that not a gang of giggles? A Jew from Chicago . . ."

Tom Spellacy nodded automatically. The real gang of giggles was when he told Des that Mary Margaret had written. Saint Barnabas had pronounced her fit to travel and she was arriving home Thursday. Des was expected to lunch on Sunday. She had decided not to wait until Kevin was discharged from the army, and as for Moira, Saint Barnabas said that using Des's influence to bring her home from the novitiate would be a mortal sin. Tell the monsignor, Mary Margaret wrote, I'm sure he'll understand.

"What do you call him?" Barry Backer said. "Your Majesty?"

"Your Eminence," Tom Spellacy said. She was always full of surprises, Mary Margaret. She had signed the letter, "Sincerely yours in Christ, Mary Margaret Spellacy," and then in parentheses had added, "(Maher)." Her maiden name.

"Hi, who's this?" Barry Backer said.

"I am 101,000 years old . . ." the voice began.

"Asshole," Barry Backer said, cutting the caller off. He winked at his guests. "We've got a seven-second air delay." Back on the air, he said, "Hey, gang, we just had someone call in and say he was 101,000 years old. It must be Danny, the dinosaur. It sure takes all kinds . . . Hi, who's this?"

"My name's Holly and I'm nineteen years old and I'm going back home to Ponca City, Oklahoma, where you find some real people."

"Why's that, Holly?"

"Because I came out here to experience the glamour and glitter and I found that this is a town without a heart and I'm going to tell everyone in Oklahoma that

302

if they don't want to end up like Lois Fazenda they better stay at home where there's some real people."

"Hey, you're a good kid, you find a swell fellow back there, right, Holly."

"Thanks, Barry."

"Gang, she's going to get married and have six kids. All those little sooners. But seriously, we've got some real people here, right, Fred?"

"Right, Barry."

"Tom Spellacy, what do you think, you think we got some real people out here in the KFIM 50,000-watt listening area?"

Tom Spellacy nodded.

"Hey, gang, Tom is just shaking his head up and down, up and down. Good fellow, Tom. A strong and silent type, he doesn't say much, but he is some kind of detective. And his brother . . ." Barry Backer whistled. "One of the really heavy priests around, Father Des Spellacy, right, Tom?"

"Right."

"Hey, he talks," Barry Backer said. "Hi, who's this?"

A voice said, "George. From La Puente. And I would like to ask Captain Fuqua what he thinks the breakthrough clue will be?"

"Hey, George, you're real people," Barry Backer said. "Too bad Holly, called in earlier, didn't meet you. Fred, that's a question I'd like the answer to myself."

Fuqua leaned close to the microphone. "George, I'm sure a shoe will solve this riddle."

"Hey, gang, hear that, a shoe," Barry Backer said. "Why's that, Fred?"

"Well, Barry," Fuqua said, "the murderer must've got blood on his shoes. That means he had to burn them, because a shoe-shine boy would have reported shining shoes with blood all over them."

"Right," Barry Backer said.

303

"And if you burn the shoes, you have to throw them away. That's what I like to call a definite pattern. So we are combing the garbage-disposal plants looking for burned and bloody shoes. I have put twenty-two uniformed officers on that detail. That's what I like to call the systems approach."

"You got it, George?" Barry Backer said. He pressed the cut-off button and said to Fuqua, "You're real people, too, Fred. My hunch is that Holly didn't hang in long enough. There's a lot more in the KFIM 50,000-watt listening area than glamour and glitter."

"Thanks, Barry," Fuqua said. He took a deep breath. "And I wonder if I might make a personal appeal to the killer of Lois Fazenda."

"Do it, Fred," Barry Backer said. "This is a first on 'Homicide Hotline.' The first personal appeal to a killer."

"Barry, I just want to ask the killer to turn himself in," Fuqua said. "We will listen to everything he has to say because it is a well-known fact that there are two sides to every story . . ."

Swell, Tom Spellacy thought. You cut her in two? Fuck it. She had it coming. It's a well-known fact that there are two sides to every story and her side isn't worth a shit.

"You know, Fred, I never thought of it that way," Barry Backer said. "I think you ought to transcribe that and the gang here at KFIM should run it every half-hour over the 50,000-watt listening area. What do you think about that?"

"That would be swell, Barry," Fuqua said. "I'll transcribe it any time of the day or night the gang here at KFIM sets it up."

"You're one reasonable guy, Fred," Barry Backer said.

"And if I may, Barry," Fuqua said, "I'd like to explain to the people in the 50,000-watt listening area just what the systems approach and the definite-pattern approach are."

"Do it," Barry Backer said. "Take all the time you want."

"Well, I have asked Lieutenant Spellacy and Lieutenant Crotty of the Major Crime Section to go over every report made so far on this case. I have also asked officers in every division to report any unusual occurrences that happened the night of the murder. Not just crimes, but disturbances. Accidents, speeding arrests, public drunkenness, narcotics violations—"

"Let me get this straight, Fred," Barry Backer said. He had a pocket comb in his hand and while he talked he shaped his hair. "You use . . . the systems approach . . . to try and find a . . . definite pattern."

Fuqua could not take his eyes off Barry Backer's comb. After a moment he said, "I couldn't put it better myself, Barry."

"Hey, that's some terrific approach," Barry Backer said. "But can you get down to specifics, Fred . . . if it doesn't get into a confidential area of your investigation, I mean."

"Barry, we are asking charwomen to report to us if they are missing any bristle scrub brushes," Fuqua said.

"That sounds like a long shot," Barry Backer said.

"Homicide investigations are a series of long shots," Fuqua said.

"You buy that, Tom?" Barry Backer said. He examined his hair in a pocket mirror.

"Yes." The Green Hornet will be chipping in with his two cents' worth soon, Tom Spellacy thought.

"The reason we do that, Barry, is because the victim's body was scrubbed with a bristle brush," Fuqua said.

"The things you guys have to think of," Barry Backer said. He pulled strands of hair from the teeth of his comb. "Hey, gang, we're in good hands, take it from

Barry. This is one dedicated bunch of guys I got here in the studio."

"And Barry, we're asking hatcheck girls to report to us if they saw the victim at any time the week before the murder," Fuqua said.

"Let me play detective for a minute," Barry Backer said. "The reason you're doing that is . . . she had to tip, right?"

"Right," Fuqua said.

"And someone had to give her the tip, right?" Barry Backer said. "A sugar-daddy type, maybe . . ."

"Right," Fuqua said. He had a broad smile on his face.

"And that sugar-daddy type just might have been the guy who . . ." Barry Backer said.

"Barry, you ought to be a detective in the Major Crime Section," Fuqua said.

"Swell," Tom Spellacy said.

"Let me ask you guys something," Barry Backer said. But first he leaned toward the microphone and whispered, "Hey, gang, I feel like Dick Grayson, also known as Robin, the Boy Wonder." To Fuqua he said, "Okay, Batman . . ."

Fuqua laughed. "It's a pleasure to be here with you, Barry."

"Swell," Tom Spellacy said.

"Seriously, guys," Barry Backer said, "let me try to add up what we got." On a piece of paper he wrote in large letters, "HAMBURGER SIDE OF FRIES COFFEE BLACK SUGAR," and held it up for the engineers in the control booth to see. "All the places she lived, we got to assume this chick was a transient, right?"

"Right," Fuqua said.

"And she liked guys, right? That's a given. She liked guys a lot. A whole lot." He whispered into the microphone, "I don't know how she missed me, gang, but she did." He held up another piece of paper on which he had written, "CHOP CHOP." To his guests he said, "And no one has ever come up with any of her clothes, positively speaking . . . unless Linda out there in Monterey Park hit on something with those personals, right?"

"Right," Fuqua said.

"And she was tied up, we know that because of the burns on her wrists and ankles," Barry Backer said. "Gang, that spells captive to me; how do you spell it?"

Fuqua said smoothly, "That's exactly how I spelled it to the Major Crime Section, Barry . . ."

The only thing you spelled, Tom Spellacy thought, was c-h-i-e-f when you looked at yourself shaving this morning. The only other thing you said was get to the station a half-hour before the broadcast, because you can't go to the bathroom while you're on the air.

"Tom Spellacy, who do you think killed Lois?" Barry Backer asked.

If I knew who killed her, one place I wouldn't be is here, Tom Spellacy said to himself.

"I'd like to answer that for Tom," Fuqua said.

"Hey, Fred, I can't say you hate air time," Barry Backer said. "Shoot, buddy. You don't mind do you, Tom?"

Fuqua did not seem to notice the barb. "First, I think I can say without reservation that the murderer is one of two things. . . ."

"We're all ears, buddy," Barry Backer said.

"The murderer is either a one-time pickup," Fuqua said, "or an individual who was acquainted with the victim and knew she would not be missed."

"That's narrowing it down," Barry Backer said. The director in the control booth made a signal for thirty more seconds.

"I think we can also say without reservation," Fuqua said, "that the crime was perpetrated in a permanent abode in a remote area."

"Hey, now we're getting somewhere, Fred," Barry Backer said. "When you say . . . permanent abode . . . you mean a . . . house, right?"

"Right, Barry," Fuqua said. "Not a hotel or a motel or an apartment or a rooming house. A permanent abode."

"Because in an apartment, someone would have heard something or seen something, right?" Barry Backer said.

"Right," Fuqua said.

"And it had to be in a remote area for the same reason, right?" Barry Backer said. The director said ten seconds.

"I call it the remote-area approach," Fuqua said.

"That's a swell thing to call it," Barry Backer said. "Hey, gang, we got to go to five minutes of up-to-the-minute KFIM news. Stay tuned to the next half-hour of 'Homicide Hotline' with our special guests Fred Fuqua and Tom Spellacy, a couple of heavyweights. See you in five. Where's my fucking coffee?"

Fuqua blanched, then when he saw Barry Backer's smile realized they were no longer on the air. A young woman came into the studio and filled Barry Backer's cup. He ran his hand up the inside of her leg until it disappeared into her skirt. A dreamy expression came over the girl's face. She did not offer coffee to either Fuqua or Tom Spellacy.

"The next half-hour," Barry Backer said, "let's talk about the guy who did it."

Fuqua's eyes were riveted on Backer's hand. "How do you know it's a guy?" Tom Spellacy said finally.

Barry Backer removed his hand from the girl's skirt and picked up his coffee cup. It was stenciled with the initials B.B. and a microphone in the shape of a woman's breast. "You're trying to tell me it's a dyke?"

"I'm trying to tell you it's a possibility," Tom Spellacy said. "We haven't found any clothes, we haven't

308

found any baggage, we haven't found any cosmetics. She dropped out of sight two weeks before she was killed. She had to be staying somewhere. Somewhere where she could find clothes and cosmetics."

"Another woman," Barry Backer said.

"I always thought she was butch," the girl said.

"Go get some sugar," Barry Backer told the girl. She sighed petulantly and flounced out of the studio. "You're going to say that on the air, she was lez?"

"No, he's not going to say that," Fuqua said quickly.

"Why not?" Tom Spellacy said.

"Because I'm doing the Cardinal's fucking mass," Barry Backer said. "Because it's a family station. Because your brother does 'The Rosary Hour,' that's what kind of station it is. Because I got the highest Hooper in my time period and I didn't get it talking about a bunch of dykes."

Tom Spellacy was beginning to enjoy himself for the first time all morning. "We could check all the dyke doctors."

"Look, I don't give a shit if she licked every snatch in town." Barry Backer's voice was still rising. "Just don't say it on my show."

"And the dyke butchers," Tom Spellacy said. "That'd explain how she got cut up so neat."

"You're dangerous is what you are," Barry Backer said. "I let you on the air with that, I'll be back sweeping out the studio at a 100-watter in Ponca City, Oklahoma, with Holly there."

Fuqua twisted in his chair and stared at Tom Spellacy. "Barry's doing a hell of a job and you're trying to fuck him up."

Tom Spellacy shook his head. "No, I just want to get things straight. What we're looking for is a family killer for a family station, right?"

"Cut the smart crap," Barry Backer said. "I make the jokes on this show."

The joke on this show, Tom Spellacy thought, is the way Fuqua's going to become chief. With Barry Backer and Dan Campion as his two leading supporters.

"You got something else we could fill up the time with?" Barry Backer asked Fuqua. "Besides a lot of dirty talk about lezees."

Fuqua glared at Tom Spellacy. "We could use the green cards, Barry."

"What green cards?" Tom Spellacy said sharply.

"It's a new clue." Fuqua ignored Tom Spellacy and addressed his answer to Backer. "Hasn't been in the papers yet."

"And you've been sitting on it?" Tom Spellacy said. "Should I tell the gang downtown to tune in? Or let them read it in the papers? Maybe Dan Campion can fill them in."

"I don't need your cheap shit, Spellacy," Fuqua said. "And why aren't you wearing your tiepin?"

Barry Backer banged his cup down on the table, splashing coffee all over himself. "What the fuck are you talking about? I got a show going back live in another two minutes, for Chrissake, and you're talking about tiepins and green cards. Why not blue cards, for Chrissake? Mauve cards. What the fuck are green cards?"

"They're the work papers Mexicans need to get across the border, Barry," Fuqua said.

"A simple question," Barry Backer said. He was trying to be calm and reasonable. "And maybe you can answer it in the next ninety seconds before we go back live." He took a deep breath. "There was this cunt cut in two, right? Now all of a sudden, I find myself up to my ass in lezees and Mexicans. *No habla Español. No comprende* what the Mexicans got to do with this broad."

"The cards were in her suitcase, Barry," Fuqua said.

"Where?" Tom Spellacy said.

"At the railroad station."

"I checked baggage claim myself."

"Well, you did a lousy job," Fuqua said. "It was in Lost and Found. The bag fell off a shelf this morning and cracked open. The cards were in it and some letters, clothes . . ."

"Sixty seconds, guys," Barry Backer said, checking the studio clock.

"Sixteen thousand green cards," Fuqua said. "All forged. Not a bad job, but you find 16,000 cards, you got to figure forgery."

"What do they go for, forged?" Barry Backer kept his eye on the clock.

"What the traffic will bear," Tom Spellacy said. Forged green cards. Where had he heard them mentioned. "Ten dollars, twenty, maybe more, you don't flood the market with them down south."

"In other words, there's a couple of hundred grand in that suitcase," Barry Backer said. "How did she get it?"

"She could've been a courier," Tom Spellacy said. "She had nice tits. They check the tits, not the bag at the border."

"Then she stiffed somebody," Barry Backer said.

"Or maybe she just lost the bag," Fuqua said.

"Somebody stood to make a killing," Barry Backer said. "And maybe that somebody knocked her off, when that dumb broad decided to pull a fast one . . ."

"We'll find that somebody, Barry," Fuqua said.

"Ten seconds," the director said from the control booth.

Barry Backer could hardly contain himself. "Nobody knows this, right?"

"Right, Barry," Fuqua said. "You're going to break it first."

Suddenly Tom Spellacy started to laugh. Now it came back to him. Turd Turner. If. If. If. He must be

311

having a good laugh someplace, Turd, telling me about the green cards.

"What's so funny, Spellacy?" Fuqua demanded.

"Nothing, Captain."

". . . four, three, two, one," the director said.

"Hi, gang," Barry Backer said. "Backer's back, and clean the wax out of your ears, because you got some heavy listening coming your way the next half-hour. . . ."

## Twenty-two

On Thursday Mary Margaret Spellacy arrived on the 2:31 bus from Camarillo. Tom Spellacy met her at the Greyhound Terminal, picked up her suitcase, kissed her on the cheek and remarked on how well she looked. She wore a dress she had bought with clothing stamps in 1943, her hair was bobbed and she had taken to wearing rimless glasses. Her face was pleasant and un-lined, as if it had been sculpted from a loaf of damp bread, and her square, somewhat squashed figure looked, as always, like a cake about to fall. Mary Margaret said that Tom looked peaked. They drove to the house in the Valley, where Mary Margaret pro-ceeded to open all the windows, air the linen, change the beds, vacuum the living room, clean the stove, rinse out the toilets, do the laundry and dust the statue of the Infant of Prague. She never mentioned that the house seemed scarcely lived in. That evening in honor of her homecoming and at her request Tom Spellacy spent three minutes on top of his wife. Friday morning he drove her to the Safeway where she bought eggs, bacon, milk, butter, coffee, sugar, oil, vinegar, bread, ketchup, mustard, a pint jar of mayonnaise, a leg of lamb, two pounds of ground round, three pieces of haddock, watermelon, sweet corn, gelatin, marshmallows, carrots, a cucumber, spinach, a package of Ivory Snow, six bars of Cashmere Bouquet and a box of Oxydol. Friday evening Tom Spellacy said he had to work late. He worked through the night watch and into the lobster trick and by the time he returned home shortly before dawn Saturday he knew the name of Lois Fazenda's killer. He did not entrust this information to anyone. Saturday night he also worked late. On Sunday Desmond Spellacy arrived for dinner.

"You remember my pa, Monsignor," Mary Margaret Spellacy said as she dished out the vegetables. "Mister Maher, you always called him. Eugene Maher is what his name was, but everyone called him Mister Maher. Except Monsignor Shea over to Saint Anatole's. My pa used to take the collection at the ten and every Sunday the monsignor would say, 'How'd we do this morning, Eugene?' And my pa would always tell him. You never kept anything back from Monsignor Shea. 'Shake the basket at them, Eugene,' if they wasn't big enough, the collections. He'd send my pa back up again if they wasn't big enough. That's how he got the job at the ten, my pa. The monsignor told Owen Curry to go up one Sunday and Owen was too embarrassed, and the monsignor said, 'That's the last time you'll ever take up a collection in this parish, Owen Curry.' Loud, you know, so that everyone at the ten could hear. 'Eugene Maher, take up the collection again.' And so there was my pa every Sunday at the ten, shaking the basket to see if there was anything but coins in it. Nickels, dimes and quarters, you know. And if that's all he heard, the

313

jingling of coins, back up he'd go. The center aisle first, so everyone could see him. Then the side aisles. He did a grand job at the ten, my pa. Mr. Maher, he was a bookkeeper, you know. At the Water Company. He had grand penmanship. The Palmer method is what he used. Palmer penmanship it was called. It's a grand asset, good penmanship, if you're going to be a book-keeper, and that's a well-known fact. The Italians don't have good penmanship. It's all those vowels their names end in, I think. It's hard to have good penmanship when you're making vowels all the time. A, E, I, O, U."

Desmond Spellacy nodded.

"And sometimes Y," Mary Margaret Spellacy said. "Like in pygmy. There's no vowels in a word like pygmy, so they use Y. There's a lot of short Italians they could call pygmies if they wanted to . . ."

Tom Spellacy stifled a cough for fear it would in-terrupt Mary Margaret's monologue. He did not want her to address her conversation to him. She's nuttier than the day she went in, he thought. A, E, I, O, U. And sometimes Y. Des looks like he's been hit on the head with a hammer. He wasn't bargaining on an Italian pygmy, I bet.

". . . cancer of the rectum is what she had," Mary Margaret Spellacy said. The segue from short Italians to a malignant rectum had escaped Tom Spellacy. Nor was he about to ask who was so afflicted. He picked up the rhythm of Des's nodding and in perfect synch began to bob his head up and down vigorously. "When she came out from under the ether, she said she was going to offer it up. She had that little bag, you know, which is what you get with cancer of the rectum. I don't know if that would be such a grand thing to offer up, the little bag. Although you offer up what you have, I suppose. And never a complaint out of her. I remember when the doctor said he was going to take

314

out the stitches the following Sunday. 'Goody, goody,' she said, 'Trinity Sunday . . .' "

Tom Spellacy tuned her out again. An occasional nod was all that Mary Margaret would need to make her think he was still listening. It was funny how things turned out sometimes. Fuqua and Mary Margaret. In a way, they were responsible for him putting it all together. The last two people in the world, he would have thought.

The green cards. That was a laugh on Fuqua. Fuqua who had not wanted him to go to San Quentin for Turd Turner's execution.

Who had insisted that Turd Turner was a nobody.

The implication being that a nobody deserved to die alone.

He remembered the holding cell down the corridor from the gas chamber.

And the cheap rye in the paper cup.

And the way Turd Turner tried to make himself out a desperado instead of the fuckup he was.

That bank job in Inglewood, Turd Turner had said. That was me.

And the hit in North Hollywood.

And the green cards.

The forged green cards.

I bet you didn't know that, Turd Turner had said.

No.

I was running them down to Mexico for Jack A.

Is that right?

Good stuff. The best. Jack was getting a hundred clams each for them from the Mexicans in Tijuana is what I hear. You got to hand it to Jack. He's got a real nice thing going with those taco heads. First he sells them the phony papers and then he gives them a job shoveling shit to pay for them. A dollar a day and a lifetime to pay. That's a Mexican's idea of heaven.

Then the rye was gone and they had embraced and

eight hours later in the presence of fourteen witnesses, Horace Turner had died in accordance with the laws of the state of California and he had not thought of the green cards again until Barry Backer refused to talk about lesbians on the family radio station that was going to broadcast the Cardinal's midnight mass at Christmas.

He should have told Fuqua, but he didn't. Fuqua was too busy telling everyone in the 50,000-watt listening area how smart he was, and Barry Backer was saying, Listen, gang, this is an exclusive, like he was Front Page Farrell. Fuck them both. One thing he was not going to do if he could help it, and that was make Fuqua chief. Sit on the green cards, check out Turd Turner's story, Jack wasn't going anywhere. There was the other side, too. With the history he and Jack had together, he had better be sure Jack was involved, a lot more sure than he was now. Brenda had said Jack was clean, and Brenda didn't owe Jack any favors. Sure Jack knew the girl and sure he was probably hip deep in the green cards—that was the sort of operation that would appeal to him—but the two together didn't necessarily add up to Murder One. Only that he liked to fuck and that he liked to make money and he wasn't too choosy about how he made it. Killing the girl was stupid and Jack had never drawn a stupid breath in his life. Nor had he ever confused a fuck with grand passion. This whole business was too neat, too much like a story on the radio, and it had been from the start. There were no loose ends, everything seemed to be connected, and that was what bothered him. Usually you locked your desk and you went home and you worried about the termites in the ceiling or the dry rot in the avocado trees or whether your medical insurance covered the piles. The hemorrhoids growing like acorns in your ass had nothing to do with a cute little number who had a rose tattooed above her bush and who just happened to be cut in two. Not this time. Everything was mixed in together. You talked about Turd Turner, then you had to talk about Corinne. You talked about Jack, you were probably talking about Des, too. Knock on Brenda's door and there was Mickey Gagnon, watch Fuqua take a leak and there was Dan Campion shaking Fuqua's dick. Crotty's Chinamen were probably in there, too, you looked hard enough.

No. That wasn't how things worked. He knew there were those who would say he was trying to cover his own ass. Fuqua, for one. Maybe he was. It would be nice to roust Jack, to make him sweat, to watch the Cardinal drop him like he was a mortal sin, but let someone else stick his neck out. Not me, not yet. A hint here, a hint there and the green card story would come out. When that time comes, sit back and enjoy it. Until then, be cautious, move slow.

All things considered, the way it turned out, a wise choice.

". . . he's sucking his skim milk through a straw, Monsignor, is what they tell me," Mary Margaret Spellacy said. Someone else at death's door, Tom Spellacy mused. She was always the first to know when the bladder didn't work or the bowels didn't move. "The arteries are so hard the blood goes banging through like he's a pinball machine. A ballroom dancer is what he wanted to be. With a roomful of gold cups from the Harvest Moon Ball. The waltz was always his favorite. But he had a hard time getting partners, with the cock eye. If it wasn't for the cock eye, the arteries would be soft as spaghetti, I bet. Because dancing is good for the veins. Blood like marbles, and you can blame it all on the wall eye. Which comes from Scully side of the family . . ."

Tom Spellacy wondered who the wall-eyed Scullys were but nodded at Mary Margaret anyway. There was a shrewdness beneath that chatter somewhere. I think we should have relations, Mary Margaret had said Thursday night. Relations. It had been two years since he heard that word and he had almost forgotten the dread it made him feel. When Corinne said "relations," she was talking about an uncle or a cousin. Someone whose name he did not have to remember. What you did in bed was fuck. It had nothing to do with relating. Maybe Corinne was the reason Mary Margaret wanted to have relations. The house obviously had not been much occupied the two years she was in Camarillo. I had to be living somewhere. Somewhere I was probably having relations. Perhaps Mary Margaret just wanted to establish that she was home. And the best way to establish it was to have relations.

The idea wasn't bad, he supposed. Just the execution.

For one thing, when he was on top of her, he thought of Corinne. Not that thinking of someone else was unusual. Often when he was on top of Corinne, he had thought of Brenda, or the girl in the Ponds ad. But when he thought of them he only thought how nice it would be to have them there, telling him how terrific he was, the best they ever had. Especially the girl in the Ponds ad, in her strapless formal. He never even wanted the girl in the Ponds ad to take off her gardenia corsage. When he thought of Corinne, in the three minutes he was on top of Mary Margaret, he remembered he had not picked up the clothes at her apartment. There was a pair of blue slacks and a brown suit and a couple of shirts and the Jockey shorts she had bought at the mid-month men's furnishings sale at Bullock's and he remembered that he had not tried to find out where she had moved or whether she had had the scrape or what she was doing or how she was getting along and he remembered how relieved he was when she said she always cut her losses and first it made him feel badly that he was relieved and then he felt

318

guilty and then he came and then he said to himself, Fuck it, never again.

It was a performance he did not want to repeat. Better to work late than to repeat it.

And so he stayed late Friday night. Stayed until he was sure Mary Margaret was asleep, lost somewhere in the folds of her flannel nightgown. The bullpen cleared out, the telephones did not ring, the teletype machine was silent except for an occasional clatter. A code 8 on West 57th Place. A 415 on the 2700 block of Hoover. A 211 on Arlington. A 447 on Devonshire. He opened the file drawers and took the manila folders back to his cubicle. The fluorescent lights made the flimsy partitions an even more sickly green than they were in the daytime. He spread the first pile of folders on his desk and stacked the others on the floor, each pile sagging under its own weight: interrogation reports, psychiatric reports, telephone logs, field investigations, confessions, statements, watch reports, end-of-tour reports, yellow sheets, fingerprint records, incident reports, arrest records, photographs, tip files, lead files, M.O. jackets, nickname files, witnesses, suspects, informers, snitches, paper, paper and more paper. The systems approach. A search for a definite pattern. Although it was not exactly what Fuqua had in mind. The systems approach to pass the time until Mary Margaret was asleep and he would not have to raise the flannel nightgown over her thighs and think about Corinne.

Let Fuqua worry about the green cards. That was a story he already knew. Let Fuqua find the thread of connections and sew them all together like buttons on a suit. He would read and not fuck his wife. The language in the reports was restful, so anonymous that it removed personality. Suspect. Perpetrator. Vehicle. Apprehended. Weapon. Surveillance. Residence. Caucasian. Male. Female. The murderer was a well-built male who

319

hated women, said the first police psychiatrist. The murderer was a well-built female who hated women, said the second police psychiatrist. The murderer was impotent. The murderer was potent. He read on. The murderer was a midget. The murderer was a twin. He ordered coffee. The murderer was a lesbian. The murderer was a child molester. He ordered a ham and cheese on rye, but when the sandwich came on whole wheat he did not eat it. The cheese curled and hardened and the bread went stale. A chief petty officer confessed, a Negro waitress accused, a deputy sheriff in Riverside County arrested. Charges dismissed.

At 11:30 he called home. Mary Margaret answered on the second ring. She said she was going to say her prayers and go to bed. Shortly after midnight he went to the all-night cafeteria on Temple. He had pot roast, mashed potatoes, gravy, apple cobbler and three cups of coffee. A drunk was asleep at a corner table. The drunk was only wearing one shoe. Tom Spellacy stared at him for a long time before he finally realized what was missing. He wondered how long he had overlooked the missing shoe. He blamed the reports for the oversight. They boiled all life's aberrations down into simple declarative sentences. The complexities were removed, the questions sandpapered away. "Subject is female Caucasian, thirty-seven years old, known only as Dildo Dot." Why was the subject only known as Dildo Dot? In the report she was no different than Mabel Leigh Horton. Female, Caucasian, age unknown. Tommy Diamond, Raymond F. Rafferty, Leland K. Standard, they were all the same. Harold Pugh, Shopping Cart Johnson, Gloria Deane, Ida Parnell, Sammy Barron, Timothy Mallory. Maybe Fuqua was right. The only way you could find a definite pattern was to plane away the knots of identity, the quirks that muddled the perception with likes and dislikes and knowing. Back in his cubicle he picked up the incident reports from the night of the murder. Armed robbery. Misdemeanor assault. Grand theft auto. Rape. Assault with a deadly weapon. Lewd conduct. Indecent exposure. The unusual occurrences of a usual night. Drunk and disorderly. Disturbing the peace. Animal bite. Arson. Burglary. Petty theft. Abandoned vehicle. Prowler. Missing child. Brush fire. Drunk driving. Dead body.

One o'clock. He wondered if Mary Margaret were asleep. The thought of her flannel nightgown made him wide awake. He picked up another end-of-tour report. Turned in by Bingo McInerney and Lorenzo Jones the night of the murder. He turned the pages of the report, wondering what it would be like working with Lorenzo. Lorenzo, whose brass was always polished and whose leather always shined. Who changed the sweatband in his cap every month. Who always used a Scripto pencil because wooden pencils broke and who always carried an extra package of lead. Whose neat square printing was perfectly matched to the unadorned language of the report. Who was going to law school at night and who Bingo thought was a pain in the ass . . .

And then Tom Spellacy had seen it.

The one thing no one had considered.


"Marshmallows is nice in molded salad," Mary Margaret Spellacy said. "Not the big kind you roast, but the little kind. Like buttons, but soft. Because they're marshmallows. Some people like the lime mold now, but I still like the strawberry. Monsignor doesn't like the lime, Tom, I'm sure of that. That's why we're having the strawberry, Monsignor. Your pa never liked strawberries, though. That's one thing I remember about him. It was the palsy he had. He couldn't keep them on the spoon, the strawberries. You don't have good balance when you've got the palsy, and that's a well-known fact. Palsy people have got bad balance. He was such a grand man, your pa. Never missed a wake. He'd be sitting

321

there in his folding chair, spilling strawberries if they gave him any. . . ."

It suddenly came to Desmond Spellacy. Mary Margaret wasn't crazy after all. She knew his father never had palsy. The reason Phil Spellacy never missed a wake was because the booze was free and there was plenty of it. Mary Margaret knew perfectly well that Phil Spellacy was only a drunk with the shakes, knew it, but still she called it palsy. Not out of any sense of delicacy either, Desmond Spellacy bet. She's just opted out. That torrent of conversation about bowel movements and Sunday collections and cock-eyed ballroom dancers was just a wall she could hide behind so that no one could ever touch her again.

He wondered if she even believed in Saint Barnabas.

How wonderful if Saint Barnabas were only an elaborate joke that freed her from the responsibility of making contact.

Take Moira. Moira wasn't fat. Saint Barnabas said Moira was a stylish stout, and all the better saints were stylish stouts. Caloric theology, Desmond Spellacy thought. He watched Mary Margaret remove her glasses. The nosepiece had worn deep grooves into either side of her nose. Desmond Spellacy wanted to knead the nose as if it were a sausage, removing the indentations. She was still a pretty woman. For a moment he felt the same sense of wonder about her he had felt twenty years before. He was sure he could get behind the wall, but then what? He knew that for Mary Margaret it was the world outside that was imprisoned, not herself. He tried to remember when she had first concocted Saint Barnabas. Probably when she discovered that Tommy was fooling around. And I bet she knows he was a bagman, too, he mused.

A philandering husband and a two-hundred-pound daughter.

Better to invent Saint Barnabas than to deal with them.

Not to mention Kev, the oldest. Kev who tended to break wind when he got nervous. Now a chaplain's assistant awaiting discharge. Desmond Spellacy hoped the general never came to call on the chaplain. It might make Kev nervous.

"Undertaking would be nice for Kev when he gets out of the service," Mary Margaret Spellacy said. "It's a grand business and you always wear a tie. Not like some businesses. Arithmetic teachers don't wear ties, I'm told. It's a new thing, not wearing a tie if you're an arithmetic teacher. My second cousin, Raymond Dennehy, was in the undertaking business and he always wore a tie. The trick kind that you clipped onto your collar. He was a driver, Raymond. 'Hearse' Dennehy, they called him. He wore a boutonniere, too, along with his trick tie. You know what a boutonniere is, don't you, Monsignor?"

Desmond Spellacy nodded.

"It's one of those flowers the spiffs used to wear in their buttonholes," Mary Margaret Spellacy explained. "Carnations, usually. Although my cousin, Hearse, always wore an anemone. They were cheaper than carnations is why the Hearse always wore anemones. He liked molded salads, too, Hearse. Strawberry, like the monsignor does, Tom. You remember how he died. At a funeral. One minute he was there and the next minute he was gone. They took off his trick tie but it was too late. . . ."

For a moment Desmond Spellacy wondered who had replaced Hearse Dennehy behind the wheel. In a certain way he could see the point of Mary Margaret's world. It was so restful. There was no Dan T. Campion to contend with, no Seamus Fargo. That was the real world. Desmond Spellacy put a napkin to his mouth and sneaked a look at his brother across the table.

Tommy's a million miles away. I wonder if he's thinking about Mrs. Morris at the Jury Commission. No, probably not. I do enough of that for the both of us. He supposed the reason she touched him so much was that she was the first of Tommy's girls he knew anything about. Other than Mary Margaret. It was just hard to think of Mary Margaret as one of Tommy's girls. Desmond Spellacy balanced a pickled peach on his fork and smiled and nodded at Mary Margaret. She had left Morty Donnelly holding Hearse Dennehy's trick tie and seemed to have segued into the Pope. It was best not to try to make a connection. Just a periodic nod until you picked up a thread. There it was. The Holy Year in the Holy City. The Pontiff. Mary Margaret seemed to have taken up calling the Pope the Pontiff. She used to call him Pacelli. And sometimes the Italian. He wondered what good deed Pacelli had performed to escalate himself into the Pontiff in Mary Margaret's affections. It seemed to have something to do with Hearse Dennehy. The Holy Year. That was it. Morty Donnelly was going to Rome for the Holy Year. Wearing Hearse Dennehy's trick tie. He had it now. Two brisk nods and a furrowed brow to satisfy Mary Margaret. Then a mental summons to Mrs. Morris at the Jury Commission. Mrs. Morris had a face. While the other girls Tommy brought into the confessional were only blank receptacles for his adulteries. He tried to remember the face. She had worn a scarf in her hair. And there were large brown eyes. He remembered them as sad but perhaps he was reading that into them. And Mrs. Morris had a voice. Goddamn you, she had said, you talk less about sin than any priest I have ever met. A thought pierced his reverie: My God, I think a lot about the uterine mysteries for a priest. The Sorrowful Mysteries, the Glorious Mysteries and now the Uterine Mysteries added to the ecclesiastical canon. He didn't suppose Pacelli would think much of that. So that was it. The envy of Tommy was a sexual envy. And all these years Tommy must have sensed it. Why else would he bring his adulteries into my confessional. Tommy. Tommy. Tommy. How difficult it is for us to love one another. If only there were a spiritual laxative to purge our guilts. Seamus Fargo would have laughed at that. Seamus didn't believe in guilt. One man, one soul, that's more than enough to worry about, Seamus was fond of saying. Still, there was no getting around it: sexual envy was a subject he would have liked taking up with Seamus in confession. Nothing ever seemed to surprise Seamus in the box. He listened. Listening was the secret of forgiveness, he had once heard Seamus say. This from a man who detested Freud. He would like to tell Seamus that Freud was the ultimate listener. Well, there wasn't much chance of that now.

". . . What I always wonder," Mary Margaret Spellacy said, "is if the Pontiff has a favorite radio program. Like, 'The Rosary Hour,' Tom. If the Pontiff lived here, he could tune in KFIM and listen to the Monsignor on 'The Rosary Hour.' And 'Fibber McGee and Molly,' too. McGee, that's a Catholic name. 'Amos 'n' Andy' are colored. They don't have many colored in Italy. 'Our Father, who art in heaven, hallowed be Thy name. Thy kingdom come, Thy will be done, on earth as it is in heaven.' It's like listening to a good tune when you say the rosary, Monsignor. 'Give us this day our daily bread.' Bing Crosby couldn't do it any better. 'And forgive us our trespasses as we forgive those who trespass against us.' If the Pontiff lived here, this would be the Holy City. And we could have the Holy Year right here. The Coliseum would be a grand place. Morty Donnelly would like that. He's got season tickets to all the games. You could do 'The Rosary Hour' at the Coliseum, Monsignor. With Bing Crosby. Bing would help out, it being the Holy Year and all . . ."

Desmond Spellacy smiled wanly. Me and Bing. A

perfect parlay, Monsignor Fargo would say. He shivered involuntarily. Even thinking about Seamus Fargo made him feel ashamed. He looked across the table. Tom Spellacy was staring at him. He probably thinks it's Mary Margaret who's making me jumpy, Desmond Spellacy thought. He probably thinks I can fire eighty-year-old monsignors without losing any sleep over it. The funny thing was, Tommy was almost right. Six months ago he wouldn't have lost any sleep over it. Six weeks ago even. It was all in a day's work. No Seconal needed to make him sleep like a baby.

Six weeks ago, he thought. That eternity ago before I made my armistice with life . . .

". . . It was a meal fit for the Queen of Spain," Mary Margaret Spellacy said. It seemed to Desmond Spellacy that he had missed a transition between the Holy Year and the Spanish royal family. "That she can be such a grand cook with all the sadness she's had to offer up. You remember her son John, Monsignor? Him that used to be His Eminence's favorite altar boy. He married a Polish girl. With all the advantages he had . . ."

Thank God for Mary Margaret, Desmond Spellacy thought. Her only concern was how to keep away from the Poles and the Italians. He tried to concentrate on the malefactions of the Cardinal's favorite altar boy, but the face of Seamus Fargo kept distracting his attention. It was not so much firing Seamus last night that bothered him, only the way it was done. At the Saint Thomas Aquinas Guild dinner. That had been the Cardinal's idea. The perfect time, the perfect place, the Cardinal had said, to announce a well-deserved retirement. After all the Guild was honoring Seamus for sixty years of exemplary service to the Church. An occasion for which the honorary chairman of the evening was His Eminence Hugh Cardinal Danaher and the principal speaker the Parachuting Padre himself, the Right Reverend Monsignor Desmond Spellacy, Legion of Merit,

Purple Heart, U.S. Army Commendation Medal, European Theater of Operations ribbon with four battle stars.

Not the kind of hit men ordinarily found on a dais.

Nevertheless.

Desmond Spellacy would wager that Seamus did not have much of a say in those selections. That was Dan T. Campion's work. Dan T. Campion was the program chairman and master of ceremonies. Which gave the evening a particularly detestable off-color shade. Sacking Seamus after trying to save Dan T. Campion—to Desmond Spellacy it was an obscene trade-off. And he had kept his mouth shut.

That was the worst obscenity of all.

Now it was Dan Campion intruding on his thoughts. Winking. Wearing his master-of-ceremonies tuxedo. Shooting his cuffs and telling Irish stories. Dan T. Campion had winked at Desmond Spellacy at the no-host bar. "Thanks, Des, you did a grand job with your brother the policeman and I appreciate it." Another wink and Dan Campion was sliding down the bar, shaking hands, moving in on Sonny McDonough and Harry Pottle. Not coincidentally both members of the Select Commission picking the new police chief. "You ask Des's brother, the policeman, he'll tell you what a grand officer Fred Fuqua is." So Tommy was right. Dan Campion was campaigning for Fuqua. "He reminds me of Teddy Roosevelt when he was police commissioner in New York." Dan Campion linked his arms to Sonny McDonough and Harry Pottle so that they could not move. "And we all know how far TR went, with his being such a grand commissioner. Fred Fuqua is the one, I'm telling you, and that's a fact. FF is what they'll be calling him before he's through, you mark my words. Like they called Teddy TR. You can fault Dan Campion on a lot of things, but you can't fault Dan Campion on one thing. Dan Campion has always been able to spot a comer. And I spotted Fred Fuqua just the way I spotted Des Spellacy, before he even knew where the front was on his Roman collar . . ."

The guest of honor arrived with the Cardinal. Desmond Spellacy wondered if he had only imagined the wary look on Seamus Fargo's face. Picking Seamus up at Saint Basil's in his own limousine was another idea of Hugh Danaher's. Showing his respect for an old friend was the way the Cardinal had put it. A way to keep Monsignor Fargo on a tight rein was more like it. "Good evening, Monsignor," Seamus Fargo had said. "Good evening, Monsignor," Desmond Spellacy had said. "I notice your friend, Mr. Amsterdam, is not here this evening, Monsignor," Seamus Fargo had said. Desmond Spellacy had smiled. You had to hand it to Seamus. He would go down with all guns firing. Sitting on the dias he was impassive. Never once a smile at Dan T. Campion's master-of-ceremonies jokes. Saint Patrick. The Mother Superior. The Catholic priest and the Jewish rabbi. The Catholic priest and the Protestant minister. The Catholic priest, the Jewish rabbi and the Protestant minister. Not the kind of stories designed to tickle Monsignor Fargo's funny bone. Desmond Spellacy checked the notes for his speech. Also not designed to amuse Monsignor Fargo. First the obligatory nod to the Protestants in the audience. Who were always called our Protestant brethren in Christ. Then friendship and common cause. The muck and the mire. No atheists in the foxholes. It was an easy transition to Seamus. A fighter in the trenches of Catholicism. A combat veteran of sixty years. Decorated by the Church. A hero in the eyes of God. An example to those younger priests of the archdiocese who were ready to take over the reins from their elders.

That was where Seamus had started and stared. He knew the jig was up then. The well-deserved retirement was only a paragraph away. All the amenities were observed. Monsignor Fargo shook Monsignor Spellacy's hand. Monsignor Fargo thanked Hugh Danaher. And his Protestant brethren in Christ. He said there were others more worthy of the honors and accolades he had received. He would strive to be an example. There was no retirement for a priest. He was always a servant of the Lord in whatever niche the Cardinal archbishop had hollowed out for him. Applause. Handshakes. The bargaining had begun in the automobile ride back to Saint Basil's. Desmond Spellacy sat in the front seat, the Cardinal and Monsignor Fargo in the rear.

My nephew, Seamus Fargo had said. Richard.

Yes, the Cardinal had said.

He's been a curate for eleven years. He deserves a parish of his own.

Not Saint Basil's, the Cardinal said.

Saint Margaret's is open, Seamus Fargo said.

Done, the Cardinal said.

My retirement?

I thought you might like to be chaplain at Saint Francis Hospital, the Cardinal said.

No.

What do you have in mind?

There's a parish in the desert. Saint Mary's.

It's bankrupt, Seamus.

I would like to die in the desert, *Eminenza*.

After a moment the Cardinal said, Done.

The limousine pulled to a stop in front of the rectory at Saint Basil's. The three priests got out of the car.

Good night, Monsignor, Desmond Spellacy said.

Good night, Monsignor, Seamus Fargo said.

I'm sorry, Seamus, the Cardinal said.

Good-bye, Hugh, Seamus Fargo said.


"The funny thing was, they were both Fords," Mary Margaret Spellacy said. "You don't often get accidents when both cars are the same kind. Two Buicks. Two

Hudsons. Two Studebakers. These were both Fords, though. The paper didn't say if they were the same year. If they were both '41s, that would have been a coincidence. At the corner of Lincoln and Devonshire. It was lucky we weren't there. Tom was there just the other day, Monsignor. That's what he told me. If it had happened the other day, he would have been killed. I was praying to Saint Anthony was the reason he wasn't at the corner of Lincoln and Devonshire. He drives a Plymouth, though, and these were two Fords. It wouldn't've been such a coincidence if one was a Ford and one was a Plymouth. . . ."

Lincoln and Devonshire, Tom Spellacy said to himself. What the hell is she talking about. They don't cross, Lincoln and Devonshire. One's in Santa Monica, one's in the Valley. He wanted to laugh. It didn't matter, they didn't cross. On this one, nothing crossed. All that work and nothing crossed, that was the biggest joke of all. Leland K. Standard jumped off the Bradbury Building for nothing. Dildo Dot accused Al C. Hopkins for nothing. Al C. Hopkins told his wife he had not seen Dildo Dot since a doubleheader between Portland and the Angels at Wrigley Field on the Fourth of July, 1943, when he fucked her in his car in the parking lot between games. Al C. Hopkins should have kept his mouth shut. The shrinks, the waitresses, the cab drivers —none of them cross-connected with Lois Fazenda. Nor did the transvestites who turned up with her underwear and lipstick containers and hair curlers. Not even Jack Amsterdam. In any way that mattered. Brenda. Des. Corinne. Turd Turner. Mickey Gagnon. The Chinks behind Crotty. They didn't cross. Not a single one mattered.

The only thing that mattered was that he didn't want to fuck Mary Margaret.

And the systems approach. That mattered. Going through all that paper. Not so much to find a definite

330

pattern as to avoid lying between the legs of someone who told him to say a prayer to Saint Anthony when he couldn't find a parking place.

Saint Anthony. The patron saint of the lost and found. He wondered if he should thank Saint Anthony. Not for finding a parking place. For finding a definite pattern.

The definite pattern.

In the unlikeliest place of all.

Bingo McInerney's end-of-tour report.

Which of course Lorenzo Jones had written up.

Tom Spellacy wondered if he even would have reread the report if Lorenzo's block printing weren't so neat. Most officers on auto patrol wrote like Bingo. Smudges. Erasures. Misspellings. Wrong names. Wrong times. Felonies and misdemeanors misnumbered. It was a wonder the DA ever got a conviction. Lorenzo's report was a model. A 927, investigate unknown trouble, at 6:43 A.M. Changed to a 927D, investigate possible dead body, at 6:47. Seven minutes from Western and Pico to 39th and Norton. A 187 reported by Officers McInerney and Jones at 6:54. A Code 3 requested at 6:55. Detectives requested, 914, 6:56, coroner requested, 914C, 6:57. Victim: female person. Cause of death: unknown. Other injuries: traumatic amputation. That was a nice touch, the traumatic amputation. He must be boning up on forensic medicine, Lorenzo, at law school. The DA would like that. And Bingo wouldn't understand it. Coon talk, Bingo would call it. Just loud enough so that Lorenzo could hear him. Not that it would bother Lorenzo. He did his job and kept his mouth shut. No witnesses. No loiterers. No unexplained noises. No strange cars. Nothing suspicious.

And no mistakes either.

Except for the 187, a typical lobster trick end-of-tour report. Tom Spellacy riffled through the other pages. A traffic violation. A domestic argument. A

331

drunk pissing on a sidewalk charged with indecent exposure. A defective burglar alarm. A speeding ticket. Bingo and Lorenzo, eight hours in a black-and-white, 11 P.M. to 7 A.M., seldom stopping for coffee (Code 7, out of service to eat, he was sure Lorenzo would write) because the male Caucasian police officer did not like to be seen at the same hash-house table as the male Negro police officer. At 5:07, a 902 reported on the 2600 block of Hoover. 5:13, the black-and-white arrives at the scene of the accident. A 901H, ambulance requested, dead body, at 5:16. Make of auto: Ford V-8. Color: black. Year: 1936. License: VOM 399. Registration: Pugh, Harold. Name(s) of injured parties: Pugh, Harold. Type of injury: deceased.

Name(s) of injured parties: Pugh, Harold.

He stared at the name for a long time.

Oh, God, what a joke.

A definite pattern and the definite pattern was a dead man. Dead even before the victim was discovered.

Victim: female person.

Cause of death: unknown.

Other injuries: traumatic amputation.

He looked at the clock: 1:30. He was wide awake. No time to think about Mary Margaret. He burrowed through the piles of paper on the floor. The M. O. file, that was what he was looking for. What was it Brenda had said? He was a walking fucking barber's college. That was it. A barber who liked to shave the pubic hair off the whores he picked up.

Pugh, Harold. Questioned, not charged, 1944.

Pugh, Harold. The suspect file. He remembered now. He had made the call himself. The northwestern directory, 529 East Colorado Avenue. Mrs. Harold Pugh had cried on the telephone. Harold was dead. Harold's car had hit a telephone pole.

Question: what the hell was a barber doing out at 5:07 A.M.?

God bless Masaryk. He had found the announcement of Harold Pugh's death in the *Times* and clipped it to the file:

PUGH, HAROLD HERMAN, passed away 15 April. Member of Encino Elks No. 672, Encino Lodge No. 272, F & AM; Encino Scottish Rite; Al Malaikah Temple; Encino Shrine Club; San Fernando Valley Shrine Club; Past Patron of Encino Chapter, O.E.S.; Artaban Shrine, Order of White Shrine; Board member Rainbow for Girls, Encino Musicale Association; Order of the Arrow, Past President of the California Barber School Association; Past President of National Association of Barber School Owners; Member Southern California Chapter of Barbers' Hall of Fame; Member of Barbers' Union, Local 1020; Legislative advocate for California Barber School Association; many times judge for local and county and statewide hairstyling contests; Barber consultant, Republic Studios and RKO Radio; survived by beloved wife Hannah (Gordon), son H. H. Pugh, Jr., daughter Mrs. Fred H. Lucchesi, now of Wichita Falls, Texas; private interment at Valley Vista Cemetery. Memorial contributions may be made to the California Barber School Association.

The Barbers' Hall of Fame. It was too perfect. Tom Spellacy wondered if there were a session on traumatic amputation at the annual convention of the National Association of Barber School Owners. The traumatic amputation of cowlicks, forelocks, pigtails, ponytails, kiss curls, topknots, ringlets, tresses, lovelocks, elf locks.

Quiff.

Beaver.

Steady. Don't get giddy. One step at a time.

He repeated the question: what was he doing on the 2600 block of Hoover at five in the morning?

Traveling at such a high rate of speed that the car was totaled.

The car.

A 1936 Ford V-8.

Black.

License plate VOM 399.

". . . Of course it's a mortal sin to eat meat on Friday," Mary Margaret Spellacy said. "Unless it's a holiday. Like Christmas. When you get a dispensation. Not for my pa, though. Mr. Maher said a rule's a rule. So that Christmas we had sand dabs. And rice pudding. With raisins. He liked raisins in his rice pudding. One thing Mr. Maher didn't hold with, and that was dispensations . . ."

Oh, Mary Margaret, Tom Spellacy thought. Listening to her all these years he must have picked up something. He had stopped questioning the inner logic that connected Hearse Dennehy and the Scully who wanted to rhumba with the sand dabs and rice pudding Eugene Maher had for Christmas. The logic was simply there. Linear thinking was irrelevant when you tried to follow Mary Margaret. You followed the bouncing ball. It would be hard to explain that to Fuqua. Fuqua would not understand how the years spent tracking Mary Margaret's monologues would bounce him inevitably from Pugh, Harold (dec.), barber consultant to Roy Rogers and Trigger and Gene Autry and Champion, to the Santa Monica Pier and Shopping Cart Johnson.

Shopping Cart Johnson, who quoted license plates.

A Reo to travel the open road. YNJ 021.

A flivver outside a Calexico whorehouse. NDS 465.

A randy nonagenarian with a Studebaker. XYL 468.

Tom Spellacy turned the pages of his notebook. He knew the license plate was there.

Ahhh.

The El Segundo barracks. Abandoned since 1944.

A 1936 Ford V-8.

VOM 399.

The definite pattern.

The lines that crossed.

Mary Margaret had been asleep when he got home. He slipped into bed beside her and for the first time in years he wanted her. He slipped his hand between her legs and she rolled over and he got on top of her. She wanted to take off the flannel nightgown and he said no. The flannel nightgown made her Mary Margaret. Who talked like a boucing ball and whom he had not wanted to fuck and those two things together led him to the lines that crossed.

Which made her fuckable.

Fucky.

Mary Margaret Spellacy.

". . . No. 10 pancake is what they use at Mc-Donough & McCarthy," Mary Margaret Spellacy said. "Shake Hands told me that himself. At Pa's wake. He looks down at Mr. Maher and says, 'He looks waxy.' And he looked grand to me until he says that. 'The powder they use at Tonetti & Leo,' he says, 'you can buy it at the five-and-dime. Which is why he looks waxy, your pa. Me and Sonny only use No. 10 pancake.' It doesn't give you the waxy look, No. 10 pancake. Shake Hands's very words. I had to do it over again, McDonough & McCarthy would do Pa. No five-and-dime powder for Mr. Maher the next time . . ."

She had been less fuckable in the morning. No freshly squeezed orange juice, he told her. No hot cross buns. No link sausage, no biscuits. No eggs, no buckwheat cakes. Not even coffee. He was on the road at seven, at the El Segundo Barracks by eight. The chain-link fence around the facility was torn and the main gate held shut only by a single strand of clothes-hanger wire wound around the gate post. There was no one about. He shouted but no one stirred in any of the four two-story wooden barracks inside the camp ground. No watchman, no vagrants or vandals scurrying for safety. Tom Spellacy unwound the hanger wire and picked his way past the broken bottles and the used rubbers. The stones lining the pebble walkways had once been whitewashed but they had been kicked away like tin cans. A breeze off the ocean bent the weeds growing between the buildings and raised little clouds of dust. On the steps of the first barracks, he stopped for a moment and peered out at the remains of the antiaircraft gun emplacements dotting the sand dunes. Inside the barracks was stifling despite the broken windows. He brushed through the dense network of cobwebs and tracked through rubble that seemed not to have been disturbed for years. A step gave way on the stairs, and he stopped and automatically reached for his service revolver, but the wood was only rotten and the top floor was no different than the bottom. The second barracks was the same, and the third. Tom Spellacy took off his jacket and cursed Shopping Cart Johnson. And himself for coming out here on a Saturday morning. Dust was beginning to cling to the hairs inside his nose and to cake against his sweat-soaked shirt. He stopped to wipe his face with a handkerchief and then he saw the small cardboard box wedged between the ground and the bottom stair of the steps leading into the fourth barracks. He pulled at the box and a colony of ants crawled from it and paraded over his hand. The box dropped from his grasp and the rotten remains of an egg roll and a single spare rib fell to the ground. With his handkerchief, Tom Spellacy wiped the ants from his hand, then settled on his haunches and stared at the cardboard box. He took a pencil from his pocket and used it to turn the box over. It was gray and crumbling, but he could still make out the faded red lettering on the box cover:

AH FONG'S
Redondo Beach
Chinese Specialties
Oriental Takeout.

It was nearly eleven before Tom Spellacy left the El Segundo Barracks. First he went to a hardware store in Redondo and bought a heavy-duty industrial lock and a large red sign that said, DANGER—EXPLOSIVES. Then he returned to the barracks, locked the main gate and wired the sign to it. He did not expect that either would keep out anyone who really wanted to get in, but the fewer people poking around, the better. That Lois Fazenda had been killed on the top floor of the fourth barracks he had little doubt. A section of the floorboard was stained a dark mahogany color by what he was sure was blood. Bugs feasted on tiny droppings of shriveled and decaying matter. Tom Spellacy worked slowly and methodically. From the trunk of his car he brought a packet of envelopes and a cardboard grocery box. He put the box on the floor and the envelopes, a pencil, a notebook and a penknife on a window sill. Then he examined every inch of the barracks, careful to touch nothing. Time was of no matter. In the latrine he spotted two strands of human hair. In a corner a votive candle melted almost to the nub. A Shrine matchbook. A fragment of wood with hair sticking to it. On his knees he examined what the bugs were feeding on. He was no pathologist, but he would bet fragments of dried skin. Gristle. Entrails. Cartilage picked white. He tried to imagine what had gone through the killer's mind, how a little innocent barbering of pussy hair had got out of hand. The thing was, he really did not care. Harold Pugh was just a name, Lois Fazenda

337

just a body. A mechanic didn't care about the Pontiac he worked on, it was just another car. He was a mechanic and they were Pontiacs, it was as simple as that. If a Pontiac hits a friend, you don't blame the Pontiac. So it was useless to speculate on the lives that Harold Pugh and Lois Fazenda had affected.

Enough of that, he thought.

Back to work.

With his penknife he scraped the skin and gristle and mahogany-stained substance from the floor and put samples of each into separate envelopes. He marked the envelopes and put them into the grocery box. The task was endless, but as always, he found the sheer tedium of it refreshing. Especially now. He was a free agent. No one knew what he knew. He could proceed at his own pace. Systematically. First the blood scrapings from the floor. Give it to an assistant in Woody Wong's office and get it typed. The ME's office wouldn't ask who the blood belonged to, he was sure of that. They were up to their ass in corpses and one more blood sample wasn't anything to get excited about. Then a photograph of Harold Pugh. There was no sense in bothering Mrs. Harold Pugh. She might get worked up if Detective Lieutenant Spellacy asked for a picture. There was plenty of time later to ask her what the Hall of Famer did at five in the morning. No. Save Mrs. Harold Pugh. The Department of Motor Vehicles would have a photograph. There was one clipped to every DMV driver's license application. A little Chinese at Ah Fong's in Redondo, then flash the badge and the picture of Harold. If he was lucky, Ah Fong would remember the face, if he wasn't, it was at least a free meal.

All in all, a pleasant way to spend a Saturday.

The rest of the material would keep in the trunk of his car. There was no hurry to turn it over to the Scientific Investigation Division. Harold Pugh wasn't

338

going to hurt anyone. And the sooner SID did a work-up, the sooner Fuqua would start taking bows.

If he waited, maybe Sonny and them would pick someone else to be chief.

When he got back downtown, Crotty was standing amidst the piles of folders in his office.

"What the fuck you up to?" Crotty said, waving his hand at the folders.

"Looking for a definite pattern," Tom Spellacy said. He knew Crotty would never believe the obvious.

"Shit," Crotty said. He picked a folder from the floor. "How's Mary Margaret?"

"Swell."

"She still cook good?" Crotty dropped the folder on the floor and picked up another.

"Swell," Tom Spellacy said. Change the subject. "What are you doing in on a Saturday?"

"One of my Chinamen," Crotty said. "His nephew leaned on a girl. I said I'd see what I could do."

"Any charge?"

"Murder One."

"Jesus, Frank."

"I didn't say I'd spring the kid, Tom. I said I'd see what I could do. Open and shut. Bang, bang. Two in the ticker. Get a good lawyer is what I'll tell him."

Tom Spellacy laughed drily. Crotty and his China-men. A full-time job. One good thing: Crotty would not get too curious about the folders on the floor as long as he was preoccupied with his partners.

"You going to read all this shit?" Crotty said.

"I'll get Masaryk to do most of it."

"Find anything?"

Tom Spellacy shook his head.

"It must be grand having Mary Margaret home," Crotty said.

The blood-test finding came up from the medical

339

examiner early in the afternoon. Type O. The same as Lois Fazenda's.

A half-hour later Tom Spellacy picked up the photograph of Harold Pugh at the DMV. The license application said that Harold Pugh was forty-seven years old, weighed 140 pounds and was five feet four-and-one-half-inches tall. The application was stamped, MUST WEAR GLASSES. Harold Pugh wore rimless glasses in the photograph and a pencil moustache.

At three o'clock, Tom Spellacy had lunch at Pup 'n Taco on Olive.

At three-thirty he was checking the records at the department's automobile pound on Temple. The record showed that the wreckage of Harold Pugh's 1936 Ford V-8 was being held at a junkyard on Vermont Avenue pending the settling of his estate.

The owner of the junkyard on Vermont said that the 1936 Ford V-8 would not even bring fifty dollars in scrap.

Tom Spellacy scraped some dried blood from the windshield of the 1936 Ford V-8 and put it into an envelope.

In the back seat of the car he found a scrub brush, two empty boxes of Chinese food from Ah Fong's and behind the seat a large kitchen knife that had begun to rust.

There was a decal for the San Diego Zoo stuck on the rear window.

The force of the accident had jammed shut the trunk of the 1936 Ford V-8. Tom Spellacy borrowed a crowbar from the owner of the junkyard and pried the trunk open.

There was more dried blood in the trunk, which he scraped into a second envelope.

Also a bloodstained two-by-four with bits of hair sticking to it.

Everything went into the grocery box in the trunk of Tom Spellacy's car.

The night-lab assistant at the medical examiner's office said he could not test the two blood samples from the 1936 Ford V-8 until after dinner.

Take your time, Tom Spellacy said. There's no hurry.

The admitting clerk in the emergency room at County General said that the blood type of the DOA named Pugh, Harold, processed on 15 April, was AB negative.

At Ah Fong's in Redondo Beach, Tom Spellacy had hot and sour soup, peach duck, Szechuan shrimp and lichee nuts.

Ah Fong said he recognized the man in the DMV photograph.

Shortly after midnight, the lab assistant in the ME's office called in the test results. The specimens were both human blood. AB negative for the first specimen from the windshield, Type O for the one from the trunk.


"You know who I been wondering about, Tom?" Mary Margaret Spellacy said.

Tom Spellacy shook his head. Looking for a dead man, he thought. The definite pattern no one had considered. The name right there in the folders all the time. Pugh, Harold. Member Southern California Chapter Barbers' Hall of Fame. 902. 901H. DOA. The numbers and letters justifying Fuqua's passion for the triplicate. Giving Fuqua the last laugh . . .

". . . That girl," Mary Margaret Spellacy said.

She wasn't a girl, Tom Spellacy thought. She was a headline. Someone to read about who wasn't your sister. Someone to get your rocks off over . . .

". . . You know the one," Mary Margaret Spellacy said.

They'd feel cheated, the people who read about her. Cheated of their vicarious vengeance because Pugh,

341

Harold, was DOA. They'd blame her. She was only a tramp, after all. And they'd wait for the next headline.

". . . The one from Holy Resurrection," Mary Margaret Spellacy said.

Sweet Jesus, Tom Spellacy thought. "She didn't go to Holy Resurrection."

"Yes, she did," Mary Margaret Spellacy said. "When Red Kennedy's sister, Mother Agatha, was principal. You saved her life, remember. The one on the Jury Commission."

So that was what she had been leading up to. And look at Des. He'd like to bury himself in the molded salad. I hope the son of a bitch chokes on a marshmallow.

"Imagine that, the Jury Commission," Mary Margaret Spellacy said. "Such a grand position for a girl from Holy Resurrection . . ."


# Twenty-three


What is she doing now? Mary Margaret had said.

Des tried to help out. Red Kennedy is an interesting case, he said. The funny thing is, he didn't get his nickname because of the color of his hair.

That girl from Holy Resurrection, Mary Margaret said.

It was the red socks he always wore, Des said.

I don't know, Tom Spellacy said.

I thought you'd know, Mary Margaret said.

Even after he was ordained, Des said.

I really don't know, Tom said.

And he didn't. Until he found the letter in his in-box Tuesday morning.

*Dear Tom,*

*It's all right. I mean, I thought you might be worried—I don't mean "worried" exactly, I mean interested—and I wanted to tell you it's all right. What made me write this letter is that I was having a drink wih a friend last night—I did have friends, you know. We never saw them, but I had them, and some of them had families and some of them were sad and some of them were lonely and some of them were happy and I suppose most of the men wanted to "get into my pants," as you never liked to hear me say, but anyway I had them, although we never saw them—anyway, I was in this place and there was a sign over the bar and the sign said, To obtain an alcoholic beverage, you must have been born before this date: May 25, 1925. And I started to cry, because I was 13 in 1925, which makes me 34 now. I wasn't crying because I was 34—there's nothing wrong with being 34—but because I was 34 and I never knew my plumbing was on the blink. It's a terrible word, "plumbing," but you used to get embarrassed if I said words like c—t and I don't know what else to use, so I use that. Specifically, it's not strong enough in there to hold a child to term, or even for much more than three months. If you've followed me so far, I think you're getting the gist. I miscarried. Naturally. I mean I didn't have to go to a doctor. I'm sorry I had to wait until I was 34 to find this out—I mean, I might have had an operation when I was younger to make it stronger, if I had known, that is—and it means I'll prob-*

ably never have a baby, but at least I didn't have to go see one of those people who would have got rid of it. All the time I was thinking about going to one of those people, I kept putting it off because all I could think of was the nuns at Holy Resurrection. That's funny, isn't it? With my track record, I mean. Everything I ever did with men, I always measured against the reaction of the nuns at Holy Resurrection. How I thought they'd react is what I mean, because needless to say I never told them what I did, except in my dreams, and that's one thing I'm glad I never had to tell them, even in a dream. I bet you never thought I was guilty about that, but I was. Just like you. You want to know something funny? I once made a list of all the guys I ever knew that way—it was shorter than the telephone book, which will probably surprise you—and I left you off. You were different; that was why. All the others never felt guilty, but you always did. It was like you went to Holy Resurrection, too.

I guess that's all I have to say. I've gone back to work and I have a new apartment and I bought a cat and some plants and a secondhand sewing machine so I can make my own clothes and I'm going to go to night school and take a course in something interesting and I'm going to teach myself to be a better cook. The problem is I've always defined myself in terms of a man, and there are times when I'd like to think they're all bastards, but they're not—or if they are, that's something I've got to learn to live with. I suppose there's somebody out there, but not knowing who he is right now is what scares me. Almost as much as what will happen when we get together. With me, it's always been like peeling away the leaves *of an artichoke. When you reach the heart, it's all over.*

*Don't try to get in touch.*

*Corinne.*

Tom Spellacy folded the letter and put in into his desk drawer. From the information operator he got Corinne's new listing. She answered on the second ring. He deepened his voice and said he was from the Welcome Wagon and when she said, "Tom?" he hung up.

At least she was safe.

The afternoon mail brought another letter.

*Dear Tom,*
*I'm sorry.*
*Brenda*

# Twenty-four

The morgue attendant pulled out the drawer and Tom Spellacy lifted the sheet. For a moment he stared at the body, then dropped the sheet and nodded at the attendant. The closing of the drawer to the refrigerated compartment echoed through the cool green room.

When the attendant disappeared through the door, Tom Spellacy said, "She had a cat."

"Dead as a goddamn doornail," Crotty said. "There was enough gas in there to take out half of downtown."

"The other one. The gas get her, too?"

Crotty shook his head. "Septicemia," Woody said.

345

"From a bad scrape. She'd been dead for four days. She must've been getting a little rancid."

Tom Spellacy knew the answer to the next question even before he asked it. "Anyone we know?"

"Lucille Cotter. Remember her?"

He remembered the cat trying to pounce on a bird that afternoon with Brenda in MacArthur Park. "Silver Tongue."

"She deserved her name, that one, she really did." A faraway look crossed Crotty's face. "It was like you died and went to heaven."

Silver Tongue. Reduced to hustling tricks on lower Sunset. She got old, Brenda had said, it happens. Silver Tongue, who had once run into Harold Pugh. My God. Nothing crossed. And everything did. "Brenda did the scrape."

Crotty did not ask how he knew. "Well, she must've done it with pliers and a screwdriver. It was real amateur night."

Tom Spellacy turned suddenly and walked out through the autopsy room, not looking at the cadavers on the tables, and down the tiled tunnel leading to the elevators. Poor Brenda. Four days with her cat staring at Lucille Cotter's corpse. She knew the penal code, Brenda. Murder One reduced at most to manslaughter. A Folsom pop at best, the gas chamber at worst. No place to go, no one to turn to. And still it took four days to turn on the gas. By the time he called after getting her letter, she was already in the morgue. And the leaking gas had nearly asphyxiated two other tenants at the Alvarado Arms.

Crotty caught up to him at the elevators. Good old Frank. As soon as the news came over the wire, he had gone to the Alvarado Arms. Just in case he might find something incriminating.

Crotty suggested they go to Wo Fat's. Tom Spellacy wondered idly if Frank had found anything incriminating, but he really did not care. So Silver Tongue had checked out on Brenda's couch and not under Harold Pugh's surgery. All it meant was that she had sucked six or seven hundred more cocks. It's nice to have someone to say good-bye to, Brenda had said. Maybe that was why Silver Tongue had gone to Brenda's. To say good-bye.

"You ever read the brassiere ads?" Crotty said after he had ordered.

Tom Spellacy shook his head.

"I read them all," Crotty said. "I can pick them out. I walk down the street, I see a girl, I see the straps through her blouse and I know it's a La Trique latex Breathe-Ezee. With matching garter belt, $5.95."

"It's a good thing to know, Frank. Useful."

Crotty held a cup of herbal tea in both hands. "Why'd she write you, Brenda?"

"The last time I saw her," Tom Spellacy said evenly, "she said she had no one to say good-bye to." He took a deep breath. "Except old whores and people she bought."

Crotty avoided his eyes. "She used to give me free ass."

"She told me."

"I figured she had." Crotty stuck a napkin in his shirt collar and let it hang like a bib. "She called Jack, too."

Tom Spellacy's eyes flickered, but he said nothing.

"The switchboard operator where she lived," Crotty said, "he was a listener. Everything went through the switchboard and I told him I was going to run his ass into the joint, he didn't tell me who she called. Your house a couple of times, but she always hung up. A woman answered, he said. I guess it was Mary Margaret."

Oh, my God, Tom Spellacy thought.

"Then there was this other number. I checked it out. It was Jack's. She asked him for some money."

347

"She wanted to open a joint in Nevada," Tom Spellacy said almost to himself.

"She told him she was in trouble and Jack said she was going to be in big fucking trouble, she didn't let him alone."

"I asked her if she wanted a reference," Tom Spellacy said. It was almost as if he were not listening to Crotty. "And she said she never had any trouble buying cops."

"She'd get herself whacked out, she didn't watch out, is what he told her, Jack," Crotty said.

They stared at each other across the table.

"And then she turned on the gas?" Tom Spellacy said.

"The next day," Crotty said.

Tom Spellacy picked up the teapot, held it for a moment and then let it drop to the floor. The pot shattered and the steaming liquid splashed over his pants, scalding his leg. He did not flinch.

"Jesus Christ," Crotty said.

"Let's nail that fucker, Frank," Tom Spellacy said.

"I don't like it," Crotty said.

Tom Spellacy explained again. The scenario was so simple. The girl had the green cards. Jack was financing the green cards. The girl tried to stiff him. The girl was snuffed. It was so logical that he could almost make himself believe it.

The bib around Crotty's neck was soiled with sweet-and-sour sauce. "I still don't like it."

"It adds up," Tom Spellacy said. It occurred to him that he had been adding it up since his days in Wilshire Vice.

Crotty took off his bib. "He didn't do it."

"He's got a motive," Tom Spellacy said. He had never believed much in motive and now he was promoting a false one.

Crotty wiped his fingers on his napkin and tried not to look at Tom Spellacy. "He still didn't do it."

Tom Spellacy did not hear. "It's Jack," he insisted. Jack on Page One. It was worth it. A grainy photograph of Jack in handcuffs. Arrested. Indicted. The headlines would wipe the slate clean. All the way back to Wilshire Vice. Even things with Des. Pay off the debt to Brenda. Corinne, Mary Margaret. The whole thing was mixed up with them, too.

"It's the barber."

It took a moment for Crotty's voice to penetrate.

"Harold Pugh," Crotty said.

Tom Spellacy slumped against the back of his chair. He took a deep breath, then a second and after a while he said quietly, "How'd you find out?"

"That stuff in your office. I read it."

"Why?"

"I'm a cop."

"You've never read anything longer than a menu, Frank. Why'd you read this? You remember what you told me the day we found her? Right here. This very table. Where the Chinks treat you like the emperor of Spring Street. You said one thing was for sure, you weren't going to lose any sleep over who took that girl out. What made you so interested all of a sudden? Saturday. Sunday. The Stars had a doubleheader Sunday. I bet you missed it, all the reading you had to do. Why, Frank?"

"It was on your desk."

"Why, Frank?"

Crotty's eyes were blinking rapidly. "My Chinamen . . ."

"What about them?"

"They pulled out of the motel."

"So?"

"I'm up to my ass in debt, Tom. I got a note due in three weeks. And not a pot to piss in."

Tom Spellacy did not take his eyes off Crotty. "So . . ."

"So I called a friend of mine at Warner Brothers. I been talking to them off and on. They think there's a picture in it. The thing was, they wanted the files."

"And if you gave them the files, they'd take care of your note."

Crotty nodded. "I'm no dummy, Tom. The stuff's right there on your desk. I see the name Harold Pugh turn up twice, I can put two and two together. I don't know how or where, but I know he did it."

"Anyone else know?"

Crotty stared at the soiled tablecloth.

"Who, Frank?"

"Lorenzo Jones."

Tom Spellacy started to laugh.

"I needed somebody to check the car," Crotty said defensively. "And he was the officer on duty that night. Plus which he's an ambitious dinge. He'll keep his mouth shut, I tell him to."

Tom Spellacy calculated the odds. Lorenzo knew, and Lorenzo knew that he and Crotty knew, but Crotty was right, Lorenzo would not be a problem. "What about your pal at Warner's?"

"Shit, Tom, I didn't give them copies of that."

Tom Spellacy probed a hole in a back tooth with his tongue. "You know what Brenda said about Jack?"

Crotty shook his head.

"She said he liked to think he was born at sixty, building cathedrals."

Crotty looked at him suspiciously. "What's that supposed to mean?"

"We're going to bring him in, Frank," Tom Spellacy said quietly.

"He didn't do it."

"Then his lawyers will get him off."

"I don't like it, Tom."

350

"He'll just get his picture in the papers. And maybe Howard Terkel will tell a few stories about him and Brenda and the old days."

Crotty said nothing for a long time. "He'll bring up Wilshire Vice," he said finally. The recollection seemed to pain him.

"Not if you bust him, Frank. I'll let you take all the bows."

"Tom . . ." There was a note of desperation in Crotty's voice.

"He builds cathedrals. He'll never admit he used to be a pimp."

"I can't go along with it."

"It'll be a real feather in your cap."

"You're just trying to settle an old score," Crotty pleaded. "And that always means new trouble."

Tom Spellacy smiled pleasantly. "You've got a note due in three weeks, Frank. And it'll be taken care of." He paused. "If no one blows the whistle on you . . ."

# Twenty-five

Desmond Spellacy checked his watch. No one had come into the confessional in ten minutes, but he was in no hurry to leave. The cubicle was like a cocoon. His own private cloister. He considered the advantages of a life of monastic contemplation. It was a private indulgence at times like this. How peaceful a vow of silence would be. Giving him time to work out his relationship with God.

Or with his life in general.

Which perhaps was another way of saying the same thing.

The primacy of self, he thought. The heresy of self, Seamus Fargo would call it.

Self.

Another thought. He wondered if he had been a better man six months ago.

No.

More efficient perhaps. More useful certainly. Useful and efficient to the Cardinal, that is. But not better.

Not that he was better now. It was just that all the skeins of his life had come together. Suddenly and without reason. Bisecting and trisecting.

The past.

The Cardinal and all His Eminence entailed. Label that the present.

Tommy. Who was the past, present and future.

And then it started to unravel. The girl, the unfortuitously dead one. It was as if she were reaching from the grave and untying all the knots and pulling all the loose threads. There was a certain theological irony that appealed to him. It was not every monsignor who was undone by a dead Christian Scientist.

There were no more moves to make, he told himself.

Or there was the other possibility.

He had just grown tired of making moves. Making moves had become an end in itself. A paralysis of the will, psychic metal fatigue. Desmond Spellacy was willing to consider all the labels. Looking at himself with detachment was one thing he had not lost the ability to do the last six months.

Hubris again, Seamus would say. Congratulating yourself on the accuracy of your self-analysis. The final act of pride.

The heresy of self.

Ahhhh.

He half-expected Tommy to tap on the mesh screen of the confessional. Tommy always did have perfect timing. They always seemed to make their peace in the confessional. Once a year, twice, Tommy came to confession. Christmas, Easter, Tommy sought him out. There was the unmistakable voice on the other side of the screen. And the predictable Irish assumption that carnal sins were the only important ones. There was the predictable adultery. With the predictable euphemism, "impure actions." And the predictable charade of non-recognition. At least until after the penance was given. And then, "That's a little steep, don't you think, Des?"

It was not so much a confession as an exorcism. A pagan rite. To Tommy, the confessional was a fraternal battleground, a mine field to reconnoiter for advantage. His forum. The place where he could be most expansive.

Tommy.

The girl from Holy Resurrection.

It seemed appropriate to think about them in confession.

In the distance he could hear a dog barking. A pedigreed dog, he was sure. Saint Vibiana's was not a parish for mongrels.

Time to leave.

Too late. He opened the screen.

"You alone in there?"

"Of course."

"Turn off the goddamn light."

Desmond Spellacy turned off the light and closed his breviary. He knew the voice. Too well. He remembered the first time he had heard it. The Turf Club at Hollywood Park. "Bay of Naples in the fifth, Father, it's a sure thing." Bay of Naples, 14-to-1. A sure thing. That was a laugh. He had put five on Ethan's Song. Bay of Naples won by six lengths. "Did you win, Father?" That raspy voice. "Thank you, Mr. Amsterdam." Who knew he had not bet Bay of Naples. And thought that knowing gave him a little advantage. If Jack gives you a tip, Des, you can put the Sistine Chapel on it, Dan T. Campion had said. He hears things.

Oh, God, how many years ago.

What now, Desmond Spellacy thought. What tip does he have to offer this time. And what does he expect in return.

Jack Amsterdam coughed.

The full force of the cough hit Desmond Spellacy squarely in the face. Ten seconds, twenty seconds, a minute it lasted. He wondered if he should call a doctor. Then gradually the cough subsided.

"Jesus," the shadowy figure on the other side of the screen said. "Son of a bitch." The voice grasped for breath. "That fucker will kill me yet."

Fourteen years I've been hearing confessions. I thought I'd heard everything. But this was a new way to ask the forgiveness of God. Maybe God thinks we deserve each other, Jack and me.

"Are you all right?"

"I want to go to confession."

"It's a strange way to begin."

"Cut the crap, will you. And listen, I don't have all day. I don't know the words. I forgot them. It's been thirty-one years since my last confession."

"Thirty-one years?" It occurred to him suddenly that with all the Church functions they had attended together, he never had seen Jack receive communion.

"I had things to do."

"Obviously."

Silence. Desmond Spellacy waited for the voice to continue.

"You're not going to say anything?"

"The way it goes, you're supposed to tell me."

"Yeah, well, I'm a married man, but I got to admit,

354

I know a few girls in my time. Five, six hundred maybe, and I'm sorry I did, it was bad . . ."

Desmond Spellacy cleared his throat.

". . . Anyone ever try to fuck my daughter, I'll cut his nuts off . . ."

"Please."

"It's been thirty-one years, it's not so bad, you remember that."

Some quick figuring. Twenty a year. And then: Almighty God, forgive me trying to pro-rate adultery.

"Is that all?"

"What's the matter, you want me to draw you a picture?"

"I mean, do you have anything else to confess?"

A cough started and failed.

"Oh, yeah, I get you. Let me think about it." The sound of heavy breathing. "I told some lies. And I missed mass. I missed mass a lot. And listen, I stole some, too, when I was a kid."

Another silence.

"Nothing else?"

"I swore."

"And that's all?"

"I got into some arguments with some guys."

"Arguments?"

"Yeah."

Desmond Spellacy waited.

"That's all I can think of. I think of anything else, I'll come back to see you, though."

Desmond Spellacy cleared his throat. He wanted to pursue the subject of arguments. He was sure the man in the laundry dryer was the end result of an argument. And Ferdie Coppola's cranes.

"How do you define arguments?"

"Shouting."

"I see." He tried to pursue it from another course. "Have you ever lied?"

"I said I did," the voice rumbled irritably.

Desmond Spellacy realized that he was damp with perspiration. He wondered what to say next. There seemed nothing left now but curiosity.

"May I ask why you're here? I mean, after all these years."

"You hear the cough?"

"Yes."

"Cancer of the throat."

No wonder he was looking for a plot in Sonny McDonough's Celebrity Circle. Jack had had the cough for as long as he had known him, and now it was going to kill him. With luck before Sonny could approach the Cardinal about giving him a sash. "I'm sorry."

"Three months," Jack Amsterdam said. "At the outside."

Desmond Spellacy repeated, "I'm sorry."

"Not as sorry as I am, Monsignor, and that's no shit, if you'll excuse my French."

Monsignor. So he knows who I am. He must've come looking for me in particular. Then he does want something.

"Are you sorry for your sins?"

A rumble of phlegm. "Sure."

"For your penance . . ." What kind of penance do you give to someone who has not been to confession in thirty-one years? Not one good deed. The irony would escape him. He would give fifty thousand dollars to the building fund and expect a gymnasium to be named after him.

Along with absolution for his arguments.

The cough exploded again. Desmond Spellacy waited. He was sweating. That racking sound. The confessional shook. He thought, He's going to die right here. The screen sieved particles of mucous and blood. Quickly: *"Ego te absolvo . . ."*

He made the sign of the cross as the coughing once

356

more subsided. Too late now to ask about those "arguments." Absolution had already been given, the arguments absolved. Jack had beaten the rap again. Using a terminal cough this time. An unworthy thought. Even for Jack Amsterdam an unworthy thought.

Desmond Spellacy thought, I don't really care.

"For your penance," he said quickly, "say a rosary. And try to make amends to all those you may have injured the past thirty-one years."

Words. Empty words.

He listened to the heavy breathing on the other side of the screen. It would be Extreme Unction soon. Maybe Jack wasn't getting off so cheaply after all.

"Thanks, Monsignor. Is that all?"

"Yes."

Jack Amsterdam fought for breath. "Your brother . . ." he said finally.

So here it was. What it was all about.

"Keep your brother off my fucking back. He's trying to drop that girl on me. That whore . . ." The words came tumbling out in one long breath. "I had nothing to do with her. I can't help it if he was on the take, your brother. Nobody twisted his arm. But you tell him . . ." Jack Amsterdam inhaled deeply. "You tell him if he grabs me, it's your ass going to be in a sling. Not mine, I'm clean. Not his. Yours. You're a priest and you knew that whore and you never told anyone. You ask your brother how that's going to look in the newspapers . . ."

Desmond Spellacy said nothing.

"I got a family. There's a scholarship named after me. . . ."

Then he was gone.

No act of contrition.

Thank God for that, Desmond Spellacy thought. Contrition from Jack was more than he could bear. For the first time since he was ordained, he felt defeated by the priesthood. The heresy of self left him ill-equipped to deal with the likes of Jack.

Amends.

Amends for arguments.

I am irrelevant.

There was a tap on the other screen. One redeeming feature about Saint Vibiana's. There would not be two confessions in a row like the last one. Honor Thy Father and Thy Mother. Thou Shalt Not Covet Thy Neighbor's Wife. Misdemeanors. Malfeasances. No amends necessary. He made the sign of the cross and opened the screen.

"Go ahead, my son."

Thou Shalt Not Steal. Thou Shalt Not Take the Name of the Lord, Thy God, in Vain.

"Listen, Des, what are you doing giving absolution to that greaseball?"

Tommy. He could always count on Tommy.

"He tell you about the green cards?"

"What do you want, Tommy?"

"How does he put it to you, he tells you he had somebody whacked out? That'd do for a start."

"Impure actions." Desmond Spellacy blurted the phrase out and he was immediately sorry. He could hear Tommy catch his breath. *Mea culpa. Mea maxima culpa.*

"You're quick, Des." A thin laugh from the other side of the screen. "A little weak on the seal of the confessional, but quick."

That was one I deserved, Desmond Spellacy thought. Six months ago I wouldn't have made that mistake. When I was useful and efficient.

"He's only got three months left, Jack, is what I hear. Tops." Another laugh. "You're going to have to start paying for your own lunches at the Turf Club."

He wondered when Tommy began to accept venality

as a constant of the human condition. And suddenly thought, About the same time I did.

"I've got confessions to hear."

"Shit, Des, who goes in this parish anyway? Some kid, he thinks he's going to be a midget, he doesn't stop doing it."

Saint Vibiana's in a nutshell.

"You want me to hear your confession, Tommy?"

"I got nothing to tell."

"It's a bad place to lie."

"Des, let me tell you something. People don't lie in confession. You know why?"

It's always "Listen" or "Let me tell you something," Desmond Spellacy thought. Snippets of wisdom from the lower depths.

"I'd like to know that, yes. Get the benefit of your knowledge."

"Because there's no percentage in lying to you, is why. They tell you the truth, what's the most you're going to hang on them. A rosary? You mumble fast enough, you can get rid of a rosary in ten minutes. For ten minutes, you're not going to lie. Not if it's going to put you in the shithouse downstairs. That greaseball was just in here, I bet he didn't lie to you. He might've jerked your chain a little, but that's your problem, you didn't understand it. He didn't lie, though. He goes into a courtroom and the judge is talking twenty years, then he lies . . ."

I am being tested, Desmond Spellacy thought. My faith is being tested. My vocation. Such as they are. Every priest expected the test at some time or another during his priesthood. Usually in a way where the choice was heroic.

Do you still believe in your God? the commandant of the firing squad would say.

I believe in God, the Father Almighty, Creator of heaven and earth . . .

Ready.

. . . And in Jesus Christ . . .

Aim.

. . . His only begotten Son . . .

Fire.

Like a lozenge, that kind of test. Easy to swallow. What the seminary did not prepare you for was your own brother in the confessional. The former bagman for Wilshire Vice.

Sanctimonious Des.

Soiled Tommy.

It would be so comforting to attribute the strain between them to that. So easy.

And such bullshit.

What happened in Wilshire Vice only crossed the *T*s and dotted the *I*s. There had always been strain between them. And fear. And envy. They were brothers. It was as simple as that.

Cain and Abel.

Always exchanging roles.

"You don't want me to hear, Tommy, what is it then?" Desmond Spellacy said. "I can pass up your thoughts on the eighth commandment."

"As a matter of fact, Des, there is something, you got a minute. Your pal, Jack, he's kind of in the shit, is the reason I'm here."

Of course.

"He left here, we picked him up. Not on the front steps, we didn't want to embarrass the Cardinal. A couple of blocks away. He ought to be arriving downtown in about ten minutes. I just thought you'd want to be prepared, you saw his picture in the paper . . ."

The sacrament of absolution. That was a laugh. Copping a plea, Tommy called it. First Jack. Then Tommy. One made him feel irrelevant, the other useless.

"One thing you can tell the Cardinal, though. He was in a state of grace and you can guarantee that . . ."

The words washed over him. Green cards. The girl at 39th and Norton. He did not understand. Nor did he try. Nor did he care.

He knew only one thing.

It was over.

# NOW

"I'm going to die, Tommy," my brother Des said.

But of course Des had begun to die that day twenty-eight years before. Jack's picture was in the paper, hands cuffed behind his back, escorted by Crotty and three uniformed officers whose names weren't mentioned, and Jack said that Des had met Lois Fazenda coming up from Del Mar and then Fuqua told the *Express* and the *Times* and the *Mirror* and the *News* and the *Examiner* that he would follow this investigation no matter where it led. They loved that, the newspapers, especially Howard Terkel. One thing you could say about Howard, he knew how to dig, and he dug up Brenda and he also dug up every construction contract Jack ever had with the archdiocese and by the time he plowed through the kickbacks and the money Jack had skimmed off the top, you got the impression that Des wasn't very smart. The Cardinal said that Des had not been personally involved in any irregularities and if you read between the lines he also said that Des had not been boffing Lois Fazenda, which is not the sort of thing Cardinals like to say about future bishops.

In other words, Des was through.

And so was Jack. Bail was refused, and by the time his lawyers were able to get a writ of habeas corpus, he had started to hemorrhage in his cell and he was transferred to the prison ward at County General and he went in and out of a coma and three weeks later he died.

Which pleased the shit out of Fuqua. Who now did not have to prove that Jack had killed Lois Fazenda. He went on "Homicide Hotline" with Barry Backer and said that the case of the Virgin Tramp was officially closed and what it proved was that his department—he was already calling it his department, even though the Select Commission hadn't picked him as chief yet—would not be intimidated by people in high places, no matter how sacred. The Cardinal got that message and wouldn't attend the civic dinner honoring Fuqua when he made chief. Which was too bad, because if he had been there, he could have given Fuqua Extreme Unction. The thing that happened was that he swallowed a piece of steak the wrong way and it got caught in his windpipe, but no one noticed because they were too busy laughing at Dan T. Campion's jokes about the Jewish rabbi and the Catholic priest and about the nun who wanted to joint the Marines, and by the time they realized that Fuqua wasn't laughing, it was too late.

Dan T. Campion died in bed two years later after a Friendly Sons of Saint Patrick dinner. With a four-teen-year-old girl. He was still wearing a funny little green cone-shaped leprechaun hat with the elastic band under his chin.

Lorenzo Jones went to law school at night, got into politics and became mayor.

As for Crotty, he got his loan from Warner Brothers, and the two of us decided that the Fazenda case really should be closed, and so we burned everything in the files about Harold Pugh.

Mary Margaret went back to Camarillo and Saint Barnabas. Occasionally, if there was a big funeral, she would check herself out and she would sniff the flowers and touch the makeup on the face of the deceased and see who was driving the funeral cars and ask how much it cost. "They paid this crowd $1,600," she would say in a stage whisper. "Sonny McDonough would have done the whole thing for twelve hundred. And made Mr. Feeney look like he was taking a snooze. Which he had a lot of practice doing, snoozing. He never was worth a plugged nickel, Clinton Feeney . . ."

I saw Corinne once. She had married again, an engineer in Water and Power, and I ran into her in the cafeteria in the basement of the Federal Building. I bought her lunch and over coffee she said she would fuck me if I wanted and I said no and while I was paying the check she just got up and left the table. I never saw her again. Crotty says that she's living in Tucson now and that she's got cataracts.

I guess that brings everything right up to date.

Right up to that grubby rectory in Twenty-nine Palms.

"I'm going to die, Tommy," my brother Des said.

And for the first time in more years than I care to remember, I broke down and cried.

I suppose Des bringing me out to the desert was his way of giving me absolution. The arteries leading to his pump were shot and it was only a matter of time. I went out to see him every week and we sat and we talked and we looked out the window at Father Eduardo, who was still trying to fix the carburetor on that old two-tone Chrysler. We never mentioned what had happened. Too many years had passed for it to matter much anyway.

Two old men in the desert.

"That's some car, Des."

"Which one is that, Tommy?"

"Father Eduardo's. He wants to plug the holes in the carburetor, he should pour some black pepper in it. It swells, the pepper."

"I keep forgetting. You know something about cars, don't you."

"I used to work three days a week for Jack Walker."

"The car dealer."

"Ninth and Figueroa."

"After you retired."

"It was a way to stretch the pension. "

"I'll tell Father Eduardo about the black pepper."

"It's a good gimmick. There's a lot of gimmicks in the used-car business."

"I didn't know that."

"A fellow comes in and trades in his old car. What you do is, you send him a dollar or so in loose change and say you found it under his upholstery."

"Is that right?"

"It makes him a repeater."

"He tells his friends you're honest."

"And he sends the friends in."

"I never would have thought of that."

"Another gimmick is, a fellow comes in to make his monthly payment, and you send him around the corner for a free car wash."

"That'll get him to send his friends. Imagine, a free car wash."

"You shouldn't be smoking that cigar, Des."

"What'll it give me if I stop? Two more weeks?"

"I see your point."

"How's Frank Crotty?"

Crotty was fine. He lived in Palm Springs and still wore the white suits. And played a lot of golf now. Mainly with Jack Decker. You played with Jack and you took a swing and missed, Jack said it was a practice swing. Jack was good about things like that. Frank said that Jack would give you a putt if your ball was anywhere within Riverside County. Which is why Frank had a handicap of twelve, playing with partners like Jack. Jack used to say that giving a guy a putt was better than being in the slam. Jack used to be Jacob Dickstein and he ran most of the semis out of LA until '51 or '52. A little highjacking on the side, and when a guy wanted to hire some muscle, he would call Jake Dickstein and Jake would give him a telephone number. Then Jake got busted for Murder One when his wife Mitzi was found in a motel in Westchester with an ice pick stuck between her tits. Frank investigated the case and he told the DA there wasn't enough to pin on Jake. Not that I think Frank tried that hard. There was a lot of talk that Frank had some of the hijack action, but I never believed it. Frank was too smart. He wasn't too choosy about who invested in his motels, but he stayed away from anything illegal. Anyway, Jake beat the rap and then he retired from the trucking business. All the way to the Springs, where he changed his name to Jack Decker and joined Thunderbird. A nice life. Golf every day with old friends. Like Frank.

"You still play golf, Des?"

"I haven't played golf in twenty-five years. I'll tell you something, though. I watch Arnold Palmer on the television, and you know what, Tommy? I think I could have taken him. Playing at Knollwood and him giving me three strokes."

"It's a shame you gave it up, Des."

"Monsignor Fargo wasn't much for golf."

"I always wondered about that. Two monsignors in the same parish."

"It was my choice. His Eminence was going to give me a parish of my own. In Merced. And I asked him if I could be Seamus's curate instead. He wasn't going to live long, Seamus, and I said I could take over Saint Mary's after he died. If his Eminence still wanted me to have a parish, that is. Of course, Seamus fooled us all, he always did. Ninety-one, when he died. He outlived his Eminence by eleven years. So I guess he had the last laugh."

"It must've been hard, Des."

He shook his head and smiled.

"He taught me how to be a priest, Tommy. I have no gift for loving God. I still don't. Seamus said that wasn't a drawback, as long as I could be useful, and out here in this Godforsaken place, I am useful. Maybe I only deal with Pinky Heffernan's bowels or Mr. McHugh's niece, the nun who wants to be a bowler, but I am useful to these people. There's a kind of peace in that, Tommy. I can't help it if you don't believe it, but it's true."

I looked out the window of the cinderblock rectory, past Father Eduardo and the two-tone Chrysler, and in the distance, way out in the desert, I could see a sandstorm beginning to build up.

"I'm sorry, Des."

He looked at me through a cloud of cigar smoke, not saying anything.

"It was my fault," I said.

Des held up his hand. "You were my salvation, Tommy."

I did not know what he meant. Still don't, for that matter. But we sat there and he puffed again on his cigar and after a while, with the smoke still hanging in the air, he said, "You made me remember something I forgot. Or tried to forget is more like it. You and me, we were always just a couple of harps."

Crotty went first. On the fourteenth fairway at Thunderbird. He was so far out on the fairway, he stepped aside and let Bob Hope and Arnold Palmer play through. It was a real thrill for Frank, seeing Bob and Arnie that way. Bob came over and shook hands and said, "How you hitting them, Fred?" and Frank said, "Frank," and Bob said, "I want you to meet my friend, Arnie, this is Frank Carter," and Frank said, "Crotty, it's a great honor, Arnie." When Bob and

370

Arnie were off the green, Frank picked his club, did a couple of practice swings and then just keeled over.

Coronary occlusion.

Des went later that summer. In his sleep. He didn't get up for breakfast one morning, and the Mexican housekeeper called Father Eduardo, she had never been in a man's room alone, she said, and the first time wasn't going to be in a monsignor's bedroom, and so Father Eduardo went in and Des was gone, peaceful, his beads between his fingers. He left a letter that said he wanted to be buried out in the desert next to Seamus. I didn't understand that, but what the hell, if that was what he wanted, it was okay with me. Being Des, of course, he had to give me one last goose. He had bought another plot and in the letter he said that he wanted me to lie out there with him when the time came.

In the middle of all that goddamn sand.

The Spellacy brothers.

A couple of harps.

The solemn high requiem mass was sung at Saint Mary's by Seamus Fargo's nephew, Richard, who was auxiliary bishop of Fresno. I tried to get the new Cardinal, but he couldn't come, or wouldn't, Holy Name Society business, his secretary, some snot-nosed monsignor, said, and the other bishops in the archdiocese were all out dedicating hospitals or shopping malls or something, which is why I had to go all the way to Fresno to get Richard Fargo.

As for me, I'm in the pink. I'll be seventy-two next week.